A Simple Twist of Fate

DEB GRAY

WITH GARRY BAKER

AF741183

DEDICATION

I would like to dedicate this book to my daughter Emma, who gave me life.

Deb Gray

WP

Published by Wilkinson Publishing Pty Ltd
ACN 006 042 173
PO Box 24135 Melbourne VIC 3001
Ph: +61 3 9654 5446

enquiries@wilkinsonpublishing.com.au
www.wilkinsonpublishing.com.au

Copyright © 2024, 2025 Deb Gray and Garry Baker

All rights reserved. No part of this publication may be reproduced, stored in a retrieval system or transmitted in any form by any means without the prior permission of the copyright owner. Enquiries should be made to the publisher. Every effort has been made to ensure that this book is free from error or omissions. However, the Publisher, the Author, the Editor or their respective employees or agents, shall not accept responsibility for injury, loss or damage occasioned to any person acting or refraining from action as a result of material in this book whether or not such injury, loss or damage is in any way due to any negligent act or omission, breach of duty or default on the part of the Publisher, the Author, the Editor, or their respective employees or agents.

Title: A Simple Twist of Fate
ISBN: 9781763688605 printed 2024
ISBN: 9781921804977 printed 2025

A catalogue record of this book is available from the National Library of Australia.

First published in Australia in 2024 by authors Deb Gray and Garry Baker

Design by Spike Creative
Ph: (03) 9427 9500
spikecreative.com.au
Printed and bound in Australia by Ligare Book Printers.

A NOTE FROM EMMA

It is with a heavy heart that I share this note in Mum's book.

Just two months after it was released, she was taken from us, following a sudden and devastating medical complication while recovering from a broken leg. She is no longer with us, but her legacy and spirit live on in these pages.

My mum accomplished so much in her life, overcoming many challenges along the way. To many, her strength and resilience were nothing short of inspiring. To me, she was simply my loving mother. She was always my steadfast supporter, my protector, and the one who believed in me when I couldn't always believe in myself.

She gave me everything she had and she did it with such joy, and a passion for parenthood. I only hope I can pass on the gifts she gave me to her expected granddaughter. She was so looking forward to meeting her, and would have been a great nan.

Her memory will forever be a part of me, and I will continue to carry her belief in me, in everything I do.

Rest in peace, Mum. I will miss you, always.

With my deepest love, your daughter, Emm.

PROLOGUE

I was born with a high degree of flexibility and dexterity, especially in my feet, lips and neck, not to mention a fiercely independent spirit. Perhaps these were innate compensations, for I had no arms and my legs were only half their expected length. If we want to be politically correct I am a short statured person with underdeveloped legs and no arms. But I adapted pretty well and people are still often amazed at the manner in which I approach each of life's obstacles in order to participate in our conformist society as an independent woman. Even those who know me and my idiosyncrasies – including my distinctive appearance - are constantly surprised by some of the things I can do.

I have had the privilege of living my life surrounded by a wonderful family, although sadly I am the only remaining member of my immediate family. Thankfully I am blessed with a wonderful daughter. My parents, brothers and grandparents, as well as my extended family and friends, were so accepting that in my early childhood years I did not understand how physically different I was. Well, physically different may be an understatement, but that's how I like to describe myself.

My parents were my guiding lights. They recognised the need to treat me the same as other developing children. They taught me strengths, encouraged my capabilities and, importantly, allowed me to skin my nose or chin as I took the first tottering steps on my life's journey.

My earliest memories include playing with mud. I loved the feel of mud as it oozed between my toes … my flexible toes. I could control its consistency and I enjoyed tossing small amounts from foot to foot, forming patty-shaped rissoles like those Mum made. Then, I'd put them into my plastic frypan and flip them with the dexterity you generally do not find in a person's feet. I just loved making those mud pies! And at the time it made no difference to me that I did not have any arms or hands, or that my legs were only half the normal length. I might have been a lot shorter than others my age, and with a different configuration of limbs, but when it came to making mud pies, my feet made some of the best.

My parents recalled it was on our first visit to the Royal Children's Hospital that possible reasons for my deformities were discussed. The medicos who treated me, and those with whom they consulted, put forward various theories about why some babies are born with various abnormalities. But there was no way they could be certain what caused mine. German measles and calcium deficiency were among possible causes, but no-one really knows. For the record, at this early stage, the side-effects of thalidomide were evidently ruled out. Over the years, many people have theorised that thalidomide is why I'm an armless little person, but it had not been prescribed in Australia at the time of my birth so, naturally, it was eliminated. Although there's an interesting twist, because it has been suggested that Mum's gynaecologist had a habit of trialling new medications, not necessarily approved for Australia, mentioned later in this book.

There was also mention of the deformities at birth being caused by German measles. But how could you know? Apparently the pregnant woman did not even have to contract German measles herself, but may simply have been in contact with someone who had it. Mum also remembers being told a deficiency in Vitamin B12 may cause defects and so her levels were checked. Mine too, I guess. But as I say, no-one really knows.

At the time I was born, in 1957, deformities like mine were quite rare, although I do remember, at the age of about four or five, maybe a little older, frolicking around the Royal Children's Hospital with a couple of similarly shaped friends. They were a bit younger than me and we only saw each other on Limb Clinic Days. Today I still recall how good it felt, knowing I was not entirely on my own … there were others who looked like me. I was not 'special' because there was more than just me living this precarious life, all because, in the words of an old Bob Dylan song, I was 'A Simple Twist of Fate'.

I want to tell my story and I want it told with frankness and honesty … the way it has been. I want to tell of the love and devotion of family and friends and in particular the importance of being accepted by the community during my early developing years and the choices I consciously made whilst trying to find people that did not feel they had to look after me and would utilise me as a friend. Then came the absolute joy of becoming a parent myself.

So here is my journey. The highs and lows; the sugar and the shit.

CHAPTER 1

Not what my parents expected

Lakes Entrance is one of Victoria's leading holiday destinations, at the eastern end of the Ninety Mile Beach where the Gippsland Lakes flow out into Bass Strait. But back in the 1950s, although it was a destination for some regular holiday-makers, it was predominantly a small fishing town. Fishing was in our family's blood. My Dad Ray – affectionately known around town as Bimbo – like his father before him, earned a living from the waters of Bass Strait as a commercial fisherman. So did his brothers.

Dad was from a large family of 13 children, the fourth youngest born to John Gerald and Lilly Marie Gray who I think were third generation Lakes Entrance-ites. So, as a Gray, I'm definitely a fourth generation and possibly even sixth.

Dad and his young wife Cammie (Christian name Camelia), lived in a little weatherboard bungalow behind a house in Carpenter Street, just a stone's throw from an extension of the Gippsland Lakes known as the North Arm. There was nothing particularly special about this little abode from the outside, but inside it was a home filled with abundant love and happiness.

Mum and Dad's first child was a son, my older brother Geoff, who was born in 1953 by emergency caesarean. It must have been a traumatic time for my parents because there were life-threatening complications including a few moments where Geoff's heart actually stopped beating. But showing typical Gray tenacity he pulled through and by the time Mum was expecting her second child, in 1956, Geoff was racing around full of life and vitality like most other three year-olds. I'm sure there must have been challenging times for Mum as she kept track of her energetic son during the latter stages of her second pregnancy. Geoff turned four years old a month after I was born.

Because of the complications with Geoff's birth, doctors suggested Mum have an x-ray in order to determine whether or not she could deliver her next baby naturally. The x-ray was performed in Spring Street, Melbourne. Nothing other than Mum's ability to deliver me naturally was discussed and nor was any other unusual aspect of the images shown on the black and white film. This is somewhat surprising as the radiologist must have seen something to indicate deformities, or that everything wasn't quite right with the x-ray, because it was noted on his report that he "would be keen to hear the outcome of this particular confinement".

The summer weather in Lakes Entrance is generally milder than many other parts of the state thanks to the breeze which wafts in off Bass Strait (Southern Ocean). January 1957 was abnormally hot. My mother was not due to give birth until the following month, so was going about life in her usual loving, friendly manner. On the morning of January 28, Dad headed down to the wharf about six o'clock and, as usual, was working on the boat with his father. In the fishing families it was common for people to be up and about at the crack of dawn or before, and early on this particular morning Mum decided to pay a visit to her mother-in-law, who lived only a few blocks away in Orme St. As they stood on the verandah, she suddenly turned and announced, "I think my waters have just broken".

With that, an urgent call went out for Dad who raced to his parents' house and grabbed the keys to his father's car – a more modern and reliable vehicle than his own – and Mum was hustled in for a quick trip to the hospital in Bairnsdale, which was 25 miles away. But he didn't stay. As was common in those days, Dad dropped Mum at the hospital and returned home to Lakes Entrance where he would keep working and await the news.

The following is based on what Mum and Dad told me:

I was born by a planned, but earlier than expected, Caesarean Section about 8.55am on January 28, 1957. As Mum came out of the anaesthetic she began to ask for her baby and after some time became increasingly agitated because nursing staff had not taken me to her. She wanted to see and hold this little bundle of joy. It did not take long for Mum to realise she was being fobbed off and naturally began to think something was wrong. It was no secret that Mum desperately wanted a little girl, but was not even told she had a baby daughter.

Even now, I reflect on this cruelty. How could you leave a Mum who has just gone through the trauma of a Caesarean birth to worry for hours about her newborn baby and wonder why she is not allowed to see it? I can only assume that no-one on duty in the maternity ward that day could face up to talking to Mum and explain the situation. They wanted to wait until Dad was there, presumably so he could offer comfort. By the time he arrived, my poor Mum was quite agitated.

As Dad recalls, it went something like this:

"They won't let me see my baby, Bim. Why?" she cried.

Dad was left to explain. "We have a little girl, Cammie, but something is wrong. She has no arms and parts of her legs are missing. The doctor thinks she might also have brain damage." Through tears of uncertainty Mum and Dad clung to each other.

After a little while of hugging and expressing their grief, Mum looked up to Dad and said, "But she's alive, isn't she? She's our little girl and I need her now!" No-one was left in any doubt what she wanted and how she felt. At this point I was taken into the ward and Mum was shown the precious baby daughter she wanted so badly, but not what she had expected.

In the days that followed my parents were strongly advised against taking me home. After all, how can you care for a baby with such deformed legs, no arms and possibly many other issues, both physical and intellectual? At least that seems to have been the thinking of the medical profession at the time. There were places available for little ones like me, they were told. Places where staff were trained to look after children who were different and relieve parents of the arduous responsibility that came with raising a child who had debilitating deformities.

Mum and Dad were always adamant about their memories of that time. From the moment they saw me, there was never any question about whether or not they would take me home. Sending me to an institution was never a consideration. Mum admits her naivety and deep desire for a baby girl may have influenced the thinking, but as far as she was concerned I was their little girl and that was that. For my part, their brave decision to take me home was the essential ingredient of the person I would become. Who knows where I may have finished up, or what sort of person I could be as a consequence of horrendous care home scenarios, which have been highlighted in the recent past, if they had taken the advice from the hospital staff.

As with most small children, I remember my youngest years were happy and carefree. When my very special younger brother Jim was born, several months prematurely and just 10 months after me, our family was complete. There was never any shortage of love in our house as Mum and Dad did their very best to raise their two sons and one physically different daughter. Nor was there any shortage of support from our neighbours or the community at large in our tight-knit little town, although in saying that there was still a degree of ignorance. Mum long remembered one ignorant and insensitive remark while standing in the small local bakery, about children born with deformities like mine being better off in an institution, and remembered just as vividly the surprise of others standing there when she did not react. Instead, the required response came from another shop patron, who quite firmly took on the reaction to berate the ignorant, pompous one. Mum felt this to be a welcome gesture of support, and she could maintain her pride and dignity.

From early on, it seemed the doctors' fears that I may also have brain damage had no foundation, but despite this my parents were still told I would be better off at Yooralla, especially when I reached school age. Yooralla – an Aboriginal word meaning 'place of love' – was an institution for people with any type of disability. But it didn't matter what Mum was told or advised, she was adamant she would have no part of it. In her opinion, children who were put into an institution only developed as far as they were allowed to. She could see no reason why her little girl could not grow up to be her own independent person and did not believe this would happen if she was 'sent away'. Keep in mind that Mum's view is from the 1950s, when families dealing with such deformities was not common.

I will always be forever grateful for my Mum's unwavering courage, determination and willingness to hold her ground, even in the face of this ongoing 'professional advice'.

Mum and Dad dug in their heels. They were not knocking institutions, but there was no way they would budge. No matter what, they had decided to stick to their guns. Mum had seen institutionalised children and said she actually thought Yooralla was a wonderful place … for those who needed it. And this did not include her daughter. She firmly believed that as long as a child had a functioning brain they should be allowed to use it, and this included children with severe physical disabilities. Mum was also firm in her view that I would not develop at a normal rate if I was institutionalised alongside other children with both physical and intellectual disabilities. Yes, her mind was made up and no-one, but no-one, was going to change it. I have read and heard many recent news articles about abuse in some of those institutions during that era, which makes me even more grateful to my parents for their bravery, love and determination. I should point out this was many, many years ago and I am sure there are much better assisted living avenues on offer today.

Dad always felt we were all extremely lucky to be living in a small, friendly, country town and I heartily agree. Had I been born in Melbourne I would probably have attended Yooralla as a day patient. Although still enjoying the benefits of living with my family, at Yooralla I would have been taught to rely on the specialised support facilities offered to those living with disabilities. No doubt this would have had a significant influence on my independence and as a consequence the standard and type of life I have enjoyed. Instead I grew up in the country in a family environment where I was treated just like any other baby, and as I grew older like any other child.

Interestingly, I was born a year after ultrasound was first used in the Scottish city of Glasgow. If ultrasound facilities had been widely available when Mum was pregnant my deformities would have been quite apparent. Ultrasound would have shown the absence of my arms, and also identified that my femoral (thigh) bones had not formed at all and that my feet were attached to tibias (shin bones) which were, in a fashion, connected to my hips, not my knees. In layman's terms this meant that I had no thigh bones or kneecaps. Therefore, at maximum height, I would only stand half as tall as my peers.

In hindsight, the absence of ultrasound was not a bad thing because it saved Mum and Dad from what would have been quite a predicament. It's something Mum and I talked about, and she was reluctantly honest as she admitted that knowing what was happening during her pregnancy could have forced her into a very difficult situation. From time to time I have wondered what Mum and Dad's decision would have been if they had known about my deformities. Somehow, deep down, I feel I know the answer. The reality is, I probably would have been aborted and the chance to love, laugh, cry or just simply experience life's trials and tribulations would have been denied. As such, one of the things for which I am eternally thankful, is that no ultrasound was available in Australia in 1957.

Although I had quite severe physical deformities it was not long before it became obvious that nature had provided me with some unique special abilities. You can imagine the surprise when a kind but ill-informed visitor brought a rattle as a little gift and as it was waved over the bassinet I swiftly kicked off my blanket, reached out and grasped it in my toes, shaking it vigorously and giggling, just like any other bub, at the vibrating sounds.

When Mum and Dad talked about those early days they did so with much joy and pride, making it hard to believe their lives were any different to other young parents. My Dad summed it up: "When something like this happens, at first you think the bloody world's fallen in on you. But there's always somebody worse off than you … worse off than Deb." I think they're the words Mum and Dad lived by, hence, me too.

Mum said I started doing things automatically, just like any other young child. She told me that when I started taking an interest in rattles, she would string them across the foot of my old bassinet where I could reach them with my toes. To me, that was quite natural.

I had great parents. They were ordinary people with no airs and graces and no pretences. It never occurred to them to be ashamed of what I looked like or embarrassed about their lot in life. Perhaps that is what made them so very ordinary, and extraordinary, because they were so determined to make sure I had a normal and inclusive life.

It didn't matter what was happening, Mum and Dad made sure life went on as usual. When I was a baby, if they went out somewhere, just like others, I went too. It was the same throughout my early years, when I was encouraged to get involved with what the others were doing. If the rest of the kids were playing down the scrub at the back of the block, then I was there too. Mum said she never saw me as anything else but 'one of the kids'. "That's our daughter," she would say with obvious pride. So my self-reliance became a natural part of life from a very young age.

When I was about 11 months old my parents were told about a visiting doctor from the United States. Professor Henry Kessler (1896-1978) was an American physician, orthopaedist, surgeon and pioneer in rehabilitation medicine and orthopaedic surgery. He focused on treating the whole person, rather than just the physical ailment. He also founded the Institute for Rehabilitation in 1947 to provide comprehensive rehabilitation for people with physical disabilities and help them achieve maximum independence. Even today, the legacy of Dr Kessler's work continues through the Kessler Foundation and Kessler Research Centre, in the US.

While he was in Australia I was taken to see Dr Kessler, with my parents anxious to learn about what my future was likely to hold. When he examined me, Dr Kessler assured my parents I would definitely be able to walk and have a relatively normal life, although I suspect his definition of 'normal' was that I would be able to eat, breathe, poop and mentally develop, as opposed to playing an active role in mainstream society. Regardless, Mum and Dad were encouraged by his words of confidence and support. They also learned more about 'phocomelia', a congenital malformation and underdevelopment to limbs and that could affect other parts of the body, including the face, ears and nose. Interestingly, a common recognised cause of phocomelia was the drug thalidomide, and over the years many people have believed I was a 'thalidomide baby'.

Officially I'm not a thalidomide victim; in fact during my formative years, we were quite ignorant to the fact the drug even existed. As I've said, I have often referred to myself using a Bob Dylan song title 'A Simple Twist of Fate'. . hence the title of this book.

Thalidomide was not registered in Australia until the year after I was born. Due to the growing global travel and immigration of many medical practitioners, with a common habit at that time of travelling with tablets in their pockets, I am not convinced that Mum wasn't given the drug, but I will never know as she had no recollection.

Thalidomide was developed in Germany in the 1940s and first prescribed there in the 1950s, before becoming available in Australia. It was a drug which was developed for something else and found to have nausea settling effects. And of course that opened the door to even more medication being sold as it now had another customer. It was soon on the market, promoted as a miracle cure to alleviate morning sickness in pregnant women, but what doctors initially did not realise was the serious side-effects of thalidomide, in particular malformation of the extremities .

At the time Mum was pregnant with me, a German-Jew doctor was living and practising in Lakes Entrance. I am told he emigrated from Germany after time at a concentration camp. Thalidomide was developed in a concentration camp. There was speculation he may have given Mum some thalidomide pills brought in as samples.

But that's all it is … speculation. We'll never know, and I was NOT included in recent thalidomide compensation.

A formal decision on this came about after I was approached by Gordon Legal, a high profile law firm in Melbourne, and asked to be lead plaintiff in a Victorian Supreme Court case seeking compensation for thalidomide victims. This was a turning point in my personality that no-one, to this day, has taken into consideration. I have even had trouble coming to grips with it myself. All of a sudden I had someone to blame for all the little hardships and disappointments I had overcome for 50 years. But after several trips to Melbourne I was dropped from the case, without further communication, when lawyers discovered I was born before the drug was registered in Australia and therefore my case would not be cut and dry.

But doubt lingers. Before the case reached the courts, Melbourne investigative journalist Andrew Rule published a feature article which provided background on thalidomide, explaining it was "linked to Nazi scientists, including war criminals recruited to Grunenthal (the German firm which made the drug) after the war".

He talked about the "black holes in thalidomide's dark history", suggested the drug was circulating from early 1956 then spent a large part of his story reflecting on my experiences, as well as others at Bairnsdale Hospital. The following is quoted directly from Andrew's story:

The possibility that thalidomide samples reached Australia in 1956 might just provide an answer to the riddle of a Victorian woman called Debbi Gray. Debbi was born in early 1957 in Bairnsdale Hospital in East Gippsland.

Debbi had no arms and no thigh bones, a condition called Phocomelia that is a classic symptom of what would later be called thalidomide deformities. When the drug was exposed five years later as a cause of birth defects, most locals assumed that thalidomide was the culprit in Debbi's case.

But the Gray family were told this was impossible. Not only did Debbi's mother not recall taking a drug specifically for morning sickness, but the official date for the drug being prescribed in Australia was some two years after Debbi's birth.

Debbi Gray was a feisty child who became a feisty woman. "You have to be when you're three foot eight high," she said. She tackled life and her disability fiercely.

For nearly 50 years she believed her birth defects were, to borrow from her favourite Bob Dylan song, "a simple twist of fate". Now she's not so sure.

Andrew Rule went on to talk about two other babies born at Bairnsdale Hospital around the same time – one died at birth - with "classic thalidomide side effects", and the fact that doctors at the time "gave drug samples to patients, family and friends".

He concluded by asking whether myself and these other two babies were "early casualties of the drug that would inflict the world's worst medical disaster?"

Lynette Rowe, who is about five years younger than me, took over as lead plaintiff in Gordon Legal's case and in the end the drug's distributor agreed to an $89 million settlement for more than 100 thalidomide sufferers in Australia and New Zealand. I wasn't eligible for any of this which in some ways is disappointing because financial stability would have made life a bit easier. For a while I thought, after 57 unsuccessful job applications in my home area, 'wow, I'm not going to struggle financially in old age and won't be a burden on anyone', which is paramount in my life. Anyway, I missed out. That's the way it goes. There's a possibility I was a thalidomide baby and there's a possibility I'm not but, as I say, we'll never know for sure. Just like I have always done, I'll get on with life,

***

Dad had some wonderful memories of our times together when I was just a little tot. I wasn't much more than two years old when I first sat on the handlebars of his bicycle, with Dad's arms held firmly against my sides to provide all the support I needed. Pushbikes were very popular in Lakes Entrance – and further afield – at the time, and Dad used to dink me all over the place, whether it was going down to the shops or visiting friends and relatives.

Mum was thrilled when a family friend knitted a pink cloak, complete with an attached hood, which I evidently wore with pride on my bicycle journeys with Dad. I have often heard people comment on how cute I looked as a toddler, especially while I was perched up on the handlebars then later, as I grew bigger and stronger, I graduated to the wrought iron seat on the back of the old bike. Lucky for me I was endowed with a presentable face and even then a persistent smile. And why wouldn't I be smiling, as I spent such precious times with my Dad, not knowing that I was any different from the next kid.

Dad also carried me on his shoulders. At first he would hold his arms up, with his fingers interlaced behind my back. It was like sitting in a high armchair from which I could not fall out. As I grew stronger he simply held my ankles because I was able to use my stomach and back muscles to easily hold myself upright, which must have been a good strengthening exercise for me.

Later, as a 12 and 13 year old I used to show off my strength by having Mum stand behind me with her hands on my shoulders. Balanced there, she would lift her feet off the ground. I guess we were both proud of the fact I was physically strong.

I have always been strong in the back and this seemed to transfer to my legs. Being so short, my legs needed to be strong so I could go the distance with my peers. This often proved quite a challenge, but it was very important to me, because I didn't want to be one of those kids who slowed everyone else down. Even at a young age, my prime concern was being able to do exactly what everyone else did. I wanted to be seen as capable and worthy of the same attention my girlfriends were getting, and I strove to be independent and prove I would not be a burden, but a valuable part of any team or partnership.

In this context I could say I wanted to be 'normal' because it seems to describe all the things that are accepted as part of everyday life. It's where nothing is different or out of the ordinary, and wherever possible that's how the first few years of my life were lived. It was a wonderful grounding. However, things were about to change. My ordinary and very normal life – just the way I liked it – was about to be re organised by those 'all-knowing' people who wore the title 'professional'. They were the ones who thought they knew exactly what I wanted and needed which, in their mind, were prosthetic arms to replace the ones I didn't have. I, at times, quite vigorously disagreed.

Now, you must remember this was in the early 1960s when I was still a young child and my parents were in awe of these 'medical professionals' who were in positions of authority. Naturally, they allowed themselves to be guided by those whom, it was assumed, knew better than everyone else. They were the experts, so why would any parent question the advice that was given "in the best interests of your child"?

Mind you, it seems there was a time when I believed I would not need prosthetic arms, despite what the doctors said. Mum tells the story of the day she found me standing in front of the window, looking at my reflection and studying the place where arms are generally attached to the shoulders, but where I only have slight bumps. I envisioned these bumps as arm seeds and told Mum I was convinced my arms had finally started to grow.

Poor Mum didn't know whether to laugh or cry. Apparently I was quite serious about this significant physical development that I believed was taking place and left Mum faced with having to assure me that my arms would never grow. I wonder now at the mind of a child. Being a country girl, I probably knew that small lizards could grow another tail if the first one dropped off. Maybe I thought something similar would happen to me.

***

Among the times I look back on with most delight are some of those I spent with Dad. He had been fishing since his early twenties but when I was young decided to take a break from the sea. He bought a truck and started transporting timber from a mill at Nowa Nowa to timber yards in Croydon. This venture proved a great success and before long he bought another truck and employed a second driver.

Dad often took me with him in his old red Commer truck. In all honesty, I'm not sure what the boys were up to at this time. With Mum also working, Geoff and Jim were possibly off with friends.

I have wonderful memories of carting timber all the way from Nowa Nowa to Croydon, which was a distance of more than 200 miles. This was before I had started kindergarten and continued during the holidays in my early primary school years. Of course the driving rules were not as strict in those days and I'm not sure we even had seatbelts, let alone laws enforcing their use. There wasn't much traffic on the roads, but nor were the roads in the condition we now enjoy. There were no dual lane highways, nor the by-passes which have been constructed to make it a quick and easy trip from East Gippsland to Melbourne. I loved the trucks and think that having two brothers probably helped make me a bit of a tomboy.

I still clearly remember travelling along on Dad's knee with my shoulders against the steering wheel; I was driving the truck. Sometimes I put my feet on the wheel and Dad let me actually have a steer, albeit for a small distance. He must have had enormous faith in my dexterity and abilities, even in those early years.

There was a particular roadhouse at Nar Nar Goon, about 60 kilometres from the end of our journey, where we always stopped. It was a very friendly place, owned by Roughy and Ann, where Dad and I used to sit out the back and eat our tucker, as if we were part of the owner's family. That roadhouse no longer exists, which is a bit of a shame as you don't seem to find that sort of place any more. Dad and I used to do a lot of singing on those trips. I still remember the songs about 'the yellow cat that wouldn't go away', and the one about 'watching the doughnut nut the hole'. I think it was also about this time that the Magpies became my favourite AFL team – thanks to Dad's influence – so I learnt the Collingwood theme song very early in life. We enjoyed lots of "Good old Collingwood forever, they know how to play the game …"

As I said, I'd become a bit of a tomboy, however I did treasure my large collection of Peewee dolls, which were so popular in that era, and played with them often. Their name was synonymous with their size and these tiny baby dolls fitted neatly in my toes. But I was more likely to be found in the back yard building a cubby house, playing in the bush or hanging out with Jim and others or Dad as he washed the truck. There was a vacant block beside our house with a big old gum tree on the nature strip at the front, and that's where Dad parked his truck. There was plenty of black dirt under the tree and when Dad washed his truck it turned to mud which is something I was particularly partial to.

I was rarely found in the kitchen helping to cook, like other young girls; that was Jim, although I do recall hopping into Mum's amazing scones or sponge cakes whenever I had the chance. She always turned out the best homemade delights. Ironically, Jim was the one to inherit Mum's culinary skills.

Despite not spending lots of time in the kitchen I did spend a lot of time with Mum. When it came to looking after me, especially when I was a toddler, my parents were excellent at sharing the responsibilities. If I wasn't in the trucks with Dad, I often went to work with Mum, who cleaned units at what used to be called the Bamboo Motel. Nobody seemed to mind when I was hanging around. In that respect, things were different in those days because that would now be generally unacceptable.

As I mentioned earlier, our neighbours were also wonderful, especially people like Merle and John Beveridge and 'Plugger' (Keith) and Patty Carstairs. One particular family we were quite close to was the Stewarts. We called the matriarch Aunty Betty and the boys were our good friends. Gary, the youngest, was around Jim and my age and Bill was Geoff's age. Sadly, he died in his late teens, which was devastating for Geoff. Ray sat in age between Gary and Bill, and Lindsay and Maureen were older. Aunty Betty was often quite happy to look after Geoff and Jim while we were away. However, Geoff once told me he spent time living with Aunty Rhonda and her husband John in Orbost, and it must have been for an extended time because he even attended primary school there. Geoff was unhappy about being separated from his family and this period held bitter memories for him. If I was the cause of this, I am truly sorry.

Despite this sad situation with Geoff, I have always believed the acceptance and support given by my whole family, neighbours and the community in general played a big part in the development of my character. During my preschool era I honestly never remember feeling any different to other children in the neighbourhood and I was often found in the homes of our neighbours, just as their children were our regular visitors. Even attending the Royal Children's Hospital was okay as there were a few different bodies there too, including a couple of girls who were physically similar to me. So even that seemed okay and it was, in fact, a relief knowing there were others like me.

CHAPTER 2

Trying to make me 'normal'

When I was only two or three years old it was decided the time had come for a range of medical and therapeutic professionals to step into our lives. They wanted to assess my function ability and discuss ways that may assist to 'normalise' me, although it always seemed their definition of 'normal' differed quite dramatically from mine. In effect, they wanted to put a square peg into what I saw as a very round hole. The medical professionals couldn't see that I did not want or need their help. The way they looked at it, how could someone so physically abnormal be able to function normally without their professional intervention? EVERYONE needs arms!!! They knew what was best for me ... at least that is what Mum and Dad believed.

What they couldn't seem to understand was the simple fact that I wanted to use my very adequate and dexterous toes. And why wouldn't I? I had no arms and couldn't even imagine what it would be like to have fingers. But I had feet and toes which worked very well doing things that, in general, was the sole domain of fingers. So my natural instinct was to use them. Despite this, my parents were being advised by the medical profession that I needed arms if I was to live anything like a 'normal' life.

One well-meaning doctor made the prophetic statement that "she needs hands", adding "it doesn't matter that her feet write beautifully, because they need to go in shoes. She needs hands!" Swayed by this type of 'professional/academic' view, my parents accepted the advice and before long they also believed I needed arms if I was to live anything like a 'normal' life.

***

My parents were always proud of their decision to take me home with them after I was born. To my knowledge they never regretted that decision, but there must certainly have been times when they wondered how I was going to cope with everyday life.

It's fair to say Mum and Dad experienced their fair share of life's ups and downs, but the day I received my new cosmetic hand was a momentous and emotional occasion. The cosmetic hand was to be a social replacement for the hook which I had on my right arm prosthesis and was manually managed, meaning the fingers had to be manually moulded into position, for example to hold a glass or pencil. The first time I tried it was an occasion my mother never forgot. Here, in her own words, is her recollection of that day when it was fitted by the team at the Royal Children's Hospital:

"Deb was sitting at a table wearing her prosthetic arm. In fact, she was wearing both arms. The fingers on the new cosmetic hand were pliable ... they could be manipulated and pushed into position so that Deb could hold things. Deb would always have to maintain a functional right hook for picking up every day things but for the moment the team wanted to see what would happen when they pushed what was well recognised at the time as a seven ounce beer glass, seen as a good shape for the exercise, into the cosmetic hand on Deb's right arm and by pushing on her arm, she brought the glass to her lips

"I remember taking a deep, deep breath. There was silence in the room and suddenly I just felt totally overwhelmed. I raced out of the room crying my eyes out. Valma Angliss, the occupational therapist, came running out to me, saying 'Oh Mrs Gray, Mrs Gray what's the matter?'

"In between some very big tears of joy I managed to blurt out that in all her life, Deb had never ever picked up a glass and put it to her mouth. And she had just done it, straight to the mouth. I eventually composed myself and Miss Angliss and I returned to the team. I'm not sure whose eyes lit up the widest when 10 year old Deb wondered aloud how many beers she could down using her new hand. We were all so thrilled with the result."

And so this marked a milestone at Royal Children's Hospital Amputee Clinic; I started training to use my prosthetic arms. When I was just four years old doctors had already taken the small toe from my left foot, as it had stuck out from the side of my foot where it just got in the way when they were fitting me with orthopaedic boots. On my right foot I still have the toes I was born with … three small toes and a large one.

***

We arrived at that stage of my re-fashioning through referral from our local Infant Welfare Centre and Medical Centre. We made numerous visits to the Royal Children's Hospital as well as the Sturt Street Limb Factory, situated just behind Victoria Barracks in St Kilda Road, which was established in World War One to make artificial limbs for wounded soldiers. Yes, it's hard to believe, but back in the 1960s it was actually called a Limb Factory!

By the time I was in Grade One at Primary School I had both a left and right arm, although the left was a non-functioning cosmetic. Dr Bob (Robert) Klein was the senior specialist at the Sturt Street Limb Factory and from the very start became my friend and mentor, as well as my limb doctor. My association with Dr Klein developed over many years and was to remain solid until the day he died. I sat with him for some time the night before he passed away and was shocked when I returned next morning to find his bed empty. He had died during the early hours of the morning. I really felt the loss.

Trips to the Royal Children's Hospital were made monthly while my prosthetics were being fitted. All the extensions and modifications which have been made to the hospital building make it unrecognisable to the cream coloured brick place I used to attend in the '60s.

The other member of my team who I will never forget was Valma Angliss, the hospital's Occupational Therapist at that time. Valma was a wonderful person and over the years our family developed a relationship with her that was based on love, empathy and professionalism, which for me continues to this day.

My parents recalled their visits to the Royal Children's Hospital with mixed feelings. These visits often seemed to coincide with days when children with mental disabilities, some quite severe, had their appointments. Mum and Dad always left the hospital with that sense of feeling how lucky we all were that I did not have the same disabilities as some of those children.

Once again, it was a measure of how Mum and Dad lived their lives. There was always someone else who was worse off, and nothing reinforced this point of view more than visiting the Royal Children's Hospital.

***

For the last few years of primary school into early high school years, still requiring many fittings, then lots of training for the artificial arms, a decision was made. Because I was a country girl who had to travel 200 miles to get to the hospital, it was organised for me to take up residence at the Royal Children's Hospital in Parkville, Melbourne, sometimes for a week or more at a time. Usually I would be placed in a large ward with three or four other children and we always had lots of fun. However, as I grew older I was sometimes given a room of my own.

I have a horrible vivid memory from one of these rooms in Ward 3 West at the Royal Children's Hospital, which occurred in later years when I was 13 years old. On October 15, 1970, as I stood on my bed, looking out the window on the south-western front corner, I watched in horror as the Westgate Bridge collapsed. It's something I have never forgotten and in my mind's eye I can still see the bridge spans as they fell to earth like little pieces of a Meccano set. On that fateful day, as I stood on my bed peering in that direction, 35 construction workers were killed as a 2,000 tonne mass plummeted into the Yarra River.

That was nine years after I received my first prosthesis which, by all the paper clipping accounts, occurred when I was four years old. It comprised a single right arm, with a tiny little rubber covered hook on the right, and had taken nearly two years to develop since the first suggestion of artificial arms had been raised. The hand was made of stainless steel and had two permanently curved fingers held together with rubber bands. It also had a thumb. As more rubber bands were placed around the fingers I could hold and lift heavier objects and have a tighter grip. Attached to the thumb was a cable which ran on guides up the arm and across my back. Pulling my shoulders forward placed tension on the cable, in turn pulling on the thumb and opening the fingers.

Another cable was attached at the wrist and also ran on guides up the arm, although instead of going across my back this cable ran down my side and hooked onto a strap around my groin. Raising my right shoulder put tension on the cable, which in turn allowed me to raise the arm at the elbow. It was all supposed to be very simple but in fact, I can tell you, it was bloody hard work!

Regardless, this is what the medical professionals wanted and thought was best for me. By the time I reached Grade One I had both a left and right arm, even though the left was merely cosmetic. It was covered in a synthetic rubber glove with wrinkles and knuckle lines so the hand looked, relatively, 'real'.

The prosthetic right hand allowed me to appear as if I was functioning like everyone else. Yes, I could sit at a table and chair, or a student desk, and look like all the other children. However, I think this is where I started to realise that the process of getting there wasn't as important as being there. It's a little bit like, you'll eat anything as long as you're hungry, or with a little discomfort you will allow yourself to be carried, just so you can reach a destination. One other way of looking at it is an adaptation of another old adage, 'it's not what you do, but the way you do it!' I was rapidly developing belief of 'it's not how you do it that matters, it's what you do that counts'. For other children writing the letter 'a' was a simple wrist movement, but for me it was laborious, and as such, an entirely different affair. My arms were rigid, so it meant my whole body had to be used to make the letter.

The fiercely independent nature which I possessed fuelled a desire to be like all my friends, but little did I realise that the early school days were an introduction to how my life would ultimately be. The entrée, if you like. But few people ever really understood how much energy I needed to perform the simple task of writing an 'a', or any other letter hundreds of times down the page. Nor did I feel that anyone understood just how alien those artificial arms were to a child whose natural inclination was to utilise the valuable assets with which she had been born … that is, my feet.

The whole prosthetic thing began to frustrate me. So too did the other word that was beginning to worm its way into my understanding. Pity. I might have been young, but I was determined I would not be pitied. It is true that empathy and understanding are a lot easier to live with than pity, but that was something I had to learn. In recent times as I have reminisced with old school mates I find it a bit sad as they reflect on my young attitude as being quite demanding.

I remember spending many hours in the Occupational Therapy Department at the Royal Children's Hospital. Activities there included everything from threading blocks and beads onto plastic string, to practising how to pour water from my tiny teapot into my tiny teacup. All that tedious work was designed to help me learn about the finer detail functions of my new arms so I could use them more effectively.

In 1963 Queen Elizabeth II and Prince Philip visited the hospital while in Australia to lead the Canberra jubilee celebrations commemorating the 50th anniversary of the naming of our nation's capital. Prince Philip took particular interest in the little girl who offered him a cup of tea from the kitchen play corner in the Occupational Therapy Department of the fourth floor. It was there I spent a good half hour, or so it seemed, with the Prince, playing with the tea-set and serving him morning tea in the little plastic cups. Realistically, it was probably only five minutes. To this day I can still visualize the extremely leggy man, perched on a child's wooden chair with his knees up around his ears. I was thrilled.

The Queen had continued on her tour of the hospital, leaving Prince Philip with me, so I suppose they caught up again somewhere around the wards. For this mere child, it was an exciting moment in my life where all the hardships of learning to use those heavy, cumbersome arms were forgotten, if only for just a short while.

***

When my artificial arms were being fitted it was really quite an undignified affair, even for someone so young. The process always began with plaster casts being taken of my upper body. I hated it from the time I was a little girl, and the hatred increased as I got older, especially from the age of 10 and onwards. It never seemed to occur to people that, yes, I did mind being undressed all the way down to my cottontails before being placed in the middle of a table like a specimen on display. From my waist to my neck, a couple of the limb factory men would wrap me in wet plaster bandage, after which I had to sit very still for anything up to half an hour while the plaster dried.

When the plaster was dry it was cut straight up the middle, front and back, with plaster cutting type scissors that used to hurt me. After the cast was removed the mucky remains were sponged off my body before I could finally be dressed again and, until I was offered hospital accommodation, ready for the arduous trip back home to Lakes Entrance. Having accommodation was convenient, however I hated time away from home. Dad would often call in to see me when he was delivering a load of timber to Melbourne. This procedure went on for many years, because as I grew my prosthetic arms had to be re-fashioned and re-fitted.

Over the years there were several doctors regularly involved with fitting my artificial prostheses. However, it was Dr Robert Klein and Miss Angliss's insight into the self-consciousness of young girls like myself and others I knew that helped us endure the fitting process. They were always included as part of the team, with Dr Klein to oversee making the prostheses and Miss Angliss teaching us how to use them.

By 'us', I mean myself, Mary Henley and Lynette Rowe, who were also under the care of this team. We used to have so much fun at the Royal Children's Hospital, in particular Mary and I. We'd go scurrying and skidding around hospital corridors and, in our own very young way, supporting each other. Mary and Lynette each had an apparatus that was like a skateboard. They had no leg bones to really speak of, just feet where the legs should start, and as such were not very mobile. On the other hand my legs, although missing the top section which is the thigh bones, were quite strong and I used them very well. Effectively I have lost the height that comes between your knee and your hips; I am not a dwarf.

Back in those days, the bed tables went up and over the bed, then down the other side and had four legs on casters. I used to get under the table and lean on the rail that stabilised the legs, while Mary would hang on to the other end. I'd run as fast as I could, then fling her around until she let go … and she'd shoot off down one of the long, wide corridors.

The other issue associated with my prosthetics was the cost. They were extremely expensive, even back in the sixties, and as I grew I needed new artificial arms about every three years which had to be made to fit my body. It was at these times that the townspeople of Lakes Entrance rallied together and raised the funds needed to help purchase my prosthetics.

The Lakes Entrance Fisherman's Cooperative instigated local appeals and the Lakes Entrance Football Club and even the Orbost Angling Club, among others, then joined in. During half time at the local footy match, I've been told that it was quite common to see four men carrying a blanket around the boundary, into which spectators were encouraged to throw money.

The Melbourne Sun newspaper picked up the story on the local appeal and as a consequence a statewide fundraising campaign started. It was a wonderful help to our family and something that has always been appreciated and will never be forgotten.

***

I also want to reflect on the time when I had reached the age where children go to kindergarten. At this point I must say how fortunate I was, when it came time to write this story, to be able to tap into my parents' memories. Some of my own recollections from those early years tend to be a little hazy. Mum could vividly recall the start of my educational years and, in particular, my first move towards kindergarten.

My first teacher was Mary Jemmeson who, fortunately, was a very forward-thinking woman. When Mum asked how she felt about enrolling me into her class she simply remarked that I would be accepted and treated just like any other child. She couldn't see any problems at all. If there was something the other children were doing that I couldn't manage then I would do something else.

Kindergarten was fairly new to Lakes Entrance when I started and was held in the old Presbyterian Church hall in Mechanics Street, where the ambulance station is now situated. At the time I wasn't being encouraged to use my artificial arms, which had only recently been fitted, outside the home. I vividly remember sitting on the wooden floor, in the old church, using my toes to colour-in pictures and to write on widely lined paper. I didn't need arms!

Because there was such little difference in our age, my younger brother Jim and I started kindergarten at the same time. Virtually from the time he was born, Jim and I were extremely close and as we grew older our bond grew stronger. It seems that despite my independent nature he was always there, ready to catch me if I fell or to pick me up and dust me off afterwards.

Mind you, I learnt from an early age to look after myself. I remember a time in the playground when I was being continuously overlooked for a turn on the see-saw. One child, in particular, was denying me the opportunity to have a go. After waiting for what I thought was long enough I gave the offending youngster a quick nudge as he was on a downward tilt and over he tumbled, thus leaving the seat vacant for me. There wasn't much I missed out on!

I've been told that I displayed assertiveness over larger children from a very early age and looking back I believe that see-saw incident was the first time I understood that if there was something I really felt entitled to, it was worth fighting to get it.

Kindergarten launched the academic years of my life. It was an exciting time where the opportunity to be included with my peers right from the start made me just like them … in fact, I was one of them. It also meant they never really saw me as being any different to what they were.

Soon after I turned five, in January 1962, I started at the Lakes Entrance Primary School alongside my friends and other kids I had grown up with in the town. All except Jim, who was a year below me at school. I turned five before April so I could start school, but his birthday was in November so he had to wait another year. At the time I was every bit as good at writing and colouring-in as other children my age, even though I held my pencils in my toes. I never wore my prosthetic arms while at kindergarten, but that changed when I went to school. I had to wear my arm every day.

Wearing the arm was okay, but I did wonder why the medical professionals were not encouraged by these good clever feet of mine. As children often do, I suppose I wondered about this, but never thought to actually ask the question. Although my feet and toes were very adept at handling a pen or pencil, apparently it was more important that I sit at a desk and write like my peers. In fact, these same professionals at the time spent many hours modelling boots to fit my crooked left foot, so both my feet could be covered up and tucked away. I figure at the time it was regarded as another step towards the 'norm', as all feet were in shoes, if you could afford them.

The other school children were very much 'in the know' when it came to my appearance, so whether or not I had my arms or shoes was never a shock to them. At school, just as in kindergarten, I was just one of the kids. In fact, there was never any shortage of children ready to help me when I needed it, which included dropping my undies at the toilet cubicle door, then I would retreat to privacy, do my business and reappear, where they would pull up my undies and off we'd go to play or class. The instability and help required was due to the weight of the arms. At home without them I was far more independent.

The teachers were also supportive. One of my teachers was Mrs Jerkins, who was renowned for being a bit tough on her students, and she left me in no doubt that I was not exempt from her wrath, especially when I didn't do my best work. I remember her classroom quite vividly, including the old wooden desks we used to sit in.

Mine was cut down to a height that accommodated my very short stature, allowing me easy and independent access.

In later years, I became particularly endeared to Mrs Jerkins, and will never forget her, because she always had high expectations of me. On occasions, as she did with others, she snuck up behind me and with a whack of the ruler over the back of the hand, in my case my metal hook, exclaimed "you can do better than that, Debbi Gray!" This was her usual reaction to students who were not working to her expectations and, although she was tough, she was fair and I also had to meet the appropriate standards. It, of course, didn't hurt on the metal hook, but it did scare me into action.

Mrs Jerkins encouraged me to write better and ensured I gave everything my best shot. She pushed me harder, with a reprimand if I was slack and praise when I truly applied myself. She was also very practical and gave me permission to take off my shoes, which was a very rare event at school but was allowed for a good reason.

We had started sewing lessons and in this class I developed an interest in embroidery. The dexterity of my toes really shone through when we were told we were to make a table centrepiece and six placemats out of yellow calico. Using my toes I painstakingly removed three threads from around the fabric, about an inch in from the edges. I replaced these with green and red thread, easily fraying the outer edges to finish off each piece. That year in Grade 2 at the age of six or seven I finished top of my class in sewing, which was an accomplishment that made both Mum and Mrs Jerkins very proud. And so was I. Mrs Margaret Rowe in Grade 3 held the same expectations but was a bit softer, and Grade 4 delivered the tough and matronly Mrs Viv Harbeck. Grade 5 introduced me to Mr Sinclair; a fabulous character who also endeared himself to me. Then Grade 6 brought a young and quieter Mr Corey.

When I look back, I can see that those teachers and fellow students who were the toughest on me were the ones who really helped to develop my ability to strive and survive. It was Mrs Jerkins who told me there was no such word as 'never' and, among other things, this may have accounted for my persistence on the greens at the local golf course.

Both Mum and Dad had always been avid golfers and were very active in the development of the Golf Club and its eventual relocation from where the Lakes Entrance Secondary School now stands, to its current location. Golf was their sport, recreation and social passion, which made the Lakes Entrance Golf Club our second home. I started playing golf, in a fashion, when I was only a toddler. On many occasions I would sit on the front of the golf buggy while Mum and Dad made the rounds of the golf course. They made no qualms about including me in whatever they were doing, and this included teaching me to play golf … or at least, letting me try and hit golf balls into the hole.

When we reached the green a ball was dropped on the edge for me to play with. Either Mum or Dad would lend me a putter, which was placed on my shoulder against my neck. Gripping the club firmly between my neck and shoulder, I planted my feet firmly on the ground, twisted at the waist as golfers do and was able to swing the club through and connect quite forcefully with the ball. Sometimes, I would shoot it across to the other side of the green.

I was certainly more physically adept than anyone expected, and this helped my efforts on the golf course. However, like all golfers I soon found there was a certain amount of skill needed to get that little white ball into the hole. Eventually I learned to play the greens and even today I still make a formidable opponent in a round of mini golf, which is a great form of recreation that my daughter Emma and I have been able to enjoy together since she was a toddler.

Many of our family friends were also golfers who had children, several of whom stand out in my memory as girls I loved being with. Among others, Julie Jackel and Suzie Bulmer - although she was several years younger - were wonderful friends and we had a lot of fun together. For as far back as I can remember their families welcomed me into their nests with loving and supporting arms. So did the families of my primary school buddies, such as Gloria Smith, Julie Waites, Lynette Smith, Brenda Buchanan, Tracey Witham and several others.

Talking of friends, Dad's lifelong mate lived up the road with his family. The Hubbards had four children and they have always played a big part in our family life. In fact, the house where they still live today was the only house on the northern side of Hazel Road at Kalimna, when we moved to that street. Kalimna is the name given to the area at the top of the hill which overlooks the lakes and entrance. Memories of these childhood years, from when I was five years old, are still etched in my mind. The yabby dam out the back of the Hubbards' house has been filled in and today the area is completely covered and surrounded by other houses.

Much of my childhood revolved around that dam. The Gray and Hubbard children could often be found trudging around in the mud at the dam's edge where we set our baits in the hope of catching yabbies. Yabbying was an activity in which I could fully participate. Using my finger-like toes I could easily tie the string around a little piece of bread, then holding the other end in my mouth I would drape the baited end back over my shoulder and with a huge forward thrust of the shoulder, fling the bread out into the murky waters.

As the bait sank to the bottom I would sit down in the mud, holding the string between my toes while I waited for a little tug. When the tug announced that something was biting on my line I would slowly pull the string into the edge of the dam where the yabby, clinging to my bread, could be scooped up in a net. That was always the most exciting part of yabbying, because if you weren't quick the yabby would let go of the bait and scurry back into the safety of the dam's muddy water.

Those were wonderful times. Like Mum and Dad, our neighbours were beautiful people with a desire for good and loyal friendships, which included much family fun.

CHAPTER 3

Fitting my prosthetics

It's funny you know, but I don't recall any real problems or adverse reactions when I attended the local schools. It seems as people got to know my personality, most had no trouble finding ways for me to fit in. Mind you, by the time I was eight years old I still had no idea of what my world would really be like as I grew older. I was familiar with the term bully but had no knowledge of words like 'discrimination' or 'patronisation', and I didn't know about arrogant attitudes or simple ignorance. Those words were rarely part of my family's vocabulary.

As a child all I knew, albeit subconsciously, was that I was breathing, I was moving and I was most certainly enjoying my young life and the environment I lived in. I had my friends and the most wonderful family life a kid could want, so why wouldn't I laugh a lot and run around with the neighbourhood kids? Keeping up with them was a bit of a challenge though, and I seemed to spend a lot of time trying to catch up. But when they saw this, most of the time the others would wait or help out. In fact, they devised some pretty interesting modes of transport for me.

I was a fairly slow walker because my legs were so much shorter than normal legs. It always felt like I was pacing quickly along, taking three steps to everyone else's one. To make it easier, Jim would sit me at the back end of the long seat on his purple Dragster pushbike and ride, sometimes hitting the infamous 'S' bend going down Jemmy's Point on the Princes Highway at top speed, or find a golf buggy which was my favourite mode of transport. It was the best way for friends to get me around quickly, especially on long distance jaunts. Although I do believe the thrill and skills learned on that Dragster instilled in me a frustrating love for riding. Later in life I would enjoy riding on the back of many motorbikes. I was a proverbial 'professional pillion'!

They could have also used a pram, but I found the golf buggy more acceptable. I had already started to display the 'don't treat me like a baby' attitude, so a golf buggy suited the image better than a pram. Also, I could easily get on and off the buggy without any help. That independent streak was growing.

***

Early in Grade 4 my parents and I were asked whether I would be prepared to trial a pair of arms which worked quite differently to those I had been wearing. They were gas operated, made in Germany and had never been trialled before in Australia.

The arms I had been using were manually operated and as such took a lot of my strength. The German arms were powered by gas and relied only on the push of buttons, or rocker-switches, which were strategically positioned inside the fibreglass jacket to which the limbs were attached. There were also switches on the outside front panels of the jacket which could be operated by pressing my chin on them.

So we decided to give the gas arms a try and they became the source of much entertainment and amusement at school, especially when I blew a hose, which was about four feet long and extended from a 20 pound bottle of carbon dioxide gas. I had to be connected to the gas whenever I wanted to use the arms. Sometimes the connection would come adrift, leaving the end of the hose whipping viciously back and forth through the air. During the last two years of primary school this seemed to particularly delight a couple of the more outgoing rascals in class, such as loveable friends Steven Ely and neighbour Wayne Carstairs. These boys, instead of simply turning off the gas, would dive on the hose and wrestle it to the floor. I enjoyed this attitude immensely as it took the more clinical view away from the situation. What did annoy me in a small way, was when they'd sneakily turn the gas off!

***

The following year it was decided by the medical professionals that I was too short and therefore needed a pair of artificial legs. Yes, in my latter years of primary school, I was told I was too short! Life would be better if I was taller, they said, and so off we went back to the Limb Factory where a pair of legs was built.

Well, they weren't legs as such, only half legs. They were made of fibreglass and therefore rigid, comprising only the lower part of the leg with no knee joint, and also no flexible ankle joint. The legs were beautifully crafted calves and designed with stability in mind. Across the top of each leg was a small, flat plate, to which shoes were attached. The plates certainly took away from the vision of 'normality'.

With a pair of little red shoes already on the feet of these legs, a second pair of identical little red shoes were attached to the plate at the top of the legs at point where a knee would be. This pair was for my feet – my real ones – to slip into. The idea of having a shoe at the knee meant that theoretically my ankle joint could be used as a knee joint. It was all very ingenious really, if I had not already developed into such an active outdoor person. I found the gait and insecurity of height, which I had never lived with before, quite daunting and extremely frustrating.

By this time Jim and I had already started attending the dances which were organised for the town's younger brigade. First there were the 'A and A Teen Town Dances' then, as an older teenager, graduating to the Surf Club Dances, which were regular community youth events and I was already proving to be quite the social butterfly. I loved dancing and believed, right or wrong, that I had better rhythm than most. I started to wonder how I was going to move like that on my new stilts!

In hindsight, the legs were never going to work. Had I persevered, I quite possibly could have achieved the right balance and gone on to walk at the standard height for my age. But this would have meant putting my feet – the ones I used so competently – into shoes and thus making them inaccessible and me, non- functional. So the desired height concept never happened. I was never stable on those legs and the longest distance I ever walked on them was down the four or five metre hallway at home.

Our local newspaper, the Bairnsdale Advertiser, wanted to take photos of me in the quadrangle at school for a feature story so my teacher, Mrs Rowe, gathered up a few of my school girlfriends to help out. Gloria Smith, Julie Waites and a couple of others rallied around me, staying close in case I lost balance. I look at the newspaper clipping of that article now and think to myself that it must have been a thrill at the time, but I can't remember ever having a feeling of pleasure or relief at being up so high. In fact, when I look closely at the photo I can see that my eyes are looking towards the ground, perhaps in anticipation of my face arriving there at any second.

By secondary school as far as I was concerned all the artificial arms I had worn for all of my primary years were limiting my ability. While attempting to achieve the desired appearance of 'normality' they prevented me from performing some of the most basic tasks such as going to the toilet on my own, dressing myself, or simply getting onto a chair.

I always found these limbs to be awkward, heavy, cumbersome, inhibiting and generally monstrous.

After the fuss from the newspapers and the announcement of new limbs for Deb Gray everything quietened down a little and, as primary school children, we returned to the usual daily routine.

Before long the artificial legs were placed discretely into a cupboard, never to see daylight again!

***

As I continued to grow so did the regular upgrading of my artificial arms. The regular fittings of my prosthetics were not events I looked forward to and these occasions really affected me at puberty, when the usual feelings of modesty experienced in the pre-teen years began to kick in. I became more aware and very sensitive to the fact there were men looking at my newly developing breasts, which were covered only by a thin stocking to protect my skin from the plaster they were smothering me in.

During that sensitive pre-teenage time I started to experience uncomfortable feelings about being so exposed. Looking back now, I know those professional men were only doing their job and would have had no idea I was struggling to understand the embarrassment I was encountering.

I never mentioned those feelings and maybe I didn't have to, because Miss Angliss just seemed to know, and from that point she was always there to cover me up whenever possible with a towel or sheet. She was a woman of professionalism who always tried her best to protect my emerging pride and dignity.

Above: 1957, 10 months old.

Above: Mum & Dad, early 50's.

Top left: Geoff (5), Jim (10mths) and me (20mths).

Bottom left: As a toddler with my dear brother Jim. We were almost like twins.

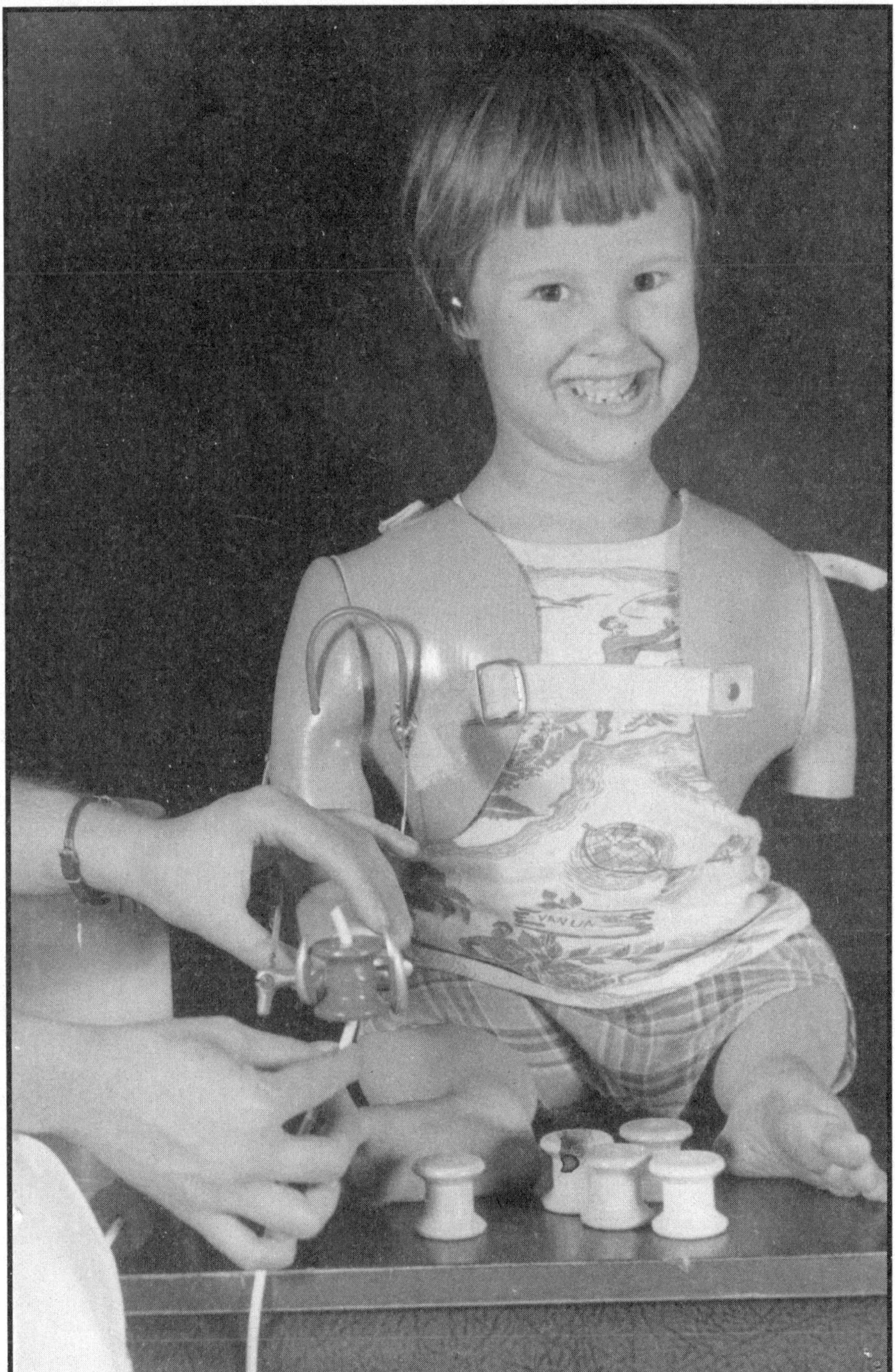

Above: Fitting my first prosthetic arms, at the age of two.

Left: That's me and my Pa Monk (Mum's Dad).

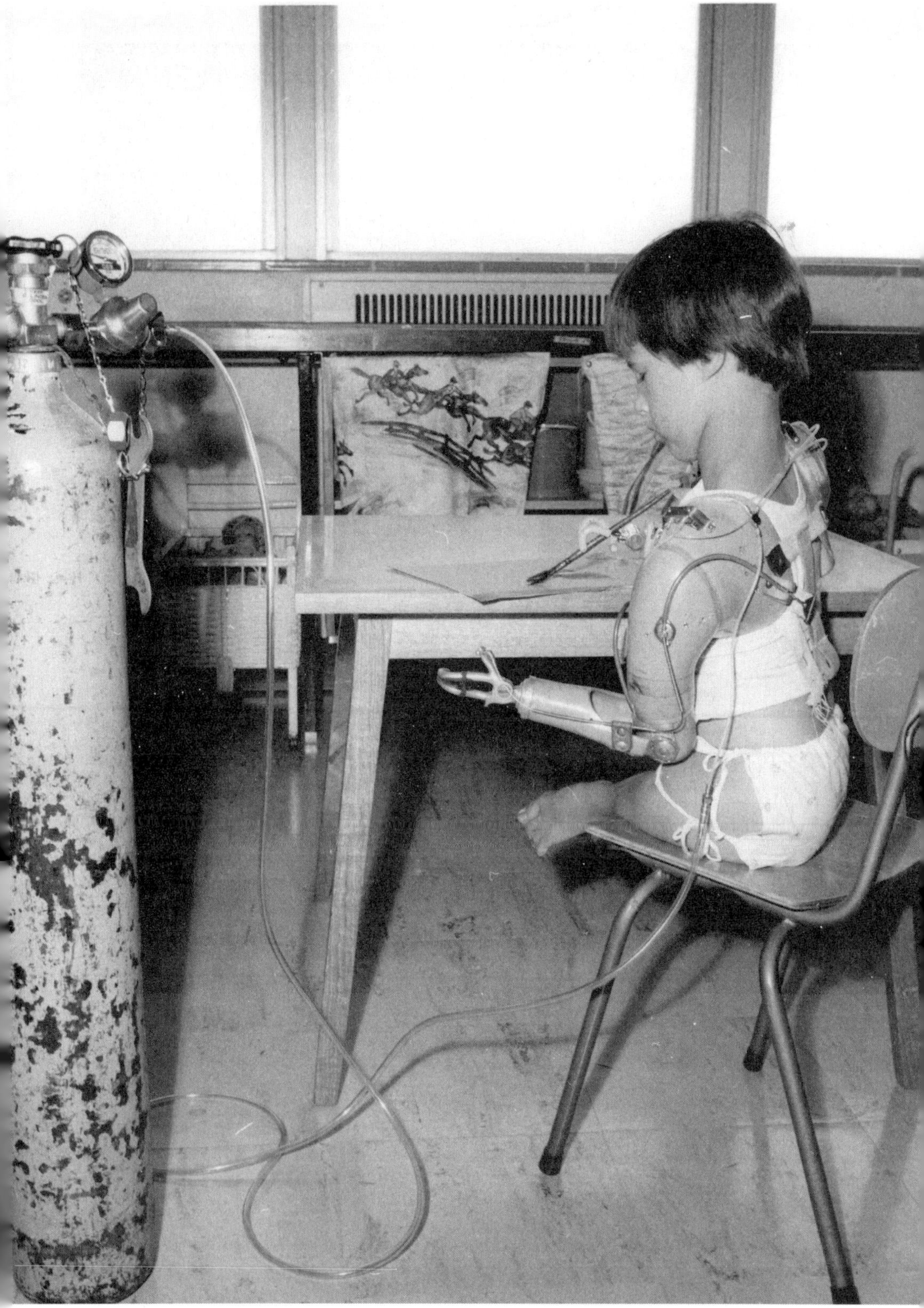

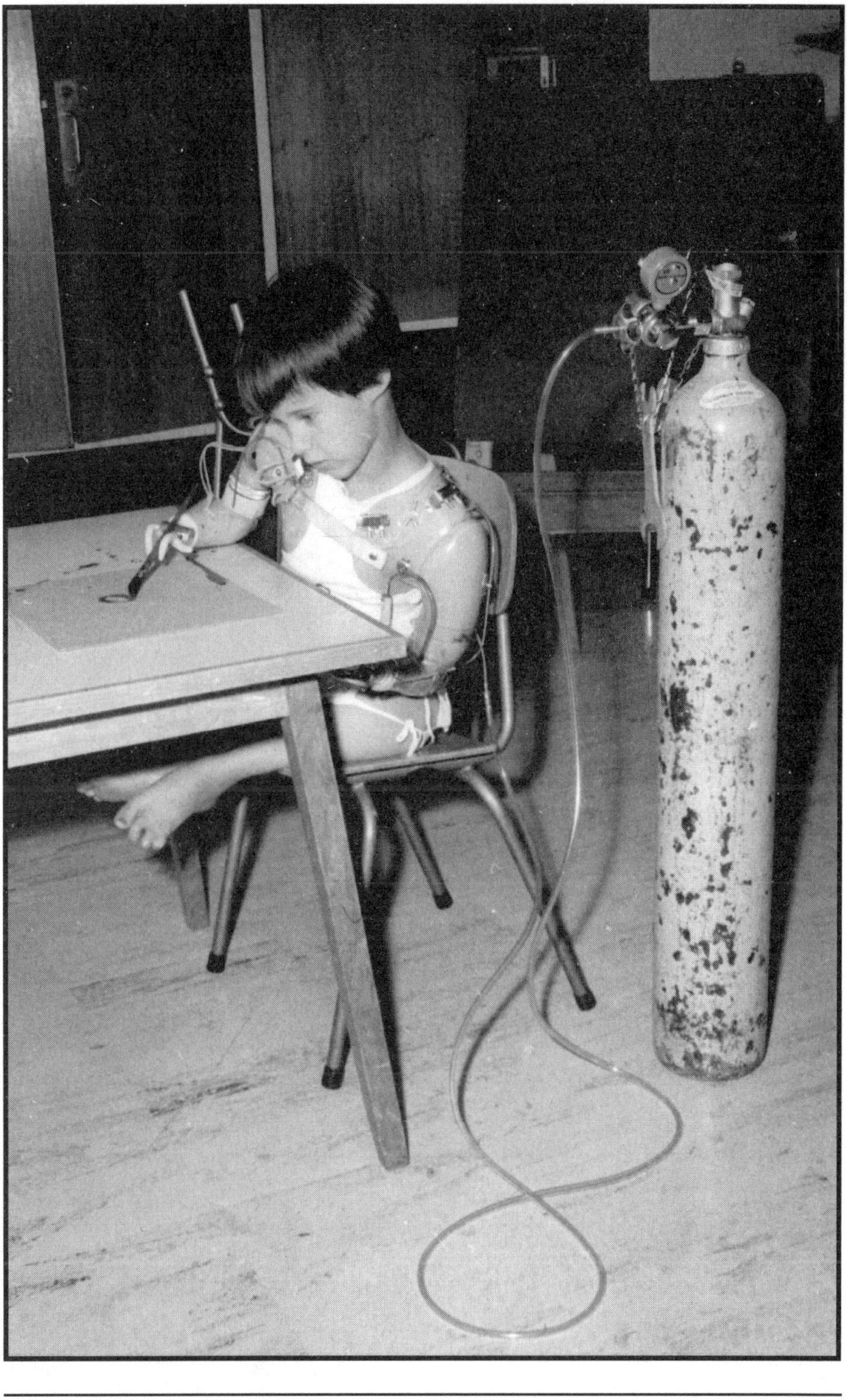

Above and left: Using my prosthetic arms at the age of 4 or 5.

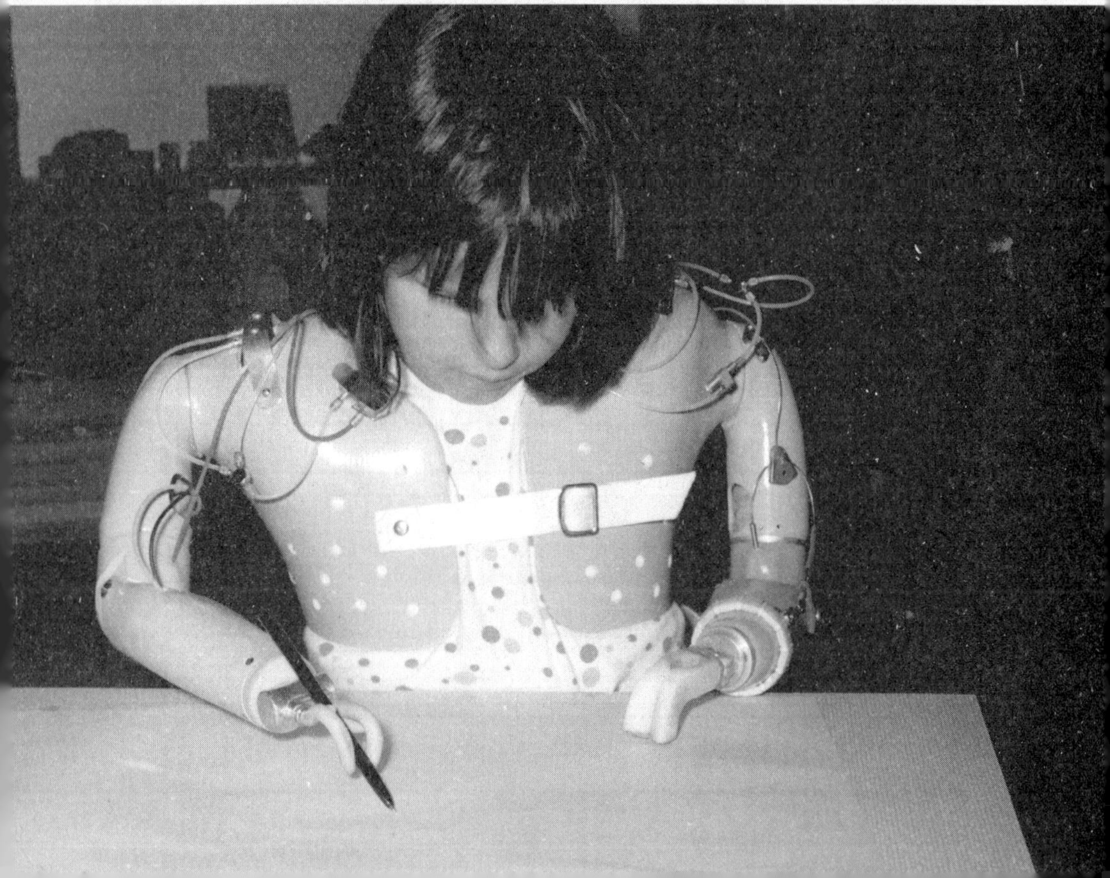

Above: Using my prosthetic arms at school, in Grade 2.

Top left: In the classroom, with the gas bottle that powered my arms on the seat behind me.

Bottom left: Using the prosthetic arms.

Above: Publicity shot with my prosthetic arms and legs.

Left: At school with my prosthetic arms and legs.

Above: My right hand had a hook. I preferred using my toes.

Top left: Enjoying a swim at Porepunkah.

Bottom left: Hanging out during the school holidays when I was 13.

CHAPTER 4

A fun loving teenager

When I was about 13 or 14 years old I ceased being a patient at the Royal Children's Hospital. Val Angliss and other prosthetic technicians at the Monash Rehab Tech Unit were now looking after my very occasional prosthetic needs. I continued under the care of Dr Klein and we went on to have a loving, lifelong friendship. I have always had great respect, dedication and love for this man and the professional support he gave me as a child.

At home, life continued as usual. I went to dances and, along with my family, avidly followed Geoff's football career, originally with Nungurner in the juniors and later with Swan Reach. Of course I also went along to support Jim when he played basketball. Jim played for the local team, the Red Raiders, and I was their number one supporter. Hence, I would get dropped off with Jim on his basketball nights at the Recreation Centre, still standing, although quite transformed, on the nor-west corner of Church and Carpenter Streets.

On one particular occasion it was hot and muggy inside the newly built Lakes Entrance Recreation Centre, where the basketball was played, so a few of us decided to go outside to the kids' playground.

Although I found most playground equipment quite difficult to use, there was a spinning wheel that we called the 'whizzy whizzy' which I could manage, even though it was a bit awkward. Basically it was two circles of tubular steel about 12 inches apart and eight to 10 feet across which children sat on as it was spun around. In the centre were a series of tubular steel spokes.

I was able to manipulate my body up onto the outer rim, but it took all my gravitational control to stop myself being flung off as the wheel went around. Sometimes the other kids would have it going so fast I had to try and hold onto the inner side of the ring with my chin and inner leg.

On May Day, the 1st of May 1970 (noted in a diary), I lay along the rings as usual, then manoeuvred into the middle to get the spinning effect, rather than being flung around in circles, with my shoulders against the spokes.

I was having great fun until I placed my foot on the ground, as we did to slow or stop the spinning. Suddenly I heard a crack and at the same time felt an intense burning sensation spread across the top of my foot. I soon discovered this was because the top of my foot's skin had been scraped off, courtesy of hooking my foot through a tree root, shaped like a loop, which had been exposed from continuous scraping of shoes on the soil. The 'whizzy whizzy' came to a sudden halt and, in all honesty, I don't know what was hurting the most – the burning sensation inside my left foot or the stinging on top.

I was untangled and lifted from my painful position by friends who carried me inside where I could sit and watch the basketball. I didn't want to create a fuss or be seen as someone who gets hurt easily so I put on a very brave front and insisted that I stay until after the game, at which time Mum or Dad would pick us up.

I struggled through with the pain until Mum eventually arrived and in her beautiful mind the fact I was able to stay until the end of the game after my little accident surely meant I had not injured myself too badly. She decided that with a couple of days' rest and keeping pressure off my foot, it would be okay. However, more than a day or two went by and I was still hobbling around, unable to put any weight on my left leg.

As a parent, I now understand how we can reach a point where we do not believe our children are hurt as badly as they may insist. In my case, this was especially true at the time because I was always keen to find any excuse which may get me a day off school. Mum probably thought I was 'putting it on' a bit, so it was 10 days later before the discovery that everything was not as it should be.

Crunch time came when Mum was enjoying a cuppa with her good friend and neighbour Betty Stewart, who we called Aunty Betty ... a beautiful, loving, loyal and homely person. I was hobbling around the bathroom trying to get undressed and into the bath, but finding it extremely difficult because I still could not put any pressure on my left leg or foot.

My moaning and groaning from the bathroom finally attracted the attention of an irate and frustrated mother. Mum was prepared to acknowledge that I had taken some skin off the top of my foot, but questioned my claim of such intense pain in my left leg!

At this point, I must say that I have become the person I am today because my parents didn't mollycoddle me. It was not unusual for me to lose some skin off my shoulder, chin, forehead or nose ... especially my chin which copped a number of bashings and still sports a few scars.

On this particular day Mum entered the bathroom, swept me up by the shoulders, lifted me away from the bath and stood me in the middle of the bathroom floor. And that's when it became quite obvious that something really was seriously wrong.

I let out the scream of the week and collapsed, crying, onto the bathroom floor. Aunty Betty had followed Mum to the bathroom and between the two of them, it was decided I had to see a doctor.

Needless to say, the prognosis confirmed the pain I had endured was not 'put on' and my complaining was well justified. The doctor advised my foot was broken and subsequently wrapped it in plaster. I cannot remember whether I hobbled around at school with the plaster on, or whether I stayed home doing catch-up homework. However, I do remember that after six weeks and another visit to the doctor in Bairnsdale, I was told the plaster had to remain in place for an extra one or two weeks. I was not amused!

Perusing my diaries, I noted the broken foot did not seem to have much impact on my weekend social activities. Funny about that! I was still able to attend the local footy each Saturday and barrack for my brothers, or get pushed around the streets on the golf buggy.

***

During my early years of secondary school there were times when I struggled with the weight of the prostheses. I had to be out of bed early each morning, giving myself enough time to get ready and up to the bus stop, then the trip into Bairnsdale High School took at least 45 minutes. Naturally, there was the same amount of time going home after school. So the days were much longer than I had been used to at primary school in Lakes Entrance.

Although I settled quite well into high school, in many respects it wasn't as easy as primary school. For some reason the days seemed hotter. Perhaps it was because Bairnsdale is several kilometres inland and 32 kilometres from Lakes, so doesn't get the regular sea breezes that we enjoyed in my home town. On top of this the school was much bigger so I had to cover a lot more ground in a day with my limited mobility.

At first I continued to use my artificial arms for school work, but as well as limiting my mobility, by the end of the day they were very heavy, especially on hot days. On a more positive note they were good when we wanted something to tie on the end of a skipping rope, which had also been the case in primary school.

It should be acknowledged that Bairnsdale High School went to great lengths to cater for my needs, though at the time I was unaware of the marathon efforts taking place behind the scenes on my behalf.

Because I was wearing the gas operated arms, necessary support equipment including gas bottles was required in the classrooms. It took a lot of consultation between my parents and the school's teachers to get this all set up. The desks, like those in primary school, would have to be cut down to accommodate my stature, and it seems every attempt was made to make it possible for me to attend Bairnsdale High.

I believe there were about 11 gas bottles, one placed in each classroom behind the desks where I sat. Despite all this effort, especially with the availability of gas and the connections for my arms, the one thing I wanted more than anything else was to be able to take off my shoes and work with my feet and toes.

***

In my first year of high school there were some significant events. I was in a French class when Neil Armstrong landed on the moon, while we all sat back and watched this amazing event taking place on the little black and white telly the teacher had brought to class just for that moment.

Even more significant, from my perspective, was the secret attention I received from a charismatic American boy. Randy Mayhall was the first boy to touch me in an affectionate way. Like my girlfriends, I was starting to notice boys and enjoyed their attention, although it wouldn't be long before I discovered they usually weren't too keen on showing it in public. It was okay behind the shelter shed or a tree, or in Randy's case visiting our house where he would sometimes sleep over and sneak to me during the night. But boys were afraid of being ridiculed by their mates if they were seen kissing or hugging a disabled girl.

I suppose by this stage in my life I was seeing a bit of nastiness in some girls, but only in small degrees, except for this one individual, whose name was Nola. She was new in town and wanted to be 'queen bee' and in her quest to be popular she singled me out for particular nasty attention, always trying to victimise and humiliate me. At some stage her brother displayed an interest in friendship and wanted to sit beside me on the bus, but his sister put a swift stop to that. I think this open resentment from his sister was my first experience with open and public discrimination, ridicule and nastiness which, to this point, had been foreign to me; so it came as quite a shock.

Generally I was quite popular, despite the occasional person who found it difficult to accept the attention I received. Most people accepted me for who I was, not what I was, never treating me differently from anyone else, which is the way I have always liked things to be. I was always included in what was going on and those who did not like my vivacious and outgoing nature simply stayed away.

Nola, on the other hand, reminded me on a regular basis I was a cripple, I was unattractive, I waddled like a duck and, in general, I had nothing to offer. One day riding home on the bus she got the better of me.

On the bus it was common to pass jokes around and she'd say "don't show Debbi", just to be spiteful. She gathered friends by intimidation and stand-over tactics, which I didn't like, and she obviously did not like the attention I received from other kids which led to her attitude towards me. She wanted the attention for herself and sometimes even managed to set me up as a laughing stock because so many girls were afraid of her.

On the rare occasions when people stared at me or talked about the way I looked I put on a hard shell appearance, not wanting to look as if I had been affected. As a young girl I had already developed an ability to generally hide my feelings, especially if I had been emotionally hurt. But several months of enduring the sister's dreadful taunts must have softened the 'hard shell' because I'd had enough.

Then, I got revenge. One quiet, calm bus ride home from school, I was the one who had the good joke and it was being handed around the bus, until Nola snatched it! She was sitting in the centre of the back seats, so I got out of my seat and approached her, asking her to give it back. But she held the note over her head, out of my reach. I was wearing my prosthetic arms and I snapped, striking her gut with the 'hook'. As she doubled up in pain she sandwiched my head between her stomach and thigh. I was trapped and there was only one way out … so I bit her! Nola screamed, while everyone else including our driver Charlie, who had stopped the bus, sat stunned. I believe Charlie defended my actions because there was not much said about the incident. After that Nola never spoke to me much, which meant an end to the nastiness I had endured, although outside of school hours I did endure several years of taunting from her and her older boyfriend, as each time they drove by they yelled shit at me about giving her rabies. Outwardly, I laughed that off toooo!

***

At school, around about Year 8 or 9, I was reverting back to using my feet more and more. I told the teachers my prostheses were broken, or simply arrived at school without them. Often I discarded them at our cubby-house near the bus stop, before boarding the bus for school, helped by girlfriend and neighbour Linda Jakobi. Then I was allowed to use my feet in the classroom which I was quite happy about.

I got away with this for several months until my scheming was undone … by cigarettes, of all things. As young teenagers Geoff, Jim and I, like many of our peers, were always on the look-out for an opportunity to have a puff. One day Dad, prompted by a sense he was losing smokes from his packet, went to the bus stop to count the cigarette butts. Not only did he find the butts … to his great surprise there was also a pair of arms hidden discretely under a bush, with nobody in them!

He decided to take them home, which of course caused me quite a dilemma. When we arrived at the bus shelter that afternoon my friend and neighbour Linda and I headed towards the bus stop cubby, to go through the usual ritual of getting my arms from under the bush and putting them back on. We were chatting away happily until we discovered the arms were missing. Then panic set in.

Those at our stop, including myself, wondered whether any of the few close neighbours who knew what I did each day had taken the arms. We searched the neighbourhood, all to no avail, as our concern – particularly mine – continued to grow. Where could my artificial limbs have disappeared to? Perhaps a couple of local dogs had dragged them away? Surely no-one would steal them, we thought. After a while it became obvious we weren't going to find the arms just lying around, so little brother Jim and I made our tentative way home, up the back steps and into the kitchen.

As we slowly slid open the back door our eyes lit up with momentary relief, for there, perched on the kitchen table, were my arms. However, just as quickly as the feeling of relief arrived it disappeared with a realisation that I was up the proverbial creek without a paddle.

How was I going to talk my way out of this one? Not surprisingly, Dad wanted an explanation. "Why were these rather expensive arms, which many people have gone to so much effort and expense to provide for you, lying under a bush at the bus stop?"

Perhaps I should briefly explain that by this pubescent time in my life I compensated much of my physical deformity with a decent dose of self-confidence. I was developing what could be termed the 'gift of the gab'. So, once cornered, I found it relatively easy to express myself and clearly convey my thoughts on the given situation. This was especially the case when anyone was trying to get me to do something I didn't want to. And I most definitely did not want to wear those arms.

As they lay idle on the kitchen table, having been rescued from under a bush by my father, I proceeded to articulate my feelings about these arms, leaving no-one in any doubt that, in my mind, I did not want or need them.

Fortunately, I had the most wonderful parents who, by this time, were also sceptical and wondering whether these heavy, cumbersome and at times painful extremities were really necessary, having seen often enough how well I could use my toes. Eventually they were convinced and supported my desire not to use the prosthetic arms at school.

At this point I should explain that in the early 1970s there were two campuses for Bairnsdale High School, with Forms 1 and 2 in the original school building at the Dalmahoy Street campus and Forms 3 to 6 in a relatively new building, which was on a much bigger site at the Wallace Street campus. At the time I was about to progress from Form 2 to Form 3. As such, if I was to use my arms the gas bottles installed at the Dalmahoy Street campus would have to be relocated to Wallace Street. Because of my persistence, and with the support of my parents, this did not occur and for the next two years I used my toes at school.

As a consequence of my insistence not to wear arms, another one of the so called 'therapeutic professionals' suggested I should be given typing lessons. I could already type well with my toes, but he thought these lessons would help increase my speed, accuracy and ability to keep a faster pace for notetaking.

I think the suggestion came about because there was an inability, even at times ignorance and unwillingness, to accept the skills that already existed in my toes. There was insufficient faith, consideration or knowledge of how effective they could be for writing, typing and many other tasks.

Anyway, as a result Mum and I went to the Royal Melbourne Institute of Technology where I participated in a rather unnecessary crash course in typing with my toes. I remember we spent three weeks away from the rest of the family, just as had occurred with my initial limb fitting and practice, at a time when I would have preferred being home enjoying the holidays with my friends.

***

Another challenge which arose just prior to graduation to Form 3 at the even larger campus was when teachers became concerned about my limited mobility and the time it was taking to get from one classroom to the next. By this stage in my education notetaking in the classroom had to be completed quite quickly and they were also worried that my toes would not be able to keep up the pace, although this was never discussed with me.

Whilst at RMIT, it was suggested that a sort of platform on a trolley could be constructed and would make it easier for me to move around to the different classrooms. And so, while I was at RMIT with Mum, the woodwork department there built me a platform on castors.

It was about 20 inches wide by 40 inches long, which was just big enough to fit a small cut-down chair and a typewriter. As it had four-inch castors the trolley was quite low to the ground. There was a handle, similar to what you have on a pram, attached to the back of the trolley. Using the handle my fellow students could push the trolley to wherever we had to go, as I rode happily along on the attached chair that was provided behind the electric typewriter.

I assure you, there was never any shortage of pushers, as my friends and fellow students enjoyed scooting down the corridors en-route to class. Like lots of schools the corridors were quite long and on many occasions my friends charged along, pushing me and the trolley in front of them to build up some speed, before jumping aboard next to me and getting a ride to the next class.

I've always had a desire to turn any small task where I needed a little bit of help into a fun experience, and I am sure it is a key reason why I was able to fit into student life at school, then later into society in general. The trolley rides were a good example.

Unfortunately, there has not always been a happy ending to my escapades. One day a group of my friends attempted our boldest and most mischievous prank, when far too many of us piled onto the trolley for a record breaking run up the corridor and past the principal's office. The laughter was replaced with a more serious tone when the principal stepped out of his office at the wrong time for everyone, forcing quick action from both sides to avoid a nasty collision. He was not amused and we had to suffer the consequences.

***

I was a fun loving, adventurous teenager who kept striving to be just like the other kids. I've always wanted to be treated the same as every other individual … don't treat me any differently just because my physical appearance is not what some may consider 'normal'.

And so because I wanted to do the same things as everyone else – good and bad - there was more than the odd occasion when I was in trouble, including the day I was caught smoking at school.

A group of us thought we had a pretty good system when we wanted a cigarette. One acted as the look-out – I had to take my turn - while the others were hiding and puffing away on a smoke. I suppose the odds were strongly in favour of us eventually being caught, and that's what happened.

The punishment for my partners in crime was several strokes of a ruler on the hand, and because I didn't have a hand for the principal to whack, I had to cop it across the back of my legs.

***

Thanks to the help of my Dad I had a great affinity with water. I loved to swim and I loved the beach, spending many wonderful hours on the sandy beaches across the footbridge at Lakes Entrance.

Dad taught me to swim, for which I am very grateful, though his methods were a little unorthodox. We had and old unused, concrete water tank which became used as our above ground swimming pool, thanks to recent access to the town water supply. It was about 8 to 10 feet deep, 12 feet in diameter, with a rope across the middle. After taking the time to ensure I was familiar and comfortable in the water, Dad tossed me in and I'd pop up and grab the rope with my toes and hold myself up, then floating became second nature.

Again, there was no mollycoddling … he had confidence in my ability and put it to the test. I became quite a strong swimmer – not fast, but strong - and was always very relaxed in the water. I don't have the usual weight of legs and arms but have lung capacity and I'm a bit like a cork. If you push me under, I'll just pop back up again. I used to dive into the water and push down as hard as I possibly could, with maximum propulsion, but it didn't matter how hard I kicked this little body would just pop back up to the surface.

I was lucky that Dad took the initiative and helped develop my love of swimming and the water, because Mum never went in above her knees. She was terrified of water after a horrific experience when she was young. As a young girl Mum and her siblings were paddling and swimming in the Snowy River at Orbost when her sister stepped in a deep hole and was sinking. Mum tried to grab an outstretched hand, but despite her desperate efforts when she almost reached the little fingertips, the hand disappeared under the water and her sister drowned.

This was another in a string of tragedies Mum had to endure. Before that she watched her little brother Terry die when he was only two years old, then later she lost her only brother Barry, plus a niece and nephew, in a shocking car accident. Yet Mum maintained her strength and, in doing so, gave me so much strength. Little Cammie always had a smile. That's what I remember.

I fortunately learnt and enjoying my swimming. I went on to be a part of the primary school swimming program and was successful at attaining the Advertiser Swimming Certificate, but due to my inability to pick up a brick from the bottom of the front lake where our lessons were held, I never achieved the Senior Certificate. 'Oh well, at least I could swim,' was the way I felt.

Among my many wonderful swimming memories are the times we went to visit Aunty Eve, who was Dad's sister, and Uncle Bob at Porepunkah, near Bright. At the back of their two-storey house the water trickled down from a creek into a big rock pool which was full of pure, fresh water. There was a gentle slope on the rock which allowed me to get in and out quite easily and feet first I would torpedo down into the clear and calming depths from higher ledges. With air retained in my lungs and a vicious kicking I would eventually pop to the surface like a cork. When we (my older cousin and I) finished swimming, we'd go inside and I would play Elvis records and write to the Elvis Fan Club. As a young 'un, thanks to Mum and her sisters all smitten by Elvis, of course I became a huge Elvis fan.

***

Some years later, as an early teen, I gained an informal adopted uncle, my Uncle Alf. He was a New Zealand merchant sailor, a single man with no family, who had read about me in a newspaper and wrote to Mum and Dad asking if he could be my penfriend. They agreed, and wherever he went around the world he collected stamps and sent them to me with his letters.

Uncle Alf literally sent hundreds and hundreds of stamps … I think he must have collected his own, as well as gathering together others from his mates.

I put them in albums, but there were so many I couldn't keep up and in the end had a big, black garbage bag full of stamps from throughout the world. Unfortunately they were all lost, along with a lot of my other childhood memories, when the house was sold and our parents moved to Sale.

Over the years I lost contact with Uncle Alf and sadly I don't even know if he is still alive. I remember on one occasion he came for a visit and brought his friend's young daughter Christine, a young Maori girl, and they stayed for about a week. Christine and I became really close friends.

But they went back to New Zealand, at a time when I was getting into my latter teenage years and always busy with this or that and, as happens too often, you lose touch. We stopped communicating. So, Uncle Alf or Christine, if you happen to get a copy of my book and you're reading this, please make contact.

CHAPTER 5

Boys and tragedies

Like any teenager I had lots of good times, mixed in with a few that weren't so good. I had fun. I had tragedies. I started learning about boys and realised I liked them but at the same time, like many other teenage girls, approached these feelings with trepidation. I had a few tears, but realised there were things I had to accept and not cry about, especially when it came to boys.

I watched my girlfriends and their boyfriends and at the age of 15 the realities of life and male/female relationships for a person with disabilities started to hit home, as did the realisation I would need to put aside a lot of my feelings … hide them from myself, as well as others. I had to hide the pain I felt as I watched my girlfriends with their boyfriends, and wished that I had one too.

To this point in my life it hadn't been an issue, but that was changing. Like many other young girls I had been kissed behind the tree at primary school and appreciated occasional male attention on the school bus. But once boys reached their mid-teens and were past the innocent age, things changed. They seemed to reach an age where there was ridicule from mates if they weren't 'going out' with someone acceptable. And usually I was not acceptable.

I discovered that if a young guy liked me, he'd been frightened to show it because, I assume, he would cop a ribbing from mates. So boys would show affection in a dark corner at a party, or down an alley-way, but not out in the open. In many respects this was my introduction to many years of frustration with the opposite sex. In later years, being on my own, I thought it perhaps wasn't entirely their fault. Subconsciously, I think I became scared. I didn't want to get too attached and then get rejected so on the occasions when a special friendship or relationship started to develop I became defensive and as a result would flick them off before we were too close.

This all started in my young late teenage years when boys didn't know what to do with me or how to treat me and, as I say, were worried about what their mates might think. So I became defensive and this mindset has continued throughout my life. Not long ago I was whingeing to a girlfriend about being alone and she told me, "it's your own bloody fault". She's probably right.

***

As a teenager, like most of my friends, I was looking for a good time at every opportunity and at this point in my life I also gained a new 'sister' to help me along this path. We had lots of fun together.

Technically this was my Aunty Keryn – Mum's sister – but to me she was more like a big sister than an aunty. Her parents, who of course were my grandparents, had died relatively young, leaving Keryn to live with her oldest sister. Unbeknown to her other siblings, the older sister then could not cope. It seems the mischievous teenager could not stay and was shipped off to Winlaton as a ward of the state. At the time this was a government run female youth correctional centre and orphanage. When Mum found out her little sister had been sent to Winlaton she went and rescued her, bringing her home to live with us.

Aunty Keryn, who is about eight years older than I am, allowed me to hang with her and her girlfriends, Yvonne Bryce, Colleen Drysdale, Cheryl Bond etc. As I recall she taught me things, such as how to smoke, amongst other things, in the old stone toilet block at the footy ground. She treated me the same as she treated anyone else. I got no obvious favours and didn't want them. In that respect, as far as my life is concerned, nothing has changed.

I remember one night when Aunty Keryn and I were at home on our own and were given a huge fright. There was a wire door at the bottom of the little half spiral stairwell, leading to the sliding back door entering the dining area, and we heard it shut. The sliding door didn't have a regular door latch to lock it, just a screwdriver which we shoved in a hole in the architrave; in a crude way, this usually kept it shut. But as someone tried to open the sliding door the screwdriver moved. Keryn jumped for the phone and I grabbed at the screwdriver, using my shoulder and chin as it was rattling around and obviously about to fall out, and butted it back in. Then, keeping my head against the end of the screwdriver to hold it in, I turned around to shove my back against the back end of the sliding door. I was grateful for a shallow finger grip that hindered the intruder, who could not get a good grasp of it. "Who is it?" we both yelled repeatedly, our voices shaking in fright. There was no answer.

We thank a combination of this grip and our efforts to hold the door shut, which were enough to convince the intruder to give up. In reality, if he seriously wanted to enter the house we could not have stopped him. It was a horrifying ideal. When police arrived they found a large footprint on the step and other footprints in the garden. We never found out who it was or what they wanted.

***

The prowler gave me a terrible fright, but it was nothing compared to the night when we almost lost Dad. At the time he was fishing on the *'Capella'* for Dick Smith. It was a 48 foot boat that had been used for shark fishing, but was converted to a scallop boat to take advantage of a relatively new, lucrative catch. The entrance back into the lakes and its sand bar combine to form a dangerous stretch of water that over the years has claimed quite a number of lives. As the *'Capella'* tried to negotiate the bar that evening with a full quota of scallops on board, 15 foot waves crashed around it. One huge wave hit the boat and rolled her side-on.

In the mayhem Dad was initially tangled in scallop gear on the deck, then dragged under as the boat flipped upside down. As he struggled in the treacherous waters Dad kicked himself free. Unaware of the boat's complete rotation he was separated from it and the current quickly swept him away. Meanwhile Dick, who was the boat's skipper, tried desperately to get him back on board. In the stress of the situation Dick collapsed from a heart attack and as the waves kept battering the *'Capella'* he was taken into the wheelhouse by his son Ted, who was also part of the crew. Sadly, the heart attack was fatal.

Dad knew there was no way he could swim to shore against the outgoing tide, so he spat out his teeth, kicked off his gumboots and swam in a westerly direction towards the Jemmy's Point lighthouse. Eventually he hit the beach, totally exhausted and barely able to crawl up onto the dry sand.

Meanwhile, amazing heroics were being shown by other Lakes Entrance fishermen and emergency service personnel. As usually occurred in these situations, the Search & Rescue Squad was quickly into action. Another scallop fisherman, John Guillot, gathered his crew and rushed out the entrance to see if they could help the *'Capella'*, while other fishermen formed a large arc off the entrance with their boats, hoping to find Dad if he had been washed out to sea.

Instead, he had miraculously made it to shore and after catching his breath started walking back towards the entrance. Members of the Search & Rescue Squad walked across the dunes to see if Dad had been washed to the western side and found him, totally exhausted, struggling towards them. Throughout the horrifying ordeal Mum, myself, Jim and other family members kept vigil on Bullock Island, which is where the Fishermen's Cooperative and search headquarters were located. Mum was supported by friends and neighbours as Jim and I huddled together, not knowing what else to do. Our older brother Geoff, who had not long obtained his driver's licence, tore up and down Jemmy's Point in his car, trying to see what was happening on the bar and keeping abreast of information at the wharf.

I can still see Dad when he was finally brought onto Bullock Island, before being taken into Bairnsdale Hospital. His skin was almost black from exposure and he was devastated by the loss of his friend and skipper.

All I wanted to do was wrap two arms around my Dad, who we thought we had lost forever, and hold him tight. But I couldn't.

***

Another great tragedy which I still vividly remember was the loss of my Uncle Barry and his children in a horrific car accident on the Paynesville Road. I idolised Uncle Barry, who was Mum's only brother. He always treated me well … the same as he treated other young people.

He was driving along the Paynesville/Bairnsdale Road, having spent the day fishing in his boat, towing the boat behind his Ford Fairlane with his only two children, Jason and Amy, and a good mate as passengers. A bloke in an EH Holden was racing down Forge Creek Road towards the intersection and apparently thought he could beat Uncle Barry. He couldn't, and ploughed into the side of the Fairlane. Uncle Barry, his mate and little Jason were killed instantly and poor Amy was thrown into a nearby paddock, which is where she passed away soon after, in the arms of a passer-by.

It was so traumatic. We were all devastated and to this day cannot get over those two kids not being here – not being able to grow up and enjoy life – because of some dickhead in his car.

Uncle Barry's wife, Janet Gargan-Monk, has been one of my life-long inspirations, for the way she picked herself up after losing her entire family in such terrible circumstances. I don't know how she survived - not the accident, but the ongoing heartache and pain – though I believe it was a strong Catholic faith that helped her keep going.

It led to one of those many moments to come, where I seriously questioned Christianity and God. If there is a God, why would he do this to someone who loved him so much? She couldn't do any more for God, if he exists, and look what he did to her.

Sadly, Uncle Barry's accident and Dad's near drowning were not the only tragedies I faced that horrible, horrible year. I also lost my good friend Suzie Pilgrim who was the 20 year-old daughter of a neighbour and good friend who was living with us while her parents were holidaying overseas. Suzie was five years older than me and in the year after her accident we were both due to celebrate significant milestones – I would turn 16 and Suzie would be 21. We were planning a combined birthday party on the Thunderbird, which is still functioning as a popular local charter vessel.

Suzie didn't make it to her 21st and the memories of the night we lost her still linger in my mind. I had been in bed asleep, but woke up suddenly and swear I saw Suzie at the window, beckoning me outside to the driveway. Sleepily, I got out of bed, went to the back door and descended the half spiral stairs to investigate the driveway. Suzie was standing beside her little canary-yellow Escort, waving goodbye, just as she did each morning before heading off to work in Bairnsdale. Soon after, and back in bed, the phone rang and we learned that Suzie, who was due home from her farewell celebration at the Bairnsdale HBO office, had been killed earlier that evening by a drunken driver in a car crash. To this day I cannot explain what I saw that night, though I do believe Suzie made a special attempt to say a final goodbye to me.

***

With Suzie's accident, again I had been devastated by the loss of a loved one. On top of everything else I had endured in just a short space of time I think it was the last straw. Week after week I dragged myself around the house, struggling to come to terms with what had happened.

Eventually, for a change of scenery, I went to visit Aunty Keryn, along with her husband and three adorable children who lived on Colquhoun Road, just out of town. We often had so much fun together and I was hoping her company would cheer me up.

About two months after Suzie's death I started getting out and about a little more … slowly but surely. Then one day, while again at Aunty Keryn's house, the phone rang. It was Mum, to tell me another one of my close friends had been killed in a car accident.

Michael French, one of the older members of our young community, owned what we all considered a 'Mean Machine'. It was better than a car – he had a classic gold Falcon. To the girls, myself included, Michael's dark hair and devastatingly good looks always made him the centre of attention. Michael's younger brother David was my brother Geoff's best friend and, like so many of the other kids who grew up together in a small country town, we all knew each other well.

The circumstances surrounding Michael's accident were strikingly similar to those surrounding the crash that killed Suzie. Again, they were innocent bystanders simply going about their business. Michael's car, just like Suzie's, was struck by a vehicle being driven by a man under the influence of alcohol. How could I lose such good friends in almost the same manner within this short space of time? I couldn't fathom it … couldn't work it out.

I thought I would never get over the deaths of Suzie Pilgrim and Michael French, especially as they came so soon after the other tragic events which I had to come to terms with. As time drifted by I learned to live without my lost friends, but they have never been forgotten. My friendship with Suzie Pilgrim was the first of three Suzies who entered my life and with whom I had a special relationship, the likes of which happens so rarely during a lifetime. Photographs of two Suzies sit on my dressing table - Pilgrim for more than 40 years and Barnes for under a decade. I pray Steedy never gets there.

***

During one lot of summer holidays I had a desire to have part-time work like my girlfriends. I wanted a job and I wanted to earn some pocket money. As young teenagers, a couple of my friends worked at holiday units in the centre of Lakes Entrance, so I started helping them out, already aware that I would have to prove my abilities in life. I remember thinking then that if the owner saw me working he might offer me a job, or at least give me some payment for what I had done. I was able to vacuum the floors and I could make the beds, even if it wasn't in the conventional way. I'm a good bed maker and I'm still proud of my 'hospital corners' - lifting the mattress with my shoulder I would take the sheet under with my head, then complete tucking it all in with my shoulders. And I had no trouble pushing the vacuum cleaner around and doing the floors, in much the same way as I held a golf club, between my shoulder and neck. Using my whole body muscles to action most daily manoeuvres has kept me fit!

At the same time a couple of older boys rented the flat in the old water tower at the back of the units, and my girlfriends and I would often hang out there at weekends, flirting with the boys, of course.

Looking back, I think working at the units was my first lesson in the harsh realities of life and work as a disabled person. At the time, even though I hoped I would get some money, it was not the main reason I was there. I was a social butterfly and wanted to be with my girlfriends and if this meant helping out a bit, well that was okay.

There was also an element of proving I could do it … showing I could do the floors and make the beds, even if I couldn't wipe the benches or mirrors.

But money never came my way, just a condescending "look at Deb; isn't she a trooper, even if she does look a bit funny with her head under the mattress".

More than 50 years later, workforce attitudes towards the disabled certainly haven't changed a lot. Back then I thought, 'gee with some lateral thinking the owner of the units could easily have divided up the cleaning tasks, allowing me to look after the beds and floors while the taller girls wiped the mirrors and benches'. But it didn't happen then and it doesn't happen now. Despite all the rhetoric we hear, as far as job opportunities are concerned the disabled are pigeon-holed and rarely given a decent opportunity to perform any meaningful task, and if you display any intelligence you are a threat. Some may not believe how much I've kept my mouth shut over the years.

Looking back now I appreciate the value of academic qualifications, which are an absolute must. Often in today's world people with disabilities are offered assistance and support with gaining a position for three months, at which point the government subsidies run out and there's a polite (most of the time) "sorry, but you're no longer required". Or they are given the most menial tasks that do not fully recognise or appreciate individual abilities.

Most employers, in an insatiable quest to maximise their precious 'bottom line', have little or no interest in any social responsibility. Governments are the same and I laugh when I hear or read about so called 'equal opportunity policies' because the stark reality is they do not exist.

***

But let's get back to some of the fun we had growing up in Lakes Entrance, just like normal country kids. Some of our adventures were perhaps a little more dangerous than our parents would prefer but we survived, including the day I crashed my face into the top edge on the side of a trailer as we raced around the paddock.

Today, Hazel Road in Kalimna is a built-up area, but in those days there were lots of empty paddocks. On the day in question Mum and Dad went to golf and left the old blue Valiant at home, so Geoff decided to hook a trailer on the back and go for a spin in the paddock next door, between our place and the Stewarts. Jim and I thought it would be a great idea to hitch a ride in the trailer.

I had no hands to hold on with, so had my shoulder wrapped around the edge of the trailer and as we bounced around I flew a few inches into the air. However, on one occasion I came down hard and my face banged against the side, causing considerable discomfort. I had put my eye tooth through my top lip and it was bleeding profusely. Somehow I must've made it to Dr Rachelman, because I remember him putting in a stitch which I evidently ate before I had to go back to have it removed. This was suggested by the doctor when he couldn't find it.

On other occasions we'd head down the Kalimna track to town and across the footbridge to the surf beach where we would flirt with Surf Club members and others who enjoyed surfing. That's what teenage girls did in Lakes Entrance.

On reflection, in some respects it's a privileged life if you can grow up in a small country coastal town. There's the close-knit community, great friends and an awesome beach to enjoy. We often pushed the boundaries and sometimes got caught, but that's also part of growing up.

One balmy December night not long before I turned 16 we had an impromptu party at the surf club. It was the year I lost Suzie and Michael, so I was feeling a bit melancholy and decided to get drunk. Until this point I had not been a kid who liked alcohol, although I had already sampled marijuana in a small way via a carnival worker. However, this night I wanted to party and bought a bottle of Ouzo, which I was told tasted like aniseed-ball lollies and was quite nice when mixed with Coke. My parents thought I was staying with a friend, but instead we were having a drink around a campfire at the beach in front of the old surf club, which in practical times, faced the ocean.

The night wore on and the bottle of Ouzo was pretty much demolished when our look-out announced the police were coming. I was pretty drunk, so a couple of guys carried me into the clubrooms where they thought I could be hidden … wedged in between two surfboards. Being small can occasionally have its advantages.

Generally, when someone is in hiding, it is important to be quiet, however in my inebriated state I began singing loudly. I loved to sing, but generally on my own! My dulcet tones wafted into a policeman's ear and before long I was being dragged out from between the surfboards, placed on an old grey army blanket and carried hammock-style back across the footbridge. A policeman we knew as 'Stan the Man' was at one end and the other, who we called 'Baby Face' carried the end where my head was. Throughout the journey he had to endure my drunken verbal diarrhoea as I continually asked him to marry me; all the way to the police station where I was locked up for being drunk and disorderly.

Mum and Dad were occasional social drinkers but certainly never got drunk, so when the police rang to advise I was in the cells and inebriated they were horrified. In fact, at first they did not believe their 15 year-old daughter could possibly be locked in a police cell in a drunken state.

After some quick consultation they decided to leave me there, perhaps to ensure that as I sobered up I may realise the potential consequences of my behaviour. I must mention the once good friend who stayed with me that night in the cell and held the bucket and wiped my sorry brow, but must add the disappointment in later years as she backstabbed our family with gossip, which was heartbreaking. Relatively early the next morning Dad came down to the station, took me home and I went into my bedroom.

Mum entered the room and was furious, as well as probably emotional with disappointment. She slapped me across the face so hard – something she had never previously done – that I landed sideways on my bed. Mum later said she believed it was a wild reaction, an automatic reflex, to seeing me in that state.

I was not proud of what I did that night, and I think the reaction and subsequent punishment from my mother emphasised again that I was treated like any other teenager. As far as Mum was concerned I had acted badly and I had disappointed her; there were no excuses.

The drunk and disorderly incident ended what had been a turbulent and emotional year. As if mid-teen years are not already fraught with enough personal ups and downs to sink a battleship, it was a year in which there always seemed to be another sensation or experience just waiting around the corner, ready to set me reeling when it was least expected.

As well as coping with the usual hormonal upheavals, I was a young teenager who had experienced her first bereavements. I was sad and vulnerable and had been further devastated when I found myself experiencing the unwanted attentions of an older man.

In many instances of child abuse the victim feels like the guilty party, and in my circumstance that was certainly the case. As a young, lonely and vulnerable teenager I quite possibly flirted, yet did not instigate what is now considered child abuse, though I felt powerless to stop it. Only after I realised the true implications of what this man was doing did I become strong enough to put an end to it.

So in my 15th year I endured some of the toughest experiences of my young life, yet with it came an awakening that I was responsible for my own actions and the decisions I made.

As time marched on not all these decisions were ultimately the correct ones, but they were mine to make and I was responsible for any outcomes or consequences.

CHAPTER 6

Into the workforce

As I progressed from school to the workforce I continued my ongoing battle to convince all and sundry not only of my intellectual abilities but also the talent and capabilities contained within my toes. To me, it was quite simple – my toes were as flexible and adaptable as the fingers of a 'normal' person. Getting others to understand and accept this was my never-ending crusade, and one which also had an impact on my footwear.

For the majority of my school life I wore prosthetic arms and orthopaedic shoes, and as my 'arms' progressed from functional to cosmetic the footwear progressed to soft slip-on canvas sneakers.

In later life, when I was able to make my own choices, I started wearing rubber thongs because they are far more practical. Now, regardless of the weather or occasion, every day I wear my rubber thongs. However, when I finished school and joined the workforce there continued this ridiculous attitude that I had to try and conform and be as 'normal' as possible.

I left school at the end of Form 4 - now called Year 10 – which, in hindsight, was one of my biggest ever mistakes. At the time no-one urged me to stay on at school and develop my academic skills, which I have always regretted. In saying this, I did not hold any grudges against my parents as we were blue-collar, working class people and they did not have the finances for academic education of their children. I was capable at school, even though I probably could have performed a little better with more concentration on school work instead of having fun and socialising. Despite that, I wish someone in my formative teenage years had talked to me about the importance of academic skills for someone with my physique.

Let's face it, when you're a tad over three feet eight inches tall and do not have functioning arms, the employment opportunities are somewhat limited. Anything with a physical element will never be included on my resume, but there was no reason why I could not have gone on to study at university.

I believe I would have made a good lawyer, or been adept at human relations. With the right training this sort of white collar career would have suited my skill set. My forte is the way I think and a clear and succinct manner of speaking, but they were never developed. Instead, I was trained as a switchboard operator, so forever and a day the majority of my workforce involvement was going to be clerical.

When I left school, operating a switchboard was considered the ideal job for a disabled person, although it's not something I did for very long. And the problem was no-one gave any thought to tasks other than the switchboard, including the challenges associated with three and four drawer filing cabinets for someone of my height. It wasn't easy being a clerical assistant when I had to drag a chair over to get into the third drawer and often cut my chin on the metal frames or my lips while trying to separate the papers.

I never worked for the PMG or Telecom on the large switchboards like many other disabled people in the 1970s. Back then, that was the 'pigeon hole' job and there was no genuine responsibility taken by business or governments to help the disabled develop their skills to help them find ongoing employment and, in doing so, provide a meaningful reason to be on this earth.

Forty-plus years later nothing has changed. In general, society thinks the disabled are there to be looked after. We are a marred product that needs to be taken care of, rather than developing greater understanding and acceptance of physical or intellectual differences. I've often been treated as if I have intellectual disabilities despite the fact I believe I am an intelligent, articulate woman. Because I look different I get lumped in the same basket as anyone else with a disability. Far too often, that's how society operates.

***

Towards the end of Form 4 I was presented with an opportunity to be trained for work at the Springvale Road Commonwealth Rehabilitation Centre, in Melbourne. I found it an exciting prospect as I had never been given a chance to earn money, which is what nearly all my friends did during school holidays. As such they had money to spend as they wished, whereas I relied on my parents for pocket money. Moving to Melbourne and the training centre soon after my 16th birthday was going to give me the personal and financial independence for which I craved.

As often happens in life, the grass is not always greener on the other side of the fence. Instead of gaining independence, in many ways I lost it.

For starters, having spent so much time and energy winning the battle to forego my prosthetic arms, suddenly they were back on. As soon as I moved to the Rehabilitation Centre it was suggested rather than use my (very adequate) feet that, for the benefit of future employment prospects, I should give the prosthesis another try.

For the next nine months I learnt how to type with one finger, that being the hook on the end of my arm. I can assure you, I was nowhere near as quick or accurate with this hook as I was with my toes but, yet again, others thought they knew what was best for Deb.

The Rehabilitation Centre was a 'live-in' facility and the time I spent there is a bag of mixed memories. For the first time in my life, and for reasons I still cannot comprehend, I became part of the 'pill popping parade'. Like everyone else, I was lined up on a daily basis and given various pills to take. To this day I do not know what they were or why I was ordered to take them, but I think we were all on a sleeping pill to keep us quiet at night; not that it worked because half of us didn't take it!

I was also not keen on the regimented nature at the centre or some of the treatment of residents, myself included, who were referred to as 'inmates' as if we were in a prison which in some respects, with the two metre high wire Hurricane fence surrounding the premises, is what it was like.

Anyone who wanted to leave the property had to seek permission from matron. The gates were all locked at night and we had to be in bed with lights out at 9.30pm. Meals were served with military precision at precisely 7.30am, noon and 6pm and there was no access permitted to the kitchen if you missed a designated meal time.

Some of us objected to the harsh rules and there were times we would rebel, which I'm sure contributed to the strong sense of comradeship which we developed.

I made good friends at the Rehab Centre, some of whom had a far more difficult boat to row in life than mine and helped to teach me the value of the abilities that I possessed. Whenever I felt sorry for myself, I only had to reflect on the challenges being faced by fellow 'inmates'.

Characters who endeared themselves to me at the centre included two motorbike riders. Billy, who was 20, had lost an arm in a motorbike accident and the heavily bearded Strop had suffered a back injury.

Then there was Zita, a feisty woman in her mid 30s who was enduring the trauma and effects of a fire. Zita had severe burns, in particular to her face and hands, and had no fingers.

Marika, a German girl, was profoundly deaf. Although her primary language was German she was learning to lip-read English. Then there was Bill, who had cerebral palsy. I fell head over heels for Bill, who had a lovely, personable nature.

They were a great bunch of people all trying to make the most of what life had dished up and doing their best to learn skills that may make their journey a little easier. I'm not sure where they all finished up, but I suspect for most it was tough going as they tried to be part of a society that can be unkind and unforgiving to those who are a little 'different'.

***

After nine months at the Rehab Centre I started my first job as a switchboard operator and receptionist at the Central Methodist Mission, run by the Wesley Church, at the top end of Lonsdale

Street, Melbourne. My workplace was conveniently located next door to the mission's hostel, where I lived independently for the first time.

The girls' hostel was known as the Princess Mary Club, a grand old building opposite the Chateau Commodore Hotel, where my little brother Jim had gained a chef's apprenticeship soon after I started at the CM Mission. About 10 years ago I was disappointed to learn the Princess Mary Club building was under threat of demolition and joined the fight to save what many consider to be a culturally and historically significant part of Melbourne's heritage. I read how it was built in 1926 and was created to help country women move to the city for work. It closed in 1988. I fully agree with a statement I read from a former resident, Ruth Davies, who was quoted as saying: "This was a great transition from my family home, to complete independence. It was so much fun. We all ate together in the dining room. It was pretty raucous at times." Unfortunately, efforts to save the building were fruitless.

Naturally, I was delighted to have the new-found freedom of a more independent lifestyle, especially after being institutionalised at the Rehab Centre. It presented some challenges, but none was insurmountable.

And wouldn't you know it, one of the first I had to address was again caused by those damn prosthetic arms. You see, I have always been able to bathe and dress myself, though I had to avoid clothes which were tied at the waist. But getting dressed became a different issue when I was wearing the dreaded arms and I needed some assistance.

I had just spent nine months at the rehabilitation centre where using the hook on the end of my arm was a mandatory part of being trained for employment. I had been taught to pull and insert plugs and chords on a PABX switch board, as well as type with the hook, and I was expected to use it at my new job.

So now, because of those bloody fibreglass contraptions that extended from my shoulders and limited my dexterity, I would again need someone to dress me in the morning and take my clothes off after work. At the rehab centre it seemed to be part of my training that someone would be there in the morning to dress me and there after work to undress me. At Springvale Road it was a chore done by the daily staff … one of the nurses. There were no personal carers at this stage.

Fortunately there was a lovely Irish lady, Theresa O'Reilly, I do recall was about 10 years older than me, who was permanently living at the hostel and working at reception. She was asked if she would mind calling on me each morning to assist with dressing and obligingly agreed to assist. She arrived at my room promptly each week day morning at 7.30 to dress me for the day, and at weekends as needed. She was a very conservative and shy young woman who was very stable and reliable. I grew to think very highly of her, however as it happens we lost contact when I left that establishment.

I quickly settled in at the Princess Mary Club, which provided an ideal start to my independent adolescent life. Before long I had a wide circle of housemates, but more importantly a wonderful small group of close mates, with most of them country girls just like me. As I said, the hostel predominantly provided accommodation for young girls who had moved to the city for work or study, so we had lots in common and I never had any shortage of helpers when assistance was required.

Like the rehab centre it had a matron, doors were shut at 10.30pm and we weren't supposed to have boys in our room, although I had learnt at school that rules were made to be bent and sometimes broken, especially if you were a physically deformed young girl trying desperately to impress the opposite sex. Sometimes you had to show them what they could have, especially if initial impressions relayed a whole pile of social misconceptions.

When Jim started cooking across the road at the Chateau Commodore, myself and other girls from the Princess Mary Club started hanging out at Bonie's nightclub.

Not surprisingly, we were often unable to make it back to the hostel by the 10.30pm curfew when doors were locked, and had to climb through a window on the first floor. That wasn't too difficult for my friends, but I did not find it quite as easy. I was grateful for the assistance but in retrospect recognise the danger we were in, as several intoxicated young women made their way up the scaffolding and back into the hostel via the open window. One girl would grab the shoulder and neck area of my clothing, while the one below pushed on my bum with her hand, as they managed to hoist me to each bar where I would balance on a bar and grip another with my chin until they positioned themselves for the next hoist up.

I was also grateful for the patience shown by my friends when I struggled to keep up as we walked around the city. Although I was very mobile, being so small presents its limitations, including the pace at which I was able to walk. My quick stroll was quite slow compared to my friends, but they were always patient. I was precisely three feet, eight and a half inches tall and without even being conscious I was doing it, when asked about my height I used to emphatically state that 'half inch', as if it was very important. In hindsight, I suppose I thought every little bit counts.

This was a wonderful time in my life, with perhaps the only downside being the fact my artificial, fibreglass arms had been reattached. It was also a time when I started spiking my hair with a kind of spiky mullet look that I thought was very 'hip'. I lived only 20 metres from my workplace and our main social outlet was just across the road, where we enjoyed lots of good times. We were well looked after at the Princess Mary Club, where our board for the week was only $17 which included three meals a day, seven days a week. There was no extra charge for power or anything like that. I was working as a telephonist, five days per week, 9am to 5pm and earning $29 a week. A packet of cigarettes cost about 70 cents and a I think a beer, which is what we used to drink at Bonies, was about 25 cents. (And for those who are good at their maths, you may have correctly deduced that I was under the legal drinking age when we first started attending the night club. But at my height, who was going question whether or not I was 18?) Those with any type of conscience never wanted to offend, which is probably why I was able to get away with also drinking at the Village Green Hotel when we used to sneak out of the rehab centre. I was only 16 at the time.

After a while we got to know some guys and girls who were in the bands which played at the nightclub and I became good friends with Lizette, who was a lead singer. I had always loved singing (although it did get me in strife on the night I got drunk at the surf club) and before long I was alongside her on the microphone. Lizette encouraged me to take singing lessons with her at Middle Park, which I did for about six months after which I moved on and lost touch with her for sometime; we are in touch today and she's still singing around the traps in Melbourne.

I would have continued with these lessons, but the shine was wearing off my work at the Central Methodist Mission reception and I was becoming unsettled. I wanted to do more than simply answer a switchboard and started applying for clerical positions elsewhere.

We all move on at various times in life and, as we get older, often reflect on certain periods and wonder why we were so keen on change when, in hindsight, everything was going along quite smoothly. That's what I did in later years when I looked back on my time at the mission and in the Princess Mary Club.

During our socialising at the nightclub I also had developing relationships with men which again, using hindsight, I could have approached a little differently. For example there was Rob, a model, who I still picture today and can only describe as being "bloody gorgeous",and a lovely guy. Unlike some of my earlier experiences where boys were afraid to publicly show affection to a short, armless person, Rob flirted openly and started taking me out. Over a period of a few months the girls helped on several occasions to smuggle him in for the night and it was all perfectly romantic and dreamy.

Rob was always impeccably dressed in a suit and when we were together there were some striking contrasts. There was his gorgeous physique, plus the fact I did not pay too much attention to the way I dressed. The rubber thongs seemed to bring me down and I must admit when we went out he made me feel a bit under-dressed which may have led to my meltdown. This occurred on a day we were going to a barbecue and Rob organised to call by and pick me up, but I said to one of the girls, "if Rob's wearing a suit when he arrives today, tell him I've moved to Siberia". That's exactly what she told him and I never saw Rob again.

About two months later, realising what I had done, I tried to track him down, but the damage was done. Rob was a really nice guy and I threw him away because, as usual, I was afraid I'd get too attached … scared he'd throw me away when the novelty wore off, so I made sure to get in first. That has happened quite a lot in my life.

Over the years there have been a few occasions when I've flicked someone after a good time looked like developing into something more and my girlfriends would say, "why did you do that? He really liked you." I don't think I could ever answer, however I feel it may have been because, again, I did not want to get too close and then have to face rejection. It was the easy way out. It wasn't a conscious reaction … subconsciously I was scared. I would have fun, then take a step back before we became too attached.

***

Throughout life I have often faced disappointment when searching for work and was again faced with discrimination when I decided to move on from the Central Methodist Mission.

I applied for jobs and attended interviews, but on arrival was told the position had been filled. I'm sure this had nothing to do with my appearance! After many rejections, like all good cripples (this word is always used when I'm being sent cynical) I joined the public service. That's what you did back then. Early in 1974 I sat for the public service exam, which I passed and was accepted as a Clerical Assistant Grade 1 typist, subsequently taking up a position in a typing pool with the Government Aircraft Factory at Fisherman's Bend, near Port Melbourne.

I had a new job and, best of all, off came the arms. I reverted to typing with my toes, again pumping out words at a respectable rate of 35 per minute. From this point Deb Gray and prosthetic arms were to be permanently divorced. We'd had some trial separations and been forced to 'make up' and live together again, but like most of my relationships there was never going to be a lifelong commitment. Farewell arms. Forever.

I was now able to again adopt a more functional lifestyle and abandon the frustrations of dressing, undressing and limited mobility. By using my chin against my shoulder, along with making the best of my mouth and skilful feet I was able to put on and remove my clothes and carry out a myriad of other activities which most people take for granted.

But with one problem solved another emerged, as with a change of employment I had to make my way daily from the Princess Mary Club, where I continued living, to Fisherman's Bend. At first the only option was public transport, even though it is not easy if you have a disability. I had to walk two blocks to catch a bus or tram, but that was the least of my problems. To get on a bus I had to scramble up steps which were as high as my waist, and this was especially difficult on Melbourne's old green trams. The first step wasn't too bad because it was fairly low, but the next one was up to my armpit.

Despite cherishing my independence I had no qualms, on a rainy or cold day, in asking for assistance when boarding a tram, often grabbing the attention of any bloke standing nearby and saying, "mate, can you take me by the shoulders and swing me up like a sack of spuds". I could always get down by sitting on my bum first. Although mostly I would stand on that first step which was a sideboard to the tram, place my shoulder into the upright grab rail and ride the side of the tram all the way down Swanston Street. I quite enjoyed this.

Independence is important for those of us who live with disability, but generally when we want help we'll ask for it. I needed assistance to get on the tram and was never afraid to make that known. If it wasn't required, I wouldn't ask. My message here is for able bodied people to be respectful of any person with disability, but don't be patronising. Wait until you are asked and when this happens provide the necessary assistance required.

Over the years many offers to help in various situations have been embarrassing and are made with no thought or consideration to my abilities. For example, on occasions I've been searching around in a handbag for my car keys or money, when a well meaning person has asked, 'do you need a hand?' No I don't. I have been removing keys from my handbag for many years and expect to be doing so for many years to come. Think about the assistance you are offering – in particular whether or not it is genuinely required – before you ask. No woman wants a stranger rummaging in her handbag … myself included.

Then there are the people who come into a roundabout and see you standing safely in the middle section, having safely negotiated the first half of the road. They stop and sit there, encouraging you to cross in front of them while at the same time jamming up traffic from all directions. I do not understand this behaviour and wonder if it is a blatant display of embarrassing, thoughtless, condescending kindness that is bordering on a patronising insult.

In making these comments I acknowledge that some people with disability need to get a better understanding of when it's okay to seek assistance with a difficult task. There is no point in myself, or anyone else, trying for 10 minutes to pick up something that has fallen if we are simply unable to do it at a dignified pace. That's the time to say, "would you mind picking that up for me, please?" But I have seen a lot of disabled people who will not ask, and by being obstinate no-one benefits.

It's all about communication. If individuals, like myself, want to function independently in society we have to effectively communicate our needs, if any, and on the other side of the coin these needs must be respected. Anyway, I'll now get off my soapbox.

***

Initially, work at the aircraft factory at Fisherman's Bend was going along okay and despite some occasional difficulties I was able to get to work and home again each day on Melbourne's public transport system. My typing pool boss was a Nana Mouskouri look alike, with straight black hair and wide rimmed glasses just like the Greek singer who was very popular in that era. After a while we discovered that 'Nana' and her husband drove close to the Princess

Mary Club and down Russell Street on their way to work each day – he was also employed at our factory – and she offered to stop by and give me a lift.

In most cars this would not have posed any difficulties, except that 'Nana' drove a slick little two door red MG. During the 70s there were no seatbelt laws and I didn't take up too much room so we managed, even though it was a little awkward. I didn't require much leg room so it was easy to sit on the passenger's knee.

I know and appreciate that the offer to give me a lift to work each day was made with all the best intentions, but unfortunately it did not end well. You see, even though I did not realise it at the time, my boss's husband quite enjoyed having a young girl sitting on his lap throughout our 20 minute journey each morning and night. In fact, it seems he found me quite cute, and as a consequence I soon had a very jealous boss who made my work situation nasty and, eventually, unbearable.

I was forced to submit a complaint to the Staff Welfare Department about the unfair treatment I was receiving and to resolve the situation I requested a transfer within the Department of Defence.

For a short time I was moved to the Commonwealth building known as the Green Latrine, at the corner of Spring Street and Lonsdale Street, where I enjoyed working. It has since been demolished, but was made famous about five years before I was there, when feminist crusader Zelda D'Aprano, campaigning for equal pay for women, chained herself to the building until she was cut free by police. Zelda drew great attention to the campaign. Maybe it's something I could do to raise awareness of inequality in employment opportunities for the disabled!

After a short time at the 'Green Latrine' I was transferred back to the Government Aircraft Factory at Fisherman's Bend. Needless to say, I was no longer getting a lift to work in the red MG and had to again endure the challenges of public transport.

Not surprisingly, this period in my working life did not end well because, for some crazy reason despite my previous complaint and objections, I was required to again work under 'Nana'. I was forced to suffer misery and frustrations in the workforce due entirely to the jealousy of one person, who happened to be my immediate superior. I started to understand how subtly victimisation in the workplace can occur.

I have long believed the insecurity in her personal life was the catalyst for the persecution and ill-treatment I received. I am unsure whether the relationship lasted between 'Nana' and her husband, but it's probably unlikely unless her needless jealousy waned. Even though I had stopped getting a lift to work, my supervisor continued to make my working day as difficult and uncomfortable as possible, yet she was very clever in how she went about it.

For example, I was allocated the largest and most boring documents to type, or given the heaviest bundle to deliver to another department even though this task was obviously more difficult for myself than any of the other girls. Her demeanour towards me was dismissive and unfriendly and in a clever way she shielded me from others, despite knowing I enjoyed the stimulation of conversation and human interaction. Her cunning and the veiled treatment I received was not always evident to others.

Before long I realised the social prejudices that I had occasionally endured in my private life were every bit as common – if not more so – in my working life, and as a consequence my self-esteem began to slide. The bright, vivacious, 'not a care in the world' Deb, heading towards the end of teenage years, was learning a few harsh lessons in life for a disabled person.

***

Outside work hours my social life remained active and I continued to have many good times with my girlfriends from the Princess Mary Club and my brother Jim who, by this stage, was sharing a narrow terrace house in Prahran with a friend.

Whenever possible we would return home for a weekend or a few days, to Sale where Mum and Dad had recently moved after selling the family home in Lakes Entrance. Jim taught me to drive while we travelled in his little brown Gemini. I used to sit on the handbrake from where I could reach both the steering wheel and the gearstick, so Jim was left to do the pedals. We would drive for miles like this. Meanwhile, Jim casually sat back with his hands behind his head. Such nonchalant and inattentive behaviour from a person in the driver's seat generated some strange looks from other motorists.

On weekends in Melbourne we were now venturing beyond the Chateau Commodore nightclub and getting into the pub music scene. It was from these outings that Cupid's arrow struck me again.

I met a fantastic bunch of blokes from Wangaratta who had formed a band and played the traps around Melbourne. The bass guitarist was a guy called Chris, aka Bandy. He had a girlfriend from Wangaratta and when we met, and for the initial several weeks of our friendship, I never knew about her. I developed a little affection for Bandy and was disappointed when I found out about Jennifer, but I needed affection and quite frankly this guy was so nice I was willing to have the dregs. It turned out she wasn't around often, only coming to Melbourne for the weekend on the odd occasion. When she wasn't there I would openly display my affection for Bandy, which he never deterred and left him in no doubt I wanted to be more than just a general mate. Before long he was reciprocating the affectionate attention I was showering him with. I was only 17 to 18 and beginning to believe this was how it had to be if I wanted anything. If his girlfriend was down from Wangaratta I behaved as a general mate. If she stayed in Wangaratta, Bandy would pick me up from the PM Club on his 750 Honda motorbike and we would go riding. We used to go to the pub where his band was playing, or a bike event, or maybe just back to the flat in South Yarra where we enjoyed partying away the weekend. I was now part of the furniture and well embedded into the South Yarra bunch of boys.

Soon it appeared I was Bandy's city companion, accepted by the boys. I knew about Jennifer, but she did not know about me. For that I was delighted because I loved him and believed he also loved me, although as a gentleman I felt he may have had trouble with the physical aspect of the relationship, because all the months we kissed and cuddled and slept together, we never made love.

It was getting the better of me and was something I felt a need to talk about, so one weekend after having a little too much to drink I went into a bedroom with a girlfriend and cried on her shoulder, blubbering into the pillow about how Bandy was never sexual with me. While I was getting all this off my chest, face buried into a pillow, I was too self-obsessed to realise Bandy had walked into the room. As I continued crying and expressing my feelings about his lack of sexuality he became the one rubbing my back and trying to comfort me. Naturally I was very embarrassed, but nothing changed.

Bandy used the excuse that he had too much love and respect for me and wanted to ensure I did not get hurt, although I knew this was just a cop out. For a while he kept picking me up on a Friday night and we went for motorbike rides and back to his South Yarra flat until eventually I realised the "I don't want to hurt you" line was a load of piffle. He was just too nice, but could not bring himself to make love to a deformed body.

By this time I had been close to a few boys, making it known I had feelings for them, and each one came up with a lame excuse to avoid getting sexually involved. They should have been honest. "Sorry Deb, but we're scared that freaky little body of yours won't be able to handle sex." They wanted to be my friend – sometimes a very close friend - but in reality I think they were all too afraid of what other people might think if this was seen to be something more intimate.

If it wasn't enough to have self-esteem issues as a consequence of workplace harassment, I now had the double blow of male rejection and an inability to form any meaningful relationships. An active social life was great, but like nearly every other teenage girl I also craved a special person in my life … a partner of the opposite sex with whom I could have a special bond.

My fellow boarders at the Princess Mary Club had always provided abundant support and understanding, but I had reached a stage where this was not enough and I again needed the strength and love of my family, which had always been close at hand for the first 16 years of my life. After two years in Melbourne, and still at the tender age of 18, I wanted to return home to the country. I had enjoyed many aspects of city life, even though some parts weren't too great when I discovered a few realities of life as a disabled person.

Throughout a childhood in Lakes Entrance I was treated by my family and community as 'just another kid'. A hunger for independence had been instilled in my psyche, so I yearned the opportunity to lead a 'normal' life. But as adulthood gradually approached so did a growing appreciation of the gigantic task that confronted me, if this burning desire was to get even close to reality.

CHAPTER 7

Workforce discrimination

While Jim and I were in Melbourne our parents, as previously mentioned, sold the family home in Lakes Entrance and bought a run-down milk bar in the Gippsland town of Sale, opposite the town's main primary school. It was a developing town and home to numerous companies associated with oil and gas exploration in Bass Strait, in particular ESSO with its large office complex.

The milk bar was tough going for Mum and Dad, who saw it as an opportunity to establish greater financial independence and worked long hours so this could be achieved. They opened the doors seven days a week, from 6am until 7pm, although customers soon knew that if you rattled the shop door after hours they would open up and help out. Not surprisingly, they soon became well liked and appreciated in the neighbourhood.

There wasn't much time for a social life, but they didn't really need one. Mum and Dad were friendly people and the shop became their social life. With dedication, friendliness and a desire to achieve, that tired little store was soon transformed into a raging business.

When I told Mum and Dad I wanted to leave Melbourne, their seven-metre caravan, which had been in storage, was towed into the neighbour's large backyard against the fence. By cutting an approved opening in the fence I had a small walk to the back door of the residence behind the shop and this caravan became my place of abode. I registered for work then started volunteering at the Gippsland Base Hospital, which wasn't far from the shop. I enjoyed helping at the hospital even though I wasn't getting paid.

Further down the track I was to learn that government policy did not allow for mental stimulation for people with disability. The emphasis was on the statistics and getting paid jobs for anyone with disability, no matter how menial the task.

I was providing administrative support in the Medical Records Department at the hospital, and this also led to some occasional typing for the Senior Medical Officer, Dr Crosby. I was happy to volunteer because it gave me a worthy reason to get out of bed each day.

My toes were very good on the typewriter and could pump out medical letters at about 35 words per minute with virtually 100 per cent accuracy. However - too often there's a 'however' - the hospital couldn't afford to pay me, even though that was not the case with its other administrative staff. Regardless, I enjoyed the work, felt useful and I was learning a lot about the medical profession, including the lingo.

The Commonwealth Government stepped in and told me I had a job at the Crestknit factory, so I had to give up the voluntary hospital position. When I started at Crestknit my sole task was pulling cotton threads out of knitted garments. Initially I thought this was okay as Mum had taught me to sew and I envisaged the factory presenting future opportunities for advancement. How wrong I was!

It was a wonderful place to work and we had lots of fun. I made friends and we got up to a bit of harmless mischief, as well as enjoying some good parties after knock-off time. As the months wore on my girlfriends were promoted to better machines while I stayed at the same table, pulling threads out of garments. At first I couldn't understand why I was not being offered a promotion as I was a competent sewer and could easily use an overlocker. All I needed was a chair high enough to get my feet at it.

Then I realised a promotion was never going to happen. I'm sure they were worried I would stab my toe … they could only see my disability, not my abilities, which seemed irrelevant and to top it off the girl I shared the work table with had an intellectual disability and I think was happy enough to be at that table forever. I was not. I could not stay at the same table, pulling out threads.

In the I end I got pissed off and left. I can only take so much. As I've said, more than 40 years down the track I have not seen the necessary improvement in attitudes towards finding gainful employment for those with disability. Later In the book I will expand on this further. I had self-value and had enjoyed helping at the hospital, even though I wasn't getting paid. I was never going to get promoted at Crestknit, so I quit and applied for a job in the office at ESSO, which was the biggest employer in town.

Before we knew it a young maintenance man from ESSO paid a visit to Mum at her shop and asked whether I would need the desk lowered or the stool heightened. Yes, I'd been given the job! Next day an ESSO public relations guy came to see us and was very excited that I would be starting work there. Mum and Dad told me how thrilled they were, and making them happy was a bonus.

But as I soon discovered, yet again despite my relatively short working career, it doesn't matter where you are or the size of the workplace, there is no discrimination when it comes to discrimination.

I shared the reception area at ESSO with two men. One was a great guy and as happy as a lark to be working alongside me. The other, who was an American, effectively refused to have me as his receptionist because he wanted a pretty young girl with long legs and nice breasts. There were a lot of Americans working at ESSO, many of whom were rude and arrogant. He fitted neatly into this category.

Before long everything erupted. The excited young public relations guy who had seen Mum and Dad only a couple of months earlier returned to their shop and, in tears, tried to explain that this more senior employee was adamant … he was not going to work with their disabled daughter. Then he had to tell me.

Mum told me later that for as long as she lived she would not forget that day as she watched, in devastation, my reaction. I walked out the back door of the shop, down the back yard and in behind the shed as I tried to absorb what I had been told. Nor would she forget the lovely PR guy from ESSO who was in the shop with tears rolling down his cheeks, so upset as he told her an employee of his company would not work with her disabled daughter.

I had previously suffered discrimination both in and out of the workplace, but there had been nothing like this … nothing as emphatic. This obnoxious, arrogant person – and there were others in the office just like him – insisted on the pretty blonde receptionist whose primary role would be to feed his ego. That may sound nasty – I guess it is – but it's reality. That's how it worked and I didn't fit his precious criteria, so I was out of a job.

At the time I remember feeling that in my wildest dreams I never expected anything like this could happen - not anywhere in Australia, and certainly not in a country town.

My parents had never witnessed that type of prejudice and discrimination towards their daughter and were terribly upset. By this stage in my life the number of discriminatory incidents I was forced to experience was increasing, however there had never been anything on this scale. I didn't want to make it any worse for Mum and Dad, so put up my 'hard shell' and told them it didn't really matter because I'd find another job. Deep down, it did.

The biggest concern my parents harboured was the potential impact this incident may have on my dream of independence and self-sufficiency. If people didn't want to work with me because I was short and armless – not the type of receptionist many men wanted - how was I going to gain meaningful employment?

Throughout my working career I met many wonderful people and made some great friends. Unfortunately, there is a very small minority who are selfish, thoughtless pigs. They are unable to put themselves in someone else's shoes, or think 'if I had a disability, how would I like to be treated?' They also forget that many people in our society who live with physical disabilities were born 'normal' but had a massive change in their life following an accident. No-one is immune. Any person can start any day in exactly the same way they usually do. Then … whoooooosh!! A car crash or workplace incident and they're suddenly a paraplegic, quadriplegic or amputee, but their dreams and desires are not affected, just the ability to fulfil them.

***

The discrimination I suffered from my early days in the workforce helped lay the foundations for the way I tackled adversity. As a young woman I was developing the mechanisms needed to cope with life and push through any obstacles as they were planted in my path. I became more adept at negotiation, innovation and communication on all levels and these skills continued to evolve during my young adult years.

I increasingly encountered the crueller side of human behaviour, but this just made me more determined to persist … to rise above it and fight for the independence and companionship for which I longed. Sometimes I let my guard down and succumbed to the injustice and humiliation, generally with a night out on the turps with friends where Tequila slammers and beer chasers featured prominently and helped erase intensifying emotions.

Apart from alcohol, another form of release continued to be singing, which I enjoyed in private. At the age of 18 I remember feeling battered, yet found solace in the many compliments I received for my singing voice. No-one could take away this gift that I loved to show off, whether among friends or, as often happened, in my little caravan at the back of Mum and Dad's shop. That was my haven, where I could express myself and just be me, without a care in the world. I sang in the shower and I sang along with my radio and records, and in doing so found a special place with a unique feeling of calm and goodness. It was my own slice of heaven.

A popular television show at the time was Kevin Dennis New Faces, a prime time Sunday night program which gave aspiring singers an opportunity to showcase their talent. Prompted by my friends I decided to audition, and before I knew it I was off to the Channel 9 studio in Richmond, with Mum and Jim for support, to perform on live TV.

I received comments about how brave I was to stand up in front of the camera and studio audience, with New Faces beamed into everyone's lounge room. But why should I be considered more courageous than any other performer? Was I especially brave because I was shorter and didn't have two arms like other contestants? If so, what does that have to do with the quality of my voice?

I waited nervously in the Green Room, alongside fellow contestants who were just as nervous – or more so – as we all anticipated our 'five seconds of fame' and perhaps laying the foundations for a future in show business, which had been achieved by former contestants like Daryl Somers, Paul Hogan, Col Elliot and, in later years, Keith Urban.

In my beautiful, smoky-grey satin gown with its gold-scalloped trim I started to wonder 'what the hell are you doing here?' Then, all of a sudden, it was my turn to perform.

Rarely on New Faces was there ever a more conspicuous and embarrassing entrance, though fortunately it was not captured on camera for the national audience. As I made my way towards centre stage, butterflies churning in my stomach and my mind focused on nothing but the words and notes I was about to utter, I did not see the camera cable which stretched across the stage. My flexible feet suddenly lost their dexterity, coming to a sudden halt as my left toes stopped against the cable and the rest of my body propelled forward, nose-diving into the floor. Without knees it is generally quite common to sway in order to lift your feet millimetres, which is enough to shuffle forward. On this occasion I did not get my feet far enough off the ground. I could not believe my television debut could start in this embarrassing manner, and despite there being some consolation as the cameras were fixated on Kevin Dennis, inwardly I was terribly upset. Silently, I berated myself for not having knees, which would have made it easier to lift my feet over the cable. I also mentally cursed those who rushed to help me, for what I felt was over the top and patronising attention. It wasn't; I just hated the fuss.

As usual, Mum was there and knew what to do. She straightened up my dress and gave me the words of encouragement I needed to carry on. "Break a leg," they say, before a thespian's performance. I almost took it literally.

The time I stepped through the Green Room doors to the time I took centre stage, with everything that happened in between, seemed an eternity but in reality was only a minute or so. And there I was, having been introduced by Kevin Dennis himself, standing in the spotlight. With all the passion I could muster I belted out the lyrics to the Tammy Wynette song which I had so carefully and deliberately chosen.

Perhaps, in my own way, I was trying to make a statement as I belted out with soft passion 'Stand By Your Man', starting with the line *'Sometimes it's hard to be a woman ...'* which I knew only too well, while shouting to the world that this was the way I would treat my man, if only one would give me the chance. I was only 18 years old.

There was also a certain cheeky twinkle in my eye, positively commented on by the judges, as I passionately sang *'give him two arms to cling to, And something warm to come to, when nights are cold and lonely'*.

As I stood silently after the final words of Tammy's song, the audience showed admirable appreciation with a standing ovation, but I was left wondering whether this recognised the quality of my performance or simply the fact I had the courage to perform and got through it admirably.

The judges said all the right things and I'm sure were awestruck by the whole episode, remarking specifically on the expression I imparted as I passionately sang the aforementioned lines. Little did they know it was something I had longed to do on numerous occasions.

I did not win that day, but I did get second place and the Encouragement Award, which was generally a gold watch. However, it was decided I should be given a $50 note which I promptly spent and therefore have nothing to show for my efforts and no evidence of the moment. (Oh shit; I hope it wasn't just a dream!) I have always felt ripped off about that. In the performance I displayed a philosophy by which my life has been lived - I had a go.

Didn't they think I would cherish and appreciate a gold watch, being a lasting memento of the occasion, just the same as any other performer, even though I did not have a wrist to wear it on? It made me ask, yet again, why do fair-minded people continue falling into the trap of unnecessarily treating disabled people differently?

***

After losing my job at ESSO in rather contemptible circumstances and missing out on another of their vacant positions as a radio operator, I returned to my volunteer work at the Gippsland Base Hospital.

Meanwhile, I moved out of the caravan at the back of Mum and Dad's shop and into a two bedroom unit which I shared with a local musician named Michael, who was a good friend. I often migrated towards musicians. He and friend Brent performed as an acoustic duo which made wonderful music around the pub circuit and at parties in the Sale district.

Michael, a flamenco guitarist, taught me to play the guitar with my toes. It began when I picked up his spare guitar and would lightly and quietly pluck away, using it on the ground I strummed with the left toes and ran the frets with my right four toes. Encouraged by this, he taught me to play the beginning riff in the Led Zepplin classic 'Stairway To Heaven'. Thank goodness there were people in the world who had confidence in my talents and, where necessary, the composure and perseverance to help me learn new skills. Life was exciting again!!

Michael was a kind and thoughtful friend with whom I shared various adventures and activities whenever we could. He was always respectful, never once showing awkwardness or embarrassment at my presence when other friends and acquaintances were around. We shared equally all the household duties and I was even expected to occasionally push the lawnmower, which I did by placing my shoulders on the bar half way down the handle, where it folded over. May I add that at this stage in my life, when I was fitter and healthier, I loved this task. It felt good to be sweating and dirty!

Born in the United States of America, of Hispanic-American blood, Michael was well travelled and possessed an open mindedness which I have rarely encountered in Australian men. I have never been sure what it is about the Aussie male that prevents him showing emotion, and often being frightened of 'what the mates might think'. There is a propensity towards conformity and a fear of being ridiculed which seems to dominate the decision making of some people. Unlike other men I have encountered throughout the world, the Aussie is often both embarrassed and fearful if they find themselves attracted to someone with a physical difference.

Mind you, over the years it has not prevented some men from wanting to experiment with someone like myself. I suppose it has something to do with the mystique and the unknown. Does she have the same hidden bits and pieces as other women? If so, can she use them? As the majority of my encounters, so to speak, have ended early in the morning, prior to other people rising, I have occasionally found it rather disconcerting when I am reminded that curiosity has been the catalyst for attention in the first place. But it is of greater concern from a societal perspective that a stigma exists which prevents any meaningful relationship from developing.

***

Losing the job at ESSO and quitting at Crestnit had a big impact. Here I was at the age of 19 without a job, without a boyfriend and craving for both. I wanted acceptance in society, the workforce and from the opposite sex, but I did not want the token acceptance I had endured in the past.

I decided to go back to Melbourne and moved into a flat in Alma Road, St Kilda with Kerri Darby. Although several years younger she was a good friend of mine from Sale and, like myself, was a strong minded individual. We had some great times together, but she moved out and I was there on my own. After the flat was burgled – which probably wasn't anything that unusual in St Kilda – I decided to move on again, this time to a place in Cubitt Street, Richmond with my little bro (by only 10 months) Jim and a couple of his new gay mates, Rodney ('Rhoda') and Michael ('Gilda'). What a fabulously fun, dramatic, busy and exciting world it had become.

Interestingly, decades later I had a phone call one night from an excited friend asking "are you watching the telly?" She repeated it before I could answer: "Are you watching the telly?" I was ordered to switch it over to Channel 9, which was screening an episode of the true-life drama series 'Underbelly' and there, on the screen, was our place in Cubitt Street, Richmond. The guy we paid rent to was a key figure on the program.

Anyway, I lived in Cubitt Street for a while and my life was still on a fairly rocky path taking in the pub scene, drugs and trying to come to grips with growing up as a little person with no arms who was striving to be 'normal'. I didn't have a job or a boyfriend, had a younger brother joyfully embracing his own sexuality and an older brother resenting it. I often longed for someone to lean on and wondered whether I would ever find someone with the courage to openly and proudly love a person with physical disability. Hence I was striving to be independent and survive as I developed a 'don't fuck with me' confident exterior, which hid a woman looking for love.

There's no denying it was an extremely difficult time in my life and, without making excuses, probably led to an incident which I have seriously regretted ever since.

It happened on what started out being a normal Friday night. We went to the pub and, as per usual, I got quite intoxicated. On this particular night, for some reason, watching loving bodies boogie together affectionately brought on a deep, intense longing. I'm a loving, affectionate sort of person and was keen to find someone who would accept the affection that had built up inside me.

But it wasn't to be and when the pub closed I grabbed a cab and asked the driver, a mid 40s to 50 largish man of ethnic origin, to take me home. He must have sensed I was vulnerable and as we headed towards Richmond he put the hard word on me. I was only 19. Regretfully, in my inebriated state, I said 'yes' and we had sex in his taxi.

As an emotional teenager there were a number of things I did not deal with very well, and my yearning for love and affection was near the top of that list. I'm far from the first person to have sex with a stranger, which I suppose in some respects suggests I am like many other young women in this and other ways. Maybe at the time I was feeling sorry for myself during a difficult phase when things weren't falling into place as I would like. It's difficult to explain, but sometimes you get to a stage in life when it is not working out as you want and as a consequence your decision-making can go astray.

At this point I needed a circuit breaker and it came when I was offered a job at HMAS Londsdale.

***

I started at HMAS Lonsdale in early 1977 as a clerical assistant and switchboard operator. It was the best job I've ever had, not so much because of what I did, but the people I worked with and the environment they created. I thoroughly and genuinely enjoyed the switchboard communications and was proud of my well respected reputation for the job.

HMAS Lonsdale was a Royal Australian Navy training establishment in Rouse Street, Port Melbourne on a portion of reclaimed land that was purchased by the Department of Defence during World War Two. The HMAS Lonsdale shore base was constructed to cope with an increased demand for recruits and services. Several years after the war its role was expanded and an additional three storey accommodation block was built, then in the early 1970s, only seven years before I started there, they established a new naval shore patrol, stores and band practice buildings on south side of Rouse Street. And, of course, they had the mess which is where we enjoyed many, many hours of fun and frivolity.

In reflection, the work environment at the HMAS Lonsdale base could be used as a shining example of how people with disability should be treated. The Navy personnel didn't give a hoot what I looked like, as long as I could effectively carry out the role for which I was employed. They were inclusive, non-judgmental and lots of fun, which probably came naturally to a group of young blokes who, in general, still had a bit of good old Aussie larrikinism in them. They also had a caring nature, both on and off the base, always looking after their workmates (including yours truly). Mind you, I did not get any favours. I was just 'one of the boys', so to speak, except for a couple of quick flings.

After getting the job I started to settle down and although I was still pretty keen on having my share of fun (plus a bit extra, if it could be managed) I became more conscious of my home environment. I moved to a place in Carinya Crescent, North Caulfield, but it turned out to be a den of iniquity that I shared with a couple of uncaring junkies. The house had a porch converted into an extra bedroom which could be accessed from outside or through my room. I'm sure most people will not be surprised to learn that I was not happy when my room was used as a thoroughfare, which was happening with alarming regularity.

To discourage my housemate I moved a wardrobe, needing all the strength I could gather to push it up against the door which led to the porch. Moving a wardrobe is not easy when you're a few inches short of four feet, but with a bit of manoeuvring it eventually settled into place, firmly wedged to ensure anyone entering the porch bedroom would have to do so from the outside door. Or so I thought.

Next day when I returned home from work the wardrobe had been moved again allowing, with no negotiation, access to a room of which I had no say in occupancy. I put it back, thinking this would convince my housemate that I was not going to tolerate the invasion of privacy, but again it was to no avail. I stood up for myself in that horrible house for long enough – probably too long – then moved out.

I was able to get a room with the Pulham family in Croydon. They were friends of my father … Mr Pulham was an old trucking mate. His wife Joy, who later moved to Lakes Entrance, was a good cook and used to leave my clothes washed and folded on my bed. It was a wonderful family nurtured environment. Meals were cooked and Joy made lunch which I took to work each day. I stayed there for a while but was keen to again live on my own, so when the opportunity arose I moved to a unit in Elwood.

This is when I had my second encounter with a peeping Tom, and being older and more brazen – though perhaps not wiser – it was approached differently to the first one in Lakes Entrance many years previous. Coincidentally, Aunty Keryn was with me during the first incident and she was visiting me in the unit at Elwood when the second unwanted visitor came by.

My unit was on the ground floor at the front of a long block of flats, with front and side windows to the lounge room which had venetian blinds, and a glass door beside a side window. We were sitting in the lounge when I glimpsed a white jumper passing the glass door and thought it must have been someone going to the back door of their unit, but then it returned, going in the other direction. The next minute Keryn saw someone through a crack in the venetian blind.

"Don't look now, but there's someone peeping in our window," she said nonchalantly, so I didn't get startled. I told her to keep doing whatever, keeping an inconspicuous eye on him and try to retain his attention, then I got up announcing a trip to the loo and slipped into the kitchen, out the front door and quietly around to the front window. He was still peeping inside when I crept up close behind and with an almighty roar of confidence, yelled, "what the fuck are you doing?" Well, he turned around in fright but didn't look down, so he didn't see me. The look of bewilderment on this guy's face was to die for. He couldn't for the life of him work out where the voice had come from.

He must have sensed I was there and his eyes dropped to my level. He saw me and took off… just bolted. We rang the police, who were beaten to the scene by the Navy cops from HMAS Lonsdale who had heard the 'callout' on the police radio frequency.

"We'll get him for you Deb!" they told me. But he was never found. Still, I'll never forget the look on this poor bloke's face. I say poor, because who with sane mind would go peeping in windows in a white jumper.

Although I lived by myself at Elwood I wasn't exactly on my own. I had two little pet terrapins, Lillian and Luther, and a cat I called Edna. It was the only time I ever, of free will, had a cat and she was a beautiful animal … I really loved her. There were the four of us in the flat and it was a time I remember fondly. After recent unsavoury experiences of accommodation sharing, especially in Carinya Crescent, I probably again needed my own space.

I also had an eclectic group of friends which in some ways epitomised my diverse lifestyle. We were a tight group who had lots of 'all nighters' on Friday or Saturday, then went to the markets on Sunday … had great times together. Our clan included Peter and Paul, who were gay, and Peter's sister Fiona. There was Kath, who was a prostitute, plus myself. I'm still friends with Kath who went on to marry one of her biker customers and they had three beautiful boys.

They always treated me like 'one of the group'. Throughout my life I've selected friends based on how they treat me, not how they look or what they do. I think this has steered me towards those who have a drink or smoke a bit of marijuana … people who are broad minded enough to let their hair down and have a laugh, or like me, finding some form of escapism.

I don't like being treated as if I'm an egg about to break. Too often, if I say "give me a lift up onto that stool" there's uncertainty and a level of uneasiness. Yet I've found this is not the case with those who enjoy a drink or a smoke … they don't give a shit and they'll wrap their arms around me and do it. They don't care about my differences.

That's how I've ended up being surrounded by some interesting characters. Mind you, I also have many friends who don't fit this mould, though I'm often less comfortable in this environment than with those who are more laid back.

On the downside, while analysing the types of person encountered and befriended through my life it has become apparent that along the way there have been some arseholes and horrible people. I suppose that comes with seeking out those who have fewer inhibitions and are less judgemental. They take me and treat me for the person I am, not what I and others are seen to be; humans, with some physical support needs that are either awkward and burdensome or restricting.

Making a simple cup of coffee is a prime example of the difficulties some people face when interacting with a person who has disability. Some of my visitors rock up and within five minutes are asking, "how about a cuppa, Gray?" So they'll take a seat and I'll go and put the kettle on and make a tea or coffee.

Others will allow me to start then hover over and want to make the bloody thing themselves, annoyingly to the point that even as I am about to grip the handle of the kettle, as per a photo in this book, a bloody hand will appear before me and take control. Don't do that!! I am quite capable of making a cuppa, which I do every day. I won't spill the boiling water, nor will I burn myself. If I may be permitted to repeat what I have previously said … if I want help, I'll ask. I've found that others with disability usually tread a similar path.

***

In my search for independence, while working at HMAS Lonsdale and awaiting a suitable car option, I devised the idea of using an electric golf buggy which provided my transport to and from work each day, a tale of which was featured in a Woman's Day magazine. Today you see lots of people with limited mobility on footpaths in their scooters. Well, I was the scooter pioneer and regret I did not patent my idea. Instead, the bloke who modified one of his golf buggies from my idea registered the patent and made a lot of money. Never mind.

I loved that ride along the St. Kilda Esplanade in my little orange buggy, even though it was always busy. I travelled on the bay side of the street, looking out over the water as I scooted along. It was a good stretch of concrete all the way and the sea wall provided protection from any breeze off the water. It was a wonderful way to begin and end each day.

One morning on my way to work I was passing Luna Park when a big white car with a blue light suddenly blocked my path. Leaping from the car, two burly policemen demanded to know where the buggy was from. Being a little smart-mouth, I told them it was a bumper car from Luna Park. They obviously took my word, because I had to wait almost an hour while they contacted Luna Park management to check out whether or not my buggy was stolen. Nothing I could say would convince them I was only being funny. I think they must have had a very tough night on the beat in St. Kilda, because they certainly had no sense of humour to spare that morning.

But I suppose they weren't bad blokes and although I was late for work, considering the environment which existed around St. Kilda you couldn't blame them for the investigation, because back then carts like mine were never seen on footpaths.

So each morning, bright and early between 6.30 and seven o'clock, I'd zip along the Esplanade from Elwood to Port Melbourne heading to work and return along the same route at night, usually after dark. This was a work environment in which I was very comfortable and, for the first time, enjoyed respect from colleagues and lots of camaraderie. I would shut down the switchboard at four o'clock, lock the room, grab my bag and wander across the road to join the boys in the Mess for a few beers … and on a Friday night it wasn't unusual to leave the Mess in a mess. Occasionally the quartermaster stopped me at the boom gate on the way out and stated firmly, but with humour, "you're not driving home tonight, Deb". My buggy was lifted into the back of the Naval Police van and I was given a lift home.

They were fun times, which is why I have such fond memories. The boys at Lonsdale were my mates and I received no special treatment, which is the way I like it. They'd throw me up on a bar stool as quick as knock me off it … there was no molly coddling.

Next morning I'd be back on the switchboard at eight o'clock, regardless of how late I arrived home the night before or the state I was in. "Deb, you've got balls of steel!" the blokes would say.

The switchboard room where I worked was only small, about 1.5 metres x 2 metres, but generally a hive of activity. Its only window was located adjacent the footpath leading to the front door of the old red administration building.

If the ancient switchboard with its plugs and cords, its 28 incoming lines and its 60 or so extensions wasn't demanding my attention, there was almost always someone scooting by the open window to toss around a bit of lip with. It might be a sailor, and his or her rank may be anywhere from the occasional Commander, to the Able Seaman. Often the younger or troubled would enter my office and sit on the ground under my window, hidden from view. They'd sip a cup of coffee and prattle on, sometimes engaging in a 'Dear Dorothy Deb' discussion, opening their heart about girlfriend troubles, the shit night they'd had, or simply say "I want to hide … I've got a terrible hangover". They just wanted to get it off their chest and I was a good listener. (For the uninitiated, Dorothy Dix was an advice columnist for 'womankind' full of "crisp, fresh ideas ... a dressing mixed of oil of kindness, vinegar of satire, salt of wit"); I felt pride with that type of reputation.

Most of the guys enjoyed my company and many used to pop in with coffee in hand for a chat. Several were deliberately flirting with me, even though they had wives back in their home town. Although I found this flirting quite exhilarating and flattering, I was acutely aware most of them saw me as a 'safe' flirt. They had no real expectations and our conversations were nothing more than small talk.

There was one occasion during my four years at Lonsdale when I had a physical relationship with a married sailor, which was a spontaneous and unforgettable experience, not unlike a typical movie scene where a couple cannot wait a minute longer to tear off each other's clothes and go at it like mad creatures.

I was giving the sailor a lift home and we were in peak hour traffic on Warrigal Road, grooving along to a full-on Phil Collins/Genesis song when I suddenly pulled to the left side of the road and we had sex on the front seat of my car. It was the most exhilarating five minutes of my life … one of those unexpected things which just happens, for no real reason and with no apparent explanation. To have engaged in a totally spontaneous, morally forbidden, sexual incident like that was amazing, and something many women never get to experience. But I did, and for that I am grateful.

There have been many other unique experiences throughout my life that I have enjoyed … a lot more than some other women with 'normal' physical attributes. An advantage, if you can call it that, of my disabilities has been a driving desire to do anything I might have done if I had been born of conventional height with four functioning limbs.

American poet George E. Woodberry once said: "Defeat is not the worst of failures. Not to have tried is the true failure." Well, I can never be accused of not 'having tried', even though some of the things I tried may not always be considered with high regard. But I've had a go at just about anything and everything, and there are lots of people – many who I know – who wish they could say the same, but can't. Should I be punished for other's inadequacies?

***

While still working at Lonsdale I moved from Elwood to live with Jim at Hastings, then we moved to Seaford. There were always Navy boys travelling from HMAS Cerberus to HMAS Lonsdale and they'd come by and give me a lift to work. I waited on the side of the road and they stopped, picked me up like a sack of spuds and threw me into the car.

It was a time in my life that I reflect on with happy memories, both at work and home. Jim and I had always been close so I was glad we were back sharing a house, even if he did give me a hard time about keeping everything neat and tidy. I had a very large bedroom and I was pretty messy … I'm not a big one for folding up clothes and putting them in a drawer, whereas Jim was the opposite. One day I came home from work and he had built me an ingenious storage area. He pulled a cupboard forward, used a broomstick and other poles for railing and dropped a curtain down which cordoned off a quarter of my room and was my new walk-in robe with low hanging spaces. Normal wardrobes are no good to me because I can't reach hangers on the rail. On an earlier occasion he had surprised me by building a photo developing area.

While I was at work Jim often went in and picked up my clothes, did the washing, made the bed and cleaned up if it was needed. I'd say "stay out of my bedroom", but he didn't take any notice. Although I went crook, he knew I really appreciated his help and his love. Living with a brother who was a wonderful chef also had its advantages.

CHAPTER 8

Travel bug bites

Young people like to travel … get out and see the world before they settle down. I had the travel bug and talked about a desire to take a trip to the tropics of Australia. My friend Anne had a Yamaha 450cc motorbike and we decided it was the ideal mode of transport for the 3,700 kilometre journey along the east coast of Australia.

Some people may see this to be rather daunting, but for these two young women it was an exciting adventure. I'd had plenty of practice as a pillion passenger on a motorbike and even though I couldn't put any arms around Anne's waist my little legs, tucked neatly under the rider's thighs, kept me securely fastened to the seat.

After careful planning we jumped on the Yamaha in April 1981 and headed for my home town of Lakes Entrance, which was the first of many overnight stops. Admittedly it was different to most as I had a nice comfy bed to sleep in at Mum and Dad's house, in stark contrast to sliding a couple of chairs together which occurred regularly during latter parts of the trip.

From Lakes Entrance our journey went smoothly as we rode up the coast road, stopping along the way whenever we wanted a smoke or saw a pub that was worth a quick (or not so quick) visit.

Deciding on the coastal road to Sydney, our only small disaster occurred when we ran out of oil at the top of the Genoa straight, as it is locally known, a long straight hill that you descend when heading north. Anne turned off the bike and we coasted to the bottom of the hill where we could pull up. Conscious of soft gravel on the roadside, we stopped on the edge of the bitumen. We sat riding the gentle glide to the side, as you do while waiting for the side peg to make contact with the ground, then realised too late that the peg was sinking into the soft surface. I quickly popped my little less cumbersome leg out of the way but Anne was not as lucky and became jammed underneath. It was pure adrenaline that saw me pop my shoulder under the tail-light block, as the bike now lay on its side, and raise it up so Anne could free herself. Thankfully her leg was not badly damaged. A passer-by helped us with oil and we were soon back on our way.

By the time we reached Byron Bay, where I caught up with an old Melbourne mate, we'd been on the bike for over 1,500 kilometres and we decided to have a break in this delightful seaside town. When thinking about how I could best describe 'Byron' I checked out a few websites and found the following, which hits the nail on the head: "*What makes Byron special is the singular vibe of the town itself. It's here that coastal surf culture flows into the hippie tide washing down from the hinterland, creating one great barefooted, alternative-lifestyle mash-up.*"

For this little party animal from the surfie culture of Lakes Entrance, it was heaven on earth. I thought Anne was also having a good time, but all of a sudden everything went pear-shaped.

Anne's boyfriend wasn't too happy about being left all on his lonesome in Melbourne and he decided to jump on his bike and chase us. He reached Byron Bay while we were still there, tracked us down and insisted that Anne get back on her bike and follow him home. Although she'd been having lots of fun (me too!!), Anne was unable to resist her boyfriend's pressure and reluctantly agreed to return south.

"Are you coming back with me?" Anne asked.

"Stuff that," was my emphatic response. "I said I was going to Cairns and that's exactly what I'm going to do."

I poked around Byron for a bit longer and via the friend we were staying with I got to know Phil, who became a good mate. We were hanging around together enjoying the Byron scene, but Cairns was my destination and I was ready to get back on the road despite having a severe shortage of transport ie. no bike, no car … nothing.

"C'mon, we'll hitch hike to Cairns," I told Phil, who was ready for the adventure.

Whenever we stood on the roadside, signalling that we would like a lift, it could be done in one of two ways. There was the orthodox method, whereby Phil would extend his arm and slowly move his index finger in the direction we wanted to travel, or alternatively I could sit on a rucksack and extend a leg. However, after getting a ride in a truck, we discovered that even more effective was seeking out a friendly truckie at local roadhouses. Forty-four and (an important) half inches of pure charm worked a treat, and as our trip wore on even Phil became more adept at approaching truckies, especially once he started to realise they often enjoyed the company.

And so we hopped along from truckie stop to truckie stop up the Australian east coast along northern New South Wales and Queensland, improving our skill levels at Space Invaders on the way. Remember Space Invaders, the forerunner to all the crazy video games we have today, where the aim was to defeat waves of aliens with a laser cannon and accumulate points? These machines were in most roadhouses and they captured many hours of our attention as we waited for a lift to come along.

I have a vivid recollection of one early morning at an 'all nighter' at Ballina, about 200 kilometres south of Brisbane. It was 3am and Phil was spacing out over a Space Invaders' machine while we waited for the truckies to wake up so we could hitch a ride through to the Rocklea terminal where we hoped to catch a subsequent ride with a furniture truck that we were told was on its way through to Cairns. (My diary noted that I had also been playing Space Invaders a bit more than is good for the soul … or whatever other part of the body these little creatures impact on.) My diary also noted that the past few weeks had been "a rage!!!!" Obviously we were having a good time.

Phil continued to amuse himself on the video game while I turned my attention to a far more serious enterprise. I got out my tarot cards to see if we would get a ride later this morning when the sun came up. Can't remember what they said. I was going to join

Phil, but instead decided to put my rucksack up on the table, use it as a pillow and have an hour or so of 'shut eye'.

I think the tarot cards must have been positive, because we were able to eventually get a lift to Rocklea, even though we spent about seven hours at that truck stop. We went for walks, played Space Invaders and drank cups of tea, complemented by toast and my daily ration of Vegemite when it was time for breakfast.

It was worth the wait, as our ride was in a huge Mack truck … it was awesome, even if getting up and into the cabin, for me, was like climbing Mount Everest. I finally made it up onto the front seat (with assistance, of course). What a buzz!!

It was an enjoyable trip with two friendly people, Joy and Bill. Joy had quit work to 'truck it' with her hubby, about three months previous. They were great mates and we enjoyed chatting to them - skinny Phil and I sharing a seat - as we headed towards Brisbane and were dropped off at the Queensland Transport Terminal (QTT).

We arrived before most people had started work, and soon discovered we were too early for the pub. We wandered in anyway, seeking a quiet beer to help us start another day, and were advised by the friendly staff that the bar opened at 10am … we had an hour to wait. After we explained it had been a long night, two refreshing glasses of XXXX were poured and we sat back and enjoyed a peaceful drink. Great place, Rocklea.

We got a lift to Maroochydore, about 100 kilometres north of Brisbane, and grabbed a motel room so we could have a decent sleep. This was successfully achieved, but it almost cost us an extra night's accommodation as it was 11.30am before we were ready to check out and the prick at reception wanted to charge us double. We told him where to go.

From the motel we went to visit a friend of Phil's, a bloke called Dave who seemed a real sweet freak, before hitting the road again. Our first ride was only a short distance from the centre of town out to a riverside park where we put our travels on hold to enjoy some fun and frivolity in the water.

I went for a dip and we hired a little motor boat for two hours. What a rage! Phil jumped overboard while I had it on full throttle, then he grabbed hold of the side and tried unsuccessfully to get back into the boat. Eventually I slowed right down and straightened up so he could flip back in, but not before zipping around in circles as we both roared with laughter.

We returned the boat and were back on the road by 5pm, getting a lift a short distance to Nambour, by which time it was dark. An interesting chick named Sandra stopped and took us another 10 kilometres up the road to Yandina and asked if we wanted somewhere to stay for the night. We accepted her offer which led to another fascinating experience meeting lovely people. As we headed to her place of abode, Sandra advised us it was the start of an alternative living community. Her partner was Brian, a super nice guy of about 30 who had two children to a previous relationship – Amanda, who was about 10 years old, and Jethro, who was about seven. After a restful night we were treated to a delicious breakfast comprising home-made rye bread and fresh honey from Brian's bees. After breakfast Brian headed off to work, dropping us off on the north side of town so we could continue our trip towards Cairns.

We picked up a few short rides before getting dropped off at a service station on the south side of Gympie, having progressed only 60 kilometres, but were lucky enough to hitch a lift in a big Kenworth which took us a further 80 kilometres up the road to Maryborough.

It took two hours to get another ride, which was with a guy in a Datsun 180ZU diesel ute who tossed out two young blokes to fit us in, saying they "stunk like polecats". He jerked us around a bit, telling us to wait while he got petrol from the depot, made a quick visit to a friend, picked up some wood (which turned out to be building blocks for his children) and had a cuppa with his Mum. Then his wife and a few mates accepted his invitation of a trip to Rockhampton, with Phil and I piled into the back of the ute for this 400 kilometre stretch on the National Highway No. 1.

It was about 8pm when we arrived at Rocky and were dropped off at another all-nighter. A young couple towing a caravan pulled up for petrol and, as I reckoned they looked pretty cool, I sauntered up and asked where they were going. They were on their way to Mackay, which would get us a further 350 k's up the road, but intended to drive for about another hour before pulling over for the night and getting an early start next morning. If we were happy with that, we could come along.

The invitation was accepted and although it was a slow trip we made it to Mackay, then got a couple of short rides before an Austrian sweetie named Helmut offered to take us to Townsville. He was in a F250 towing a 26 foot caravan and on the terrible roads up north at that time it took us nearly seven hours, only averaging about 70 kilometres an hour.

You meet some intriguing people on the road. Helmut was a photographer, travelling throughout the Outback and visiting Aboriginal schools where he took school portraits. He helped get us to yet another all-nighter at Townsville, arriving a bit before 9pm where I put a couple of chairs together and caught up on some shut-eye.

The final leg, from Townsville to Cairns, was with a couple of obnoxious Americans in a rented Gemini. The driver raced along at 140 kilometres an hour, then hit the anchors as he kept stopping to photograph dead kangaroos on the roadside. At one stage he asked Phil to take a photo on their Polaroid, which he didn't know how to use, as they both stood with a foot on the roadkill. Phil and I found this scenario quite hysterical and our faces flooded with tears of laughter. I suppose you had to be there! As we approached Cairns the clouds and drizzling rain over the mountains looked amazing.

The maniac driver had kept hassling me for my Melbourne address, which I had no intention of divulging. When we hit Cairns I asked if they would drop us off at the Criterion Hotel. We arrived there just before one o'clock in the morning and I piled quickly out of the car and lost myself in the bar, leaving Phil with our transport hosts in the carpark. They soon left and headed back to Brisbane for a return flight to the USA. Yes, in just one overnighter, these guys could tick Australia off their 'bucket list'.

There was no-one I knew at the pub and it was about to close, so we grabbed some cans of XXXX and walked to the nearby Post Office where we sat on the steps, enjoyed a cold beer and made a few phone calls.

A bloke who we later discovered was aged 63 stopped for a chat. He was on his own in Cairns and seemed pretty lonely. Anyway, he dropped us at the Australasian Hotel and as we walked in the door the first thing I saw was a guy whose quiet but confident demeanour attracted me, like a bolt of electricity. I'm talking unusual, but magnetic, attractive! My jaw dropped and my heart throbbed with such intensity it nearly vibrated my sarong off. I grabbed my pack, we strolled over and I had my introduction to Reeves. He was gorgeous with a capital 'G'.

Reeves was one of the first men I saw in Cairns and after our initial meeting I really didn't care much about any others. I quickly learned he was a local fisherman who, fortunately for me, was on a short break. After a few beers he was showing open affection towards me, which is not something many males have been prepared to do. I spent five or six nights with him camping in his tent on the beach and it was very romantic, especially when we made love in the tropical ocean waters. My time with Reeves helped make the trip to Cairns one I will never forget.

But unfortunately all good things must come to an end, or so I'm told, and far too soon for my liking it was time for Reeves to get back on the fishing boat and head out to sea. A wonderful experience came to an end, so Phil and I packed our bags and headed for home.

***

After the Cairns trip I returned to work at HMAS Lonsdale and soon after was nominated for Disabled Person of the Year. It was in 1981, which had been proclaimed International Year of Disabled Persons by the United Nations. The intent of this proclamation is to be applauded, but I don't think it had any lasting impact on how society treats the disabled community. In its resolution a key objective of the United Nations General Assembly was "promoting all national and international efforts to provide disabled persons with proper assistance, training, care and guidance, to make available to them opportunities for suitable work and to ensure their full integration in society".

More than 40 years later I would have to question whether we have made much progress, in particular making available "opportunities for suitable work".

The Disabled Person of the Year Award was instigated by the Australian Council for Rehabilitation of the Disabled, aiming to highlight the achievements of disabled persons and help to raise public awareness of their ability and potential as contributing members of society. Adverse publicity surrounding those who received social security benefits was perceived as putting people with a disability in a bad light, and as a result ACROD decided there should be more emphasis on capacities and abilities.

The aspirations for what they wanted to achieve were well founded, though it's a shame we have not seen more concrete outcomes. Anyway, I was nominated, primarily for my work at HMAS Lonsdale, the independent life I chose to lead, and my commitment to disability awareness. Since 1979 I had been addressing secondary school students with my Ability Awareness presentations on my rostered days off.

Ironically, amid all the hype surrounding equal employment opportunities, I started at HMAS Lonsdale as a Clerical Assistant Grade 1 and left in frustration, nearly six years later, because there never seemed to be any chance of experience in another position offering advancements or opportunity for promotion, while others around me got to act in each other's position as absences occurred. There was no reason that I could see for this to happen, other than disability discrimination.

I went to Sydney representing Victoria for the National Disabled Person of the Year Award, but was pipped at the post by a lovely, married lady with paraplegia who had recently given birth and was raising a child with assistance from her husband. I think she may also have been a bit more entrenched in the politics of disability arenas than I was at the time. I greatly admired her achievements, however it seemed the panel was so awestruck by the fact a paraplegic woman had given birth, they seemed to overlook the achievements of many others who didn't have the family or partner support, but nevertheless had achieved great things throughout their lives.

Although I participated in these awards, I did so with some reluctance because it went against my natural desire to be no different to any 'normal' person. I actually considered them quite stupid, but they provided a vehicle by which I could make my Mum proud. I have always had a tinge of regret for the many things Mum missed out on because she happened to have a disabled daughter. I wish I had been able to give her grandchildren earlier, and perhaps even bring a son-in-law to the fold so she could enjoy the fuss and excitement of planning a wedding. Mum suffered a lot because of me and didn't deserve it.

Despite my misgivings, I would not be honest if I didn't admit the extrovert within me had agreed to be Involved in awards, hoping the media coverage and public interest was going to open doors for many living with disability. My display of happiness, in part, was fake! But to this day friends and acquaintances have always perceived in their own minds that I lapped up the attention I received throughout the award process.

I was rather thrilled to have images appearing in newspapers and magazines that showed me working the PBX switchboard at HMAS Lonsdale, as well as larger-than-life banners on trams that cruised around Melbourne, even though this did convey in some minds the view I was working at a telephone exchange. This campaign and subsequent images displayed to the world showed a different but competent ability to perform quite technical tasks, by a person classified as disabled. It's important that I provide some clarification regarding my work as a telephonist. Over the years a number of people have talked about the memories they have of the time they worked with me at the telephone exchange in Melbourne. In fact, I never worked with any national telecommunications organisation in any form. I'm sorry if this revelation has burst anyone's bubble. Only recently I was reminded, not for the first time, of the skateboard I used to get around on. I have NEVER used a skateboard as a mode of transport.

In saying that, I do admit to being a frequent visitor at the telephone exchange in Russell Street, Melbourne. My good friend Peter was employed there and I often called in to say hello while he was working. This was during an era when the workplace was less formal than it is today, as I don't think modern bureaucratic establishments would allow someone to pop in for a chat and waste the precious time of their workers. And to be honest, back then I could often get away with more than most people with my friendly, outgoing and sometimes cheeky nature that included a lot of gusto for such a tiny frame. I think because of this I wasn't initially considered a threat wherever I went as a young woman until I got too much attention - sometimes publicly, sometimes personally.

CHAPTER 9

Getting behind the wheel

I would like to tell you about my journey with cars which, at various times, has been interesting, intriguing, exciting and frustrating. As I discovered, when you have extremely short legs and do not have arms, getting behind the wheel becomes a challenging exercise.

Despite not having a licence I bought my first car in 1976, at the age of 19. It was a second-hand blue Ford Cortina from the late 1960s that cost $600. The car was going to give me more independence and cut down my reliance on friends and public transport to get from point A to point B. I had driven vehicles in the past (well, kind of) so didn't foresee any problems with the modifications that would be necessary to get me on the road. How wrong I was!

For two years the Cortina sat idle, though I think it was teasing me a bit because whenever I looked at that little blue car it seemed to be saying 'c'mon, get behind my wheel … I want to go for a spin'. Just like the VW in the 'Love Bug' movies, my car had a personality and was trying to coax me into the driver's seat.

Inevitably, I had to weaken, which occurred when Jim's former fiancé Robyn, who remains a good friend of mine, came around for a visit. Robyn was only 16 or 17, but that didn't seem to faze me as I suggested she could work the pedals – which wouldn't be difficult, as the car was automatic – while I looked after the steering. I was comfortable with that, having driven Jim's car many times.

We decided our first stop would have to be the service station to fill up with petrol, and as this wasn't far away it would be a handy practice run. I must say, we managed the journey extremely well with Robyn in control of the brake and accelerator while I handled the steering wheel. Unfortunately, when we arrived at our destination before proceeding on a longer, more exciting trip our plan went a little crazy.

Before we had finished turning into the service station my co-pilot got a bit panicky and put too much weight on the accelerator. As our pace quickened I had no time to straighten the steering and we ploughed smack, bang into the bowser, knocking it around quite badly, but not quite off its stand. At this point the panic levels, like the car's speed a split second earlier, accelerated rapidly. We had two choices – get out of the car and fess up to the service station owner, or get out of there as quickly as possible. As neither of us was licensed we chose the latter, and in great haste reversed away from the bowser and got the hell out of there.

Despite a rather stressful drive home we managed it safely, deciding on the way to park the car around the back, leave it there and hope no-one saw the damage. We ran inside, pondering the consequences if we had been seen. Thankfully this occurred before the days of CCTV and we never heard a word about this incident. Nor did Robyn and I take a trip like that again.

***

The whole process of getting me behind the steering wheel of a car took more than six years of tears and heartache, going through numerous avenues as I tried to find the right organisation or person who could develop a way for me to drive. In hindsight, it's amazing how difficult it was to deal with what should have been a relatively easy and straight forward process.

I worked with a couple of organisations to design the modifications, including the Victorian Disabled Motorists Association and the engineering department at Royal Melbourne Institute of Technology and although they had the most honourable and best intentions they were generally stuck in an academic mindset and could not shift the paradigm into practicality. There was exceptional technical knowledge, but no matter how hard I tried I could not convert their thinking away from using a joystick, moving it back and forward like an aeroplane … much the same as

I now do with my wheelchair. I did not want a joystick; I wanted a steering wheel.

Mind you, it must be acknowledged that this was in the late 1970s and early 1980s when the entire concept of someone with my limitations being in control of any dangerous machinery, including a car, was fairly new and, for many people, quite daunting. I understand they were doing their best, but in my mind this was not good enough.

After two years of complicated and unsuccessful consultation with the VDMA I gave up, left my little blue Cortina in their yard and walked away. I could not convince them that my feet were strong enough and could be used when I was driving, provided the controls were within reach. I left in frustration, never returned and did not see my precious first car again.

About six months later I bought a white Holden station wagon with power steering and spoke to personnel at the RMIT engineering department about the modifications I required. I suggested it could be a good project for engineering students, as I thought they may not be clouded with preconceived ideas like I had experienced at VDMA.

When I handed over the vehicle it was immediately apparent the teacher wanted to take it on as his personal project, thus defeating the purpose of my initial suggestion to tap into bright young minds. Consequently the project went dormant as the teacher became obsessed with the manner in which I should enter the car, rather than the more important issue of being able to drive it. He did not understand that getting in was not a problem … it wasn't back then. I could simply lean on the car's door to step on the sill, then place the left leg over the seat. It's similar to getting on a bike.

I persistently argued that he should get his priorities right and concentrate on a modification that would allow me to drive the damn thing, and if I looked a bit awkward making my way into the driver's seat I really did not care. I kept telling him that I'd been 'throwing a leg' to get into cars since I was a little girl so don't worry about that part of it. Regardless, the teacher could not get over his own view that I should enter the car in a more dignified manner.

His 'solution' was an electric door opening system. Once the key was turned in the lock it would automatically begin a process to open the door and unfold a step which lowered to ground level. If I stood on the step the automatic process would continue as it lifted me up to the seat level. There were two issues with his wonderful invention – firstly, of course, I did not need it. Secondly, when the door automatically opened I had to step aside to avoid getting knocked over. It never came to fruition.

I tried extremely hard to convince this person that I would dearly prefer his engineering expertise and experience to focus on developing a way for me to drive the vehicle, as this was the one and only problem I would like solved. Alas, my efforts were in vain. Over a year later my Holden station wagon was still sitting on the floor of the RMIT engineering department without any modifications that would allow me to drive it away. In frustration I walked away and left it there and, just like the blue Cortina, never saw it again.

Giving up is not in my vocabulary and, rest assured, I had no intention of abandoning my efforts to drive a car and gain additional independence.

The media coverage which had been generated from the electric golf buggy I drove to work at HMAS Lonsdale attracted a lot of attention, including interest from an executive in the customer service department of Mitsubishi Motors. He wanted to help get me into a vehicle and offered to sell me one at fleet price, which I thought was quite generous. It would allow me to get a new vehicle at an affordable price and in return Mitsubishi would get some publicity for helping me out, which was reasonable.

Before long I was the proud owner of a canary yellow Sigma station wagon for a bargain price of only $2,000. I fell in love with my beautiful new car, but still had no idea how I was going to drive it. I approached the vehicle registration authority – today known as VicRoads – and discovered it had become quite common for vehicles to undergo all sorts of modifications to suit individual requirements. On my behalf, the authority agreed to contact engineering experts who could assist and ensure any work carried out met their legal standards.

They put me in touch with a man called Andrew Enkelman who was a consulting engineer with VicRoads and who, about 15 years ago (several decades later) yet again signed off my vehicle modifications as they were transferred from my last car to my current vehicle. At our initial meeting in 1981 we met and discussed what I needed, but he immediately indicated the design required for me to drive a car was not something he could get his head around. I was disappointed, until he said, "I'm not going to do it, but I know just the man who can". Soon I was introduced to Lindsay Head, at the time in his mid to late 60s, who is best described as an academically untrained grease monkey who had dropped out of school at a young age and spent the rest of his life in the garage working and playing with cars. What he didn't know about motor vehicles was not worth knowing, and his innate love of mechanics which started as a hobby became a lifelong passion and very successful career, particularly building, maintaining and driving stock cars.

God bless this little man and his son Doug, who I had the pleasure of meeting down a narrow street in the Melbourne suburb of Moorabbin where numerous parked cars inhibited the flow of two-way traffic. Lindsay and I sat opposite each other on rickety wooden chairs in his pokey, grease-ridden office, with lots of paper and invoices scattered across his desk. We talked about many things which, I guess, was his way of getting to know me. After a while Lindsay held out both hands, palms up and placed them under my feet. He asked me to put my feet in his hands and push down as hard as I could, which I did. He then asked me to put my feet under his hands and push up. He gauged my strength in four directions - up, down, left and right – and quizzed me about how I thought I might be able to drive a car. I explained that what I had envisaged involved an automatic transmission, meaning only one foot was required to stop and go, and pedals I could reach from the seat.

This was the first time anyone had asked my opinion on driving. Others had been quick to tell me what they thought I needed, but rejected outright any suggestions I made. I'm sure at times they weren't even listening to what I said. Lindsay was so different and for that I will be forever appreciative.

I made a couple of other visits to his garage and it was only about four weeks after our first meeting that he phoned with the good news: "Your car is ready to be registered." It had power steering and power brakes, with extensions to the pedals hinged off the dashboard which allowed me to steer with my left foot and use the pedals with my right foot. Forty-plus years later I still used the same modification, which Lindsay built as one unit, that unbolts so it can be fitted to another car.

So at last, after six years of frustration, I was only one step away from controlling my own transport and, as I saw it, not being a burden on anyone. As a bonus I wouldn't have to ride on the cold, old Red Rattler … the common name for the Gippslander train which I often took on a Friday night when no one with wheels was heading from Melbourne to Lakes Entrance. All I had to do now was get my driver's licence.

I can still remember the excitement and jubilation I felt when the phone call came through with the wonderful news my car was ready. I could anticipate the freedom it would bring and the progress I could make towards the strong desire for independence. The feeling is so difficult to explain, but I suppose it could best be described as a combination of cheerfulness and absolute adulation. In a nutshell, I was over the moon.

As such, with this excitement bubbling over, it's probably not surprising that I decided to celebrate. I called Janice, who was a relatively new friend I had met when working a temporary position a year or two earlier, and we planned our Friday night out at my first choice watering hole, the Station Hotel in Prahran. At the time it featured artists including Matt Taylor, Richard Clapton and my favourite, Broderick Smith, who happened to be performing on Friday night. A big session was on the cards, and being responsible young women we made a conscious decision to take a taxi instead of Janice's car so there was no risk of drink driving. But alcohol can screw up even the best made plans, can't it?

We had a fabulous night as I celebrated with gusto, knowing I would soon be behind the wheel of my yellow Sigma. We partied, boogied and drank to our little heart's content. Janice and I were a pair of social butterflies who danced and chatted to people all over the place. Eventually after the music stopped and the bar had served last drinks, we wandered outside, both extremely 'under the weather', and waited for a taxi to take us home.

While we stood there a friendly woman, who we had met and befriended on the dance floor, pulled up and offered to give us a lift and we were in no condition to make a sensible decision regarding whether or not we should accept. We'd taken a taxi to avoid the dangers of driving under the influence of alcohol, then jumped in a VW Beetle which had a driver under the influence of alcohol. It wasn't a smart move and Janice and I lived to regret our foolishness.

Turning left onto Punt Road from Greville Street, we travelled south and crossed Dandenong Road before attempting a left turn into Alma Road, in East St. Kilda. Travelling about 55 km/h, we veered into the left lane to make the left turn into Alma Road when the VW, with Jance and I in the back seat, were smashed into the rear of a parked car. Adding to our stupidity of getting a ride home with someone who had been drinking, neither Janice nor I bothered to put on our seatbelts.

The force of the crash propelled both of us into the back of the vehicle's front seats. Janice went face first and smashed every tooth out of her mouth, which I'm sure caused considerable pain and ongoing distress.

I was sandwiched on the floor and delirious with pain, especially in my right leg. Although relatively hazy about what was happening, I recall I stubbornly would not allow anyone to touch me.

I had a very close male friend from the Navy, Charlie, who lived around the corner. Someone went to his house and explained what had happened and Charlie was soon on the scene. He was a big man and lifted me out of the car, at which point I blacked out and did not wake up until the following morning. I was in the Alfred Hospital with my right leg plastered from the toes to the groin.

When the accident occurred I had impulsively lifted my right leg to protect my body and stop myself from going forward. As a result, this leg took the full force of the collision and my right ankle shattered, the joint splintered in several places.

I never saw Janice again. She did not visit me in hospital, or phone to see how I was going. I suspect, rightfully or not, she blamed me for accepting the ride home and obviously harboured a lot of resentment. I can't blame her for this reaction because what we did was very foolish and, perhaps like Janice, I have never been one to easily suffer fools. Whatever the reason I will forever regret what happened to Janice in my company.

I spent seven weeks lying on my back in the Alfred, with complete dependence on the nursing staff. Ironically, for a number of months a stupid decision on my night out to celebrate some newfound independence temporarily robbed me of all independence. And my independence is not all that was robbed. While I was recovering in hospital some mongrel broke into my house and stole all our LP records, including a high percentage owned by Jim … a collection that numbered somewhere between 200 and 300. I also had many, many miniature cacti, of which I was attentive and proud, and these were all destroyed, squashed into the carpet of the beautiful sunroom I had adjoining my bedroom. How senseless was that?

During my time in hospital Jim was very attentive. I don't know what I would have done without the physical and moral support of my caring little brother. Charlie, my sailor mate from HMAS Lonsdale who had rescued me from the car crash, also called in daily after work and I thought our relationship was going places.

At the time of the accident I was living on my own in Elsternwick and it seemed practical for Jim to pack up the house as I had a long road to recovery and wouldn't be needing it for at least a couple of months, and probably longer. It was then decided I should move back to Lakes Entrance and stay with Mum and Dad until my recuperation was complete and my independence had been regained. They had by now re-sold the shop in Sale and were live-In managers for the Manchester Unity Caravan Park in their beloved Lakes Entrance.

My brother Geoff had married his fiancé Diane in a ceremony conducted by a celebrant in our parents' lounge room, in front of a small family gathering.

My car was still waiting for me and this was the driving force as I did all the physio and worked hard towards my immediate goal of being able to walk again.

When the time to leave hospital finally arrived Charlie arrived, as planned, to pick me up, and to my surprise he was accompanied by my friend Kaye. Charlie had no trouble lifting me into the front of his car, which had a bench seat, and encouraged me to move into the middle.

I think I had developed suspicions that Charlie and Kaye had become more than friendly acquaintances – even though Charlie and I had been very close – and as I joined in with the light-hearted banter I couldn't help but feel the vibes as they made eye contact from either side of me.

Of course I was right and another potential partner had been lost. Charlie, like Janice a couple of months previous, never did explain why our relationship was unable to evolve. Although I was devastated, I had experience with this situation and played their game, then left for Lakes Entrance to recuperate. By this time in my life I had suffered a lot of heartache and I'd learned to cry like hell, and move on. It wasn't long before I heard Charlie had left the Navy and moved to Bundaberg with Kaye where they opened an antique/second hand furniture shop.

***

My recuperation from the accident was long and difficult, in particular my ability to become mobile again. Most people with a broken leg or similar injury will hire a pair of crutches and use them to get around, but crutches aren't an option if you have no arms.

So here I was, 25 years of age and completely reliant on my mother's help for everything, as if I was a little girl again. Whether it was toileting, eating, dressing or getting in and out of bed, my Mum's help was needed. Another task where I needed her assistance, as I could not weight bare or get the plaster wet, was bathing, and the thought of the first bath made me very nervous.

You see, I knew Mum would discover the tattoo I had on my breast and I did not want to disappoint her or like a child explain a personal choice. I also figured she would not be impressed. It was a little mushroom, which I'd had for about five or six years, and symbolised my employment frustrations at being 'kept in the dark and fed shit', which particularly related to my inability to get any sort of promotion to professional, managerial or supervisory ranks, at the same time as I watched co-workers with less skill, but no disability, climb the corporate tree.

When Mum saw my tattoo she nonchalantly asked, "this does rub off, doesn't it?" to which I replied in the negative. My dear Mum then responded with, "oh darling, you've marred your body for life". I remember her comment having an impact as I realised she never saw my body as being marred, even though it is different.

Not surprisingly, during my time at home I received overwhelming support from Jim who was my hands and legs, carrying out any necessary task to make life easier. However, he was working on the Bass Strait oil rigs with a 'week on, week off' shift and as such was only around to help for half the time.

When he wasn't there I had a select group of friends who made life bearable, and I'm not sure what I would have done without their support. They came around home, lifted me into the car – which wasn't too difficult as I only weighed 25 kilograms - and provided a release from the boredom of being housebound.

Despite this being a difficult period in my life I have some fond memories of these times. If anyone who assisted back then is reading this book, I want you to know your support and friendship meant so much to me, and it is this type of behaviour and acceptance that has contributed immensely to my overall enjoyment of life.

***

After what seemed a long and arduous journey I was eventually back on my feet, with a focus on getting my driver's licence so I could return to Melbourne and enjoy the modified yellow Sigma, soon to be forever referred to as 'Sal' or 'Sally'.

As previously mentioned, my main driving experience had been with Jim in his Gemini, and I have forever been grateful that he was brave enough to let his big sister sit on the handbrake, from where I could easily access the wheel, and steer his car for miles upon miles as we came home from Melbourne. Jim's job was to run the clutch, brake and accelerator pedals which, of course, were well out of reach for my tiny legs.

I also received driving instruction from a short, stocky family friend by the name of Warren Corbett – better known to us as Booey or Boo - who I had known since I was a child. When Jim was off-shore Boo would pick me up and we'd go to the Eastern Beach carpark where he gave me lessons in reversing and parallel parking. He was only about four feet six inches tall, so only his head protruded above the 44 gallon drums that I had to manoeuvre around. He would half tip and roll at least four bins into the middle of the road and I had to weave in and out, both forward and backward, or reverse park between them over and over again.

When my leg was almost fully mended, but still bandaged, I spent time every day in what I called 'Sally's Cockpit', practising all the driving motions. I grew confident I could pass my driving test, hence the day and time was organised, and it was to be conducted under the watchful eye of our long-time local police sergeant Adrian Lalor, who knew me quite well. He put me through the ropes, going up Myer Street, which is quite steep, for some handbrake starts, then I had to reverse park several times, plus three-point turns and a few other things. May I say, I executed each one with confident precision.

We returned to the police station where Sergeant Lalor nonchalantly announced he could not fault my driving and advised I had passed the driving test with 100% score. I could not have achieved this without the help I received from Jim and Boo.

The feeling of independence this gave me was indescribable. It was out of this world. On my first solo drive I took my yellow Sigma to a secluded place overlooking the beautiful waters of Lakes Entrance. I sat there, all alone, stared out the window and cried like a baby.

Only a few months later, while I was in the final stages of recuperation at home in Lakes Entrance, Boo was killed in a senseless, tragic car accident. I was lucky not to be involved and later, although devastated, was slightly relieved because I could also have lost Jim and my dear friend Suzie.

The four of us were known as the 'Four Amigos' and on the night in question we were all heading to a friend's farmhouse at Swan Reach. Boo had a small, sporty type of car and I took our St. Bernard dog, Pluto, in my station wagon. Four people (even including a small person such as myself) and a big dog were not going to fit in Boo's car, so I said I would follow.

As we passed the Nungurner turn-off Boo put his foot down, and as I came along a straight stretch of road just before the sweeping right hand bend at the top of the rise, just east of Bennett's Brook, there was a reasonable distance between us. When I came around the bend Boo's tail-lights were nowhere to be seen, and as there was about 50 metres to the next bend I assumed he had gone even quicker and was well up ahead.

I continued another five or six kilometres until I reached the farmhouse and was quite surprised when no-one was there. After a few minutes, when they hadn't arrived, I decided to retrace my tracks, thinking they may have broken down and I'd missed them. As I came around the bend to the east of Bennett's Brook I was confronted with a horrific scene, with the flashing lights of emergency vehicles and the road blocked.

I swung through, nosed up to the police car and could see someone on a stretcher was being loaded into the back of an ambulance. Sergeant Lalor approached my vehicle with an extremely solemn look on his face and told me Jim was on the stretcher. I wasn't sure what had happened to Boo or Suzie and was in a bit of a daze as the roar of sirens announced the departure of the ambulance carrying my beloved little brother. At that point I didn't know whether he was dead or alive.

With my heart racing I excused myself from Adrian, jumped back into the car, did a quick U-turn and raced off after Jim, having no regard for speed limits or my own safety. All I wanted to do was keep up with the ambulance. I'm not sure how I managed to arrive in one piece at the hospital.

When I did, I learned Jim's left arm had been severed so badly that it was only attached by a small piece of flesh at the back of the bicep. After a frantic emergency department assessment he was rushed to theatre for microsurgery, in the hope his arm could be re-attached and saved.

While he underwent surgery I tried to find out what had happened to Suzie and Boo. As for Suzie it was relatively good news. Although her condition was listed as serious, the main injury was a broken leg in several places. She was on her way to surgery but expected to make a full recovery.

Boo was not as lucky. He was dead. OMG!! When would tragic accidents stop taking away my friends? Here I was in the middle of this strange, sterile hospital with people running everywhere. It was a hive of activity ... the place was buzzing, but to me it became a blur. I climbed up onto the nearest chair, sat down and I cried and cried and cried. I had known Boo all my life and now he was gone. My little mate was gone forever.

***

As the emergency department continued to buzz around me I sat alone, waiting for other members of the family to arrive and trying to get my head around what had happened.

As time progressed we (ie. Mum, Dad and I) were told Jim's surgery was successful, although he was still in a coma and in a critical condition. Doctors were confident he would wake from the coma, but didn't know how long it would take. They told us when he woke up he should not be told the true circumstances of the accident, including Boo's death, until he was more stable.

I knew I had to pull myself together, get over my grief and be in a position to support my little brother through his recovery, just like he had done for me not so long ago. I don't remember much more about that day or those that followed, except that I spent the entire week sitting next to Jim's bed, waiting for him to come out of the coma. I sat and watched as he lay there peacefully sleeping, his re-attached arm supported in a sling and hanging from a frame. I don't think I showered for a week.

I can't remember the actual moment when he regained consciousness, but I recall agreeing with Jim as he spoke about his recollections of the accident, even though they were incorrect. He had been in another car accident several years earlier, when he was in the car on his own, and in his mind he thought that's what he was recuperating from. He had no idea what had happened.

This continued for another week and I made no mention of Boo or Suzie, as per the medical advice. I would tell Jim I was going for a cigarette break, and instead went to see Suzie in a nearby ward. I'd then return to Jim and not mention her name. He was heavily drugged, extremely groggy and for several days after regaining consciousness was not really aware of anything.

Jim gradually improved, at which time he was told about the accident. He was terribly upset. As for Suzie Barnes, she hadn't recovered so well, as her leg, which had been fully plaster casted, began to rot. In fact, it was Mum who brought attention to the horrid smell surrounding Suzie as it had begun to intensify. She demanded the plaster be removed and it was! Within hours Suzie was urgently flown to Melbourne where surgeons immediately performed surgery to save her leg, and life, which as a result of a full plaster cast over a compound fracture were now under serious threat. A compound Fracture is when the fractured bone pierces the skin, creating what is called an open-wound, which should have been attended to daily and it wasn't, thus gangrene had taken hold.

Police investigating the accident could find no clear reason why Boo's car crossed the road, flipping and rolling 100 metres into the paddock, coming to rest against a tree stump. And as the driver was killed there were no legal ramifications. Suzie and Jim received life lasting injuries with Sue's leg amputated and Jim's nerves to his arm ripped from his spine. Reattaching the arm left him with intense spasmodic pain and no hand functions. Maybe I influenced his ability to soldier on, as after that he capably continued with his career as a chef. It is sad that, as time went on, heroin gave him so much relief!!

I remember feeling sorry for my parents who, in that one year, had suffered the worry and heartache of car accidents with their two youngest children. It must have been a difficult and trying time for Mum and Dad.

From my perspective, after many years and numerous battles, I finally had a car and a driver's licence. I won't say I was back to normal after such a traumatic period, however it was time to get back on my feet and back to work.

CHAPTER 10

More work, more travel

After a lengthy period of recuperation I was finally ready for a return to work at HMAS Lonsdale. I had endured a huge 12 months. There was the accident and my recovery, I had lost another very close loved friend and almost lost my dear brother. On top of this, plenty had also happened on the home front.

If I can digress for a minute, I was given the opportunity to meet a family of dwarfs who lived opposite Diane's parents in Mooroolbark. Lyn was around my age, but not the type of personality that I connected with, although I formed a close bond with her mother Jean. Miraculously, I was taller than both of them.

I remember having lots of fun and laughter with Jean and I could relate when she said one day as I was leaving, "it's nice when someone doesn't have to bend down for a kiss".

Jean became a close friend and I remember with sadness the day I sat loyally by her side until she took her last breath, having suffered from the dreaded cancer. Unfortunately it was not going to be my last experience with this terrible disease. Over the years I have supported three people to their last breath from cancer and feel honoured to have given the comfort.

***

So, as I said, I was at last ready for a return to Melbourne. But just before I left, after jumping into my yellow Sigma to wind my way back up the Kalimna hill and onto the highway, I had a sweet surprise.

A little explanation is required here. Like my Mum I had a minor addiction to sugar and always put 2½ teaspoons in my cup of tea.

Growing up I always drank Milo or tea, never coffee, to which I had an utter disdain. For many years I couldn't even stand the smell of coffee, let alone drink the stuff, although I must confess that as I matured and travelled I developed a liking for the aroma of freshly roasted coffee beans, especially in the arcades of Melbourne's CBD.

As I slowly reversed out the driveway, starting my trip back to the city, Dad tapped on the driver's side window. I hit my fabulous electric window switch allowing Dad to lean over, obviously keen to tell me something.

"By the way, you're now down to drinking tea with only half a teaspoon of sugar ... that's all you have had for the last two months." My immediate reaction was one of slight annoyance that Dad had taken the liberty to gradually reduce my sugar intake. However, my attitude changed to one of gratification when I was back at work and made the brave decision to give up sugar altogether. I no longer had to drag the kitchen chair across to the table, located in the corner of the tea-room, so I could climb up and reach the sugar bowl. It was worth the effort for 2½ teaspoons, but certainly not half a teaspoon. So, thanks to Dad, I was weaned off sugar.

***

At HMAS Lonsdale I had many friends and was regularly part of social and recreational activities. The Port Melbourne depot greeted numerous foreign ships which presented me with the opportunity to meet some wonderful people. These included two American sailors, Johnny and Peter, from the USS Hector who invited me out to a delicious lunch. So guys, if you happen to read my book, I hope you are pleased that I still remember.

Johnny and Peter were both extremely honourable and, unlike many other sailors, never made any inappropriate moves or suggestions. They seemed to enjoy my company as a female which made me feel very much like a woman and, at the time, helped restore a sometimes shaky faith in mankind. I still did not have a boyfriend, so the attention was welcomed. The day following our luncheon date the USS Hector set sail, but not before I received a warm-hearted kiss goodbye from them both.

At weekends, crew from HMAS Lonsdale gathered to socialise. We went to the Mess or at a bar in Bay Street we all called the 'Hole In The Wall', though I'm not sure of the hotel's proper name. It was the last pub on the left heading south on Bay Street, before you reached the water.

We also went to Defence Forces' football matches, which were a hoot. The Navy had two sporting categories, one for officers and the other for juniors, and we had lots of good times at official and unofficial matches.

It was also about this time, I'd been licensed for a year or so, I received a call and was asked to visit a chap called Harrow Morgan to discuss designing a car for Mary Henley. Mary, Lynette Rowe and I attended the Royal Children's Hospital together when we were young to have artificial prosthetics fitted. At the time Mary was living at Yooralla, while Lynette and I had the good fortune to be in our loving homes. As children we used to terrorise the occupational therapy and outpatients departments and were called, among other things, "the tricky trio".

I'm not sure if the discussions I had with Harrow were instrumental in getting a result, but I know Mary was successful in her attempts to get a modified vehicle. Many years later she drove to Lakes Entrance and stayed with me for a weekend.

I remember reading an article in the Melbourne Age who interviewed Mary after it was claimed the German company, Grunenthal, ignored and covered up warnings about the anti-nausea drug thalidomide that her mother took while carrying her in 1961.

In the article, Mary said she was "incensed" to discover that her disabilities could have been prevented. "I'm outraged," the report read. It went on to say that any compensation, while welcome, would never take away the pain she and her family have suffered. "It's not going to give me arms, it's not going to return a childhood that was very different, it's not going to give me the husband and children that I didn't have," she said.

And she's right. Money can help provide for your care, but it can't replace what has been lost, nor make up for the indignation suffered too often by too many individual human beings who, through no fault of their own, have a disability.

In my case, I didn't receive any thalidomide compensation because, according to the law, the drug was not available in Australia at the time I was born. Whether or not it caused my physical differences will forever remain a mystery.

However, what doesn't change is the need for many people in our 21st century society to think a little harder about how they treat their fellow human beings who live each and every day with disability.

Personally, I have generally steered clear of disability groups and organisations, probably because of my desire to live an independent and normal life which is something I can proudly say I have achieved despite the discrimination I have had to face. Society tends to lump the disabled in one basket, making incorrect ASSUMPTIONS about the support that may be required or the SKILLS they may possess.

I know there is a strong view in some quarters that more help is needed for the disabled, and the National Disability Insurance Scheme is, supposedly, designed to address some of the shortcomings. I hope the good intentions of this scheme do not forget to properly acknowledge and understand the uniqueness of every single person, as the needs and aspirations vary enormously. From what I hear so far it is purely a path to make additional funding a taxpayer obligation.

However, if the Government stopped allowing selfish executive wages and inappropriate bonuses to publicly funded positions, and sorted the archaic justice system, we would be able to support the less fortunate in our country. If they deported those who broke our contract agreements of entry, we would not be looking after so many criminals who spit on our freedom and way of life and take resources from Australians who are entitled to them.

It is imperative that we foster independence and individuality, as sometimes the support mechanisms become too onerous and limit a person's ability to grow within society. I have lived on attitude, not disability, and I do not want or need to be catered for as a disabled (definitions are: dicap, weaken, cripple, damage, paralyse, impair, debilitate, incapacitate, immobilize, put out of action, disempower, enfeeble, render, inoperative, deactivate, disarm, defuse, make safe) person. That's my call and I expect others to have respect for it. I have had event organisers phone and ask "do we need to cut your sandwiches?" They may be well-meaning, but they're also unnecessarily intrusive. If I want someone to cut my sandwiches, I'll ask. What I do not want is people foreseeing or forethinking what I may or may not require, simply because I have a disability. Although I do acknowledge, this may be required for some.

While on the subject of disability attitudes, those in authority also need to have greater understanding and compassion towards providing for the individual, not the masses. It must be about the person, not ticking another bloody bureaucratic box or maximising the profit for a company making millions as it services a lucrative disabled industry.

Here's an example. A number of years ago I had to get a new wheelchair … well, I didn't actually need a new chair, just a bit of patch-up work to the old one. But no, we can't do that. When I asked for some repairs to be carried out, including a new motor and fixing a wheel, I was told the old chair had to be 'written off' and I'd get a new one.

The replacement chair was from unmodifiable mass production which did not suit my unique individual requirements. Unfortunately, from my perspective, that's simply seen as bad luck. I suspect the rules and regulations are put in place by bureaucrats who have never used a wheelchair, and nor will they seek expert advice from, or employ, a wheelchair user.

So they refused to fix my old chair and instead I had to place an order for a brand new one, worth $19,000, that has this amazing LCD display telling me how many kilometres I have travelled and whether I'm going fast or slow … a tortoise and hare set-up to make it simple for us simpletons. Do you think I give a shit if I'm doing 1.6 kilometres an hour or I've travelled six or seven kilometres? Nor do I care about the time. I've never worn a watch on my wrist - it's a bit difficult without a wrist – and, put in plain English, I did not need this convoluted, obtrusive control panel on my wheelchair.

What I did, and still do want, is a small, simple control unit; bells, lights and whistles not required! To explain, the smaller unit, as on my old chair, did not inhibit my ability to front up to tables and benches or manoeuvring in confined spaces, whereas the larger one does. Also, with the toggle lever for steering located at the back of the unit I need to hold my foot firmly pulled back so it is not in the 'go forward' position. This also inhibits my ability to hit reverse, which requires a readjusting of my seated position. Does anyone really understand the intricacies of being a physically unique person in need?

If I was allowed to accept the new chair and buy a new more suitable control panel, or swap the control panel from my old chair, that would be fine. There was nothing wrong with the old panel. But you're not allowed to do that because it would contravene an arrangement between a government agency and the manufacturer.

Isn't it reasonable for me to ask, "hang on, who are you here for? Is your prime responsibility to me and my mobility, or is it more about making money from my disability through mass production?" The world has become so obsessed with bureaucratic process that we seem to have lost sight of who we are trying to assist and how individual scenarios can be best addressed. Again, it's lumping people with disability into one basket and ignoring extensive diversity which exists in the real world.

I know people are sometimes offended when I express my strong opinions, especially those who genuinely believe they are doing the right thing. All I'm trying to do is provide some education … help develop a better understanding. If you are dealing with a person who has physical disability, like myself, look past the physical and treat them like any other person. Most persons living with just a physical difference know when to ask for assistance; we know when it's needed. And most of us know that an order for a hot drink will be hot!

It's a simple message. When interacting with a person who has disability, especially of a physical nature, treat them with respect, just as you would (or at least should) treat any other person.

***

In the early 1980s it was becoming more common for young people to get bitten by the travel bug, though not to the extent they travel today. I loved visiting new places, making friends and generally having a good time.

Another trip I remember fondly, at the age of 25, was across the Nullarbor to Western Australia, then inland heading north before heading east to the coast at Onslow and up to Karratha.

I think the catalyst for this trip was a yearning to enjoy my car. It had taken many painstaking years to get my modified vehicle, yet before I had a chance to experience the independence it was going to provide, the accident and subsequent broken leg interrupted this dream. Now I was back at work, looking out the window all day at my precious Sigma, which sat idle in the car park. I couldn't stand it and applied for holiday leave and took off on a road trip across our vast nation, accompanied by a couple of good friends.

Three of us left on a Sunday morning ... Kerri Derby, Sue Alexander and yours truly. Sue and I have been lifelong mates, and before our trip shared a house in Middle Park. We also worked together at HMAS Lonsdale where she was a gardener.

We raged along to Ararat, bought a supply of fruit and decided to go via the Grampians where we camped the first night at Lake Wartook, nestled at the top of the mountain range. We had the camping ground to ourselves and it was serene and peaceful, with nothing but the noise of the surrounding bushland and the bubbling stream just 40 metres away. I went for a walk in search of firewood and found an old cart with big iron spoke wheels and solid wood chassis, bolted together with huge iron pins. It was embedded into thick overgrowth and this indelible piece of Australian history had obviously been there, untouched, for years. Later, Sue and I went for another stroll and sat on a bridge, our legs over the side as we mused about the peace and beauty of wind, wildlife and the sounds from a manmade miniature waterfall which was only 10 metres upstream. Just Sue and I, with Kerri back at camp, in a pristine part of the world … no-one else for miles.

Our world surrounded by nature was broken when we heard a humming sound in the distance, getting gradually closer and louder as it rumbled down the mountain. Suddenly it was almost upon us, then a car flashed around the corner and across the bridge as we sat in silence, our legs still dangling over the side.

We listened as it drifted further away and enjoyed a few seconds of silence before the car's engine again broke the evening air. It came closer and we realised it had turned around and was again heading our way. As it approached the bridge the car slowed down and I could see a man and a woman inside. This time, instead of racing passed us the car entered the bridge at a crawl before stopping, as we sat with trepidation.

Then suddenly the driver exclaimed, "hi Debbi!" as he wound down the window. 'Well fuck me!' I thought, looking in to see Laurie Mooney, who was the brother of a high school friend, and his girlfriend Cindy. We had a rave about 'it's a small world' and that sort of stuff, and learnt they had been in the Grampians for a week, staying in a nearby caravan and camping park. Laurie and Cindy left after telling us "we'll be back soon". We sat and absorbed some more bush silence, before sauntering back to camp where Kerri, being a cook by trade, had the fire blazing and our tea under preparation. We must have all been good Girl Guides. Laurie and Cindy returned and we had a great night sitting around the campfire and singing along as Kerri strummed her guitar. I love the bush.

I also love being able to wake up and get out of bed when you feel like it … no pressure. It was 11.30am when the tent flap was opened next morning. We lit the fire and cooked some brekky (well, it was really brunch), then I ignored the 'no swimming' sign and took a dip in the crisp, clear water of the lake. It was so fresh and exhilarating.

After a quick detour where we bid farewell to Laurie and Cindy, we limped into Horsham with the petrol gauge on empty, filled up at 40 cents a litre (wouldn't you love that today!) and continued on our journey, crossing the border into South Australia just before five o'clock.

That night we stayed in Naracoorte at Kerri's destination, with her brother and sister-in-law, Damien and Annie Derby. The intention was to head off the following afternoon, but it didn't quite happen which was of no concern. As planned from the beginning, Kerri was not continuing any further than Naracoorte, and it was easy to delay our departure a day or so while Annie made some curtains for the car, which Damien fitted, giving us additional privacy and making it easier for us to sleep in the back of my very much loved, canary yellow Mitsubishi Sigma station wagon.

From Naracoorte Sue and I continued on our journey through Keith, on to Tailem Bend for petrol, then Adelaide which we went straight through and only got lost once (which we thought was a pretty good effort). Our intention was to camp the night at Port Wakefield but apart from a servo there was nothing there so we continued another 50 kilometres to Snowtown. This was about a decade before the infamous Snowtown murders when 11 people were killed and their bodies put in barrels.

Like Port Wakefield, Snowtown had nothing of interest to us and looked a boring, barren place. We stopped at the pub for an ale and while chatting to a local he suggested we keep driving another half hour to Crystal Brook. It wasn't palatial, but at least it was a reasonable camping area just off the National Highway with lovely big gum trees and a nearby creek bed which, like everything else this side of Adelaide, was dry. After erecting the tent Sue and I laid back and enjoyed the cool evening breeze, which was welcome relief after a warm day.

We were nearly 600 kilometres from Ceduna, but decided to get an early start next day and make it that far, ready to tackle the Nullabor. Anyway, you know what they say about 'the best laid plans …' We didn't make it to Ceduna, instead taking a detour off the highway and finding a neat little caravan park where we pitched our tent right next to the beach at Streaky Bay. I had become adept at getting the tent up and banging in the pegs by putting the hammer across my shoulder with the handle firmly positioned under my chin. By leaning over the peg and moving my shoulder up and down I could get the peg into the ground. As a bonus, when I used the hammer I never had to worry about whacking it on a finger.

Before we ventured across the Nullabor I decided that maintaining hair on a camping trip was an arduous task I could do without so, with Sue's help, out in the bush one day it was all hacked off with a razor blade. Although my head was not shaved, my hair was very, very short for the first time … but not the last.

There were a couple of nights camping along the way until we reached the little town of Eucla, just a few kilometres over the West Australian border, where we again set up camp and slept in the back of my car.

The drive across the Nullarbor Plain, on the edge of the Great Australian Bight, stretches more than 1,000 kilometres and although the scenery sometimes gets a little monotonous, there are stretches of extreme beauty. I savoured every one of the many miles behind the wheel; just two crazy young gals with the wind in our hair via open windows as we cruised along, taking our time and driving until dusk.

We continued on to Perth and stayed with another friend called Sue Hobson, who had her 21st birthday party while we were there. It had a 'green' theme and was lots of fun.

From there it was a long trip to Karratha as intended, to visit cousin Col, but not along the coastal route. We travelled inland, heading north-east on the Great Northern Highway to the old gold rush town of Mount Magnet, camping along the way. It was primitive living, with just a single burner gas Primus to cook our food and hopping into the back of the car and onto the mattress when it was time for shut eye.

I've always loved the outdoors which is probably why I have such wonderful memories of that trip. Whether it was erecting the tent, which we did occasionally, or preparing our food I always managed to do my fair share.

At meal time I laid out the cooking tarp and chopping board, Sue filled the dish shaped bucket with water to wash my feet, then cut and diced our food or peeled the spuds. This was all lumped into the saucepan which I placed on the stove in a similar manner to hammering in the pegs, which I described earlier. Quite simply, I held the saucepan of the frying pan handle on my shoulder and under my chin, and lifted it onto the cooker. At some of the places we camped there was a barbecue or hot plate which we used if it was easier than lighting the Primus. The only area where I relied on Sue to do most of the work was lifting our gear out of the car, or re-packing before we moved on. But I think one of the most enjoyable aspects of this trip was our sharing of responsibilities. Sue and I made a great team ... as I said, we were great friends over 30 years ago after working together with the Navy and have remained lifelong friends ever since.

We continued on our way to Newman before heading east to Karratha, on the coast, where we spent a week with one of my cousins. After a week in Karratha we headed south, following the coastal route to Perth, then gradually made our way back across the Nullarbor, through South Australia and back to Melbourne. It was a fantastic journey that I will remember forever. We covered more than 10,000 kilometres in three months and, as Sue was unable to drive my modified Sigma, I was the driver for every single one of them. I didn't mind a bit as I made up for lost years not behind the steering wheel.

CHAPTER 11

Off to America

After our journey to the west and back, I somewhat reluctantly returned to work at HMAS Lonsdale. Although I loved my job and the people with whom I worked, after five years there I had decided to apply for positions elsewhere. I was suffering from employment stagnation and needed to move on, again due to an inability to get promotions.

There were limited opportunities at Lonsdale, with its civilian workforce only comprising the senior gardener and his assistant, plus the captain's secretary, two clerical positions in the Reserves Department and my job as base switchboard operator.

If anyone in clerical was ill or on leave, one of the others usually took on a relief role and I became frustrated because even though others would temporarily cover my tasks if I wasn't there, I was never given the chance to step in and fill their position. "Why not?" I started asking myself.

I have often reflected on my time at HMAS Lonsdale and still consider it the best job I ever had. But I was driven to become more than a switchboard operator. If the Department of Defence refused to acknowledge I had the skills to do more, I would find someone who did.

This all led to life becoming pretty miserable at work, even though I still enjoyed the company of my work colleagues. I guess it was all about my nature and the implicit desire to go further … to achieve.

Before we left on the WA trip I began perusing the Commonwealth Gazette and applying for jobs that would at least give me a promotion from Clerical Assistant Grade 1 to Clerical

Assistant Grade 2. Several of these positions were as a project officer which suited my experience and physical limitations. None of the applications was successful.

My efforts to achieve a promotion finally bore fruit when I received notification that I had been offered Clerical Assistant Grade 2 as a telephonist/receptionist at the Coonac Rehabilitation Centre. As an establishment directly working in the area of disability, assisting people to grow and overcome employment and living issues involved with having a disability, I thought the environment would be supportive and encourage my ambitions. I accepted and left HMAS Lonsdale only a week after returning from our holiday, excited that a new phase in my life was about to start. I thought it would be an easy transition from one job to the next. How wrong I was. I felt really honoured to have been formally presented with a RAN HMAS Lonsdale plaque in appreciation of my service to Lonsdale, which hangs proudly on my wall today.

My new workplace was in a magnificent historic building on Clendon Road, in Toorak. It was built in 1867 in the tradition of the early Italianate mansions in Australia, and from 1948 to 1986 was home to the Commonwealth Rehabilitation Centre. I read a few years ago that Coonac had become one of the few remaining mansions on its original Toorak block and comprised 20 rooms in 130 squares, plus a tennis court, pool, park-like gardens and sweeping lawns, all of which I recall.

The building's grandeur is one of few positive memories I have of Coonac, which is a shame because it was a rehabilitation centre staffed by people who were supposed to understand the needs of those with physical challenges. They were supposed to help others living with disability but in reality this did not happen … instead they were patronising and placating.

I was employed as telephonist and receptionist and apart from looking after the phones was required to attend to the reception and administration needs of clients, staff and all visitors, and occasionally typing as requested.

I started at Coonac full of my usual vibe and enthusiasm but after a few months I felt this was resented by some office peers, though I was not sure why. Rather than appreciating my enthusiasm, skills or abilities there was a begrudging attitude. In retrospect I could see why someone continually asking for tasks may be annoying for those who like to sit and chinwag, ring a friend or give oneself a manicure.

Nevertheless I battled on and continued fulfilling my duties, and sometimes those of others. During my second year at Coonac there was a vacancy for a full-time transport officer under the classification of Clerical Officer Grade 4, which would give me another promotion. The primary role was dealing directly with clients to coordinate taxi travel, and at the same time ensuring each taxi being booked was utilised to capacity. It involved determining the best route so more than one client could be picked up or delivered during a taxi's trip.

The incumbent sat next to me in the reception area and I had often been called upon to do this task when she was on leave or out of the office, so I was well versed in everything it entailed. After six years in the public service I had only progressed from Grade 1 to Grade 2, while being constantly leap-frogged by others in the promotion stakes, even though there seemed to be no justifiable reason for this, apart from my physical appearance. In this instance, however, I expected to be given the transport officer's position, even if this meant that the arrangement we'd followed as I occasionally did the sorting, booking and display board, would need to be made a permanent, but small, task for another person. Once the board was set out with taxi numbers and their passengers, I would ask another staff member to carry the metre square board several metres outside of reception and hang it on the wall.

No such luck! There was a nurse on staff who, as everyone in the office knew, or so it seemed, had a drinking problem and was finding it difficult to effectively fulfil her medical duties. I assume management was not prepared to sack her, and instead she was transferred to administration and given the job I had my heart set on.

This really got my hackles up. I had six years seniority in administration and had effectively and efficiently carried out the duties of transport officer on a part-time basis. I thought, "I'm never going to get past CA Grade 2" and could see that if I stayed at Coonac I would still be telephonist/receptionist in a decade.

Perhaps I should have been satisfied with that, but I wasn't. My brain wanted more. When I achieved a task that had been tackled it was time to move on and find the next one. Throughout life this approach has helped keep me going and cultivated self-worth. As I conquered a challenge I wanted another one and in this way I did not dwell on what I did not have and could not do, no matter what effort I put in, simply due to physical limitations. But I always looked at it with a view that nobody on earth can do all there is to do. I really longed for intellectual stimulation, and I had aspirations for management.

Being overlooked for the transport officer's role had a profound effect. Before long I was suffering from depression. I only connected positively with one co-worker at Coonac, a lovely older lady called June, who could see what was happening, befriended me and we often enjoyed a coffee and chat outside work hours.

I appreciated and accepted her support but it was not enough to stop me having a breakdown which forced a move away from Coonac. Ironically it was during this time that I was temporarily transferred to the staff welfare department at an office in North Melbourne, working as Clerical Assistant Grade 5. I worked successfully alongside two social workers and thoroughly enjoyed it until the woman I was filling in for completed her maternity leave and I was sent back to Coonac.

When I returned to this horrible working environment, knowing I should have been the transport officer rather than receptionist, my depression worsened and I had a more serious breakdown. That was more than 30 years ago and it saddens me to think attitudes in the workforce towards disability may have not changed. Organisations that employ people like myself will not let us in, and I cannot understand why. We are not a threat, but I think in many cases that is how we are perceived.

It took me many years to admit the contrast which often existed between my exterior and interior. There was a smile on the dial, but in reality this was a “fake it until you make it” veneer, often covering how I felt inside. I often went out and made sure I had fun so it looked like everything was rosy.

***

For a number of years I had realised that not continuing my education was a big mistake. I wasn’t the type to be moping around on an invalid pension and needed constant challenge to keep my mind active.

When you do not have the physical capacity for many jobs it is important to have academic qualifications which can slingshot you into the workforce. I decided to improve my qualifications by undertaking a Diploma in Social Welfare, at what was then known as the Gippsland Institute of Advanced Education, at Churchill. It later became a campus of Monash University, and more recently is called Federation University.

I enjoyed the challenges of returning to study and really applied myself, but it did not take long to realise this was a mountain too high to climb. For three weeks of the month I studied at home, which was okay, but for one weekend per month we had to attend lectures on campus. Have you seen the size of the social studies books that were a compulsory part of university? I can assure you they are quite large … far too big for a short person with no arms to lug from one lecture room to the other, at a time when there weren’t support services for students with disability and before my days of having a wheelchair to assist with mobility.

For a year I desperately tried to adjust to the challenges of being a mature age university student. Most of the obstacles I could overcome, but my inability to get huge text books from the carpark to the first classroom, then the next, was overwhelming. I completed the first year of my degree, then bowed out.

My time at Coonac tipped me over the edge and I thought, “I’m going mental; I have to take a holiday”, so took 12 months leave from the public service. I was thinking rationally enough to know that resigning was not an option because it may leave me without a job when I was ready to return.

In 1985, at the age of 28, I'd had enough and was no longer coping. My attempts to get meaningful work were continually frustrated by people who looked at my disability, instead of my ability, and attempts to advance my academic qualifications were also thwarted by the limitations of my physicality. I had to get away from it all. I had to get right away … out of the country. So I went to Flight Centre and bought a one way plane ticket around the world. Planning the trip with the travel centre staff, then buying the ticket, was a time filled with anticipation and excitement.

I also tried to help out my flat-mate, who I thought could look after my unit in Carnegie which I had gone in to debt and purchased a year or so earlier, but was luckily able to payout with insurance money from the car accident. I offered her 12 months free rent while I travelled, on the condition she both look after the unit and go back to school. We had shared home tasks and we were living together well. I knew she had the perfect attitude to work as an occupational therapist, so encouraged her to enrol at Lincoln Institute and spend the year studying. She made her way into the professional world, although I was a little disappointed that she then found our friendship was not needed and vacated my life.

But getting back to my travel plans, I was going to show everyone that I didn't need anyone. I didn't need a carer or helper; the public service might think differently, but I knew I was a capable individual and would prove it.

So here I was planning a travel journey far greater than anything I had undertaken. Sure, I'd been on road trips to Queensland and Western Australia, but this time I was going to travel the world. My rather large, lime-green backpack was packed and I was ready to go, not exactly sure where I would end up, apart from the International Disabled Persons Conference in the Bahamas due to start in a week or so and the fact my first landing would be in Los Angeles. America, here I come!!

***

Despite the burst of confidence, walking down the gangway onto the plane was one of my life's scariest experiences. When I boarded the plane a flight attendant put my overnight bag in the overhead locker, but it didn't stay there long. I had to ask a fellow passenger to get my bag down so I could use it as a step to get into the seat. I sat back waiting for take-off, and as the Boeing 747 thundered down the runway my heart raced. What was I doing? It was too late to turn back.

I was allocated an inside seat which was not ideal, as getting out to use the toilet or go down the back to eat a meal was difficult. After a while I was swapped to an aisle seat. Once I settled down I enjoyed the flight with the help of airline staff who were marvellous, giving me all the support I needed. At meal times, if I wanted to use a knife and fork with my toes, I was able to sit on the floor in the kitchen area where my food pack was opened and I could stretch out as the attendants stepped around me.

When I used the bathroom an attendant placed my overnight bag in front of the toilet and I used it as a step. Toilets in aeroplanes are quite high and not user friendly for the disabled.

The assistance I received from flight attendants, one in particular, continued when we arrived in Los Angeles and I faced the first major challenge of my world trip. I waited and waited at the carousel for my luggage to come around on the conveyor belt and eventually realised it was not going to appear. When the airline staff realised my predicament one of the flight attendants kindly offered me accommodation at her house until my luggage arrived. It took a several days.

Her name was Kathy and she lived in a beautiful house at Redondo Beach with her husband and two children, who were both college students in their late teens. They were at the centre of my first international adventurous experience, and one which left the trepidation of getting on the plane pale into insignificance. In fact it was one of the most extraordinary self-controlling experiences in my life.

The teenagers appeared to be polite, well grounded youngsters and when they invited me to a party a few days after my arrival I was happy to accept. Little did I imagine the outcome. It blew my mind … literally. And I thought they were straight, well behaved young college kids!

I was handed a pipe and told it contained hashish. I'd smoked hash before and said "okay", not realising it had been laced with Angel Dust, or at least I'm fairly sure that's what it was. Phencyclidine, commonly initialised as PCP and known colloquially as Angel Dust, is a dissociative drug. I remembered seeing a sparkle just before the pipe was lit, but didn't take much notice. On returning to the party the hallucinogenic effects of the 'dust' were kicking in. As I conversed with people I could see my lips were talking back at me from the other side of the room and it took all the mental strength I could muster to remind myself that I was simply tripping!

I was tripping and a long way from home. At this point all the years of keeping my emotions under control gave me the strength I needed to understand what was happening. It took all my brainpower to remind myself I had been laced and keep a certain level of control until it eventually wore off. We made it back to the teenagers' house and I realised America was going to be a wild ride and I would have to stay focused.

While staying at Redondo Beach I was introduced to a family friend of my hosts who, despite heading towards the elderly phase of her life, was a bit of a swinger. She was contemplating a road trip to Mexico and after we chatted about this for a while I agreed to tag along. We left soon after my luggage was recovered.

Everything went smoothly for a few days until we met Carlos who showed me a lot of attention which led to a burst of jealousy from my travel mate. Consequently she wanted to move on, even though she knew I wanted to stay … that's what we each did.

I was smitten by my Latin lover Carlos and I stayed several days with him in a resort in Baja California, a Mexican state on the Baja Peninsula which borders California, until it was time for me to again move on. I headed to nearby Guadalajara, the capital and largest city in the Mexican state of Jalisc, with the intention of getting to Guademala which was further south. However Mexico was a wild enough place and I felt unusually vulnerable so I didn't stay long before jumping on a plane to Los Angeles, then flying to Florida on the other side of the U.S. for a three day Disabled Persons International Conference in The Bahamas.

When I was thinking about where I should go – this is before I left Australia – I discovered this conference, which was of particular interest, and decided it was worth attending. That was the catalyst for making America my first destination.

I attended as an independent Australian and as such paid my own registration and accommodation for the conference, which was a fantastic event that stretched over several days. While in The Bahamas I was under the guidance of a local chap called Coffee, a delightful person who showed me around his native island in this archipelago. In The Bahamas, like numerous other places around the world, tourists only get to see the resorts and not what happens in the less privileged areas.

I wanted to look behind the front streets, and Coffee was able to show me the poverty and primitive living conditions under which many people suffered. I especially wanted to see what their disability rehabilitation centres were like and this was quite confronting. Coffee took me into a basic cement sheet house, probably full of asbestos and with torn, worn linoleum on the floor, which in reality was nothing more than a slum. Elderly residents sat around in the front room on old chairs with their walking sticks or frames nearby. It was an eye-opener, and made me realise how fortunate we were with our rehabilitation centres back home. This one must have been only for the elderly because there were no children to be seen.

Coffee also introduced me to the most delicious seafood I have ever tasted. It was called a Conch, a tropical marine mollusc with a robust spiral shell, the meat looked and was cooked similar in some ways to a scallop, although from my perspective there was one huge difference … I didn't like eating scallops, which back then were caught in large quantities off Lakes Entrance. But I just fell in love with the conch and ate them morning, noon and night.

I stayed in The Bahamas for a while after the conference before making my way back across the small stretch of ocean to Florida where I was meeting up with a team of seven others from Trek

America for a bus camping trip across the continent. We assembled at a hotel in Florida and were paired up ready for departure. My original tent-mate was Meg, a social worker from Adelaide, although our camping union did not last.

Throughout the trek we stopped each afternoon at our camp location where the first task was erecting the tent and setting up our bedding, after which there was cooking on a roster basis. Being an experienced camper I was able to handle these tasks without much difficulty. Meg was a flirty type who had eyes for the tour guide, and early in the trip she started using me as her 'charity case' during the day, trying to impress the guide by giving me unnecessary attention and assistance. Her behaviour was less thoughtful when camp was being set up, especially with my bedding which she occasionally ensured was upside down or short sheeted, leaving me to fix it before I retired for the night.

I put up with Meg's antics for a while but one day spat the dummy and demanded a new tent-mate. The guide paired me with a wonderful big Dutch chick named Yolanda ... or Yollie, as we called her. Yollie and I became great friends.

The trek started in Florida, firstly heading across to the Mississippi state of Louisiana, staying for a few nights at the French Quarter in New Orleans where we were keen to get involved in the night life and music scene for which it is so famous. Unfortunately I got a little bit too carried away and on reflection appreciated the serious consequences that could have been suffered.

On our first night in New Orleans we went out to a bar in the French Quarters – what else would you do? – and one of the waiters, a very cute African-American by the name of Malcolm, was paying me a lot of attention which I lapped up. He finished work and joined us for a drink or two before inviting me to go home with him, which I accepted. I have always been open to affection and loved passion, and at this stage in my life I was yearning male company and found it difficult to dismiss the male advances which occasionally came my way. I craved for the open and public attraction and affection which my life had been deprived. And so it was with Malcolm, as I enjoyed a memorable night of unbridled bliss.

I discovered African-American men sure know how to treat a woman. They don't seem to care about shape or size – the focus is on providing gratification and contentment for their partner. Malcolm was a gentleman and an amazing lover.

I had a wonderful experience with Malcolm so the following night, longing for a re-run, I returned to the bar where he worked in the hope of a repeat performance. Unfortunately he wasn't working and, in the heat of the disappointment and the moment, I foolishly left the bar with one of his mates and we went to a motel. Although it is no excuse, I blamed a cocktail they served called a Hurricane for my lack of judgment. It's a popular New Orleans' drink made with rum, fruit juice and syrup or grenadine and I know I dropped my guard after too many Hurricanes.

We spent the night at the motel before my newfound lover friend – I use the word 'friend' loosely - vanished at 5.30am without paying the bill, using the excuse that he was going to get a Coke. I was left on my own in a dishevelled state and never saw him again. I felt used, abused and sluttish … but that was not the full extent of what I faced. I couldn't reach the shower taps, or the mirror to see if I looked as horrible as I felt, all the while suspecting it was worse. I was lost and helpless, then went outside and realised I was in the slum area of all slum areas. What was I going to do?

Top priority was to get the hell out of this dive. I slid along the wall, snuck past the peekaboo reception window and ran down the street as fast as my little legs could carry me. I walked through the slums – it was terrifying – before finally reaching a main road where I hailed a taxi. He didn't stop. Nor did the next, or the next, and I realised I obviously looked so dreadful that none of the New Orleans drivers wanted me in their cab.

Walking further along the road I spotted some activity, with people boogying on the footpath outside a hotel, which was down a side-street. Knowing I had to talk to someone and get help, or find a taxi that would take me to the hotel where my trek mates were staying, I headed towards the revellers. Our trek bus was leaving at 8am which was less than two hours away.

As I approached the people on the footpath I realised it was a rather unsavoury crowd and once more my worries escalated. Then, a stroke of luck, when a taxi pulled up on the opposite corner and a man opened the door to get out. I raced across the road and when there was enough room between this passenger and the taxi door I darted through the gap and dived across the car's back seat. There was no way that driver was not going to give me a lift to our hotel, regardless of how bedraggled I looked.

He gave me a weird stare as I wiggled my backside into the seat and blurted out the destination. That taxi was my saviour. I made it back to the trek hotel, cleaned myself up and before long we were back on the road again and I had learned a valuable lesson. I had lost touch with myself in New Orleans and considering the AIDS crisis that followed, felt very lucky that I hadn't contracted any STDs and wasn't pregnant. Never again would I put myself in that situation.

From that point I had a wonderful trip. Yollie and I enjoyed each other's company as the seven of us rode our little bus across the mighty U.S. of A., from previously mentioned places like Florida, across the Panhandle of Alabama and the bottom of Mississippi, Louisiana for a few days, to the wonderful bluesy and sexy city of New Orleans, then travelling on to Texas, New Mexico, Arizona, north to Utah and across to Colorado. Then it was further north to Montana and across the panhandle of Idaho to Washington, trekking from south-east to the north-west - what a fabulous time and experience in many, many ways.

In Denver, Texas we had a night out at the pub with some locals playing pool and, of course, drinking and smoking 'pot'. I think the Texans were impressed with my prowess on the pool table which had been developed over many years of practice in Melbourne and Lakes Entrance. I used to stand on a wire glass rack which I borrowed from behind the bar, placed the cue on my shoulder against my neck similar to the golf club grip and, looking straight down the cue, gave a little sharp twist of the shoulders and stabbed the cue forward, making fairly controlled contact my with the white ball. If it was a long shot I put the bridge or spider on my left shoulder and the cue on my right. If anyone does not believe my unique method of playing pool can be effective, let me know and I'll challenge you to a game at the local pub, although I'm not sure how my form would be 30 to 40 years down the track. I'm not sure why I kept getting attracted to some scenarios and situations, although admittedly in the mid 80s 'pot' was rampant across the U.S. More great memories!

After a couple of games one of our new-found friends sidled up to me with an irresistible invitation in that typical Texan drool. "Ya comin' out for reefer, gal?" Next minute I was sitting next to him on the footpath, back against the wall, sharing a 'reefer', after which we sauntered back inside and continued thrashing arse on the pool table.

From Texas we continued on to Arizona and a special experience when I sat my bum down on four states at the Four Corners Monument which marks the quadripoint where Arizona, Colorado, New Mexico and Utah all meet. Yes, I know it's a dumb touristy thing, but it was still a great feeling.

As we entered Yellowstone National Park, in Wyoming, we were warned that a Dutch woman had recently been mauled to death by a bear so caution was needed. We wisely decided against pitching our tents, instead opting for the protection provided in the park's cabins. It was a wise move, because the following morning we awoke to find a bear just outside our front door. That was interesting.

Yellowstone, with its canyons, alpine rivers, lush forests and gushing geysers provided some exhilarating sights and experiences, but this was just one of many across the U.S. Not surprisingly, the Grand Canyon was a favourite and I also enjoyed Lake Powell Canyons in Utah where we hired a boat and took in the immense beauty of the lakes and surrounding mountains.

Yollie and I were an exaggerated version of the early 20th century comedy duo Laurel and Hardy, and as we stood together at the top of a mountain it must have looked quite funny.

Our trek ended in Washington, where Yollie and I stuck together for a few days before I headed up to Canada. That was the last I ever heard of Yollie, which is regretful but that's the way it happens when you are travelling. You meet people and move on, which is something to which I had become accustomed. Also, at that time communication was only via letters because we did not have email, Skype, FaceTime or mobile phones. We swapped addresses and Yollie may have sent me a letter, but the chances of it reaching me were slim because I moved around a fair bit when I returned to Australia. I clearly recall the day we parted, and the photo shoot as we lined up on the hotel steps. With backpack firmly strapped I was ready for my journey's next phase.

***

During my time at the conference in The Bahamas I met some wonderful people, including a blind guy called Hugh who, like myself, didn't mind a party. He lived in Vancouver, a bustling west coast seaport recognised as one of Canada's most ethnically diverse cities, and suggested that when my trek was finished I should make my way up there for a visit. So I did.

Not surprisingly, soon after my arrival Hugh hosted a wonderful party where I met a lot of his friends including Alan and Mia who lived in Victoria, on Vancouver Island. Anyone who travels is well aware that you meet some very friendly and welcoming people, and Alan and Mia fell into this category. They invited me to come and stay, which I accepted.

Alan worked in the timber industry and spent a lot of time travelling around Vancouver Island, so I tagged along for a couple of days. We went to lots of Canadian beaches, although I was surprised to discover they were covered in black pebbles and a stark contrast to the beautiful sandy Ninety Mile Beach back home.

My intention was to go inland from Vancouver to Banff and possibly on to Calgary but, to put it simply, it was too bloody cold. It had been snowing and I was not enjoying the weather so jumped on a Green Tortoise bus that was going south where it would be warmer. And there started another fascinating chapter in my North American travels.

The Green Tortoise bus company still operates today, though I suspect their tours are no longer as liberal as those in the 1980s and the vehicle fleet has been upgraded.

I was on a dear old big Bedford bus that effectively had two passenger sections. At the front were little tables and chairs along one side, with a few seats on the opposite wall, and the rear half of the bus was a platform on which there were mattresses where passengers would lie around and smoke pot ... talk about peace, lovin', and sleep! No-one, including the driver, seemed to mind, but there was a strict ban on alcohol.

I travelled on this hippy bus from Vancouver to San Francisco, which took several days. We stopped along the way at natural springs and spas for our daily wash. This is one of the most peaceful, wonderful trips I have experienced, and it was with the most amazing bunch of about 30 people. Everyone was helpful and there was never any fuss or stress, it was just a lovely, easy going environment from start to finish.

There wasn't one man on that bus who I could not comfortably ask, "hey, throw me up on there, will ya?" And they were all happy to grab me by the shoulders and toss me up onto a mattress so I could also lay about.

I left the bus in San Francisco and met up with my girlfriend Christie, which led to another unique experience I will remember for life. It was near the end of January which meant I was celebrating a birthday. Christie picked out a pub on the other side of the Berkeley Bridge and suggested that, because it was a special night, perhaps we could order a limousine to get home, though no firm decision was made. We did a bit of cocaine and by the time we left for our big night out I was full of excitement and exuberance.

It was a fairly flash pub that, I believe was owned and ran by famous singer Sheena Easton who, at the time, was good friends with pop star Prince. They had produced a song together and there were suggestions of a relationship, although she denied this.

Christie and I had a super night. We drank and danced and the night wore on. When it finally reached time for us to depart we were pretty well under the weather, so to speak. We walked out the hotel's front door – staggered might be a better description – and as soon as I stepped onto the footpath my eyes lit up. There, right before me, was a long, luxurious, white limousine.

"Christie!" I yelled, almost hysterical, "you ordered my limousine!" It didn't cross my mind in that split second of exhilaration that this luxury vehicle may, in fact, have been for someone else. The back door was open so I raced as quickly as possible, taking into account the limitations of my short legs and the alcohol which had been consumed, making a bee-line for the opulence that lay within.

I nose-dived through the open door of the 'limo' in not dissimilar fashion to the manner I had entered the taxi after my regretful night in New Orleans, hitting the floor with some force and, at virtually the same time, looked up to see a familiar African-American staring down at me with a mix of shock and bemusement.

It was Prince. Yes, the one and only Prince ... American superstar. He said "hello" as he stared in bewilderment while I came to a sudden freeze on the limousine's floor and the obvious conclusion that my assumption it had been ordered by my good friend Christie as my birthday gift was misguided.

Very few times in my life have I been seriously embarrassed. This was one of them. I mumbled, "oh, so the limousine's not for me" – more of a statement than a question - and sheepishly retreated, amid a realisation it was being shared by Sheena and Prince, the latter waiting patiently while she ducked into the hotel. By this point Christie, who knew she had not ordered a limousine, was coming to my rescue. She graciously poked her head in the back of the limo, grabbed me by the shoulders and assisted with my red-faced back pedalling. We went home, more than a little drunk and more than a little nonplussed at how my birthday night out had ended. I'll never forget it ... including the look on Prince's face.

I had met Christie's awesome friend, Rastafarian taxi driver Waverley Logan, who Christie believed would be a good match for me. A few days later I left Christie's place to spend time with Waverley, who had become a close friend, and spent a glorious three weeks lapping up his adulation. I thought Waverley, a taxi driver, was about eight or nine years my senior but discovered he was much older, like 15 years. He was a Jamaican and held his age extremely well. He was a beautiful man who wanted me to stay but, as usual, I let go and moved on. At this stage of my life the relationship between Waverley and I was the most romantic, passionate and normal connection I had ever experienced.

He often ran me a bath with rose petals and every night when he returned home from work he brought flowers and I had dinner on the go. I thought, "I could live like this forever". But that's not how the world works and after several weeks I was forced to leave this tiny slice of heaven and make my way to New York, from where I was flying to London to meet up with another camping trek through Europe.

I boarded a Greyhound bus in San Francisco for a four day journey to the east coast and, wouldn't you know it, took my allocated seat right next to a big, friendly Negro. Several hours into the trip, after we'd been chatting away and were by now well acquainted, he took out of his pocket a little pipe in which he inserted the tiniest amount of hashish. It was smokeless, and as our bus made its way across one U.S. state, then the next, we puffed away to our heart's content. Mind you I have always considered my usage as recreational, I could take it or leave it, and as such do not consider myself to be like hard drug users often portrayed by the media. In fact the man beside me was a successful, professional businessman.

A German tourist seated across the aisle kept staring at us. It must have got the better of him because he went into the toilet at the rear of the bus and next minute the smell of marijuana was wafting through the ventilation system. The driver was furious. He immediately stopped by the roadside and marched down to the toilet, grabbed this guy and exclaimed "no smoking drugs on my bus … you're off!" And out the door the poor German went, in the middle of nowhere. We kept puffing away on the hash until we reached New York.

My intention was to spend a week with a friend in New York before flying to London. However, getting off the bus at the Greyhound depot in the Empire State I felt uncomfortable and unsafe. I did not feel safe on my own in New York. The bus depot was a scary place, with flagrant sleeziness and desperate people… so much was being offered I could have bought a pound of anything, and I wondered "if the police cannot control a bus depot what will it be like out on the street?" That was in 1986 and I believe New York is a lot different today.

I hailed a cab and asked the driver to take me to the nearest decent hotel where I checked in. Making a judgment call, the following day I changed my flight schedule so I could leave almost straight away, headed to the airport and flew out to London.

CHAPTER 12

World travels continue

Sitting on the plane as I left America I reflected on the many people I had met and places I had seen. My mind wandered back to the day I landed in Los Angeles, wound my way to Baja California and had the pleasure of my first Latin lover. I'd had loads of fun with lots of new friends, especially Yollie and others on the camping trek, and I wondered if they ever classed me as a burden or would they do it all again. I hoped it was the latter.

My only regret was not getting further into Mexico, although a couple of experiences in Baja California were enough to make me realise I should not travel there alone. One day I will return with a friend and visit Mexico, I thought.

It was late December and the middle of winter when I landed in London. It was bloody cold! Fortunately I was wearing a pair of boots which I could slip on and off easily. They also came in handy across the colder states of America. I made my way to the luggage carousel with some trepidation, hoping there would be no repeat of the lost bag in Los Angeles, and was relieved when my lime green backpack dropped on the conveyor belt.

"Would you mind grabbing that pack as it comes passed?" I asked a nearby traveller, who obliged and helped position it on my back. As I left the airport I was aware that some strange looks were focused in my direction but, as usual, chose not to respond. I'd encountered enough of human comments and attitudes to know they were looking at this short woman with no arms and in a patronising manner either mulling it over in their head or communicating to their companions, "isn't it wonderful to see such people, with a body like that, out living life … and she's smiling!" I left the airport and hailed my first little black cab.

I rented a room in the suburb of Earls Court, which was an area of London frequented by many Australians. It was in a typical London street lined with narrow houses, packed tightly side by side. I paid the cab driver, got out and saw there were a couple of steps to the front door.

As a younger person I was able to climb in and out of cars and onto buses, and getting up steps was not a huge problem. I even lived in terrace houses in Melbourne where the steps didn't bother me much, although I'd bypass living upstairs if I could. Today I have to avoid steps whenever possible.

I made my way up the steps to my temporary London home and knocked on the closed front door which I was unable to open. This was a regular occurrence throughout my travels and I generally knocked or waited for a passer-by and ask for assistance. Someone heard my knock and let me in to a terrace house that was similar to many in Melbourne's inner suburbs with a narrow hallway and rooms along either side. There was a stairway on the right and a community kitchen towards the back of the building.

I was sharing my room with a young New Zealand girl called Lindy Mason who was very conservative but had a great fun nature. I spent several weeks in the hostel where fellow travellers were always happy to help me out when needed and even arranged to tie strings on the door-knobs so I could get in and out at my leisure. There was always someone at the hostel to let me in when I returned from my daily adventures and at night my roomie would help out by leaving the door ajar. It seemed safe to do that back in the 80s.

I was in and out all day every day, except when it was snowing, and spent a lot of time sightseeing, especially in the mornings. Many afternoons I could be found relaxing at the bar in the nearby The Prince Of Teck Hotel. I had a fantastic time hanging out at the 'Teck' and was spoilt by the pleasures of another holiday romance. There were several nights when I did not make it home to my own bed, but had to put a stop to the developing relationship when I realised my suitor was getting possessive and a tad too serious. I called on some mates at the 'Teck' who helped me scare him off. I must admit I was a bit chuffed that, due to his persistence, getting rid of him was no easy task. When he finally took the hint I did not see him again. Although he was bloody gorgeous and very romantic it was easy to let go because I am not compatible with someone who wants to possess me and spend every waking hour by my side. I had spent too many years rowing my own boat!

It was cold and sometimes awkward when I was out and about as I had to wear my slip-on ankle boots which made it difficult when I needed to use my toes. The boots were black with black and white fluff around the collar and despite the inconvenience I didn't mind the look, as opposed to thongs. Fortunately, by balancing on my right leg I could quickly and easily shake off the left foot boot when I had to access my bag or wallet.

London has so many incredible historic sites and I had lots of fun days visiting places such as Buckingham Palace, the Tower of London, St Paul's Cathedral, Westminster Abbey and others. With the awesome ancient history it was a great beginning to my European experience.

One day my roommate Lindy and I took a trip to Dover where we had a picnic on top of the amazing White Cliffs, although the most spectacular view of the cliffs was some weeks later as I looked back while sailing on a ferry to Europe.

During my time in London I discovered that a good friend from Sydney named Adrian was living in a place called Elephant and Castle, squatting in a rundown vacant flat in a low socio-economic, crime ridden public housing estate. He was burdened with problems and I think his only solace was living rent free. I stayed and watched this squatting lifestyle unfold for a couple of days, then gladly returned to the hostel.

Before long it was time to check out and say goodbye to friends I had made. We again promised to keep in touch but I still had several months of travelling and lost most of their details after returning home, so that didn't happen.

I moved to a hotel from where my next adventure would begin, taking a European and North African tour on a double decker bus. On the first evening tour participants were asked to gather in the hotel bar at seven o'clock for a 'meet and greet' which was a good ice-breaker. Several of us connected almost immediately and probably spent a bit too much time getting acquainted. Our 'punishment' was a hangover for the early morning start next day.

The double decker bus was not just our transport, but also our home, with sleeping quarters on the top deck. At the front of the top deck was a row of seats which provided the prime viewing area as we travelled along, though you had to be quick to secure one. The bottom deck was our living quarters and comprised a lounge, day area and kitchen, with a toilet at the rear under the stairwell. It was such a well-equipped bus and ideal for our tour.

Our driver Steve and guide Glenn were both Australians. Glenn was an attractive young guy, quite aware of his resemblance to Richard Gere whom I saw as very much enjoying the attention he received from the opposite sex. It wasn't long before he had a 'secretary', Bronwyn, who was another Australian girl travelling with her friend Rosie. Other Aussies in the contingent were Sally and Neil, both also travelling alone, as we three immediately connected and discovered we all had three things in common … our solo traveller status, nationality and the fact we were all in for one hell of an adventure together.

Early on the morning of our departure (with hangovers) we left London and headed to Dover, where we boarded a ferry to cross the English Channel to Calais, in France, where I got that second extraordinary view of the white cliffs of Dover and upon arrival took my first step onto European soil. From Calais we travelled the southbound to Paris through beautiful quaint countryside meandering along narrow roads that, at times, weaved between houses with hedged fencing along the roadside. On other occasions the countryside opened up to the horizon with harvested fields.

This first day was very exciting as we cracked drinks and got to know each other while travelling along in the double decker bus. There was a window between the driver's seat and the back of the bus so Steve was not left out of the banter unless he wanted a break, in which case he would shut his little window and continue along in peace and quiet.

Then we arrived in the beautiful city of Paris. Perhaps strangely, before I travelled I had never given a lot of thought to the concept of 'big' and 'small', despite definitely being in the latter category. However, by now I appreciated how big some natural phenomena could be, like the huge canyons in America, and in Paris I was to get another lesson in size as I stood under the Eiffel Tower and marvelled at the height of this man-made structure.

I thought about the height of my house as I looked straight up, thinking it was tiny in comparison. I looked up to the top of the tower, all 324 metres of it stretching towards the sky. I hadn't in my wildest dreams thought a mechano-like structure could be so tall.

We left Paris and travelled east into southern regions of Germany, making our way to Dachua where we stopped for a tour of the first concentration camp opened by the Nazis before World War Two. I left feeling this was the most inhumane and horrid environment I had ever seen. In the 12 years of its operational existence, from 1933, over 200,000 people from all over Europe were imprisoned at Dachua and subsidiary camps and 41,500 were murdered. The huge ovens and massive pits were indelibly etched into my mind for a long time after we left Dachua. In fact to this day I am realistically aware of the horrors both historically and now that mankind can do to each other. This was the most emotionally draining and horrific day of my entire year away, even though I am pleased we went there so I could gain a greater understanding of what other human beings had experienced. If there was ever a tiny racist bone in my body it was certainly erased that day.

We stayed in nearby Munich and, like any group of young travellers, ensured we had a visit to Hofbrauhaus Munchen on our itinerary. It is one of Munich's oldest breweries with a beer hall established back in 1589. Many young visitors have since graced its halls and I am sure, just like ourselves, spent considerable time enjoying the German ales. Some of my newfound friends helped me up onto a mantelpiece where I was perched for several hours being fed large German steins. It was another outrageous social night in this huge beer hall that was packed with drunken revelry.

After a couple of days in Germany we were back on the road and heading for Austria. We arrived in Salzburg and enjoyed Austrian sight-seeing, which was a pleasant change from the previous hectic few days. No visit to Salzburg would be complete without a 'Sound of Music' tour, taking in the breathtaking scenery where this famous movie was shot back in the 1960s. We went to the von Trapp residence where I performed a sing-song, including a little pirouette, in the centre of the gazebo, much to the delight of my companions. (I thought the journey would be incomplete without one of my favourite past-times, singing, at such a famous location.)

Back on the double decker bus, we continued our tour south through Austria and on to Italy where we stopped at Venice, the capital of northern Italy's Veneto region. I spent a lot of time here with my fellow Australians, Sally, Rosie and Neil, taking lots of photographs, although there are few in which I am included. We all had a ball floating through the streets in our own gondola and under the Bridge of Sighs, which was breathtaking. This enclosed bridge is made of white limestone and has windows with stone bars. It was built in 1600 and was the last view of Venice seen by convicts before their imprisonment. There's a local legend that lovers will be granted eternal love and bliss if they kiss on a gondola under the Bridge of Sighs as the bells of St Mark's Campanile toll. Unfortunately I never had an opportunity to test the validity of this legend.

From Venice we continued south to Bologna, Florence then Rome taking in some of the Italian beauty and history along the way. Although I marvelled at some of the sights on our journey to the Italian capital, when we reached it and toured the ancient Roman buildings I was speechless.

First there was the Arc of Constantine, built between the Colosseum and the Palatine Hill to commemorate victory in the Battle of Milvian Bridge on October 28, 312. I was in awe at the brutality of the Colosseum itself, the Roman Forum in the centre of the city, the 26 metre high Trevi Fountain and the Spanish Steps ... all 135 of them.

As I absorbed the historic beauty of these ancient structures and reflected on other buildings we had seen throughout Europe I thought about the mud-brick building course I had completed a number of years previous in Melbourne and it all combined to reinforce my desire to eventually have a home constructed of earth or rock.

The next leg of our journey was a long ferry ride from Italy across to Tunis, North Africa, then south to the region where Star Wars movies had been shot. We had many amazing experiences in Africa, but one night let our guard down and narrowly avoided a horrific incident. Rosie, Sally and I were enjoying a night of Arabian liquor in a hotel where the pub scene of Star Wars had been filmed. We became friendly with some local guys who bought our drinks and answered direct questions about their culture and living style.

One of them said he still lived at home with his mother and invited us to go with him so we could meet her and get a first-hand look at their living conditions. He seemed genuine, so three inebriated tourists said goodbye to our friendly barman and headed towards the hotel's front door. Before we'd gone far the barman yelled out Rosie's name and when we turned around he had a strange look on his face and said "there's a phone call for you". We found that rather crazy - who would be calling us in a Tunisian hotel? – and as we nattered away about who would even know where we were, staggered back towards the bar where we were quickly guided passed it and through the kitchen to the back door, which was pushed slightly ajar. There, eagerly awaiting our arrival with the guys who had befriended us, were eight local men. We had been saved from a pack rape. We thanked our lucky stars that our friendly barman was prepared to save us, then went straight to our room.

The next day we started on a journey that was the key reason why I had booked this trip ... we were going to cross the Sahara, the largest hot desert on earth. As expected much of the desert was seen from our bus window as we travelled along. We spent one evening surrounded by the walls of some old ruins, sheltered from the filthy hot winds and sand that were whipping across the land. The mythical view I had of an oasis was at that moment dispelled, but the red and blue from horizon to horizon as we approached a widespread desert was amazing. However, it returned, as we eventually spotted from a distance and approached a treed oasis about as big as an acre of land, sitting in the middle of a horizon to horizon land of sand.

We reached the Algerian capital Algiers, on the west side of a bay of the Mediterranean Sea, then continued on to Morocco, approaching and crossing the spectacular Atlas Mountains which stretch for 2,500 kilometres across north-western Africa spanning Morocco, Algeria and Tunisia as they separate the Atlantic and Mediterranean coastline from the Sahara Desert. The scenery across North Africa was such a stark contrast to what I had experienced a short time ago in Europe, yet both so stunning and breathtaking in their own special ways.

While in Morocco we visited Marrakesh, drove up to its largest city Casablanca on the Atlantic Ocean then inland to Fes which is famous for its walled medina and the medieval architecture. I hired an Arabic guide with his own mule and rode like Mother Mary on a donkey with my Arabian leader guiding me through the many, many alleys which were all part of a market the size of a city. Interestingly I discovered the word medina means 'town' or 'city' in modern day Arabic. I bought many items at the markets, including rugs, and had them directly addressed to my residence in Australia. They beat me home because I did not arrive back for several months.

It was sad leaving Fes as this was nearing the end of my African adventure. We travelled back to Morocco's northern coastal town of Tanger Med and boarded a giant ferry to cross the iconic Strait of Gibraltar to Algeciras in southern Spain. We did not have seats on the ferry and Sally, Rosie, Neil and I spent the trip freezing out on the deck, where all faggers suffered for their cause.

Once in Spain we made our way north-west to Seville which is famous for its flamenco music and dancing. Not surprisingly we had a night out taking in this local culture. It was then on to the coastal city of Lisbon, in Portugal, before returning to Spain and its famous capital Madrid. Our tour included attending a bullfight and despite some apprehension I decided to go along, rather than simply relying on my uneducated views on this 'sport'. I guess I believed then, as I do today, the adage 'when in Rome do as the Romans do'.

I do not have fond memories of that bull fight. It was an appalling event and I could not believe what I was witnessing. I found it unfathomable that people believed it was 'manly' to ram a knife between the eyes of a blood-drained bull that was already near its death. I felt such empathy towards this poor bull that when he was still in the contest and tossed the matador in the air I enthusiastically jumped up yelling "yeah!!!"

The tour guide, sitting in the adjacent seat, quickly slapped my feet from under me and I was brought swiftly down on my bum. With a hand on my shoulder I was tersely instructed "bury your head" which I did, but not before taking in piercing glares from many in the surrounding audience. To their eyes my actions were tantamount to cultural insult, for which I was truly sorry, however I was sorry only for this perception and not my actions as I believe that bull fighting is an unnecessary, useless and cruel pastime, although I somehow maintain my respect for cultural and historical behaviours and habits.

Heading up through Italy we went to Pamplona, famous for its 'running of the bulls' every July. Thankfully we were not in Pamplona in July because I view this senseless event in the same manner as bull fighting.

From Madrid we made our way back up through France staying closer to the coast as we had been inland and to Paris early in the tour. We arrived at Calais and took the ferry back to England where our journey came to a sad end. Looking back it was a fabulous trip with fabulous people and it's a shame we did not manage to keep in touch because it would be interesting to sit back now and reminisce. Rosie, Sally, Neil and I were kindred spirits; mischievous with blurred boundaries in the name of fun. Our other fellow travellers were also a super bunch and we had plenty of enjoyable times together, but it was our 'terrible four' that stood out.

Throughout this unbelievable trip there were numerous memorable events and occurrences, in fact far too many to recount in this book. But there is one memory that stands out above all else … I do not remember any time or incident where I felt my physical challenges were resented.

***

Once back in London I returned to the Earls Court hostel for a couple of nights before catching a flight to Athens where I stayed several days to take in all the popular tourist spots including the Acropolis, Poseidon Temple and Temple of Olympian Zeus.

I wanted some relaxation time before heading home and decided to chill out for a few weeks on the Greek island of Paros, in the Aegean Sea. Paros is described as having unrivalled natural beauty, beaches with crystal clear waters, unrivalled Byzantine footpaths connecting traditional villages and breathtaking landscapes. It was all that and more and an ideal location to take it easy before returning to Australia.

On the downside, it was not conducive to someone with my physical limitations. Reaching taps was a particular problem and accessing water was at times limited. So I swam a lot. The island was hilly with big steps which made it somewhat difficult for me to get around and this was exacerbated by the absence of taxis.

At first I booked a room in which I managed quite reasonably. As usual I used a chair to reach the hand basin taps which allowed me to wet facecloths for a wash down, but I was unable to take a shower because its taps were inaccessible. Within a couple of days I had made some new friends who talked me into visiting tent city, where they were staying. It was like a backpackers' camping ground and I realised it provided more suitable accommodation. I bought a tent for $2 from a couple of English girls who had ended their stay on the island.

The camping ground was merely a paddock of tents with a typical European earth building which housed the basic amenities.

I must confess, unlike many Aussie travellers I did not mind the in-ground European toilets … no need to be too personal but I'm sure you can understand this convenience. The shower, of course, had taps at shoulder height for the average Joe Blow so for me they may as well have been in the sky. However, there was a tap at a more reasonable height on the side wall which I assume was for washing feet. I found if I took an extra towel into the amenities block to sit on I could manoeuvre myself under the tap and get a decent job done. Because the weather was so warm my wet towel would easily dry for the next day.

As such I found it easier to live in tent city than in the apartment. There were no steps, no doors to tackle and at least I could get water flowing over my body even if it was cold (which was no different to showers as they also ran cold). Thankfully the weather made it all possible and acceptable.

The only real issue I faced with tent city was its location, being at one end of the beach and a two mile walk to the nearest bar. I am to this day grateful for the outgoing nature with which I was born, which allowed me to be open, honest and friendly to people who never had any hesitation helping out if I was finding the trek to the bar, or back, too long. I made two special Aussie friends, Mick and his mate, who helped transport me each afternoon from the beach to the bar by taking it in turns carrying me on their shoulders. Life truly was fabulous on the island of Paros!

For a number of weeks my days were spent meandering between the beach and a local café where breakfast always comprised fresh Greek bread and tzatziki. Then it was off to the beach and after a stint of sun and swimming we made our way to the bar. I had been away from Australia for nearly a year and this was the most relaxed, easy going time I had enjoyed since I left.

The beach was so much fun with its eclectic population and happy-go-lucky social scene. It was not unusual to find nude or topless bathers of varying ages and shapes in an environment where I felt totally at ease, which is probably why I could also be found lounging around in nothing more than my bikini bottoms. I loved every minute of not having to worry about putting on that extra item of clothing. I lived in a sarong, which was so easy to wrap around my small body and as a bonus was very comfortable.

One day on the beach I was approached by a good looking local guy with a brown case who offered to pierce my nose for only $5. I was feeling relaxed and adventurous so I agreed, but sadly the stud fell out before the day was over. For many years I intended to replace it which, to date, I have not done. But you never know … I'm not dead yet.

During this time in my slice of paradise friends came and went and before long it was my turn to depart. I have never forgotten Mick and was so grateful for his friendship and muscles, which came in handy during our many walks to and from the pub with me sitting on his shoulders.

All good things must come to an end, so I packed my gear and prepared to leave Paros. I sold my tent for $2 – the same amount I'd paid – and as such my entire accommodation bill for three weeks on Paros was the few dollars it cost for a room on the first couple of nights. I guess that was the eighties and I'm sure you could not do it now, adding to a belief that my generation has really had the best time in human life.

On leaving Paros I returned to Athens, then flew to Australia with an overnight stay in Singapore. Not being one to spend my evening in a motel room I ventured to the bar below and it wasn't long before I was enjoying a drink with a few colourful friends. I was very familiar with the social world of homosexuals and transvestites, having frequently accompanied my brother back home, and I soon found myself laughing and enjoying the company of the local transvestites of Singapore, known at the time as 'Billy Boys'.

I had a fantastic night being transported with half a dozen boys as we headed for the famous Bugis Street in a rickshaw. We went from nightclub to nightclub until the early hours of the morning, when I was due to fly out. My new friends stuck with me through this sleepless night. They helped pack my bag and acted as shopping guides as we found a duty-free store where I could buy a new stereo system, before escorting me to the airport as we laughed and giggled all the way. As was generally the case with many friends I met during my travels, we never maintained contact.

CHAPTER 13

Meeting David

Holidays don't last forever. So in 1986, after a fun-filled year trekking around the world it was back to reality.

I returned to work but found it difficult settling back into 'Coonac' life. Sadly, I found the situation at work had not changed at all except that my good friend June – one of only two administration staff members who I respected and found enjoyable company – had passed away. She was a mature lady who I was very fond of and I missed her terribly around the office. In fact, her absence made the workplace unbearable.

I started attending staff welfare counselling sessions, after which I managed to secure a couple of really good temporary positions, but due to their nature I would inevitably return to Coonac Rehabilitation Centre where the work situation had become untenable.

Eventually I applied to the public service for a compassionate transfer, seeking a position closer to my home town of Lakes Entrance. It was some time later, but finally I was notified of a position with the Commonwealth Employment Service in Bairnsdale where I would be a clerical assistant at Grade 2 level, running the switchboard, plus common clerical duties including typist for the office manager and assistant manager. This seemed the answer to my prayers, moving back home to the country with a good job to boot.

The half hour drive to work and back each day didn't bother me and I was in the familiar territory where I grew up. Little did I know what was just around the corner, when workplace discrimination raised its ugly head again.

What I did not realise at the time, but did before too long, was that the position I accepted had been ear-marked by my boss for his mate and he was none too happy when it went to little Deb instead. In fact, it's fair to say he was downright pissed off.

As such, from day one my time with the CES in Bairnsdale was made difficult. This was supposed to be a boys' club and my presence was resented. The stress this placed on me was almost impossible to cope with.

I was given the toughest tasks as part of a deliberate attempt to make sure I knew my presence was not wanted and I was the subject of bullying and harassment by my superior, that should not be tolerated in any workplace. I think what still hurts most about that period is the abuse born through a vindictive person whose nature could not by-pass his own comfort, and with that in mind he took great pleasure in delegating me to tasks that taxed my physical structure to the maximum.

A prime example was allocation of two important duties, the first one keeping up-to-date job flyers in their respective compartments on a display board, and the second was filing index cards which were held on each of the hundreds of unemployed clients. Remember, this was pre-computers when filing and displaying were manual tasks.

It's not hard to understand that I found it difficult putting flyers in their compartments on several large, free standing, partition-style display boards. For starters, these job boards were upstairs, and with that point in mind I was not the ideal person, which should have been obvious during the delegation process. Any thought at all would have recognised the reaching that was required. To be honest, the top of my head was level with the lowest of four rows of flyers on all three partitions. I struggled as I was forced to reach a good metre or more off the ground on a regular basis to place information flyers on various occupations into their correct little pocket. This task would take me most of the day as I had to drag a kitchen-size table across to each partition, then drag a chair across and use it to climb onto the table. Using my shoulder and chin I removed the flyers from their pockets and laid them on the table, then had to get back down on the floor where I would again use my chin and shoulder to take the flyers from the table, one occupation at a time, take them over to a corner out of the way and lay them out on the floor. Once all hundred or so were there I would refresh and insert new ones, placing them in alphabetical order. Then I had to re-install them in the partitions. This was all in the upper level of the office, so when it was done I had to make my way back down the stairs. These days were physically draining, but I was not going to let the boss know he was getting me down.

On the other hand I found the filing of client cards quite easy with a chair adjusted to table height. We had an index card for each client and they were filed in alphabetical order in a large tray that was about 1.5 metres long and maybe .75 metres wide. During the day employment officers would pull out the cards they wanted, then toss them in a tray after they were finished with that client. The clerical staff would return files in alphabetical order, ensuring everything was in its correct place. If filed incorrectly, they were nearly impossible to locate. I had no difficulty with this task and because I was meticulous the cards would go back in their rightful place, in contrast to what occurred when they were returned by the other clerical assistant who was a trainee with a known literacy problem.

It would have made more sense to use the trainee for the occupational flyers as they could be visually checked for alphabetical errors if not in order. This was the most logical decision, because we were losing client cards due to his poor filing skills, while at the same time I was slogging my guts out going up and down stairs and trying to get the flyers up onto a board that was too high for me to reach.

But logic and common sense didn't come into the equation. The manager was not going to listen or act on any suggestion I made and, to be frank, I think he was quite happy that my job was being made more difficult than it needed to be.

The antagonism towards me increased to the point where I had to stand up for myself and the breaking point came on the day I was called into the manager's office for a 'dressing down' because I had been laughing too much. This was quite a belittling experience and I quickly became emotional, at which time I asked him to open the door so I could go and wash my face, after which I would return to continue the discussion. I was unable to reach the handle to open the office door and when asked to help he refused and openly stated that he would not open it until he was finished with me.

I only vaguely remember picking up a chair and aiming it squarely at the plate glass wall that separated us from the main administration office. I threatened to let myself out, whatever it took. In shock, he opened the door, by which time I was delirious and left the building. I submitted complaints through the proper Public Service channels, but the Regional Manager was his mate and my complaints were placated. In the end I left the CES for stress related issues and found myself without a job.

What was frustrating at the time, and still annoys me, is that it was so unnecessary. Some empathy and a small dose of common sense is all that was needed, but because I had been given the job instead of someone's mate this was never going to happen.

As I have said before, I'm not sure much has changed in the workforce. Instead of helping to find the right role for those with disability our employers tend to ignore their skills, nor do they effectively listen when someone says "this would be a better task for me". As a result we have too many on a disability pension, which is often not their preferred option, instead of playing an active role in the workforce.

After that terrible episode I ended up in a psychiatrist's office where it was decided that for psychological reasons it would be best if I was placed on an invalid pension.

This was a pivotal moment in my life. After all those years of struggling for, among other things, the same economic rights as everyone else here I was, aged 29 and on an invalid pension, as it was called at the time. In the same way I had approached these situations for many years, outwardly I made light of the situation and the fact I was now classified as 'in-valid'. The English dictionary has some fascinating descriptions of this word with meanings such as 'unacceptable', 'unenforceable', 'illegal', 'worthless', 'unsound', 'void' and 'null and void'.

Today, it has been changed from 'invalid' to 'disabled' which is again a rather offensive dictionary description of a person that includes the likes of 'incapacitated', 'restricted', 'inactivated', 'deactivated' or 'put out of action'. Oh my God, how do you expect anyone to strive to be human when they are carrying such labels? I sure did try.

***

When you're out of work it does not take long for boredom to set in, and unfortunately the next step can be depression. That is what I faced after I left the public service, brought on predominantly by the way I had been treated. I craved for challenge; I wanted to be meaningfully employed and given promotions as I earned them, the same as the next person. This didn't happen because I didn't look like the next person.

There was a condescending attitude within the public service; an ingrained culture with a view that they were doing disabled persons like myself a huge favour just by giving us a job, and so it was unrealistic for us to expect equality. It was like 'be happy with what you've got because we're doing you a great service'.

No they weren't! They were doing myself and others a disservice by not treating us the same as any other staff member. It was workplace discrimination and if you're disabled there are often two choices – accept it or get out. I eventually chose the latter.

After a while I started shaking off the depression in the knowledge I had to get on with life. I had $30,000 on hand from a superannuation pay-out I had received and spoke to little brother Jim about opening a retail shop.

And so Gray's Shop Three was born in an arcade off Carpenter Street, in Lakes Entrance. It was a groovy place where we sold kitchenware and other household items, with our niche market being lots of unusual objects, including giftware. We built a false floor behind the counter so the cash register was at a height I could easily use.

Initially, at least from the customer's perspective, our little shop was going along just fine. We developed a reasonable clientele of locals plus the tourists on whom Lakes relies, admiring what we had on offer and making enough purchases to suggest the business could be viable.

We had the right ingredients to succeed. Jim was excellent with décor and I had strong customer service skills, so we were able to complement each other quite well. Also, having grown up in the town we knew lots of people and this can often help in a small community (though not always).

We quickly became one of the trendiest gift stores in Lakes Entrance, then Jim branched out into floor and wall tiles to expand our housing décor range. Before long we split the shop in two, allowing Jim to concentrate on his tiles and I looked after the giftware. That was okay for a while, until we started running out of space and Jim suggested he should relocate to larger premises in Whiters Street.

So Jim moved and I spread out in the shop. Unfortunately, this arrangement did not work as there was a rather large issue having a significant impact. Before we started Gray's Shop Three I knew Jim had a hard drug problem and deep down I hoped the shop would give his life more purpose and help him stay away from drugs. But it didn't. All I achieved was giving him and his buddies access to more cash.

When he moved into his own shop the situation worsened. I was lonely on my own and missing Jim's daily company, and at the same time I was worrying not only about his personal issues but also the financial situation that was rapidly developing.

At this point I would like to digress for a minute and talk more about my dear little brother. Jim and I were as close as twins and my relationship with him had everything you would want from a male, but without the sex. He loved me and cared about me. When we were living in the same house Jim often came home from work with a gift he'd picked up on the way – a scarf, a new top or a pair of earrings. It's the type of attention you expect from a loving boyfriend, more so than from a kid brother.

I think we were so close for a couple of reasons - firstly, because he was only 10 months younger and secondly he seemed to have an innate desire to support my endeavours.. When we were young I was very much the talk of the community and regular comments were made about the support I received from my brother. I still fondly remember people talking about the fact Jim was always 'there', quiet as a mouse, in the background. He was ready to lift me up if I needed help, pick me up if I fell, hand me a toy that I wanted and, in general, make sure I was okay. Mind you, I feel I must remind people that, until much much later, in fact not so long ago, I had no awareness of any adverse impact my very being may have had on others within the immediate or extended family, and if this has turned out to be the case, I'm sorry.

We went to school together in Lakes Entrance and Bairnsdale. Jim was a year behind me all through school and we had our separate network of friends.

While I was still in Melbourne Jim made the transition to Sale with Mum and Dad, starting in Form 4 at Sale Secondary College. That's where he met a special friend, Robyn, and a number of years later they were engaged. I still treat Robyn like a little sister, even though the wedding never took place. All wedding plans were called off when Jim came out, to his friends, as homosexual. He gifted Robyn the engagement ring and the three of us were like brother and sisters until the day Jim died.

She knew about his homosexuality and in many respects gave him permission to come out ... do what you have to do and be what you have to be. Robyn never held any grudges.

Upon leaving school Jim moved to Melbourne and started his apprenticeship as an a-la-carte chef at the Chateau Commodore, in Lonsdale Street, which I have previously referred to. He went to Melbourne because I was there and he wanted to stay close by. It's as simple as that.

And he kept following me, even when I was seeking more independence. He was always there for me ... never far away. I didn't begrudge this because if he wasn't around I missed him. The only time that changed was when he found himself in trouble with drugs and I decided to bow out of my surrounds for a while and give him some space. In reality, I tried to run away.

That's when I put on a brave front and bought the one-way ticket around the world. On the surface I was travelling to prove my independence, but deep down I was running away from my brothers, who both needed to get their act together. I wanted to leave Jim on his own in Australia for a year, during which time I would be unreachable.

What I didn't know at the time was that Jim jumped on a plane several weeks later and followed me … he followed me all around the world and I never knew. Years later, while talking about this journey, we discovered our paths crossed at London's Heathrow Airport, where we missed each other by minutes. His plane from New York landed while mine was on the tarmac, waiting for clearance as I headed for the Mediterranean. Somehow he found out I was in Greece, probably when he spoke to Mum and Dad, so that was his next destination. He thought I would go to the Isle of Santorini, which was a well known young people's party place and a bit of a gay scene, but instead I went to the island of Paros, about a hundred kilometres away. I spent six weeks at Paros while Jim was looking for me on Santorini.

I was away for a year and Jim and a couple of his friends followed after me for much of that time, but to no avail. Hed was unable to catch up and I was unaware he was trying. He arrived back in Australia not long before I got back. But that's the sort of thing Jim did. As life goes, Jim was a gift to mine!

Which brings me to our older brother, Geoff. The close relationship between Jim and I was hard on Geoff because he didn't have a brother … the type you would bond and grow up with as there was a five year gap between them. His brother was always with me, so that bonding never really eventuated. We loved each other, and even through difficult times Jim and I loved our big brother and just wished we were all better bonded.

We had a different dynamic than most families, which is something that's common among families where one member has a disability. This is an important issue that needs to be considered and addressed in disability circles and among support networks. Education programs are needed to assist parents with decision making.

In a family where uncontrollable circumstances deliver a child with special needs there are issues around giving the right level of attention to each child. I received more than Geoff or Jim, through no choice of my own, even though Mum and Dad did everything within their powers to treat me the same as anyone else. I'm sure this had an impact on Geoff, in particular, which was exacerbated because Jim and I were so close.

To try and balance the ledger Geoff was given favouritism in other areas. For example, for his 16th birthday he was given a horse and for his 18th he received a car. Jim and I were never gifted such extravagant things. Yet as I've discovered through life, additional gifts don't work. They can never replace love, attention and time together.

Geoff passed away suddenly in April 2016, leaving me the sole survivor in our family. In his final years our relationship was difficult for many reasons, which was a huge disappointment for me, but not my decision. The day Dad died was the day Geoff was able to stop putting up a front. I felt sorry for Geoff, because it wasn't his fault that he had to play second fiddle to a demanding sister with disability.

I think I understand where he was coming from and why he developed a disconnected attitude towards me, and I wished there was something I could have said or done to change it. Now, it's too late.

Importantly, I will always love him and retain fond memories of times together during our childhood. There will always be a place in my heart for Geoff. I think boys can walk away from such situations, but girls cling to a glimmer of hope forever.

***

Now, let's get back to the situation with Gray's Shop Three. Like Jim, it was going downhill and the combination of these two was causing me a lot of stress. I was near breaking point and had to get out.

I spoke to Mum and told her "I've got itchy feet and I need to get out of here". Mum agreed to look after the shop, so I contacted my good friend Sue Steed and said "let's go to America", and that's what we did.

I suppose I ran away again … ran away from Jim, just like I had done on my previous overseas trip. I had so much loyalty to Jim but there was only so much I could take. It had reached a point where I couldn't take any more.

So in 1988, at the age of 31, off I went with Sue Steed, back to America. We landed in San Francisco after a few days in Hawaii, one night of which is another story, perhaps (with tongue in cheek) another book! Hiring a car we headed north across the Golden Gate Bridge to San Rafael to catch up with a friend of a friend called Jonesy, who sold us an old Ford LTD which we nick-named 'Fran'. Sue and I lived in that car for the next month as we cruised the west coast of California heading north, hoping to get to Banff, in Canada. She slept in the front, I slept in the back and as the back of the front bench seat was about eight inches wide we used it for a table.

Each night we lit a candle and enjoyed a candlelight dinner, followed by the traditional cup of tea after boiling water on our little gas burner, mostly looking out over the ocean. We took the coast road and usually stayed near a beach, occasionally at the top of a cliff. At times we were inland a bit and as we got into Redwood country we intentionally turned off the main road to spend a night amongst them. What a mystical, magic environment in which to camp, with a full moon to boot. Whenever possible, we'd light a campfire … we were having a wonderful time along the Californian coast.

Our pleasant meandering struck a snag when 'Fran' decided to break down in a Safeway carpark at 11pm one Thursday night in Crescent City, which is about 550 kilometres north of San Francisco and about 50 kilometres south of the Oregon. We called a tow truck operator, went into the supermarket to grab some stores and returned to 'Fran', setting up our primer in the carpark so we could have a cuppa.

Before long the tow truck pulled up and out jumped this great big American guy. I mean, he was huge … the top of my head didn't even reach the bottom of his bottom. He introduced himself as Vestel Scaggs and we soon discovered he was one of those delightful gentle giants. He was a lovely, lovely man. So here we were, two vivacious, adventurous Aussie chicks in a supermarket carpark in the middle of the night, and we found ourselves with an amazing, albeit rather large, American.

Vestel hooked up 'Fran', threw me up into his truck like it was nobody's business and asked us "well, where do you want to go?" Sue and I looked at each other, not really knowing the answer, until Vestel explained that he could take us to the yard and park us amongst a myriad of wrecks, but the mechanic would not be able to work on the car until the following Monday.

"I can park you in there among the wrecks and you can stay with your car over the weekend. There's a security guy who can let you in and out of the yard," Vestel advised, although neither of us thought that sounded much fun. He then gave us a second option. He would tow 'Fran' down the coast a bit, leave us and the car near a beach for the weekend and come back and get us Monday morning. It did not take long to make a decision.

Vestel towed us to a beach south of Crescent City, where we enjoyed our weekend. At that time along the American west coast it was common to have caravans and other RVs parked along the coastline for as far as you could see, and we were just one of the crowd. Some were permanent campers, others passing through, all taking advantage of the free camping on offer. Over the weekend Vestel returned each day with bread, milk, beer and any other supplies we needed … he was such an awesome guy; he has since passed away, as has Tommy, another new friend who is mentioned further on. May both lovely men be resting in peace.

That weekend Sue and I had an interesting experience and thought we may have 'won' a cute little girl who was about three years old. We met her parents at the beach camp and became friendly. On our second day there, they asked if we could look after their daughter, whose name I can't recall, while they ducked into town. Although this seemed a bit strange as they really didn't know us from a bar of soap, we agreed and off they went. Two days later the little girl was still in our care and there was no sign of her parents. Eventually, late in the afternoon, they returned and apologised for taking so long as they explained "we got stuck at the hotel".

On Monday morning Vestel returned, hooked up 'Fran' and took us into the wrecking yard where a mechanic was on duty. He introduced us to Tommy, the security man, who had a caravan on site and an old, primitive shower in the corner of the yard. Over the weekend we had only been able to splash ourselves with water, so were most grateful when he asked if we would like to take a shower and perhaps rest with a hot drink in his van. We also decided to stay in the yard and continue sleeping in 'Fran' for the next couple of nights while she was getting repaired.

Later that afternoon, while we were enjoying a coffee in Tommy's caravan, he came in and told us he had a friend who comes over most nights for a drink and "he'll be here soon … I hope you don't mind?" My life was about to take an amazing twist.

The second that Tommy's friend, David, entered the caravan the sparks between us were flying. In many respects it was quite surreal and something I had never previously experienced. We connected in a way I did not think possible. I know we read about 'love at first sight' and watch it happen at the movies, but it doesn't happen in real life, does it? Well, I can assure you, it does. Within three seconds of looking at each other, before he had even put both feet into the caravan, David and I were in love.

Later that evening Sue took a photo of David and I cuddling and I still look at that photograph and marvel at the love and affection which is so obvious in his face. It was beaming. Sue has often spoken about the electricity between us on the afternoon of that first meeting. To this day I still hope for love because that day I discovered true love and will forever know that special feeling.

David was the Auto Collision Repairman (a panel beater extraodinaire) for the business. He and I quickly became an item and before long Sue had hooked up with Tommy, although their relationship did not last long. For the next couple of weeks I would go home each night with David, while Sue stayed with Tommy in the caravan. She then decided to move on, heading off to a friend in Texas and on to Scotland, but I wasn't going anywhere.

I moved in with David and our love blossomed. This was the man I wanted to spend the rest of my life with and I was sure he felt the same way about me.

After nearly a year together my visa ran out so I had to return home. David came with me and we spent the following year together in Australia, then went back to America. We had so much fun and so many wonderful times together.

We rarely had any issues, perhaps apart from his possessiveness. When we were living in Crescent City I would occasionally visit friends Mike and Mary up at Big Flat, a 30 mile drive through the beautiful Redwood Mountains. When I returned David used to drill me about where I had been and what I was doing. Then, when we were in Australia, he had trouble coping with the number of friends I had, which he saw as competition for his affection.

David wasn't entirely comfortable in Australia so I shut the shop, sold off all the stock and we returned to America, accompanied by my little red kelpie Cuppa, who was my best mate and, bar my absence with Steedy, was always by my side. I had found Cuppa at the local pound when I went there with my nephew Luke, looking for a dog not long after moving to Lakes from Melbourne. We saw her as soon as we walked in the gate and I turned to Luke and said, "I reckon she's just my cuppa tea". And that's what I called her … Cuppa. She'd already spent a lonely year during my 1988 trip with Steedy, but this time in 1990 she took this trip with me as we moved to Crescent City, California, for a new start.

Once back in the USA I quickly settled into a wonderful matrimonial style life and, as I couldn't drive Fran, the LTD Steedy and I bought, at some stage we sold her and David modified a Chrysler Malibu station wagon for me. I named that car 'Malcom'.

Looking back, I have wondered how such an independent person as myself could accept David's possessive nature, but I think that sub-consciously I knew I had pushed many men away and wasn't going to do it again. I was 34 years old and wanted a long term, loving relationship and, most importantly, I wanted a family. I was desperate to start a family.

So although it could be difficult, I put up with the occasional attitude which surfaced when I wanted to do something or go somewhere without David. If I ventured off without him, it was always "why don't you want to be here with me?" But I knew he loved me and I knew I loved him back. His inability to cope when I was not around was the only issue we had in our relationship.

Well, at least that was the case until the night we had a conversation about starting a family. Until that point everything I had done in the relationship, and I suppose my life in general, was geared towards a burning desire to have my own family.

I remember the night clearly because I asked David in almost a humorous way with a question like, " do you think you'd like to be a dad again?" In many respects I asked in a joking manner because I was trying to feel out the moment … trying to gently discover his thoughts on parenthood.

There was no 'feeling out the moment' with David's response, when he told me he had an irreversible vasectomy 20 years ago "so it won't be with me". He said he did not want a child under any circumstances. He already had a daughter and through this experience had doubts about opening his heart to a child that could be whipped away. Rather than risk it, he had the vasectomy.

At the time I felt for David and what he had endured, and in fact I still do. He was a man of circumstance. He married his childhood sweetheart and they had their daughter, but after a disastrous marriage his wife cleared out with his little girl when she was only two years old and he did not see her for the next 13 years. One day, when she was 15, his daughter rang and said "daddy, I need your help". She was addicted to heroin and in all sorts of trouble. David hired a plane, rescued her and helped get her cleaned up. Then one day she ran away, taking his 10 speed bike. After all his help, she stole his bike and took off and he seemed unable to forgive her. I think because they missed out on that 13 years of parental bonding it was easy for David to just say "no, I don't need you in my life". Nor did he want any other children. Full stop.

David had such a lovely nature in so many respects, but he had been through a fair bit in his life and he'd lost a lot, especially when it came to family and relationships. He loved me with such intensity and in a selfish kind of way I have since wondered 'why didn't I find a normal man to love me that way?' Then again, what's a 'normal man' and perhaps if he was untouched by heartache, disappointment and pain. he would not have been interested in me.

In some ways I have been a victim of perpetual circumstance and it's all relevant to my disability. I realise that big, strapping men with confidence – the type I have always enjoyed being around – want a 'good-looker', or at least someone capable of looking after them and their children. Their dream is around a stereotypical family that does not include someone who looks like me. David was different and that's what I loved about him.

For two years we had an amazing life, just like any young couple who were madly in love. He went off to work each day and I'd wash the clothes, do the housework and have a meal prepared when he arrived home. I spent a lot of time in between with Diploma in Journalism studies by correspondence through the International Correspondence School system. By the time I departed the US I only had a year to go, but never completed it.

Our life for those two years was like pure matrimonial bliss. David had built a proper wooden cedar sauna in the back yard which ran with a firebox and steam, and sometimes when he arrived home I had the sauna fired up. Yes, we had a great life, but it all fell apart because he didn't want to be a dad. It was as simple – or complicated – as that.

Above: That's 18 year old me, with 15 year old Robyn Boulton (Jimmy's fiancé to be) and Robyn's sister Margaret.

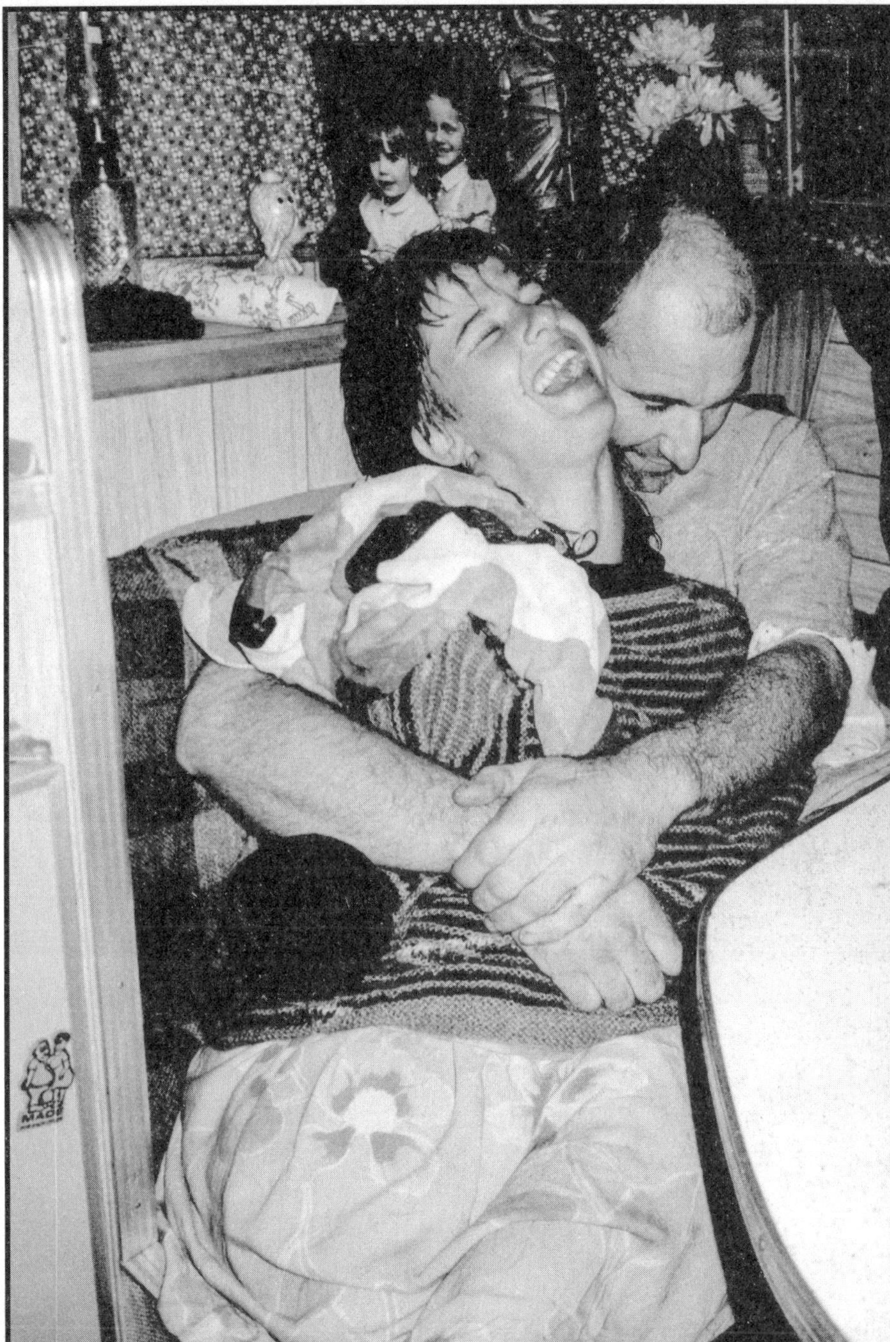

Above: With David … a bit of fun on our first night.

Left: My PABX switchboard at HMAS Lonsdale.

NORTHCREST AUTO CENTER
EMERGENCY
AAA
ROAD SERVICE
464-2146

Above: David and I … already feelin' in love.

Top left: Our car 'Fran' broke down south of Crescent City, Highway 101, by the beach.

Bottom left: Hooked up and ready to go for repairs, with our tow truck driver, Vestel.

Above: For a while, the car was our home in America.

Left: Albert Collins jumped from the stage and gave me a special performance at the Golden Gate Bridge Blues Festival in 1988.

CHAPTER 14

I'd be a good Mum!

I wasn't the type of person who ever wanted to trap a man into loving me. I could have tried that on many occasions, including by means such as controlling my contraceptive etc. However I didn't, but now I knew David was the only man I would experience true love with. Although he had made it clear that he did not want to be a father, I prayed hard and harder than I ever had before that he would, as I had seen other men do, which was change their mind and stick by their woman. After all, he loved me so much.

I was alone and gutted, and almost at the end of my battle to succeed in love, but nothing was going to get in the way of my dream to have a family. I had another good friend who I was quite close to in Shaleen, a bar worker at David's favourite local social spot, Burger King, which had its own bar and poolroom. I arrived on her doorstep in tears of dismay, and we talked. It was Shaleen who informed me: "Deb, you're in America now and anything's possible!" On Shaleen's advice, I decided to visit the Sutter Coast Hospital social worker who we thought may be able to shed some light on any options or methods that may be available. And if I wasn't going to have a baby with David, I thought I would need help to find a way to let go of my maternal desires. But I found a welcoming option at what is now called the Center for Reproductive Health at the University of California, San Francisco. I attended and was placed under the care of Dr Eldon Schriok.

I explained the situation and told him I wanted to have a baby, asking if I would be a candidate for donor sperm. I would not even consider getting access to sperm through casual sex. I was in love with David and enjoyed his sex too much to envisage sharing my body with anybody else. Dr Schriok considered my situation and raised his concerns, but concluded there was no reason to suggest it would not be successful. The Australian system would not have allowed me to consider any supported insemination treatment because I was disabled for a start, but also classified as a single woman. I would automatically be ineligible in my home country, but that level of discrimination did not exist in America in the early 1990s.

Before the treatment could proceed I had to undergo two psychiatric assessments that the doctor explained was normal procedure for single women and had nothing to do with my stature. David accompanied me to the second one of these and it was heartbreaking to sit, silently sad, as I told the psychiatrist, while pretending confidence and comfort, that my partner was not going to be involved in the process.

In fact, his objection was so strong we agreed that when I fell pregnant it would be best if I returned to Australia for the birth. In a nutshell, David refused to have anything to do with fatherhood, so my child would mean the end of our dynamic relationship. We were both up front with the psychiatrist. David told him clearly, "nope, I'm not having anything to do with it", and I explained I would be going home to Australia where I had a good supportive family (who at this time had no idea of my endeavours).

The psychiatrist was happy with our honesty and I was over the moon when I saw his report come back and written on the front of the manila folder in bold, red texta colour was "200 percent should be a mum". Dr Schriok then gave me a thermometer and a chart, explained what changes I had to look out for and said, "the moment you see this change get your arse back down here". It was an eight hour drive which didn't worry me in the slightest.

But before we go any further I have to relate an incident which occurred on my first trip to the psychiatrist, when there was only Cuppa and I in the car (Cuppa accompanied me on these trips, which I found exhilarating). At the time I smoked quite heavily and as I puffed on a cigarette heading towards San Francisco it slipped out of my mouth and down beside the seat. I panicked a bit, thinking the car might catch fire and I tried to spit on the smouldering cigarette, but of course that didn't work. "What am I gunna do Cuppa?" I asked, not expecting her to provide an answer. Then we came to a truck stop so I pulled up, raced inside and yelled "quick! I've dropped a smoke in the car and need a glass of water". Well, several big truckies stood up and raced out with glasses of water to put out a fire which, thankfully, had not ignited and as it turned out didn't exist. They were such friendly blokes. With the danger over I went back inside and had a cup of tea and a bun with them – they even let Cuppa in the café – before getting back on the road to my appointment.

Anyway, I did as Dr Schriok instructed and when my body changes occurred I was back on the road to San Francisco and inseminated with donor sperm on, ironically, my young brother Jim's birthday - November 21, this was 1991. Two weeks later I rang the doctor and told him excitedly "I'm pregnant … I'm pregnant". Naturally, he said it was too soon and tried to convince me I was wrong, but I knew even at this early stage that I was going to have a baby.

"Well, how do you know you're pregnant?" Dr Schriok asked and I said, "because my boobs are sore; and they never get sore". He told me to phone back in a few weeks. Several weeks later I took a pregnancy test and called to advise Dr Shriok it had confirmed I was pregnant. I was carrying a new life inside me.

This was a time of immense pride and joy, but before long there was also apprehension and sadness as the realisation hit home that my relationship with David was about to end. I tried hard, but was unable to convince David he would make a good father and was left with no choice but to fly home where I would give birth and raise my child. I was determined not to be neurotic, emotional, demanding or, God forbid, force a man to spend a life with a woman he didn't still love, or for his own reasons didn't want to share his life with.

Although David had been open with me about not wanting children I was still gutted by this decision and the absolute determination that his mind would not be changed. I was 34 years old and motherhood was a goal which had been dear to my heart for many years. In fact 12 years earlier, at the age of 22, I fell pregnant to a good friend as a consequence of a one-off, out of control encounter. Although I had not yet informed the father of the pregnancy, I had decided to keep the baby. Arriving back in Lakes to break the news to my family, I was again to be gutted as both parents did not support my decision. Hence, an aunty and Mum escorted me to the Queen Victoria Hospital where my heart lay shattered as the abortion was performed. I went on to enjoy travel and many experiences that I would have missed if the time had been right, but I have never forgotten the little being I wanted and had, but could not keep. Now the time was right and, just as David was adamant he would not be a father, so was I that I was going to be a mother … and a good one. I strongly suspected that David's reluctance to have a child was from the enduring hurt he encountered from losing his daughter and the fear something similar would happen again. Eventually, I had to accept our fate.

I have asked the question on many occasions – why did the only man in my life who was so proud to call me "his woman" have to possess such a negative attitude towards parenting? In my circumstance it was such an insurmountable problem because of my strong, even extreme, maternal instinct. Even today my boobs pump if I glimpse a baby, let alone smell one, and as all my friends know only too well, I simply love children. I had to have a baby and not even the love of my life and the man I will love until my dying breath was going to stand in the way.

***

We had a final Christmas and New Year together and quickly it came time for me to board a plane and fly home to Australia. That day – Tuesday January 7, 1992 – will be forever etched in my heart. In many respects I had subconsciously prayed it would never come to this, but it did and there was no turning back.

The previous day David, Cuppa and I drove from Crescent City to San Francisco and booked into a motel for our last night together. We sneaked Cuppa into our room and the three of us snuggled up to watch television. It was all so friendly and loving, yet between us was a broken bridge that could not be repaired. In some ways it seemed so small - this bundle of joy growing slowly in my womb - but in others it was a chasm that could not be crossed and would cause an irreparable separation.

As we cuddled in that motel room I still dreamed of having both David and my baby, but it was not to be. That night I tried to encourage his love, however by this stage he had lost his sexual appetite for me, which occurred soon after I spoke of my strong desire for conception, and it could not be rekindled.

So I lay there with David and Cuppa in silent reflection. I thought about the packing up and pre-departure days and was proud of the way I handled what could have been an awkward situation. I maintained our home, prepared our meals and looked after my much loved herb and rose garden. I even continued my habit of bathing at 3.45pm each day so I was freshened up when David arrived home from work about 4.30. My mind wandered back to our passionate days, when David would sometimes slip home early and at times jump into the bath with me. Oh, the passion and excitement of it all! But the passion had all gone.

The next painful morning, as we drove silently to San Francisco International Airport, Cuppa sat as usual between us, oblivious to the change that was also about to engulf her life. I was numb with the fact that this was it. Here I was, leaving the closest thing I'd ever had to a lifetime partner. Perhaps the closest I would ever have to a lifetime partner. And here was the man of my dreams, so internally hurt and angry that I had chosen motherhood over him that he just couldn't speak.

As David pulled my Malibu station wagon into the unloading zone at the airport he suggested I hop out and he would go and park the car. A porter stepped forward to lend a hand as David was lifting out my suitcases, while I said goodbye to my best mate Cuppa, who returned to her usual position in the front passenger seat.

David handed my cases to the porter and jumped back in the car. Standing by the front passenger door I looked through the open window and said quietly "hurry back, my love". As he put the car into gear I stepped back onto the footpath and watched the two most precious things in my life drive away. My precious David … the man of my dreams. My precious Cuppa … the best canine mate a woman could ever have. Today, more than 30 years later, the image of those two heads – just the back of them through the rear window – remains implanted in my memory and will be forever so.

I waited for David to park the car and return. I waited … and waited. Surely he was going to come back and see me off? Was I never to feel those passionate lips and feel the security of his loving arms as we said goodbye? And so I waited some more, standing there and wanting to feel David's lips against mine to remind me how special he had been, and still was.

He didn't come back. I stood there for at least 20 minutes and eventually my waiting time ran out, as the porter so courteously reminded me, with a suggestion that I hop on the luggage trolley, and with an ache in my whole body I simply rode along as the trusty porter checked me in and made sure I reached the gate on time.

Making my way down to the plane I prayed for an aisle seat. Although I missed the view, it was so much easier to get in and out, giving me a bit more swing and wiggle room. Again, using my little backpack as a step, I wiggled like hell into my seat.

As I settled into the aisle seat which had fortunately been allocated, a silent river ran down my face as I realised David had no intention of suffering any more hurt with an airport farewell. And as I later reflected, I came to understand that it would have broken his heart into tinier pieces than it was already in. The tears continued to flow for half an hour from a hurt deep inside that was more intense than I had ever experienced. I ordered a Scotch and Dry, something to help me let go of David and the hurt. Then I drank another one and as the burning amber spirit lifted some weight off my shoulders I thought about the wonderful years we had enjoyed together. It was nearly four years I will never, ever forget. It was the matrimonial experience in my life and has allowed me to look back and say "I know what love is". I don't miss arms because

I've never had them, but I miss love because I've had the feeling and often long for it to return.

***

Although my heart was broken I could look forward to having my baby, and this helped me survive a difficult time. Physically, David also survived, and I am deeply sorry that our fate caused us both a lot of pain in parting.

Cuppa was not as lucky and not long after my departure was placed on heart pills, before she died less than a year after I left America. When I had first travelled to the States with Steedy, Cuppa was staying with my parents, a couple of kilometres from our home in Australia. Little was I to know that she continued to escape, finding her way back to our home where they would find her on 'her' veranda. So eventually they left her there, returning to feed her once a day. There Cuppa stayed, waiting for me to return. On that occasion she survived, but it was obvious she couldn't live without my love again, pining for my company and with no desire to live without the person who rescued her from the pound.

Just as humans become very attached to their dogs, so do dogs get attached to humans, especially when they spend most of their time inside. My dogs have always been my close companions, but none closer than Cuppa. She was on heart pills less than a month after I left America and died about nine months later. I feel responsible because I know Cuppa died of a broken heart.

***

I flew into Tullamarine Airport and was soon heading down the Princes Highway to Lakes Entrance. I'd travelled that road many times but never with such a heavy heart. Although I was looking forward with eager anticipation to motherhood my mind was still overcome with sorrow from the sudden departure at San Francisco, and not getting the opportunity for a final goodbye from David.

I moved in with Mum and Dad, who by this stage were living in Gold Ring Road on the eastern side of town at the edge of a high ridge overlooking Bass Strait. It was a brick home with all wood interior, designed and built by Dad who was a master craftsman.

As you can probably imagine, as my baby grew inside I looked increasingly like a beach ball. Well, when there's just over three feet, eight and a half inches in height, it doesn't take much additional width to give a rather circular appearance.

I had a perfect pregnancy, under the watchful eye of my obstetrician Dr Elizabeth Boyd, with Dr Graham Bromwich coming in towards the end as he would perform the pending caesarean. The three of us were a great fit, which I suppose made everything easier. I would really and truly have loved to have experienced a natural birth, however following the footsteps of my grandmother and mother who had also given birth by caesarean, I didn't have much of a chance.

I knew I was having a baby girl several months before the birth, thanks to Mum and Aunty Keryn who accompanied me for an ultrasound in Melbourne. Initially I told them I did not want to know whether it was a boy or a girl. As we sat in the lounge room at Aunty Keryn's place in Corio after the ultrasound, where I had asked them not to divulge the sex, Mum kept saying, "go on, you want to know don't you?" In the end I said "okay" and under great pressure phoned the clinic where the ultrasound was done. I said, "look, I've changed my mind and I would like to know what sex I'm going to have". Then all of a sudden I had second thoughts and handed the phone over to Mum.

"Don't tell me," I told Mum and Aunty Keryn, but they couldn't keep it to themselves. Everyone was so excited. Anyway, I didn't believe it when they said I was going to have a girl because I was convinced it was a boy.

I was able to have a say on the delivery date because I was having the birth by caesarean section. Caesareans are always easier if they can be performed before the baby enters the birthing canal and I was due in early August, but Dad's birthday was July 27 so I decided to give him a special birthday present … and a Leo, just like Pa. At the time, the star sign was no consideration at all, but as I reflect back now I can sometimes see that stubborn Leo character in my daughter.

I was so proud when I walked into the Bairnsdale Hospital the day before the birth … no wheelchair or any other form of assistance. I was walking on my own two legs, even though I was a bit sluggish.

I had been born in that same hospital 35 years previous. I grew up and was educated in Lakes Entrance and Bairnsdale so I knew lots of people, including many staff at the hospital, and had a fairly high profile due to the media attention I received over the years. This all made for an exciting, fun-filled time as I prepared for the birth of my baby on the following day.

Once settled into the hospital I had a visit from Dr Elizabeth Boyd, who had guided and cared for me throughout the pregnancy. Alongside her stood Dr Bromwich, or Dr Brom as we affectionately knew him, who was going to perform the surgery which was scheduled for around 9am.

My adorable baby was born at 9.05am on Monday July 27, 1992. It was an amazing day … the only disappointment, which left a sad space hiding in my heart, was accepting that my little bro Jim was stuck offshore at work and would not be present for the birth. I was surrounded by family members, including Mum and Dad and a couple of aunties, plus television cameras from the Seven Network, although Mum was the only person allowed in the room during the birth. Life was just a buzz, and here I was about to introduce a precious life into the world. I thought, if this little one is born with a good strong body and my tenacious and loving way of thinking, the world will be her oyster!

With the guidance of Dr Bromwich I had the epidural and stayed awake during the birth, with Mum sitting by my side. I cherished each moment and felt skin-bursting excitement as my baby came closer to its first look at life on the outside. It was such a joyous occasion and, to this day, it has been impossible to verbalise how I felt.

But as precious as it was, I remember my mind kept turning back to Jim and David as I thought, "I wish they were here", as deeply and silently my heart ached. No doubt this was a reflection of the great love, respect, understanding and caring nature of my relationship with my little brother and my lover. They are relationships that I will forever treasure, and as I sit and ponder I am unable to find words to express that gratitude I have for the fact he was my brother and David my open and honest lover. Jim gave me a lifetime of love, caring and companionship. And David - no other has ever shared my heart, body and soul, so completely, as he did.

Straight after the birth, for a fleeting minute I thought I had been correct with my prediction several months earlier because Dr Bromwich lifted up the baby and said "it's a boy". I looked at Mum and gleefully stated "see … told you so", then Dr Bromwich quickly took back his claim as he advised us that "no, sorry, that was the umbilical cord … it's a girl". Mum turned to me and went, "thank God for that"; referring to a penis that could be as large as the umbilical cord. We all laughed.

I didn't care, as long as I had a healthy baby. And I did! A 6 pound, 9 ounce healthy, happy bundle of joy. All the pain and heartache of life now seemed worthwhile, as they lay my child across my chest. It was hard to believe, but I was a Mum and my darling girl was perfect. I named her Emma Camelia, after her Nan.

We were wheeled from the theatre to our single room in the maternity ward where a lovely surprise awaited. My close girlfriend at the time, Catherine, lived with her partner and two young children about 15 kilometres out of Bairnsdale at a little place called Clifton Creek. When their children were young they slept in a wonderful antique wrought iron cot which had metal post and rail sides and opened on hinges, like a gate, instead of the usual cot sides that slide up and down. Catherine, a bit of a Bohemian who loved her art and antiques, had brought in this cot, which was perfect for me because I was able to open the sides. Straight away I was able to manage getting Emma from my bed to her cot and I didn't have to deal with the awkward hospital bassinets.

The Seven Network's current affairs reporter Jackie Quist, who was working with 'Today Tonight', came to Bairnsdale to film the birth and do a story. Disappointingly they weren't allowed into the theatre during the birth and I resented then and continue to resent today the pompous senior nurse Isobel, who would not budge, despite my protests. However, they were filming when I was wheeled out with Emma who was only five or 10 minutes old. As my thoughts wander back to the second the theatre doors shut, I remember feeling disappointed that the cameras could not capture the birthing experience … not for public viewing, but for my own private celebrations and so Jim could experience this special event. As this most personal part of the birthing day was not captured on film it was not worth holding anything else back for private viewing, so I allowed Channel 7 to use whatever they wanted to highlight such a "wonderful" achievement of this armless, height deprived woman. Jackie Quist and I kept in contact for a while, but as often happens you lose touch. She was pregnant at the time and had a son, Michael, a couple of months later.

From the start I found feeding quite easy, with just a modicum of help from one of the nursing staff. I would get up on the bed and the nurse brought Emma over and sat her on my lap. It was then just a matter of hanging my boob over so she could latch on, and drank beautifully.

I also quickly adapted so I could carry Emma around, or move her, using skills I had developed with my cuddly doll when I was a young girl. I picked her up by gathering the clothing in my mouth … especially the singlet, because it didn't stretch too much. I had practised this during the pregnancy to make sure I had the balance right so her head wouldn't slip, or she would not slip out of her clothes. So, for a short time I gathered the fabric from between her armpits and across her chest and lifted her, similar to a mother cat carrying her kitten, onto her wire framed, net covered bouncinette.

I have often laughed at the way mothers fuss over holding a young baby's head, because it's not a problem if they pick up their baby gently. People with arms only need to hold a baby's neck because they pick it up too quickly, forcing the neck to snap back. They just need to take it slowly. Emma learnt to hold her head up and I always lifted her gently and steadily so she had time to adjust the strength into her back or legs.

Before long I could get Emma onto my shoulder and hold on to her clothes so she wouldn't roll off, and as she got older she learnt to dig her elbows into my back for extra grip. I also had a baby's carry backpack which I was able to put over my shoulders, allowing me to cart Emma around on my back, although I never carried her far.

She adapted, just like monkeys and other animals do as they cling onto their mother. They swing through the trees and the baby manages to stay on board … I never did anything like that, but in a similar way Emma adjusted to my body and we were able to get around okay. As she got bigger she would hang on around my neck and I was able to take her weight on my hip. Then before we knew it, Emma was walking.

***

I have forever been grateful to the American system which allowed me to become pregnant with Emma, and reflect with a tinge of sadness that other single women in Australia, at the time, were not given a similar opportunity. In America the doctor treated me as a normal person and was happy to proceed with donor sperm insemination. This is not an IVF treatment.

It is largely due to this type of attitude that I love America. When I was over there men would show a flirty interest and didn't care that I was physically different, which is in stark contrast to how Australian men treat women like me. While I was overseas I had a couple of flings with foreign men, but for various reasons walked away from them.

I'm not physically attractive or seen as independently capable and 'normal' enough for most men and that has been painful. They don't mind a bit of fun behind a closed door, but don't have the guts to take the ridicule from their mates to get publicly connected. I've had plenty of attention from men, both married and unmarried (the former I have not shown any interest in, apart from the one spontaneous incident during my time at HMAS Lonsdale), however it wanes as soon as there's an inkling that it may get into the public arena.

***

The feeling when I took my Emma home was indescribable. I knew there were some challenges ahead, but nothing I couldn't handle. I'd been used to facing up to challenges from the day I was born and this was just another one.

As I explained, we managed to get around together okay. Emma's bouncinette used to slide easily on the carpet so I could move it around without too much trouble. An older friend of the family, Colin Kleehammer, a most gorgeous natured and extremely clever woodcrafter, built me a wonderful change table, which was a larger padded version of a Lazy Susan - a small spinning table you use in pantries, or for condiments on a dining table. I'd lift Emma onto it, only inches off the floor, and spin it around. I sat on a small stool and, using my hand-like feet, dressed or changed her, one side at a time. This parental, loveable bonding moment was never a problem. If we were out somewhere and I didn't have the Lazy Susan I just had to get up a lot and move around her, moving from one part of her body to another. It was a bit difficult, but it wasn't going to be a life-long task, was it? And I didn't mind because I had my darling daughter to look after, she kept me fit.

Emma grew up a very confident and competent character. As a toddler I dressed her using my teeth and shoulders, gathering the back layer of an upper body piece of clothing onto my shoulder, which would then expose my shoulder through the neck hole and allow me to place my shoulder on Emma's head and drop the clothing over her. During the very early toddler stages I would then tug it down with toes or teeth, guiding her arms to the appropriate outlets. However, just like most children, it wasn't long before she instinctively knew how to get her arms into the sleeves or her head through a dress. She was a very astute young girl and I think she advanced rather quickly because she had to adapt to the way we lived. There were various assumptions and comments, prior to birth and continuing even today, that Emm is just as helpful to me as most kids are, and if not a little less helpful. You see these assumptions told me, and maybe subconsciously told Emma, that society was looking at my pregnancy and her very being as a personal slave making venture. This first started with comments made to me whilst pregnant, like; "My that baby will be a good help to you!" Then when Emm was born people would do the "coochie coochie coo," adding "my you're going to be a good help to your Mum". Finally we were then stuck with, "my you must be a good help to your Mum".

An example of where she did learn a little earlier than most kids was learning potential dangers in the kitchen. I had a ground level kitchen sink, which means hot and cold taps are within easy reach of toddlers, but by the time Emma was 18 months old I had taught her not to touch the taps. When she had young friends around she acted as guard to ensure they did not go near the sink. By the time Emma was two she could turn on the kettle if she wanted her bottle heated and was able to let me know when it was ready.

I breast fed Emma for her first seven months and she was feeding well until one day she didn't get enough milk and I soon learnt I had dried up because I'd gone into menopause. This also meant I never had the chance to give Emma a little brother or sister, which was very disappointing. I had sperm from the same donor waiting for me in America and my intention was to return there because I wanted a genetic sibling for Emm, but it was not to be. So much was 'not to be'.

***

In early 1993 Michelle Lollo, from Woman's Day magazine, paid us a visit and wrote a two-page feature article that appeared in the April edition (which, by the way, had photos of Elle Macpherson and Princess Diana on the cover). I thought it was worth reproducing because it sums up quite succinctly what life was like, although there are some small statements I disagree with. For one of a few discrepancies, I never changed Emma on a bed. That's the media!

When it comes to loving and caring for her dream baby there are no drawbacks for this Victorian woman.

Debbi Gray can't sit still for a moment.

The fact that the gutsy woman, born without arms and only parts of her legs, finds it easier to stand than sit has nothing to do with it.

Like any new mum, Debbi can't help fussing over her baby daughter Emma.

The seven-month old giggling bundle is what Debbi has been longing for since she was 13.

And although the courageous mum has no arms to cuddle her little girl and has only her feet to wipe away Emma's bedtime tears, it seems to have had little impact on their relationship.

"I have wanted this baby for so long," Debbi says, nibbling at Emma's tiny ear.

"I can't cuddle her with arms but I snuggle with her and she grabs hold of my neck and gives me cuddles.

"I don't think we're missing anything at all. I'm sure she knows how much I love her."

Debbi, 36, was born with a congenital birth defect, leaving her with no arms, and legs with knees and feet where her thighs should be.

Doctors have been unable to offer any reason for her handicap.

But as the amazing woman uses her mouth to lift Emma out of her chair and place her on the bed to change her nappy, it's obvious she doesn't allow her disability to get in the way of the daily demands of raising a child.

In fact, seeing Debbi's life-long dream of having a baby become a reality surprises no-one – least of all herself.

Before the baby's birth Debbi already had a reputation in the Victorian holiday resort town of Lakes Entrance for her determination to tackle things that would daunt even "normal" people.

Along with horse riding, motorbike riding (as a passenger) and working as a typist using her feet, Debbi stunned friends and family in 1985 when she announced she was going to travel the world – alone.

And travel she did, from Europe to North Africa, Canada and New York.

As Debbi uses her mouth to spoon-feed Emma, so matter of factly and without awkwardness, the lack of limbs goes almost unnoticed.

Carrying her cup of tea on her shoulder through the toy-filled living room, Debbi laughs off the suggestion that her unflustered way of coping with a child is an inspiration to all new mothers.

"I'm used to doing things with my feet. They are like your hands and I'm very good at using them," Debbi says.

"I've heard other mothers saying how hard it is to raise children and how draining it is.

"There was never a moment during my pregnancy that I thought, 'I won't be able to handle this.'

"If you want something badly enough, you adjust."

For Debbi, little Emma's cheery disposition is all the proof she needs to reassure herself she's doing a good job.

While friends are constantly popping in to the home she shares with her brother Jim, 35, she admits there is one thing she can't do.

When it comes to bathtime, friends or her mum Camelia and dad Ray, who live just a few minutes away, place Emma in a bath and help get her out.

"I bathe her, but I do need help getting her in and out. Everything else I do myself though," she said proudly.

When Debbi decides to go shopping or get some fresh air, she places Emma in a pouch, puts her shoulders through the straps and off they trot.

"Emma giggles all the way. It's a bit bouncy, but at least we can go out and do things together," Debbi says, showing how it's done with ease.

Although there's no shortage of friends and family ready to pitch in, it is easy to spot Emma's favourite.

When her grandad Ray – whose birthday is on the same day as Emma's – walks in, her cherubic face lights up.

And if he doesn't come straight over for a cuddle Emma lets out an almighty scream.

"She loves her grandad and she hates him leaving her. He dotes on her more than I do I think," Debbi laughs.

When Debbi became pregnant last year in America, she moved back to Australia without a moment's hesitation.

The decision to have the baby on her own was not difficult.

"I never looked upon having a baby on my own as frightening. For me it was something that was always going to happen, it was just a matter of when.

"It didn't matter if there was a husband or boyfriend. I have had boyfriends before, but none prepared to be fathers, so that was just that," Debbi says.

"Some people might think I'm selfish. It would be nice to have someone for Emma, but it wasn't to be and with so many people around me who love Emma, I don't think she's going to want for anything."

Like any new baby, Emma takes up most of Debbi's time.

But even that hasn't stopped her from trying to achieve more.

With the donation of a computer, software and printer from three Australian companies, Debbi has started writing books on helping children deal with other people's disabilities.

"I'd really like to make people more aware that people with disabilities can achieve an awful lot.

"There are always going to be limits for handicapped people, but what they have to do is make the most of what they have got.

"The learning has to start from an early age and hopefully I can make a bit of a difference."

NB: Please keep in my that this was written by a journo with an obvious sense of the literary, including that last sentence.

***

When I brought Emma home from hospital we spent the first few months living with Mum and Dad in Gold Ring Road, but eventually we moved into a two bedroom house I owned in West Crescent, having bought it using funds from the sale of my unit in Carnegie. It was a lovely place, albeit a bit small.

Jim was also living with Mum and Dad in Gold Ring Road, although he spent lots and lots of time at our place. He absolutely adored Emma and was like her surrogate Dad. Jim and I got talking and we decided to sell the West Crescent house and buy a block at Kalimna, with the intention of building. So in the interim, Emma and I moved back in with Mum and Dad and Jim, who by then had moved to O'Neill's Road.

Before long construction started on our house in Kalimna, on the eastern side of Lakes Entrance. A number of years previously I did a mudbrick building course in Melbourne and wanted an earthen home. So bricks were made on the property and we had a great local brickie who laid them for us. Jim was still working off-shore – week on and week off – and when he was home he'd help out, while I also did plenty of watering and was involved with making the bricks.

On December 7, 1994, when Emma was nearly 2½ years old, I received a phone call advising the house was completed to lock-up stage. The bathrooms were finished and we had a kitchen sink, but at this point there was no stove or kitchen cupboard. I was so excited I borrowed a small Primus camping stove from Mum and Dad's place and Emma and I moved in, spending the first of many nights at the new house. Jim was off-shore at the time and moved in with us when he came off the rig a week later.

The early days in our new home were almost like camping, with only the Primus for cooking and no beds, just mattresses on the floor. During the day internal work was being finished off around us, and it wasn't long before it was completed. For the first time ever I would not be climbing to access the stove; I had used the stove display concept and had a stovetop under the benchtop stove that I could pull out and use then slide back into a cupboard. I had also installed a low sink, as we had in West Crescent, and for the first time I had an en-suite vanity within easy reach. It sure beats cleaning teeth and spitting into a dunny! Other than that, there isn't much difference to any other home.

On top of this I would share our house with my adored two year-old daughter and my dear, younger brother Jim, or Mimmie as Emma would say. Life was good.

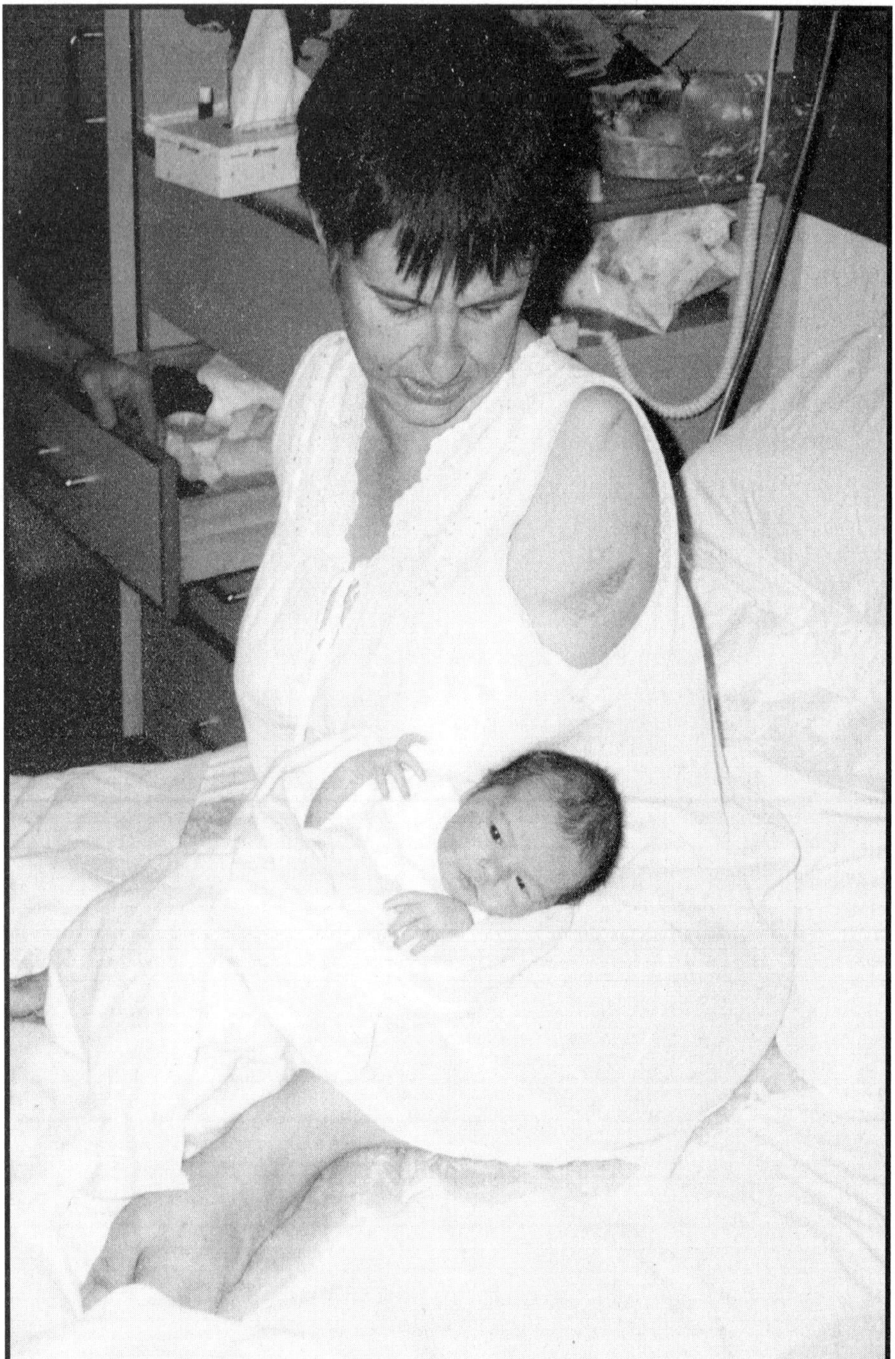

Above: My darling daughter Emma, soon after the birth.

Right: Emma enjoying her bouncinette.

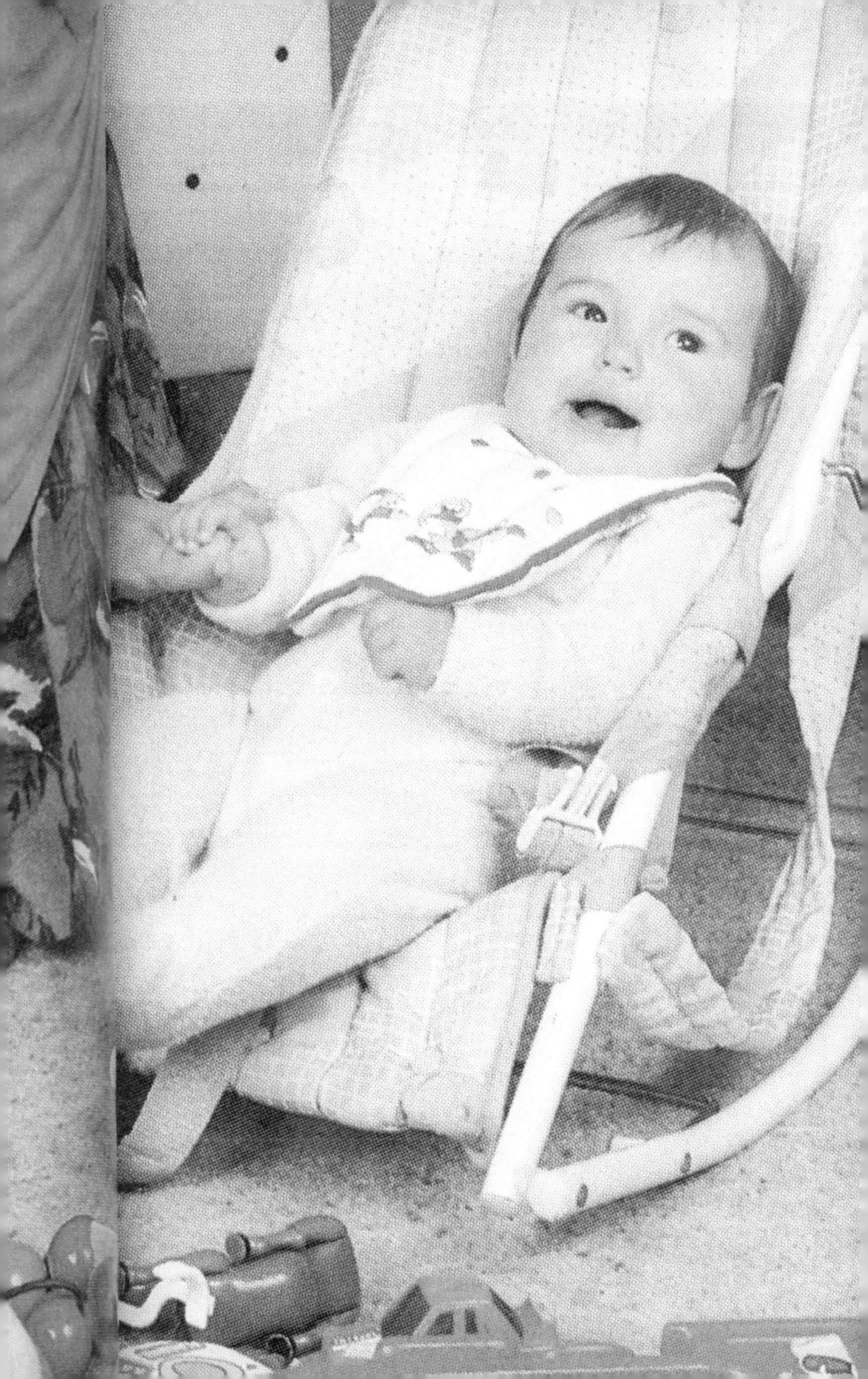

Above and right: Looking after my darling Emma.

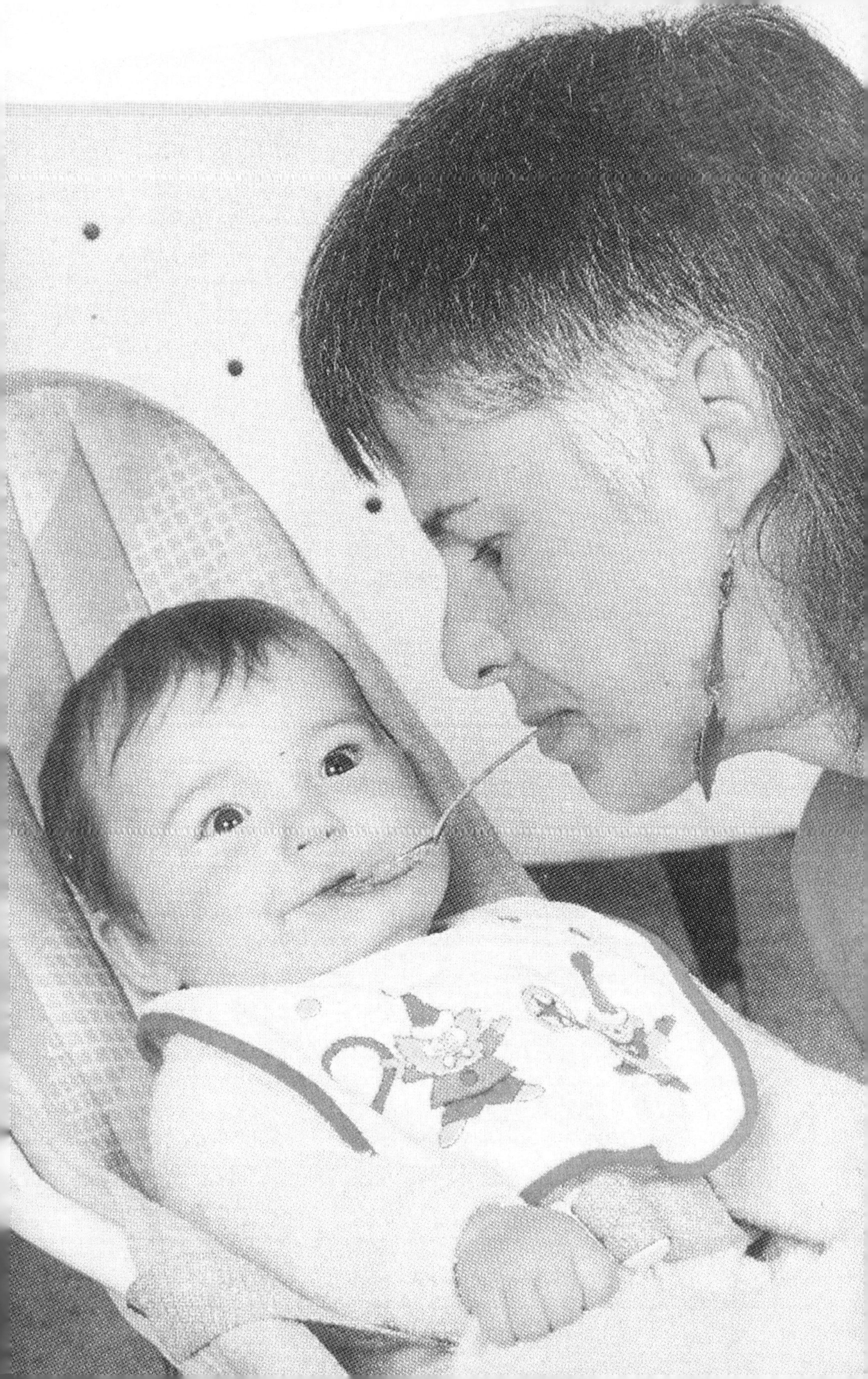

Above: Doing some work on the computer.

Left: Time for a feed. (Photo from Woman's Day article.)

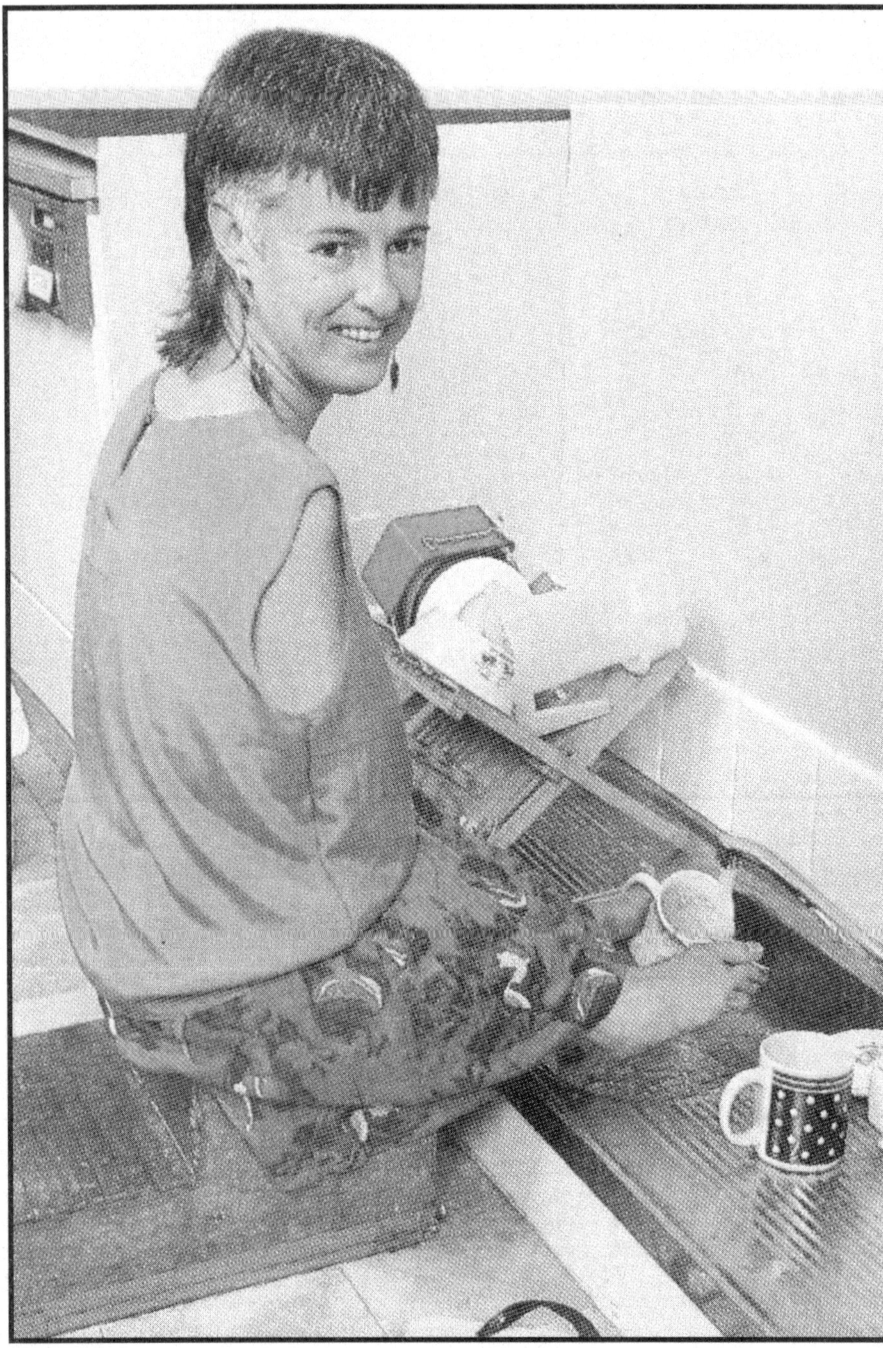

Above: Time to wash the dishes.

Top right: Jim loved his adorable little niece.

Bottom right: Jim, Emma and I.

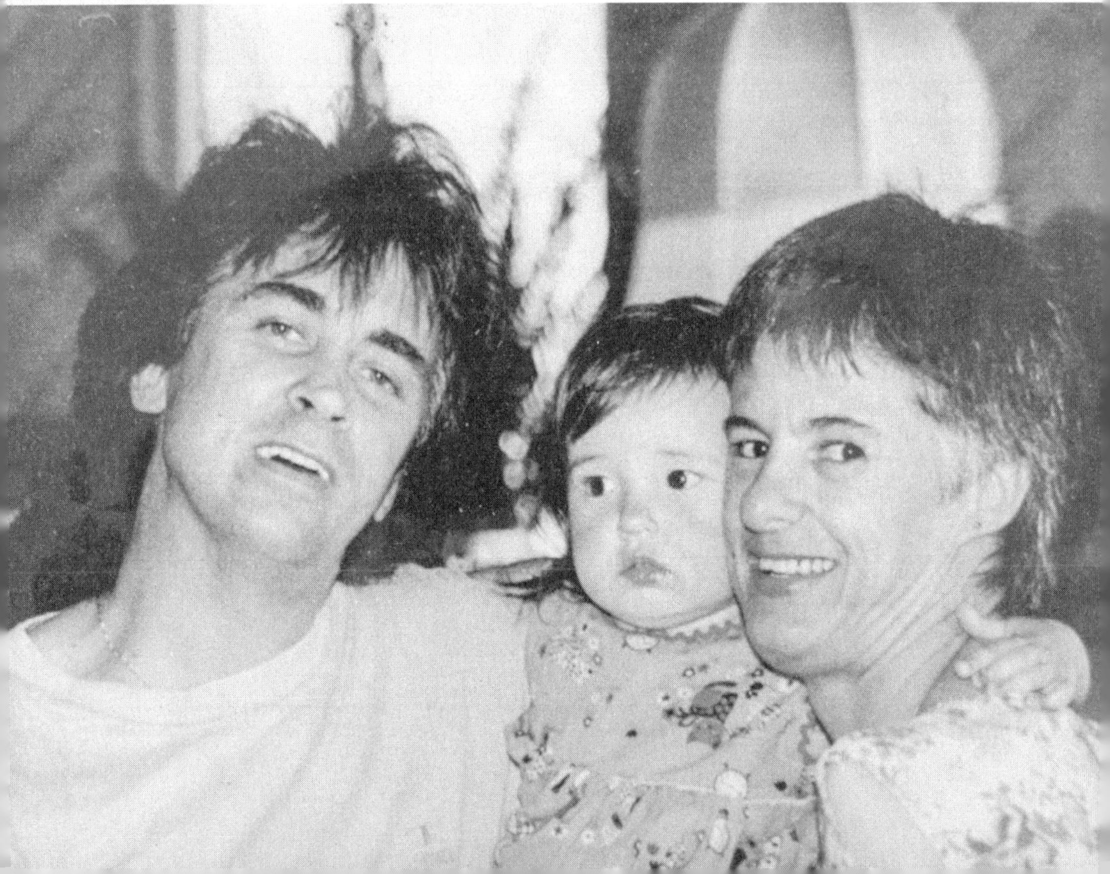

Above: Jim, Emma and I.

Right: Developing a special bond.

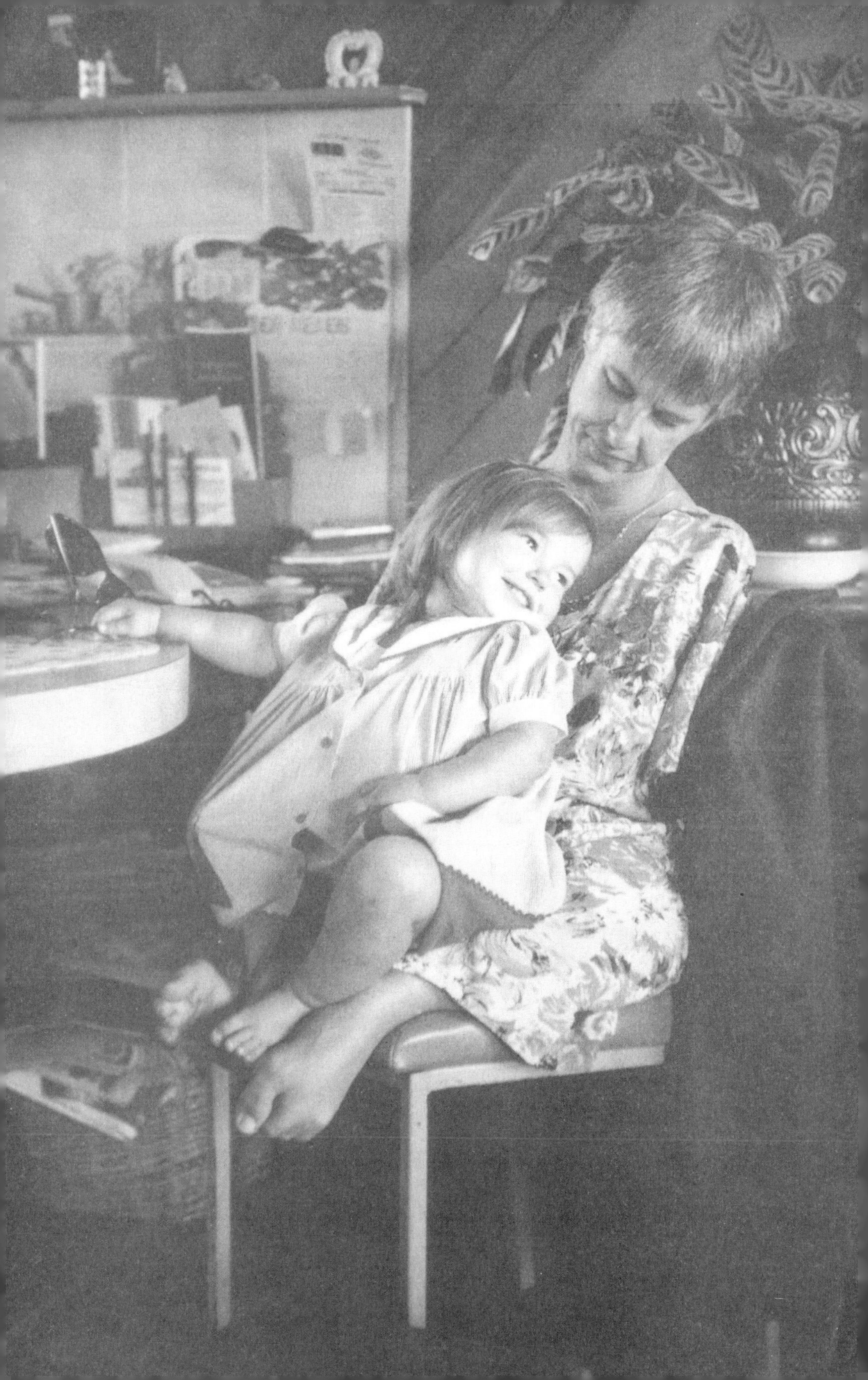

Above: A special moment on the jetty.

Above: Life in the opposite … Emma giving me a whizzie (Photograph © Ponch Hawkes 2000).

CHAPTER 15

Losing my little brother

Life was good, but I was about to be hit with a sledgehammer. The kitchen was finished, we had a fabulous house-warming party with lots of friends around and enjoyed the remainder of summer and early autumn in our new house. Then, the day before Anzac Day, my world came crashing down.

It started as a normal day. I was on a bit of a fitness kick and trying to keep strength in my body, so I purchased membership at the Lakes Entrance Aquadome where I could use the gym, which I did quite regularly. I utilised mainly the stepping machine and weights, or did a 25 lap swim. At the start I booked Emma into the Aquadome creche while I exercised and later she also attended Heatherlea Grove crèche for two mornings a week, giving her an opportunity to play with other kids and also give me some time to myself.

This particular day I dropped Emma at the crèche and headed for the Aquadome. Giving myself a physical challenge and pushing my body to its limits gave me a fantastic feeling. As funny as my little legs must have looked as they pumped on the steps and pulled on the ropes, it was a rare enjoyable moment that, regardless of how I actually looked, I felt sweaty and sexy, which helped me savour these work-outs.

It was late Monday morning, April 24 1995. I drove home as normal from the Aquadome and was entering the front door as Jim's mate, Mark, coming for a visit, pulled into the driveway behind me. I entered the house and as Jim wasn't answering my greeting I walked up the hallway towards his room, yelling "wake up sleepy head, it's nearly lunchtime". There was no response. "Jimmy!" I yelled, and when there was still no response I went into his room and quickly realised the bed was empty. As I turned to head back down the hallway Mark was right there in front of me. He dropped to his knees, so his head was at the same height as mine, put his hands on my shoulders and with a look in his eyes that is so hard to describe but told me something was terribly wrong, he said softly, "I've found him … don't go in the laundry".

I shook myself free of his grip and raced straight to where Mark had told me not to go. Before I reached the door I could see Jim's legs lying across the floor. Mark gently lifted Jim out from underneath the ironing board and placed him on my lap. That's when I really realised he was dead.

I massaged, rubbed and prodded the one inch deep dent in his forehead where his head had hit the leg of the ironing board as he fell, but I couldn't get it out. The spoon we used to feed our beloved cat, Patsy, was still in Jim's hand. As I later discovered, the gear Jim had used for the heroin injection he self-administered a short time previous was still sitting on the kitchen bench. It seems that after the injection he went into the laundry to feed Patsy as the massively potent heroin kicked in, sending to sleep every muscle in his beautiful body, including his heart. I tried to wake him; I tried and tried and tried. But this time no-one was going to bring Jim back.

I started crying and was yelling his name. "Jimmy! Jimmy! Jimmy!" He couldn't hear me. For a while I was screaming and delirious, then I sat with Jim in my lap and talked to him, telling him how much I loved him and asking: "Why? Why did you do this?"

Jim had been the most wonderful little brother for practically my entire life. As I've said a number of times, I was only 10 months old when he was born and in many respects we were like twins. I suppose I was a bit of a novelty in Lakes Entrance and certainly very well known in the community, and as Jim and I grew up together he was often around, always ready to lift me up, pick up something that I couldn't manage and generally make sure I was okay. As we got older there were occasions where I felt sorry for the position in the sibling order that Jim was tossed into, growing up so close to such a determined, tenacious, self-righteous and sometimes bitchy sister. But it never stopped him from being by my side. He looked out for me and, as big sisters do, I looked out for him, though try as I might I could never get him to kick the heroin habit.

So now it had killed him. While I continued to nurse Jim on my lap Mark called the police. I remain eternally grateful for the sensitivity and compassion displayed by the officers who attended that day. They looked down at Jim, then at me as one of the policemen asked, "Deb, are there any other drugs in the house?" I said there was a bit of pot in the lounge room cupboard. He then found a pillow in the lounge, slowly lifted Jim's head and eased it down onto the pillow and calmly told me "go and get it, Deb, and put it in your bedroom". He followed me to the cupboard where I took out the small pipe which I wedged between my neck and shoulder, picked up the bag of dope in my teeth and headed off down the hallway, then came back and whispered a heartfelt "thank you". That gesture meant so much to me and was a prime example of common sense policing. He could have thrown the book at me, and with Jim still lying there I'm just not sure I could have coped.

We later learned the batch of heroin which killed Jim had slipped through the cutting stage and he was one of many addicts who suffered the same fate on or around April 24, 1995, which was no consolation, except it did help ease my quiet suspicion of suicide.

The rest of that day, and the weeks which followed, remain hazy in my mind, apart from the day I buried my brother and best friend. Such a sad, sad day. A vacant place was left in my heart that has never been filled and, I know, never will be.

My good friend and USA travel buddy Steedy and her boyfriend Jack moved in to give me some support. I was in shock and struggling to cope … devastated and at the same time afraid of what the future would hold without Jim in my life. Susan and Jack slept on the fold-out couch in the lounge-room for six long weeks, a time when simple survival was my aim each day. I am still so grateful they were there for both myself and Emma.

Although that six weeks remains a blur, looking back I presume I slowly came to grips with a life which did not include Jim and the grief was gradually easing. After all, I still had to care for my daughter.

***

As Emma quickly grew up we revelled in having fun times together. We became avid campers and if we couldn't head off to one of our favourite spots in the forest or along the coast we would have a camp-out in the back yard. On some of these nights we'd simply pull a mattress out onto the veranda, then drop our trusty mosquito net down and tuck it under the mattress to keep those biting little pests at bay.

I had an awesome nephew, Luke, with whom I had a special connection, who also enjoyed camping on a regular basis and often invited us along. As Emma and I organised our own camping adventures, we welcomed along anyone else who wanted to take part. At different times we went out into the Colquhoun Forest, which wasn't far from home, up to Cape Conran near Marlo in far-east Gippsland, or to Blue Duck near Anglers Rest, which is about 30 kilometres north-west of Omeo.

***

When Emma was three years old I was nominated for the 16th annual Tattersall's Award for Enterprise and Achievement. The awards, which were established by Tattersall's in 1980, were aimed at encouraging and rewarding individuals and groups who, in the view of judges, had decided to 'have a go', even when the odds seem overwhelming against them. I received the January award and was then eligible for the annual award, which was presented in October. I attended a presentation ceremony with the other 11 finalists, including swimmer Tammy Van Wisse who, among other achievements, swam nearly 100 kilometres across Bass Strait which is one of the world's most treacherous stretches of water. There was also Peter Wearne, who worked with street kids in St Kilda; Phillip Maisel, a holocaust survivor who captured the stories of other survivors on video; Ruth Padgett who established Junior Neighbourhood Watch; and Bernarda Stevenson who was helping the disabled enjoy better access to everyday facilities and services.

I really felt so undeserving, as I saw these people as more worthy recipients, and even though I was honoured to be announced as the 1996 winner, most importantly I received $20,000 for the charity of my choice, which I subsequently donated to Lakes Entrance Surf Life Saving Club. I felt the awards and recognition gained for my many years and many miles travelled in order to raise ability awareness for people with disability were important for my Mum. I wanted to make her proud of me, even though in many respects I find awards of this nature to be patronising and placating - isn't she clever, doing all these things with no arms – when all I really wanted was to be normal, and be seen as being normal. Anyway, it made Mum happy and the Surf Club received a healthy and unexpected donation. As a result I received an Honorary Life Membership and began a new phase of involvement with the Surf Club, this time a bit more responsibly. I joined the Committee of Management and sat in several positions including treasurer and secretary/publicity officer. After a few years of this involvement I was in hospital during committee membership election time and outvoted on the seat I nominated for; and I haven't heard from anyone at the club since.

Later that year the Shire of East Gippsland hosted a civic reception in my honour to recognise the award, which was addressed by the Shire's Commissioner Duncan Malcolm. It's worth repeating part of his speech, as recorded in the Lakes Post, because he made some pertinent comments about differences and disability.

Mr Malcolm said: *"It is fair to say that although we may be created equal, none of us is quite the same as another. The extent of our differences can be measured in many different ways. Differences are measured by different attitudes, different backgrounds, different relationships, different physical characteristics, different talents, different skills, different levels of patience, perseverance, determination, stubbornness, different levels of acceptance, tolerance and understanding. Someone meeting Debbi for the first time may be tempted to think that her physical appearance is her most notable difference. I am sure, however, that those who know her well, who have grown up with Debbi and shared part of her life to date, could nominate quite a few other differences which to them are far more significant. Her indomitable will, her adventurous nature, her determination, her perseverance, her capacity and willingness to communicate with and inspire others, her intelligence and her personality."*

Like many who have to live with disability, I didn't want to be recognised for being different, in my case being short and armless, rather for 'normal' human traits such as the ability to communicate, operate radio, telecommunication, computer software, organise, be prepared, stay safe, watch for obstacles … caw blimey, when I think about it, intelligence. That is why I was so angry a number of years later when awarded an Australia Day Centenary Award. During the presentation by a prominent politician I sat amongst the many others to be awarded. He spoke only about "Debbi's lovely smile". Who wins an award for having a nice smile? It was insulting, and when I arrived home I snatched the medal out of its fancy display case and threw it in the bin. After expressing my disgust to the appropriate authority, I was convinced to retrieve the medal which is now in a drawer for Emm to deal with when I'm gone. What does it mean anyway; many years down the track I am still unused in a valuable capacity?

The Surf Lifesaving Club used the money I donated from the Tattersall's Award to buy a new Mazda B2600 ute that was fully equipped with oxygen and associated resuscitation equipment, stretcher, two rescue boards and rescue tubes, radio, extensive first aid kit and knapsacks. I think it was the Surf Club's first 4x4!

***

Looking back, 1996 was certainly a big year. In March that year I accepted an invitation to holiday with Mum and Dad on King Island, where Dad was catching up with an old fishing mate. On the Saturday night I accompanied Sharon, the mate's wife, to a girls' night out and went to the pub, meeting up with a group of guys who were in town for an air show. Before I knew it a friendly bloke called Tony, who I discovered was a pilot flying planes for the parachutists, was hitting on me. I appreciated the opportunity to engage in conversation with such an intelligent man and we had a wonderful night together. He was comfortable in my company, which he showed as he placed an arm around my shoulders and moved in for 'the pash'. We parted the next morning, as I caught up with the folks and we flew back to Victoria.

The fleeting moment in time I spent with Tony gave me the impetus to pursue another long-time dream to try sky diving. One sunny morning at 10am on the 10th day of the 10th month I was taken 10,000 feet up in an aeroplane from a private strip along the Princes Highway near Bairnsdale. While strapped to an instructor, we jumped, and ohhhhh what an exhilarating feeling it was as we went into freefall. I remember the amazing floaty feeling as we rolled head over heels before levelling out and flying through the air at an incredible pace, the wind pulling your skin backwards to what I envisaged as an unwrinkled youth look, to a point. Then the parachute was released and we floated to the ground. I'd love to go sky diving again, but unfortunately the budget hasn't allowed it. Maybe some time soon. I never saw Tony again after our night on King Island, but I have often reflected on that, our fabulous night together and silently thank him for giving me the motivation to jump out of a plane.

***

My other big adventure in 1996 was a very long drive. Not long before being advised that I had won the January Tattersall's award I saw an advertisement on television for Variety Club's VicBash 1996 from the Melbourne suburb of Chadstone to Kakadu in the Northern Territory and thought 'I'd love to be part of that!'

I spoke to a lovely local couple, Peter and Lorraine Hobson, who I knew had an interest in rally driving, and asked how they thought I would go in a Variety Club Bash. Peter invited me to come along the following weekend as his navigator in a local event. Peter and Lorraine were extremely supportive and after the test run as the navigator in their vehicle I was determined to give the 'Bash' a go.

The following weekend I drove to Sale, armed with a few thousand dollars I had inherited from a small insurance policy that Jim left me, and found my ideal vehicle … a 1964 Valiant Safari station wagon.

I had to get together a team and sponsorship, and the latter received a boost when I spoke with Lance Beehan of Tattersall's, who had presented me with the January achievement award, and he encouraged me to submit an application. So I put my proposal in writing and soon received a positive response, which led to Tattersall's and Powerball logos being splashed over the vehicle. A friend of brother Jim's and now a friend of mine, Jim Howell from Coongulla, near Maffra, and his 76 year-old father George made up our team. One of my many joys during the trip was to look in the rear vision mirror and see George sitting up in the middle of the back seat with the biggest grin on his face as we ripped through the desert.

The Bash started on August 7 and at 6.30am that day we were up bright and early checking the car over and making sure everything was ready to go. The start at the corner of Warrigal and Waverley Roads in Chadstone was a hive of activity with all the crazy cars and their crazy drivers anticipating the big drive ahead. Our first night was in Deniliquin where I caught up with a couple of old friends, Garry and Pat Baker, who had moved there from Lakes Entrance about six years previous. Now here we are nearly 30 years later and Garry, an experienced author, is working with me to help edit and publish my ramblings. We enjoyed typical country hospitality that night in Deniliquin, though it was bloody freezing so we decided to book a room for the night. On most other nights George and Jim pitched a tent and I slept on the front seat of the car.

We had a fantastic time on the Bash, raising funds for sick and disadvantaged children. There were dress-up nights, with plenty of jokes and frivolity along the journey. There I was, in my element behind the wheel of an outback vehicle, heading for the exhilarating environment of the desert. I drove relatively hard and with many other competitors encountering a few 'out of control' moments I felt proud we had no such disasters. I felt even better as we passed a rolled Holden driven by none other than Mr Frank Green, the Assistant Commissioner (Traffic and Operations Support), who was a most amiable bloke. Everyone was okay and we roared out some cheek as we flew by, knowing the sweeper truck would be along to assist in getting the car upright again. I loved every minute of this driving experience and must admit I found it very hard to share the driving, and even harder to sit through Jim's careful, restrained and slow sessions at the wheel. Hence, poor co-pilot and navigator Jim got a bit frustrated with the boredom. But my team-mates were both great men and we had a lot of laughs.

At the end of the Bash we had a finale in Darwin, where I was met by Mum, Dad and Emma who had flown up to greet me. I'd had such a great time and wanted the adventure to continue, so decided to drive home with Emma by my side … and we wouldn't be in a hurry. My co-pilots Jim and George were happy with this arrangement as they'd had enough of the Outback heat, dirt and dust, whereas I'm a bit of a desert rat at heart and loved it!

I put my four-year old daughter in the car and said "c'mon Emma, we're going for a drive back to Lakes Entrance". We pulled out from Darwin at the same time as Peter and Lorraine, as well as other friends Ray and Mary, and these guys would catch up with us each night until we reached Ayers Rock. We headed down the Stuart Highway from Darwin with no set itinerary, just a determination to take our time and work our way steadily back down south.

We travelled about 400 kilometres from Darwin to Mataranka for what was supposed to be a brief overnight stop at the caravan park. But when I discovered the thermal rock pools, where it was so easy for me to get in and out, we decided to stay a bit longer. I was in paradise and we spent many leisurely hours in the warm, relaxing waters. We slept in the back of the station wagon so the cost was negligible and we were well looked after by the park owners. After a beautiful time at Mataranka we reluctantly decided to continue the journey.

We were on a Thelma and Louise style road trip, albeit without the trouble they encountered, flying along the highway in the Northern Territory where, at that time, there were no speed limits and no requirement to wear a seatbelt. Emma was either perched up beside me on the front seat or in the back where she played with her toys or had a sleep. And oh, how dangerous that sounds today!

Along the way we encountered lots of road trains and Emma, very outgoing for her age, loved getting on the CB radio and having a chat with the drivers. She was gorgeous, pressing the button and in her sweet young voice saying, "hello road train, this is the purple Valiant" and often getting a response like, "hello purple Valiant. What are you doing little girl?" Then they'd chat away as we went down the highway. On one occasion when we must have been driving more slowly than usual a road train passed us and soon there was a voice over the CB exclaiming, "hey, purple Valiant, why has your mother got her feet up on the steering wheel?" Quick as a flash Emma replied, "because she's got no arms, you bloody idiot" and I laughed and laughed. The road train driver also saw the funny side and stayed on the line babbling away with us for a while, then we later met up with him at Eridunda Roadhouse for a coffee.

When we reached Eridunda, at the intersection of the Stuart and Lassetter Highways, we decided to stay for a night and then take the three hour drive to Uluru, but it was such a friendly place we extended this out to a few days. It was run by a lovely couple who offered to let us stay in a caravan they had at the back of the roadhouse. There was also a swimming pool, so again we had found another little utopia.

Eventually we took off to Uluru and checked out the big rock. Yes, I did manage to climb a small portion, perhaps a hundred metres, and Lorraine, another VicBash 'basher' en-route home, took Emma a little further. It was certainly not far, but we did get to enjoy the experience. We said goodbye to Peter and Lorraine, as well as Ray and Mary, before returning to Eridunda and spending a few more days in the roadhouse caravan park before continuing on towards Port Augusta. Once we crossed the South Australian border I had to be a bit more wary of our speed, as I didn't want a ticket and we'd set a pretty solid pace in the Territory.

We made it to Port Augusta, then drove east through Adelaide, stopping over at Murray Bridge and Horsham on our way back to Melbourne. The last night before arriving home was spent on the banks of Lake Glenmaggie at Coongulla where we called in and caught up with my Bash team members, Jim and George. It took us more than six weeks to get from Darwin to Lakes Entrance, along the way having lots of adventures and meeting friendly people. It was a trip, or should I say, an adventure, I will always remember and treasure.

CHAPTER 16

Emma goes to school

We returned home and had to get back into a routine after the buzz and emotion of our long journey. Every Sunday night we had dinner with Mum and Dad which we relished, with Emma especially adoring the time she spent with her Nan and Pa.

Generally I was okay at preparing our meals, but very, very slow at it. Emma was rapidly approaching school age so I rationalised and let go of some more of that independence that I had fought so hard to keep for a lifetime. It was time to extend the support I had in house cleaning to include meal preparation, as I knew good stable meal times would become more important. Although I'm competent in the kitchen, as I said I'm very slow and to get a meal on the table for Emma by six o'clock I had to begin the preparation about 2.30. I therefore contacted Home Help and they came in for a 'meal prep' hour each morning and afternoon. Because I have developed other needs as I've aged I have continued using Home Help to this day.

Before I knew it Emma was ready to start her education and was off to Lakes Entrance Primary School. I like being active and involved so almost from the start I was helping out at the school, first by reading to the preppies and typing stories on the classroom computer, and soon I was also involved as a member of the parents' committee. I especially enjoyed the school fetes where I volunteered to paint faces, and for several years charged 50 cents then later a dollar per face. The kids loved my artwork, which turned their faces into all sorts of favourite cartoon and movie characters. Unfortunately my face painting days came to an end when an art teacher, who fancied herself as a professional artist, offered to help out. She became the expert and I was offended when she promoted her faces, at times not as intricate as mine, as being worth twice my price. Personally, I didn't think her face painting was any better than mine, even though she charged the children $4 each.

By this time I was also getting active on the speaking circuit. After the Variety Club Bash I was asked to address a number of organisations and found it rewarding, and also appreciated the interaction it gave me with a wide range of people.

I worked extensively for quite a few years, doing many lonely miles delivering Motivation and Ability Awareness presentations at both secondary and primary schools, as well as to community groups and corporate arenas always trying to educate and inspire society to value their own skills and abilities and those of people with different abilities. In the meantime I also applied for various full-time jobs and although I was often able to reach the interview stage, that's as far as it went. It seemed no-one wanted to employ a little person with no arms. I have often wondered why I was well respected for speaking engagements but not considered appropriate enough for many jobs, in particular project coordination positions. I had by now seen many folk offered positions and the training to go with it, but not me....... ever!

Among the schools at which I gave presentations were Xavier College, Parade College, Vaucluse College, Penola College, Sale Secondary College, Salesian College, St Joseph's Boys College, Mount Scopus College, Carey Grammar, Bethany Primary School, St Patrick's Primary School Stratford and St James Primary School Oakleigh South. I also addressed the Gippsland Business Women's Summit, Disability Rights Victoria and White McKail Business Centre, among others. I had by now also addressed an International Prosthetics Conference.

In June 2000, having enjoyed numerous speaking engagements and finding there was increasing demand for this service I launched my new business venture, titled 'Liv to Liv', with a small presentation and evening, hosted at the White McKail Business Centre in Bairnsdale. The Bairnsdale Advertiser attended the launch and wrote the following article:

A solo parent with no arms and standing a mere 3' 9" tall, Debbi Gray's realistic and positive attitude has enabled her to tackle tasks that most would think twice about.

But a deep self-acceptance and willingness to push past the limits has seen Debbi become a highly motivated person and she has embarked on a new venture to share this with others.

'Liv to Liv' was launched by Debbi in Bairnsdale last week and the Lakes Entrance resident is making herself available for consultancy and speaking roles in motivation and ability awareness. Debbi communicates three powerful and enduring ideas:

We all have gifts and abilities;

Have a positive attitude on life;

Be grateful for what you have and what you can do.

Organisations wishing to speak with Deb regarding appearing at functions can contact her at PO Box 235 Lakes Entrance, 3909.

I have derived great satisfaction from talking to people about what you can achieve if you really want to, and in particular highlighting the importance of not treating someone differently, just because they have a disability. It has primarily been a process of education, but also motivation if people want to take this from what I have achieved, even though from my perspective I have only wanted to be seen as normal and, importantly, treated as normal. I am not ONLY what my body portrays!

I also gave various presentations to schools in the East Gippsland region. I recall an address to Nungurner Primary School which was titled 'Smile to communicate for a better chance to educate', and an ongoing program at Bruthen Primary School based around the adage 'You Can Do It'. I found working within these programs especially satisfying because it wasn't about me, it was about the philosophy.

I was enjoying the work in schools and at other speaking engagements but unfortunately my legs were deteriorating and I had increasing trouble with mobility, so I had to reassess my direction. I was more and more reliant on the wheelchair and it became too difficult … getting the wheelchair in and out of the car and trying to cope in the confines of a motel room was just too hard. If I was rich enough, or making sufficient money, I may have been able to employ an aide to help out, but this was not an option.

I was still able to do some of this work, but on a greatly reduced scale, and continued presenting at the Alpine Leadership Schools in Dinner Plain and Marlo a few times each year.

After one of these trips a young man named Tom, from Maffra Secondary College, posted the following on the campus website:

Debbi Gray came to the Snowy River Campus yesterday, on the day that I was student leader! It was awesome. The glow and the energy that she emitted were incredible, and she inspired a lot of us. I should start this off by briefly saying who Debbi is. Debbi is a woman who was born without arms... none what so ever, this meant that she had to learn to live life without hands, but with feet instead. She stated that when she was little, her mother's friend dropped by with a present for the baby... a rattle, she had no clue that the child was born without arms, but Debbi, as a baby, reached up with her feet and grabbed the rattle, just like you or me would have with arms, she did with feet.

Debbi talked to us all about her life, living without arms, becoming a mother, a rally car driver and going skydiving, all against the odds of her ever achieving anything without special assistance. She also spoke to us about the discrimination and the bullying that she received at school, and in the workplace, which was monumental, compared to any of us. Debbi inspired tolerance in all of us. She proved yesterday that we can't judge or assume anything in anyone. And for that I thank Debbi.

***

Some years prior to the launch of Liv to Liv I was invited by Disability Advocates, Vi and Bill, from the Latrobe Valley area, to help set up one of the first independent disability advocacy services in Gippsland, and before long Gippsland Disability Advocacy was born. It is now referred to as GDAI, in acknowledgment of its growth and incorporation,.

I was a founding member and went to Morwell for lots of meetings, but once it was up and running I had little involvement because it was based in the Latrobe Valley and that's where its interest was concentrated.

Generally I have worked hard wherever possible to support any programs or initiatives that may benefit people with disability, though the politics of it all leaves me – and many others – pretty frustrated. For example when Sheryll Garbutt was Community Services Minister in Steve Bracks' Victorian Government I attended a three day conference in Benalla where she was the guest speaker on the final day. It was in early March and I had waited for three long, hot days to talk with the Minister.

She spoke to the conference about helping people with disability live independently, the government's Accommodation Innovation Grants and what she called its 10 year vision to support the rights of those living with disability. Ms Garbutt also talked about how we should get stronger and stay committed to our advocacy roles, assuring us she was listening to our concerns. Of course, I had heard this government rhetoric many times before and when Ms Garbutt finished her speech, myself and others in the 500-strong crowd were ready and willing to ask a few pertinent questions.

A lot of time and effort had been spent by various individuals preparing questions, as this was a unique opportunity and most had exhausted local and so-called 'proper' channels to have their views heard. From Ms Garbutt's perspective it also offered a chance for her, as boss of our sometimes pathetic support services, to hear from the heart what really matters in a disabled person's life.

But this wasn't going to happen. After her brief address – I could have said in one sentence what took her more than 10 minutes – the Minister exited the rear of the stage. The MC announced question time and I asked loudly, "who is going to answer our questions?" We were told this role would be filled by the local Member of Parliament.

Instantly disgusted with the token appearance, I raced out of the building to see if I could catch the Minister before she was whisked away in her flash, taxpayer-funded car. I tried to get a few minutes with Ms Garbutt as I explained to one of her 'minders' that I appreciated she was very busy but wanted to ask about a couple of pressing issues. Not likely ... she was on her bike and wasn't coming back. She was in the car and I was very angry, because there were a lot of people who needed questions answered from the top. In my trusty Zappy wheelchair I decided I needed to stop the vehicle from leaving until she spoke to me. I positioned myself behind the vehicle, hoping to stop them from leaving. I was sure the Minister would see the passion and at least say something, but instead the driver simply drove up on the gutter and around other vehicles to make the escape. I was disgusted and frustrated and felt sad for those inside the conference centre, many of whom had gone to great lengths to attend and rightfully wanted their questions answered.

In more recent times I have tried to convince our Member for East Gippsland, Tim Bull, of the unique needs of real people in our community who live with a physical disability and the lack of appropriate recreational and respite accommodation and long term residential services. As it stands today, the options are aged care or supported residential housing, shared by many with age, behavioural and intellectual differences.

It is unjust that some very smart younger people are surrounded by such debilitating and, for some, demoralising environments. They do not want to be put in a nursing home with old people who are moaning and groaning all night, and old men who wander into the room and put their hand under your blanket. I know this sounds harsh, but it's reality and at the moment for many it's the only option. The idea is pushing me towards an armed robbery, as you're better looked after in jail, where you seem to have more rights and stimulation.

I had architectural drawings prepared and took a business plan to a local MP outlining how a suitable accommodation centre for the physically disabled could be built and how it might work. As usual, nothing happened.

***

As Emma continued in Primary School I kept helping out whenever possible, even though it became more difficult as my once strong, agile and flexible body continued to deteriorate. Try as I might it was becoming harder and harder to live the active, independent life for which I had always strived and lived.

Towards the end of the 20th century, at a time when the world was rejoicing as we headed towards a new millennium, I was under the care of a psychologist. I needed this outlet, as it was someone to whom I could vent all my frustrations at a time of very low self-esteem. I was in desperate need of being needed and my inability to gain ongoing, meaningful employment was the centre of many sad moments that dragged into hours, then days. It didn't matter how many jobs I applied for, the answer always seemed to be the same, which was very depressing. Thankfully, when she was not at school my young daughter needed me.

By the time Emma was 10 years old and getting towards the end of her primary school years she had developed into an extremely confident, outgoing young girl. She was very energetic and always ready and able to be involved in a vast range of sports and activities. As soon as she could Emma joined the netball team in an informal but competitive environment and I soon became the number one supporter and, before long, took on a role as unofficial coach.

Emma was also involved in Scouts and I eventually agreed to take a seat on the Committee of Management. We had been regular campers for many years, so we enjoyed the Scouting Movement and often took part in the group's organised events. It was on one of their camps that a fellow Scout's father started showing a little extra interest in me. Over the course of the weekend we were often sitting together and he was very accommodating and willing to help me out whenever necessary, including meal times, when he collected our meals from the cooking area and delivered them to our eating spot. In fact he was doing everything I generally witnessed from a male towards a female when they were at work on 'the pick-up'. Of course I look back now and in retrospect I see he was just a very caring man and was just looking after the disabled, I guess.

I was thrilled and to an extent felt privileged at this very rare and public display of behaviour and personal attention, but kept my feelings under wraps. This turned out to be a most enjoyable family weekend and I was pleased when the attention did not stop after we returned home. The man in question, an offshore worker who was a divorcee and father of two lovely boys, kept in regular contact and I did not mind the phone calls I received a couple of times each day or, when he was at work, each night to check that everything was okay on the home front as we chatted away, enjoying each other's conversation, for half an hour or more. Naturally this made me feel special and quite upbeat as I thought at last something may be happening on the love and partner scene.

For many weeks we continued our phone calls when he was offshore, then when he was home we were regularly at each other's house for meals – he would often bring lunch around - or just paying a friendly visit. His youngest boy was about the same age as Emma and also in Scouts, which gave us something else in common. It was also great to have a man around the house. Emma was playing basketball, so I supplied the materials and he built a basketball ring which still stands in my back yard as a permanent reminder of our short time together. But he was here one day and gone the next.

I soon realised that it all happened too quickly and I felt he was unable to get his head around a sexual future with someone like myself. He did what I had seen all too often in times past. He went for a better body. Sadly, I have lived with this type of thinking for many years. Others had not been as gentlemanly as this fellow, but the result was the same … as a relationship developed it didn't take long for them to start thinking about sex, and when this thought process started most were quick to walk away because they were unsure what the future might hold in this regard. In their mind it was easier to get out before things got too complicated. With my male friend from Emma's Scout group it was more difficult to accept than usual. At the time it was unexpected, even though I had been abandoned before. Yes, this one was harder to take, but life goes on.

What I did not appreciate as a fall-out from our liaison was the way it affected my relationship with his ex-wife, who I worked alongside on the Scout Committee, of which I was now President. I also knew her fairly well through other local activities and events. Her boys often came to our place to play with Emma, but she soon put an end to that. One particularly nasty incident that I recall was when, as Scout Secretary, she changed the venue for our Scout meeting at the last minute and told everyone except the President. I eventually found out where the meeting was being held and by the time I arrived everyone was waiting patiently so we could get started. I wasn't going to play silly games like that, so resigned as President and never again attended a Scout meeting. Sadly the organisation developed political issues that affected its support to the extent that it was forced to fold. I found this very unfortunate, and especially felt sorry for the dedicated Scout Master, Dianne Sinclair, who had worked tirelessly in that position for so many years.

***

Despite this failed relationship and a few other personal issues, I was keeping busy and overall it was not such a bad time in my life. Emma kept me active with all her sport and I was getting more involved in my painting, having finally set up Jim's room as a studio. Mum and Dad still loved their golf and started to involve Emma in the game when she was a little girl, presenting her at some stage with her own little golf stick. If they had an early morning game planned she often stayed the night with them. Over the years her game improved immeasurably, after initially taking about 180 shots to play the difficult front nine on the challenging Lakes Entrance course, and 150 to play the back. Eventually she reached the point where she was able to submit three handicap cards and was getting quite proficient on the golf course. She started with a handicap of 45, which was the maximum, but was playing well for one so young. This was helped by some excellent coaching which included a train trip one day with her Nan to Oakleigh Golf Club, in Melbourne, for a junior golf day.

My golfing involvement with Emma continued to be at the local mini-golf where we had many fun outings. I got pretty good at it too, if I do say so myself ... placing the putter grip between my chin and my shoulder and pushing the stick through with my shoulder I would send the ball towards the hole, just as I had done in my younger years on the golf course with my parents.

***

Around this time I had one memorable event, though certainly not one I look back on with any fondness. Over the years I had done everything possible to take good care of and retain my teeth, but despite my best efforts this was not going to happen as every few months I would return to the dentist for another extraction. When it got to the point that only eight lower originals remained, and one of them was to come out, I made another tough decision - they would all be removed.

So it was a sad day when I sat in the dental chair and the eight teeth were extracted. As an armless person who uses her mouth a lot it was imperative that new ones be available immediately. It was a tough few months adjusting … but hey, what doesn't break you, makes you! Again I survived and again I thrive.

By this stage my work on the speaking circuit was limited and generally on a volunteer basis after I deregistered the ABN number for Liv to Liv. Mobility was an increasing problem as I became even more dependent on a wheelchair to get around, and when I travelled to schools for a speaking engagement it was often by train and wheelchair. That was difficult when I went to places such as Geelong, Ballarat and even Harrietville, up on the Great Alpine Road (I couldn't take a train on that trip, as there isn't one! I was driven by a friend).

Adding to the insults that life regularly dishes out, the fabric on my wheelchair had the word 'karma' - the brand name - written all over it which internally I dealt with every single day it was in my possession. I found it offensive, but to avoid conflict I treated it as a joke. The dictionary tells me that karma refers to "the spiritual principle of cause and effect where intent and actions of an individual (cause) influence the future of that individual (effect)". Can anyone tell me how there's karma from being born with physical deformities like mine? Anyway, I thought at the time

I had to be grateful for my wheels, which had been provided at no charge.

Increased reliance on the wheelchair was symptomatic of escalating physical problems as I crept gradually towards 50 years of age. As my body started to wear out, I developed back trouble which led to a stint in the Latrobe Regional Hospital with the prospect of surgery to relieve the pain. Whilst awaiting a decision on the surgery, I was placed under the care of a physiotherapist to relieve the pain, caused by the lower spine curving out to the left. The specialist's report described me as having "gross abnormal deformity". What an insult! The pain was becoming difficult to manage and I was extremely grateful for the common-sense approach by the physiotherapist who simply suggested I get a built up thong for the right foot. This simple adjustment to my spine proved to be a successful physiotherapy treatment. I was also seeing a psychologist to help me deal with numerous issues that provide a challenge for anyone who is my height and does not have the use of arms for the everyday tasks which most people take for granted.

***

Emma graduated in 2004 from primary school as an A grade student who was very popular with fellow students and her teachers. The following year she started Year 7 at the Lakes Entrance Secondary College.

Throughout her primary schooling I had been involved in reading to students, typing stories and various other school duties, so I suppose it was only natural that I would quickly get involved in secondary school activities.

I was soon on the school committee and also started assisting with some motivational work, in particular with students who were having difficulties at school and with life in general. The Education Department had developed what it called the VCAL program – an acronym for Victorian Certificate of Applied Learning –a hands-on study option for students in Years 11 and 12 with components that focused on work-related skills and personal development skills. The principal asked if I would assist with VCAL revolving specifically around improving school engagement for a group of Koori students. We wanted to do something worthwhile that encouraged those involved to take a greater interest in their education with the help of VCAL.

I did not have teaching qualifications, however I had my Art Diploma and believed I had the ability to develop a level of rapport with the students that could ensure the course's success.

Naturally, to be effective we needed an appropriate space, but for some reason the school could not make this available. On top of this I was unable to access all the necessary equipment we required. At this point I started to wonder whether the school was serious about the project, or was it just a 'tick the box' exercise? We had no permanent location – which was essential – and there was no structure nor expected outcomes, which I found disappointing. Eventually I went to the Assistant Principal and asked "what outcomes do you want? What are we trying to achieve?" I pointed out I did not want to be part of a 'box ticking' project. I was told, "well, you decide what the outcomes should be". They left me floundering and without the level of support that was needed if the program was to succeed.

Unfortunately, those who suffered were the students I was trying to help, as I realised that from the school hierarchy's perspective, all the system wanted was a program that kept these students in the school grounds, or encouraged them to at least attend on more days than had previously been the case. There was no genuine support or assistance, so inevitably the program drifted towards obscurity.

This was such a shame because I was helping these young adults in a voluntary capacity, believing I had empathy and an understanding of their frustrations as they grappled with challenges that life throws up. Similarly, they could see the challenges which I had been forced to deal with and developed a respect not only for Deb Gray as a person, but as someone who had faced these challenges head-on and refused to let them hold me back. But despite being able to effectively engage with my students, the support, resources and structure in the timetable were not forthcoming.

People have asked: Why would I involve myself with a program like VCAL on a voluntary basis while everyone around me was getting well paid in their mentoring roles? Quite simply it was another attempt to be involved in my community and the people around me as I continued striving to be a team member and find my place on this earth. I didn't want to sit around the house wasting whatever time I have in this short life that we are all given. None of us are here for long and for most of my life, in particular the first 50 years, I didn't want to waste a minute.

***

But let's get back to some of the wonderful times I had with Emma, who was growing up to be a smart and gregarious young girl and, in her early secondary school years, setting goals and like most girls in their early teens trying her hand at various activities.

At some point most country girls want a horse and in this regard, God bless her cotton socks, Emma was no exception. As any parent whose child has been involved in this unique past-time would know, this is not an inexpensive hobby. From where I sat, the fact her Mum had a disability that wasn't conducive to riding was not going to stop my daughter pursuing her dreams and having a 'normal' teenage life. So, as you do, I agreed that Emma could have a horse and join Pony Club. However, this was at a time when I was also teaching Emma financial responsibility and I told her I was happy to offer as much support as possible and be a 'Pony Club Mum', but made it clear I couldn't afford to buy the horse so "you'll have to help me out here".

The maturity and commitment Emma showed for a 14 year-old made me a very proud Mum. She immediately went searching for work and soon had a part-time job at Baker's Delight, with money earned being saved so she could buy her horse. Before long Emma was the proud owner of Stanley, a handsome 14 hands high bay gelding and so started another awesome bonding journey in our lives.

However, Stanley soon taught us a lesson or two about the vagaries of this sport. When we bought him, the previous owner paraded Stanley around the paddock and assured us he was a lovely, quiet young steed; ideal for a learner. Going for a short ride alongside the seller, he was well behaved and as I could wheel right up to his chest without a flinch from him, we both felt very at ease in buying him. But we were proved to be quite naïve and it didn't turn out to be that easy. After we arrived home Stanley realised his new owner was inexperienced and quickly decided he would show her who was boss. As a result, before long Emma was dumped from the saddle to the ground, as Stanley, who had become cantankerous and stubborn, put on a display more akin to the rodeo arena. Emma bravely persisted over several months.

It was a time during which Emma was growing into a mature young woman and showing an impressive level of responsibility and commitment. She had saved her money to pay for Stanley and displayed a Leo like dedication to overcoming Stanley's behaviour. Then another issue immediately emerged ... how are we going to transport him? Pony Club events are held throughout the region and Emma was keen to get involved in gymkhanas and other eventing. Her Pa, so impressed that she had worked hard to buy a horse, came to the rescue with a $1,500 loan so we could buy a horse float. Pa had even greater admiration – if that was possible - for Emma's integrity when, 12 months later, she repaid him with money she had earned. From a very early age I tried hard to teach Emma respect and appreciation of her grandparents because you do not know how long you will have them. I was always so proud of the special relationship she developed with my parents, especially her beloved Pa; she thoroughly enjoyed his company as they worked on various projects, building or fixing something.

Once a tow ball was added to my car we were off to Pony Club on a regular basis. We had our Lakes Entrance Pony Club events and, like many of the members, there were regular trips to places like Buchan and Bruthen, as well as various agricultural shows. Often we were away camping for the weekend, so we had an awning made for the side of the float.

As usual with an organisation in which Emma was involved, when it came time for the Annual General Meeting and parents were being recruited for the committee I put up my hand, so to speak. I wanted to be a valuable club member, even though I could not ride a horse or help in some other active areas such as setting up jumps and courses. For a while I was heavily involved undertaking any task that I could, although unfortunately my years on the committee were cut short when the committee decided to accept an offer from a seemingly influential member to hold Pony Club meetings at the new offices of her husband's business. My interjection that this would be inaccessible to me, considering it was a two storey building with office at the top and no elevator, was greeted with hesitant offers to carry me up the stairs. I was a mature aged woman surrounded by other women and did not at all feel comfortable with that option, envisaging future back complaints for which I would carry the guilt. Why, I ask, could we have not stayed at the Bowls Club where the meetings were central, accessible and catered for, with tea and coffee and maybe a biscuit?

By this stage my mobility was such that climbing stairs was not possible. However, this did not stop me from continuing to play a role in Emma's enjoyment of Pony Club until the inevitable day came, as it usually does, when children leave home and head off to university.

Before this occurred, to try and overcome Stanley's three year-old feisty nature we called in help from those more experienced in horsemanship, A lovely young school friend of Emm's, Lizzie, had a lot more riding experience and confidence and took him on for a while. In the meantime, Emm began to ride another friend's, older and quieter bay gelding. While waiting for Stanley to settle, we bought an older 'grey'. Jake, at 20 years old was not ideal, finding the showjumping a challenge. After finding Stanley's behaviour was still not getting any better we accepted an offer from Karen Vickers to settle him a little more. Without Lizzie and Karen's assistance, there's little doubt we would have had to sell Stanley and cut our losses, as it was, we eventually had a good horse in him, and Jake went off to a quiet retirement in the mountains. When time came for Emma to move to university, Stanley was sold to a good local horsewoman, Robyn, who went on to win many events with him. As for answering questions as to how does a mother without arms raise a child who desires such a large animal, I'm not sure how I could. While growing up Emma had several types of animals and timing is the most important thing when you make a decision to get an animal for your child. As you could imagine, I was limited in how I could help her physically. She is lucky that she grew into such a capable child. I'm hoping I had something to do with that and it makes me proud.

One area where I was able to assist and be involved was as the chauffeur who was proudly towing a float with a big animal. This responsibility was mine to treasure and feel proud of. We enjoyed our time together in the Pone Club scene and it was with a heavy heart that Stanley was sold and another chapter in our lives was closed.

Above: My HMAS Londsdale Badge.

Following pages: Some of my certificates of recognition and education.

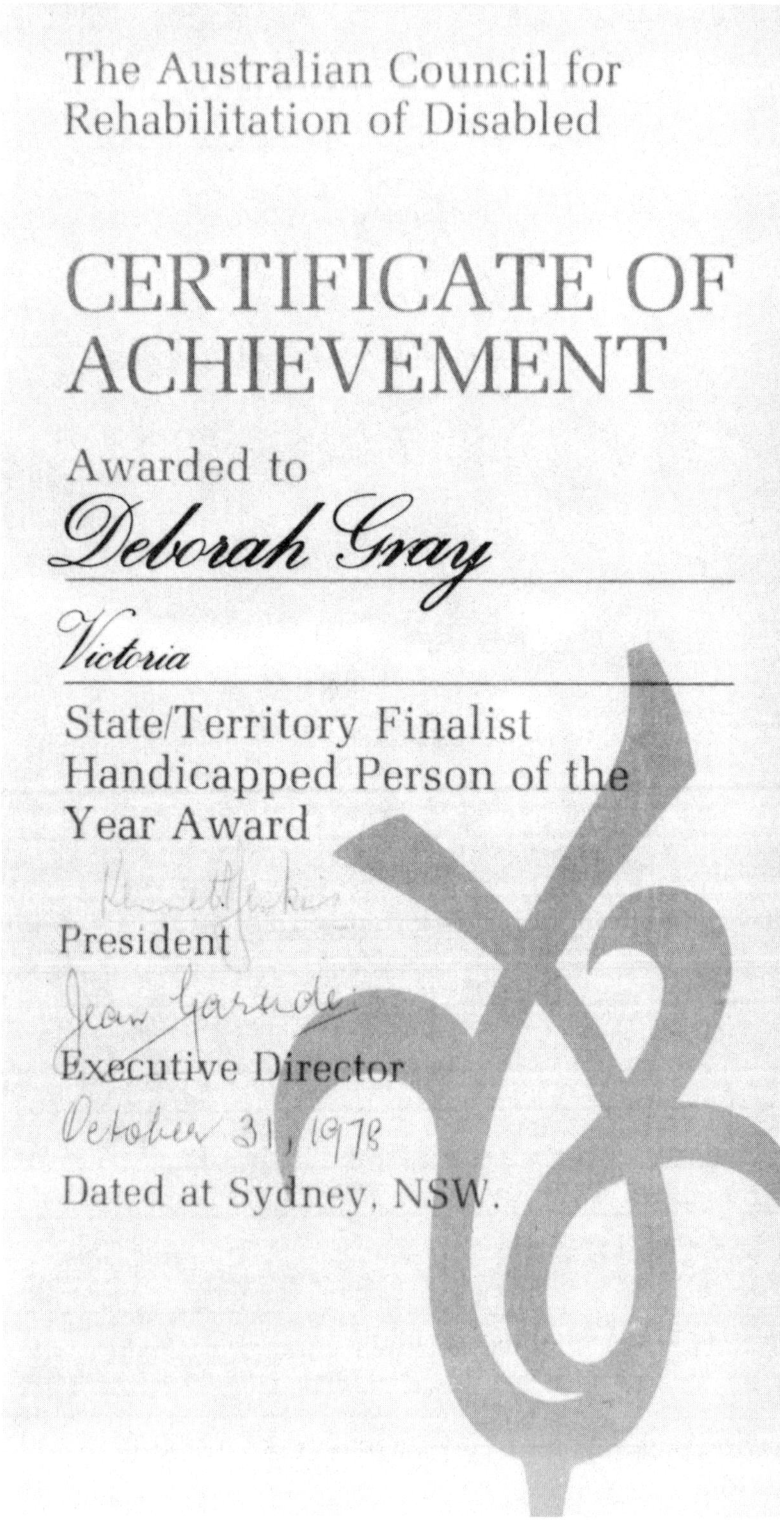

The Australian Council for Rehabilitation of Disabled

CERTIFICATE OF ACHIEVEMENT

Awarded to

Deborah Gray

Victoria

State/Territory Finalist Handicapped Person of the Year Award

President

Executive Director

October 31, 1978

Dated at Sydney, NSW.

EAST GIPPSLAND
SHIRE COUNCIL

CERTIFICATE OF RECOGNITION

PRESENTED BY THE

CHIEF COMMISSIONER, COMMISSIONERS

AND CHIEF EXECUTIVE

OF THE EAST GIPPSLAND SHIRE COUNCIL TO

DEBBI GRAY

IN RECOGNITION OF OUTSTANDING ACHIEVEMENT

IN WINNING THE

"1996 TATTERSALL'S AWARD FOR ENTERPRISE & ACHIEVEMENT"

Duncan Malcolm
Commissioner
4 November, 1996

MONASH University

Centre for Biomedical Engineering

In recognition of

Deborah Gray

for

significant contributions to the annual
Clinical Management
of Upper Limb Amputees Course
over the last decade

A/Prof. Ian T Brown	*Prof. David Morgan*	*Dr. Andrew Nunn*
Director, MUCBE	Research Director, MUCBE	Clinical Director, REHABTech

May, 2005

EAST
GIPPSLAND
INSTITUTE OF
TAFE

This is to certify that

Deborah Gray

has completed the requirements
for the award of

Diploma

of

Arts (Visual Arts)

12857VIC

EAST GIPPSLAND INSTITUTE OF TAFE COMMON SEAL

Director Angela Hutson

Council Member

Register No. *54500*

The qualification certified herein is recognised within the Australian Qualifications Framework.
National Provider No. 3070

PO Box 886, Bairnsdale Vic. 3875, Australia

12 September 2006

NATIONALLY RECOGNISED TRAINING

Quality System
Quality Endorsed Company

To

DEBORAH LOUISE GRAY

Greeting

WHEREAS Her Majesty Queen Elizabeth The Second, Queen of Australia, has instituted an Australian medal to commemorate the centenary of federation of Australia; I DO by this warrant award you the Centenary Medal.

Governor-General of the Commonwealth of Australia

By His Excellency's Command

Prime Minister

CHAPTER 17

Challenging times

For a large part of my life I have been involved with numerous organisations in a voluntary capacity, and after returning to Lakes Entrance in 1986 I never stopped trying to find meaningful paid employment. I was forever searching for job opportunities and submitting applications for anything deemed suitable. For most individuals who live with disability it is a depressing and sad reflection on our society that an offer of meaningful employment is not something we can generally look forward to, regardless of skill set.

Employment is a huge issue, especially frustrating for those like myself who have a physical disability but no obvious impairment to their intellectual levels.

If society in general was at all interested they would be making a better effort to make those with disability feel worthy and a valuable part of the world in which we all live. There's a social responsibility element here that governments and the business community are missing. This desperately needs to be addressed.

For starters there is the financial aspect. If people with disability are gainfully employed they are a lesser burden on the taxpayer, although it's actually more than that. It's giving a person a reason to get out of bed in the morning and get involved with other people. As much as anything it's helping with social development and alleviating the loneliness and often depression which are, for some, by-products of living on your own. On the way to work you might meet the postie, say g'day to a neighbour or interact with other members of your community. In my case, now in my sixties, it is a combination of loneliness, worthlessness and pain, contributing to increasing bouts of depression. If someone had offered me a job 10 to 20 years ago, when I so desperately wanted a meaningful career that helped with my financial independence and self esteem, I'm absolutely certain I would be in a better headspace today.

To be effective it is not imperative that full-time work is provided for those with disability, including myself. In some instances just a couple of hours a day is enough to make a difference in a person's life. I would have preferred more than that, but anything would have been better than nothing … which is what I've had to live with since I returned to my home town. Not one of my buddies, old or new, entrenched in positions within this community ever displayed a real desire to have me work alongside them. However other friends, often unskilled, were employed and given necessary training. On the other hand, maybe my ostracised feeling within the East Gippsland region has stemmed from a couple of conciliation cases I have successfully brought about. I wish sometimes I didn't need to be the one to make the stand, but if I do, I do!

I think we're at a point where business and government has to be told "this is what you must do to expect a person with disability go ahead feeling they are a worthy part of our great nation AND this is how we can do it!" The message has to come from the people with disabilities, not well meaning social workers and bureaucrats. We have to stop putting this issue in the 'too hard basket' and do something about it. There are many tasks I am able to effectively perform, so why is it so difficult for employers to make adjustments in the workplace to cater for unique needs? The same applies to many others with disability.

Part of the process needs to be education to improve community acceptance of abilities, rather than focusing on disability, and giving the person with disability a chance to show and reach their potential. This is not something that can be ignored. There is an increasing number of people living with disability and we're all getting older, bringing with it a growing risk and financial burden on the nation as a whole. Helping the young disabled of today get into the workforce must be looked at as an investment in the future, not a present day financial strain.

I submitted 57 job applications … every single one of them a job I was capable of doing, yet not one was successful. The reality, which we must accept and change, is that I suffered discrimination because potential employers saw my disability, not my ability.

I have completed diplomas in business and art, then thought I would study for a Disability Cert. 1V which would get me into a sector I know fairly well. Unfortunately I could not complete that certificate because it required that I have a workplace environment to go to at least once or twice a week in the disability sector. Go figure! I rang the only service provider with an actual office in our town and asked them for an appropriate space for me, but this was to no avail. I do commend one organisation for being honest and informing me it was perceived that it would be a breach of confidentiality, considering I was a client. Oops, I forgot, people with disabilities are unable to abide by conditions of the Privacy Act.

So I could not attain the qualifications I need for that industry. I have lots of experience but it seems experience means nothing if you are less than four feet high. What is particularly frustrating is that I have dealt with too many people who are inexperienced and unqualified, or both, but can get a job. The same people who employ them will not give me a chance.

One of my Home Help girls recently told me she asked her superiors if she could give up the physical side of her work but continue employment with the organisation. She was switched from providing outsourced care to a role in the office, primarily answering phones. They knew I wanted a job, which made me ask why someone couldn't phone and say, "Deb, we have a job for you". But of course they can't do that because I'm a client and it's a breach of their confidentiality and privacy policies. These policies, by the way, are a joke. Clients aren't supposed to know the identity of other clients, yet I was aware via other service users that some Home Help workers left their rosters, which is a list of clients, on a bench or table, making no attempt to hide it and going off to work in another room while it sits there. The sheet lists all their clients for the day, including their names and addresses. How confidential and hypocritical is that?

To address that anomaly for my few services, I was referred to as client 414. However, it still had my address and the list was still left lying around for anyone in the house to read. In a country town you generally know who lives at a particular address so you don't need their name to identify the person. I even got mail addressed to Client ???. These examples highlight the double standards that exist within our social sector. On the one hand I cannot be employed because of privacy concerns, yet on the other the privacy they practice is severely lacking any serious rigour.

On a rare occasion over 30 odd years ago, when in my thirties, I was accepted into the workforce with a disability organisation run by able bodied people. They were supposed to help those with disability find employment, but didn't have a clue what living with disability was all about. I was ostracised in the workplace and given zero support. Before I started I was promised a desk at the same height as my chair, so I could work with my feet. It was never provided, yet every day I'd be told "get rid of that unprofessional mess on the floor". What was I supposed to do with my paperwork if I didn't have a desk? One of my tasks was to type client resumes, which I could only do if I was sitting on the floor, as I had no desk. When clients came in to see me, they'd come behind the front desk and sit down with me which was okay, but not the most professional way to talk with those who we were supposed to be helping. Despite this, all my requests for the low level desk which was promised when I started the job were ignored.

Case workers became jealous and intolerant when clients came in and wanted to talk with me. I believe clients were comfortable with me and maybe felt I might have a better understanding of their troubles. While I would not encourage too much discussion, I was never rude or discouraging with a client. Often a Case Worker would come out and ask them, "do you want to see me?" They'd reply, "not today, I came in to see Deb". I'd then get some negative comment about talking to the clients and not doing other work, even though at this stage of the new business there was not a great deal to be done and our conversations were never employment related.

In this position I was also embarrassed and incensed by some of the language that was used. For example, I witnessed a person with a mild Acquired Brain Injury who came to discuss their job prospects with one of our employment counsellors. When the client left, the counsellor blurted out, "thank God that moron is gone". In the end this 'counsellor' was considered suitable to be working with those who have disability, but I wasn't. This same counsellor was happy for me to make his coffee, but I later discovered he had complained that he "nearly puked" when he drank it because I stirred his coffee with the spoon in my mouth; I do not dribble!

This disgraceful behaviour and attitude is what you have to try and live with in the world of disability and, in my view, it's a fairly pitiful reflection on too many able bodied individuals in today's society. Cultural change is needed and this can only be achieved when you accept those with disability for what they can do, and work harder to ensure they lead a positive, contributing life.

When my three month probation with the disability employment provider was completed I was told I would no longer be required. This experience was among the worst cases of discrimination I have encountered, though it's a long way from the solitary one. I knew I had not been given a chance and, in my view, other 'counsellors' – and I use the term loosely – did not want me around because I was more in tune with clients. Sadly, due to my own physical disposition, this was true and my empathy was genuine. This was recognised early in my employment so every attempt was made to ensure I did not fit in or become entrenched in this workplace. I am not a person who pursues litigation unnecessarily or easily, but I felt I could not possibly allow this type of treatment to occur without expressing my views in the strongest way.

I complained bitterly to management about the lack of professionalism and what I perceived as a disregard within the organisation for those with disability, whether this be towards colleagues or clients. My complaints were ignored and the manager made it clear she did not like the cold hard truths which were being laid bare. I realised there was not going to be any support coming in my direction and, in frustration, took my case to conciliation. I received financial compensation for the way I was treated, which is what I was instructed to accept, but that is not what I was seeking. My sole aim was recognition that in the disability environment, individuals must be shown respect, regardless of their mental or physical capacity.

Without sounding arrogant, I think I have enough personal and professional experience to understand what is required in the disability sector and by those who live their life with disability. Those working in the sector need to be private and professional. It is okay for a support person or carer to become friendly with their client, but they must retain an appreciation for the role they are playing and empathy towards the person they are assisting. I have had carers with a condescending 'look what a good person I am' attitude, patting themselves on the back because they are helping someone with disability. I've also suffered the indignation of effectively being put on show.

On one occasion a support worker in an art class brought her daughter along to show off 'how I help out little Deb'. The child then went to school and, as a paranoid imagination might feel, told other kids how 'my Mum helps Deb and gets her brushes and when Deb has finished painting my Mum goes back there and helps clean everything up'. This gets exaggerated and misconstrued and by the time it's at the end of the grapevine a support person who gets out brushes at the start of the class and returns to clean up at the end is said to have brushed my teeth, wiped my arse and looked after every other little personal task we all have to perform throughout the day. Believe it or not, I've had to deal and cope with such degrading gossip. (And for the record, I don't need any assistance with personal hygiene and trust I never will.)

In the employment sector the attitude towards all clients should be the same; that is, they are not a number, nor a means towards another bucket of government funding. Every effort should be made to assist their pathway into a meaningful career. Too often, that does not happen.

***

So I was told my services were not required by an employer in the disability sector who did not want a person with disability in the office, and this was followed by my failed attempt to get a Disability Cert. IV because I couldn't get work placement. That's when I gave up, which is not something that had previously been in my psyche. Deb Gray, for 50 years, did not give up! If a task was tough or the going proved more challenging than usual I had an in-built determination – a fierce independence which had been nurtured by my parents and fully supported by my little brother Jim – to fight on until the challenge was beaten. But following 57 job applications with just one opportunity, from which I was forced out after a three months' game of bullying, intimidation and discrimination, I had to wave the white flag. I don't care whether a person is three feet eight inches tall, or a physically strong six footer, there's only so much emotional bullying you can take. I'd reached my limit. That was many years ago and I've since been writing, painting a little, and looking after the house.

And before I get down off my 'disability discrimination' soapbox, I want to make the point that I feel some people get annoyed with my enthusiasm and ability to do a job well. I've wondered whether it makes them feel inferior when they see the capabilities of a little woman, perhaps because they are not doing their best and making the most of opportunities in front of them.

I have excellent references from positions I held that speak in glowing terms like "bright, intelligent, very capable and a pleasure to deal with". Similar comments are in every reference, yet I left the public service as a CA2, with only one promotion over all those years. Why? Because of physical disability, not lack of ability.

A number of years ago I was asked to help a woman who had bravely left a domestic violence situation. I spent a considerable amount of time on the phone to a social worker at Centrelink resolving various issues. Interestingly, I think all the Centrelink social workers are now employed in call centres … you don't actually get to meet someone. When our rather lengthy discussion had finished the Centrelink worker asked, "who do you work for?" When I replied, "no-one ... I haven't been able to get a job" he responded, "that's a shame". I hung up the phone and cried, because I am sick of being told "gee Deb, you do a great job", yet I sat at home relying on being needed by friends for happiness; they never came. With too many idle hours trying to fill in each day, it was hard.

In 1981, the International Year of the Disabled, I was the Commonwealth Public Service pin-up girl, featuring in promotional material including being pictured at work on the side of Melbourne trams. But were they fair dinkum about providing opportunities for the disabled? No, I don't think so. It was all words and blabber. I do acknowledge there is a better support system for those with all states and levels of disability wishing to upgrade or continue on to academic skills. This in itself gives a person a better chance of being placed in a less laborious career.

But there is no genuine community desire to provide employment for those with disability. I sometimes wonder whether this is due to laziness - it is easier for people, particularly in the corporate sector, to donate some of their millions rather than rearrange tasks and provide a position for a fellow community member.

I certainly do not want my life to end as a lonely unproductive or non-contributing spinster ... and nor it should for a person who has worked very hard to be independent, lived a normal life and wanted to be seen as someone who has the same needs and aspirations as the woman next door.

***

Let's get back to Emma. Before her first year was completed at Lakes Entrance Secondary College I had some niggling concerns about her development. A spelling test – which was like a game we had played from the time Emma learned to talk - brought everything out into the open. When she was a little girl I regularly taught Emma small words, then harder ones as she progressed into primary school. By the time she was at secondary school her spelling was above average. I picked her up one afternoon from school and on the way home, as was often the case, I threw a word at Emma and asked her to spell it. She got it wrong and did likewise with the next word, which was very unusual.

Later that afternoon, while we were at home, I asked Emma how she was going at school, in particular in English class where she had always excelled.

"I don't know, Mum," she responded, "I feel like I'm slipping a bit." I had already been hiding some quiet concerns regarding the priorities of the school and was prompted to ask Emma what she felt we needed to do about it. I then asked if she would consider attending Nagle College, which is a highly regarded Catholic co-educational school in Bairnsdale, a 45 minute bus trip away. She responded quickly with "yes" and by the end of the following week was enrolled in Nagle where she spent the rest of her secondary education.

After graduating from Nagle, Emma went to 'schoolies' in Queensland with a couple of her fellow graduates. They had a great time and were on top of the world when they returned. In fact, Emma enjoyed it so much she decided to go back to Queensland for her gap year. At the time I had a bit of an 'empty nest' feeling, but of course had to accept the reality that my dear Emma was not going to stay by her Mum's side forever. I wanted her to fly and encouraged her to take the gap year, enjoy it and return in the right frame of mind to settle into university studies.

In hindsight it was actually good for me, too, because she took our two beautiful Border Collies, 'De Boyz' Chips and Archie, with her. I was able to get out and about and spend time as a mature Mum without the responsibility that comes with children. Naturally I missed Emma, which is to be expected as our lives had been so intertwined for the past 18 years. She was the one I poured my love on and I had committed everything to ensuring she would be raised as a normal child, with no restrictions from having a Mum with disability. I cannot comment on my success … I guess we would have to ask Emma.

After six months in Queensland, Emma and De Boyz returned home. She got a part-time job at Macca's and enjoyed this short period before continuing her education at La Trobe University.

She completed a Bachelor of Veterinary Bioscience and was then accepted into Melbourne University where, in 2019, she graduated with a Doctorate in Animal Veterinary Medicine.

These days I don't see Emma as much as I used to – and to be honest, as much as I'd like to - which is sometimes difficult for me to deal with, especially when I'm feeling lonely. She now lives in Melbourne and leads a busy life between working at the Lort Smith Animal Hospital and a social life that is very active and in many ways similar to my own at that age, although I'd say hers is a lot healthier. As much as I love the outdoors I'm not that energetic in it and I know she likes to go hiking a lot, which is something I could only dream about. I am so proud of what she continues to achieve. I must say that to be honest "I'm a wee bit proud" that despite all the challenges I was able to raise such a bright young person who I know will be a great asset to the veterinary world and her community in many ways. Emma has grown into a good-hearted and humoured, strong woman who I will love and cherish until my dying breath.

***

While Emma was at Nagle College we suffered the unexpected and devastating loss of my dear Mum in 2009. It was on the evening of July 28, a day after Dad and Emma share a birthday, when I received a phone call from my older brother Geoff about 6pm telling me "something's wrong with Mum". I sensed it was serious, jumped straight into my car and screamed down Kalimna hill at speeds I'd never previously attempted on that dangerous stretch of road. I raced along the Esplanade, almost screeching the tyres as I took the left turn In Myer Street, passed the police station and up to Mum and Dad's home at the top of the hill.

I ran inside and to my left were Geoff and Dad, seated at the dining table, and on my right was the lounge where, just over the top, I could see a couple of heads and immediately realised they belonged to ambulance paramedics. I raced around the couch to where they were working on Mum. Not wanting to intrude, but needing to be with her, I sat on the floor at her feet, stroking them will all the love, respect and gratitude I could send to her through my touch. Each time they had to use the defibrillator 'electric shock' I had to let her go and as they prepared for a third hit I shook my head. “No,” I said softly, knowing it was all too late.

I later discovered that Mum, as she did each evening, had taken Dad’s meal to him in the lounge room, placed it on his knee and returned to the kitchen. She picked up her own plate and was turning around when the aneurysm hit.

“Ohhhhh love!” she exclaimed to her beloved husband before collapsing towards the floor with flailing arms. Dad raced to her side, catching her as she went down and carrying her to the couch in the open plan living area, then making the heart-rendering decision to leave her side and grab the phone as she pleaded, “don’t leave me Bim, I’m scared”. But he had to call an ambulance. By the time he returned she was gone. As I was beside my Dad and nursed him to his own passing, I know he regretted his decision to leave Mum and go for the phone until he could regret no more.

I lost my precious Mum, then six years later Dad was diagnosed with cancer. He was soon being treated at the Peter McCallum Cancer Centre in Melbourne where he and I spent a couple of six week stints while he underwent chemotherapy. During this time in Melbourne, Dad would stay on his own in Heidelberg, where cheap accommodation was provided for country folk getting medical attention, while I stayed with an old secondary school friend and his most accommodating flatmate, who was also owner of the house. Being old school and a gentleman, I guess, Dad could not share a one room twin bed motel-style room with me, as to why, I can only speculate. Emm stayed with him as often as she could and Dad loved it

During these treatments Dad had medical transport arrangements, so I didn't need to back track and pick him up. I would leave John and Watto’s in Preston bright and early at six o’clock each morning, thus missing the peak of the peak hour traffic, and also have time to get to Peter McCallum Hospital and get a park for the car. As I am unable to function in John and Watto’s kitchen, I would then,grab my first cuppa for the morning adding my habitual toast and Vegemite. After attending to my culinary needs I headed to the foyer and transport area where I waited for Dad to arrive by Red Cross taxi. I was by his side throughout every day of his treatment. In fact, when we finally returned home, except for two small respite trips away towards his end, I stayed by his side for the next 18 months.

At this point Emma was doing her final year at La Trobe Uni and she was fabulous with her Pa. By the time we were at our final stages of Dad's last treatment the radiotherapy was starting to knock him about a bit, so Emma, again, would go and stay at his unit for a couple of nights and give him some extra support. As the treatment and illness took their toll Dad started becoming more vague and he went from knowing exactly where he was and what was going on to having increasing lapses in coherence. It took me many sleepless nights, with concerns from others, to start making lots of phone calls and annoying the doctor before Dad was sent for further tests and it was discovered the cancer had progressed to his brain. Another small stint in the local hospital was arranged.

During the discharge process from the hospital, and a meeting involving the occupational therapist, social worker and several family members, it came as a disappointing surprise when it was realised I was the only family based option for care and support, hence Dad moved into my house where I could look after him. Before going to Melbourne for the treatment he had been living alone in the house he had shared for many years with Mum, before her passing. I knew I couldn't cope with Dad on my own so rang my close cousin Sandra, a single Mum who lived in Tasmania, and asked if she could help. Sandra arrived within 36 hours and stayed with us for 18 months until Dad passed away. I will never forget her amazing, loyal and dedicated love and support.

Dad's health gradually worsened to the point where we knew he would not be with us for much longer. We enjoyed our final Christmas together in 2013 and early in the new year Dad was requiring quite a high level of care. Despite this, he continued to live at home and nurses paid a visit to assist with washing.

As his final days drew closer my Aunty Merle, who had been a regular visitor, again came to visit. By this point, each night Sandra and I were generally taking four hour shifts by Dad's side. Sandra would spend four hours with him, then come and wake me up and I'd take over, and occasionally we'd stay longer than four hours to ensure we each had enough sleep.

On the night of February 16, 2014 Aunty Merle wanted to stay into the evening and told both Sandra and I to get some sleep while she sat with Dad. I went to bed around 10pm, planning to get up and take my usual stint with Dad from 2am onwards. Sandra was usually awake until I took over at 2am, so stayed up as normal. When Sandra went in about 10:30pm to have a chat with Aunty Merle and see how everything was going, she noticed Dad's breathing was irregular and he was restless, so she came and woke me up. As was routine, I gave Dad another jab of morphine to help him settle. On realising it was the last prepared injection I called the after hours contact and Penny, the nurse, arrived to help draw up some more injections that I would administer to Dad if he showed signs of discomfort. I told Penny I was concerned about Dad's colour and breathing and she confirmed he may not make it through the night. I called my brother Geoff who came straight around.

Still sitting by Dad's side, his hand draped warmly around my foot, while quietly conversing with the others I kept a check on his irregular breathing rate of 'in 1,2,3,4 … and out, 1,2,3, …' I was counting to myself and, surprisingly,I realised I had got to seven. I stared at Dad's chest and looked at his face. I turned slowly to Geoff, Aunty Merle and Penny and whispered, "he's gone".

Then, a beautiful thing happened. Penny stood up and asked, "do you mind if I open the door so we can let his spirit run free?" I immediately responded with a nod and a quiet, "yes please". When the door was opened, I could almost see Dad's spirit flowing out of the room. It was quite surreal; quite amazing. I'll never forget it.

CHAPTER 18

Life's not always easy

I found the next 18 months after Dad's passing to be quite a challenge. I lost my vibe and was certainly not in the same positive, inspirational frame of mind that dominated my life and way of thinking for over half a century. I was lonely, often sad and suffering bouts of depression that dragged me down to a level that I struggled to rise up from.

Earlier I spoke about the joys of growing up in a small country town as an innocent young girl who was often the centre of attention. The support from family and community helped mould me into a fiercely independent, determined individual. As I wallowed in grief and depression I felt like that same town had deserted me, at the same time as my body was deteriorating and mobility became a greater challenge. I wasn't getting out like I used to and apart from Home Help I rarely had visitors.

No-one ever placed their arm over my shoulder and said "come on, mate, I've got a job for you and you can learn as you go", even though I had seen this same thing done for many of my friends over the years. I have even often felt that my voluntary efforts weren't valued. In fact I have more often felt the opposite. Occasionally, I felt as if people saw me as a person who should be more grateful to be given something to do. I was an active part of the pony club, but they relocated meetings to an upstairs office and from that point I couldn't attend. How do you think anyone would feel? When I received the Tattersalls Award I gave $20,000 to the Surf Live Saving Club and helped out in other ways, including time on the committee. The donation was my way of saying 'I have a heartfelt passion for the surf club and I appreciate and admire what you do'. This involvement also put me back in touch with a childhood passion … I loved hanging out with the crew on the beach, even though my active participation was obviously limited. I was made an Honorary Life Member of the Lakes Entrance Surf Life Saving Club as a thank you for the financial contribution from my Tattersalls Award. I responded by applying for a seat on the committee and was honored to hold a couple of positions on committee, including Publicity Officer and Treasurer. I was so proud and happy to be a part of this team. But then there was a change in administration with the club and I was pushed aside; no longer needed. I never hear from anyone at the club, and even as an Honorary Life Member do not get invited to presentation or anniversary functions.

I sit at home like many others, wondering why I no longer have company. Perhaps it's because in earlier years I was a bit too confident and outrageous for most country people. I also believe I have lost friends because in some circles I am considered a bit of a know-all, yet in reality this perception stems only from my need to be well organised and planned every day. Out of necessity I've always had an innate sense of what is going on around me – I sit back and carefully take in my surrounds - which perhaps has made me more observant than most people. Coupled with a natural propensity to express my opinions, regardless I suppose of whether they are wanted, has had an impact on how I am perceived.

The careful planning has been from necessity. When I lived in Melbourne the first thing I did when I woke up each morning was to think about and plan my day. Where was I going? How many doors will I have to go through and where are they? Would there be someone around to open a door? If I have to access a building that is remote, will I have to phone in advance and get them to meet me at the front? What about an accessible toilet? Remember, there were no mobile phones when I was young and although I was able to find a way around most situations, when you're three feet eight inches and have no arms, opening a pull-open door (which most people take for granted) is generally impossible.

Having had such an active mind for so many years, always carefully planning ahead and thinking about any challenges I may face, made it even more difficult when I was spending so much time at home on my own. I was sitting around in my wheelchair getting bitter and angry, which is not the happy go lucky Deb of the past, and wondered why my friends didn't come around and say, "c'mon Deb, enough of this crap, we're here to pick you up, dust you off and help you move on." Instead I thought they had walked away, because that was easier.

On top of this, as my mobility becomes more limited it's harder to get around … more difficult for people to pick me up and toss me in the back of a car, because the wheelchair has to also come along for the ride and it's a pain in the arse trying to get it in or out of the boot, especially if we encounter a shower of rain. Years ago I never worried about the fact that I always had to wear thongs while others strutted around in their funky fashionable shoes. But you don't fit the business world if you are in a wheelchair and wear thongs. Instead, you're considered in the class of pensioners. And don't get me wrong, I'm not denigrating pensioners here; after all, I've been one for a while. What I am saying is that people get pigeon-holed and it is extremely hard to move from one 'hole' to another.

I am on the pension because I need that money to survive. It's an essential necessity ever since I moved back to my home; it's not a preference. I've been told numerous times, "you deserve the pension, Deb", and I say, "why the hell do I deserve it?" Can anyone tell me why I deserve to be on the pension, rather than spending my days like most people in a paying job that helps maintain a reasonable lifestyle? I have worked voluntarily for primary and secondary schools, I was a founding member of the Association for Employees with Disabilities and I've been involved with a whole host of organisations in an attempt to make a worthwhile contribution to society and the community of folk with disability. I'm not sure that qualifies for "you deserve to be on the pension", because in actual fact I deserve to be working.

Naturally, on the outside I am seen as being different, but for many years people have failed to understand that my disability has not affected my brain, nor my heart and soul. In fact, by necessity it's probably made it a lot sharper. I have conversations with people I've just met and they say, "you're pretty smart, Deb … who do you work for?" And the answer, of course, is no-one because I'm short and have no arms. I don't know for certain that my disability is the reason I cannot get a job, but I can't think of another one, especially when I try so hard and witness so many in positions for which they obviously don't have the skills. So I sit here on my own, asking myself time and again, "why won't anyone employ me?" And as I do this my state of mind continues to deteriorate. All I have ever done is strive to be as good as anyone else and to want the same as anyone else … have the normal life that my bloody head tells me I'm entitled to.

Although it's a shocking way for a person like myself to think - especially with my history of 'life is for living' and all that blah, blah, blah – I have to confess that in the past 20 years or so, on various occasions I have thought it would have been easier if I had an intellectual disability to go with my body, as this would have perhaps sheltered me from deep and meaningful expectations. It tears me apart to say that, but it's how I felt have at times and something I needed to acknowledge and deal with.

I also believe the issues I have faced are symptomatic of a broader national concept where large sections of the population have trouble dealing with any person who is different. I have a very kind cousin, but I've known since we were children of the troubles he has when I enter the room.

Maybe when this book is published it will give me a new lease on life, and those who I have befriended and tried to help over the years will have a better understanding of how the world looks from my eyes. I hope so. I reflect on events like the VCAL program at the local secondary school and see them as my attempts to find a worthy place on this earth, because until recently, sitting around and wasting whatever it is that I was born with has not been an option. I have always been prepared to answer questions, to pass on my experiences, abilities and thoughts to others, in the hope they may be of some benefit. In fact it was persistent requests from others to write a book that got me started on this project.

I was a vivacious, out there kind of character. As a little girl I spoke up, which was possibly an unintentional and sub-conscious reaction to being half the height of other kids. If I didn't speak up I could, and at times was, trodden on. To some people I was nothing more than a smart little bitch, but looking back I believe I was only trying to reinforce my presence and independence. And it was only a minority who didn't like this side of me. Most people liked my happy, fun nature and some admired what I was able to do, or at least trying to do. For example, as I've said, in my twenties I could ask any young athletic bloke who was nearby to toss me up onto a bar stool, a tram or bus. I felt the glares and caught disgusted looks, but I ignored the patronising remarks of nearby women as these guys wrapped their arms around me. Now that I'm considerably older it's a totally different kettle of fish because such a look of fragility seems to provoke a more uncertain response, now carrying the extra marring of older age.

Throughout life there have been many things I could not do or be part of, but I came to think of it as sharing the load and would ask the general public for help when or where it was needed. If I put forward an unsuccessful 'please' I just had to accept it. My philosophy was to take an optimistic approach, understanding that what I lost on the see-saw I'd pick up on the merry-go-round. For example, when I travelled in Europe others in our double-decker bus group went on a night walk and although, back then, I could get around pretty well on my own, a long walk after six or eight hours on the bus was a bit too tough. So, I said, "you guys go along and I'll wait here". By the time they returned I'd made friends with locals or other tourists wandering by who had shown an interest in the bus and we were having our own little party. I missed out on some night sights, but I'd get around and have a look the next day and certainly didn't miss out on having a bloody good time. That's what life has been all about.

Despite this, there have been niggling regrets at experiences and occasions I have been unable to live and enjoy - things I can't reach or touch - like that romantic image of walking along the sand, hand in hand on a secluded beach with a special man, sharing that intimate moment in its sparseness, with the sound of waves rolling onto the sand. Being a beach lover, that has been a loss to my life. It's something that I had thought about – closed my eyes and wished – but I stopped thinking about that romantic walk because it can never happen, though this is not to say I have not experienced my own romantic and passionate moment in the surf under the moonlight. Don't worry, I'm happy I'm not the only one that may have missed that moment.

I'm sorry if this is sounding too melancholy, but I did not want this book to be just about the good times that I have enjoyed, especially in the younger years of my life. Recent times have not been easy and it is important that some of the mental health challenges which often come with disability are better understood and accepted. I want the book to be honest which is why I have to admit there have been occasions when I thought ending my life was an option, although this has always been overpowered by my love of life and, since her birth, my love for my daughter Emma. Again, being brutally honest, I went through a period of feeling that if I wasn't here there is probably not another soul on earth who would suffer any major loss in their life. I'm not saying many people wouldn't be sad ... they'd be sad thinking about the vivacious little girl who loved life so much, yet finished up so depressed, but other than that it would not make one iota of difference. Anyway, if you are reading this book don't worry because, hopefully, I am not going anywhere any time soon.

With luck my autobiography has been a smashing success and taken away the dark side that has plagued my thoughts not just in the last couple of years, but for a period before that. In some respects there has been an impact since Jim's death and it was camouflaged while I remained active. Since the struggle to get around has intensified and I spend too much time in a wheelchair dreaming about what might have been, the sombre thoughts bubbled to the surface like an erupting volcano.

My apologies if the honesty has been a bit too confronting, but from the day I decided to write this book I was determined to ensure it was a warts and all account of my life and my views. I felt there were things I had to say to the world, with no beating about the bush, so those who know me and those who don't can understand what life has done to me. If this helps societal education and improves the attitude of just one person toward those living with disability and how they need to be supported and treated with respect, then the exercise has been worthwhile. I know I'm not Robinson Crusoe - I'm not the only person with disability who has suffered depression and loneliness - but I genuinely believe there needs to be greater understanding of why people like myself get to this point.

It's not dissimilar to what happens with a lot of elderly people who have been very active for many decades, whether it be working, raising a family or being involved in their community. Often it's a combination of these three. Then all of a sudden they're old and unusable and cannot get out and about like they used to. No one NEEDS them anymore.

***

When I was young and determined I wasn't going to let anything get in the way of a 'normal' life. Over the journey I have discovered there are many people - certainly and thankfully a minority - who make this quite a challenge; an adventure. In some quarters the lack of empathy and understanding for those who live with disability is quite mind-boggling. For starters there are comments people make.

So may I respectfully suggest the need to put your brain into gear before making comments to or about others with disability. I generally try to adopt an empathetic, not sympathetic, approach knowing that often a comment which may offend was not meant with any malice. Sometimes it's a matter of asking myself whether there was a legitimate reason for what was said. For example, I get called short arse and that's legitimate. Well, it's true, isn't it? If someone says, "hey, short arse, get over here" I won't be offended if it's in the right tone. It's the same with "oh, she's armless". Why would I take offence when that's the way it is? But then there's the "Be careful it's hot" comment when I am delivered a cup of tea 'I' ordered. For God's sake, I know tea is made with boiling water.

I've always felt sorry for the narrow minded ignorance of those who either bully or patronise, hence never been stressed about people making judgments because I am short or do not have arms, though 'tis not to say that some comments in total innocence can be painfully offensive. And there are days when I won't give two hoots, yet others when I may be more sensitive. I suspect most people who live with disability are the same. Does that make it more difficult? Yes, perhaps it does. But it does not excuse the manner in which the disabled are patronised, or some of the brainless words that can flow from an able bodied person's mouth.

Recently I was asked: "Do you know such and such, who lives in Darwin?" My natural response was, "why would I know this person?" I was then told "they have no arms?" Why, may I ask, am I likely to know a person in Darwin simply because they do not have arms? Did the person who asked this ridiculous question think about what they were asking? I'd suggest the answer is 'no'. Maybe they assumed I would be attached to a 'no arms' disability group of which all the 'no arms' people in Australia are members.

I've also been referred to as "Debbi … the one with no arms or legs". I could ask, how do you think I walk around if I don't have legs? I'm not like John Coutis. He zips around on a skateboard because he doesn't have legs and even though mine might be only 10 inches long, I do have them. It makes me wonder how stupid some people can be. How do they think I get around … on a ball or bubble under my skirt? Nah, it was a skateboard, so I've been informed. When my back first began to give me trouble and I started using this wheelchair more frequently, several comments from several school acquaintances were made to me, such as, "oh wow, …..that's an upgrade from the skateboard". May I say right now, my only skateboard experience was in my early twenties down Market Street in Sale where I probably managed five metres, at the most, before I flew into the air and slid the rest of the way on my bum. I've never done it again.

It's these silly, ignorant comments that are annoying to myself and others with disability, and all I ask is for a greater thought process before words flow. If you are meeting a person with disability for the first time, take a couple of seconds to think about what you might say, rather than opening your mouth and offending. I know we are all human beings and none of us is infallible, but I also know you can try harder to be more understanding and less offensive. Most people with disability have to be very tolerant and patient and learn to occasionally smile and walk away.

Then there is the employment situation. I must admit, I'm at a bit of a loss to know what we are going to do about this in Australia. In a nutshell, society does not have the essential programs that we need to provide meaningful jobs for those with disability. We need to be self sufficient and independent, which will not happen if we do not have effective policies to support these aims. Society has to make a choice – do you want to provide worthwhile choices for those with disability or do you want to keep driving us towards government dependence? If you choose the latter, the time will come when our great nation can no longer afford to keep those with disability, as the financial burden continues to grow.

From my perspective, the only solution is to recognise our abilities and structure workforce roles accordingly. This will not only give those of us with disability a fulfilled life of worth, but also the means to be financially dependent and emotionally stable. We need a paradigm shift in the way employers and governments think and act because at the moment, in the vast majority of cases, they do not know how to tackle this problem.

I understand there are efforts to be proactive and find solutions, and around this there has been a lot of publicity about lifting the profile of people with disability and what we're all about, but in reality there has not been enough progress. I have, both in the past and present, often seen resentment of my enthusiasm in all aspects of life and wonder of the human ego's part to play in keeping the physically, not intellectually, marred people dependent or isolated by the lack of willingness to compromise, maybe? That has to change. Too often from a government mindset it's all about ticking a box instead of truly appreciating and implementing what is required. Instead they should look at what has to be done to make it work … look at the needs and abilities of each individual and what actions have to be realised and issues resolved to ensure they can become part of society, let alone the workforce.

In my opinion the only way this can be done is for programs to be developed by those who have to participate in them. If a program is to support a person with disability you must have someone with disability involved in its design, instead of getting a bureaucrat with a university degree to write a hypothetical policy that might look okay in the text book but doesn't work in the real world. I've said for many years that we must involve people who have 'walked the walk', but governments won't let us in, so nothing changes.

They make these incorrect assumptions that people with disability fall into particular categories. No we don't! We're all individual, we all have different types and levels of abilities and because of this we also have very different needs. It is imperative this gets recognised by governments, otherwise in 10, 20 or 30 years the only change will be the financial burden of those with disability on the rest of society. Governments need to be far more proactive in their search for solutions and these must involve considering the abilities of each individual and tailoring their work accordingly. There are tasks within all organisations, even if they may seem small and menial, which can be put in one basket and allocated to a person who may not be able to handle more complex or physical roles.

Everyone can be productive, we just need a more individualised system as well as one in which there is the appropriate level of respect and support. We must also get rid of disability support personnel like the one I worked with who refer to their clients as 'morons'. It is the responsibility of managers and colleagues to eliminate this discriminatory attitude. What also needs changing is the manner in which disability employment support is funded.

At I write this, the job provider's priority is getting a person on a three months trial, regardless of the job's suitability, so they can get a subsidy. What happens after the papers are signed and the subsidy is approved doesn't matter, which means the required level of follow-up support generally doesn't exist.

It would be interesting to survey the number of people who get into subsidised employment and compare it with the number who remain in their positions after the subsidy runs out. I'd suggest the numbers would be staggering, again because our system is designed around 'ticking a box' rather than providing purposeful, permanent employment. The cycle continues and nothing changes.

We must develop a system that encourages and supports employment permanency, and we also need a revolution in the way managers and others in the workplace treat their colleagues who have disability. During the years of my working life I often felt like I was seen as a threat, whether this was to another worker or a manager. I wasn't put in a position where I could shine. I'm not sure why; could it be that there was a fear this could highlight an abled bodied person's inadequacies? They didn't want little Deb, with no arms, to show them up or appear smarter, so I felt like I was kept under control a compartment.

As such it was impossible for me to reach full potential. And there's a double whammy if you're living with disability, because if you complain no-one will take the complaint seriously. So if the system is to be fixed it needs a complete overhaul, accompanied by a new approach that gives those with disability some confidence that they have a productive role to play and their abilities and contribution are appreciated. It's no different to the way any human being expects to be treated in their work environment. The impact of ignorant people on me has always been something I faced alone and in more recent times I was surprisingly and sadly rejected again, because people find it hard to see those that are different as a valuable inclusion to our community, let alone society. With an interest in various forms of artistic creation, I answered the advertisement and made a phone call regarding the call for interested thespians to be cast in a theatrical piece, titled the

'The Waiting Room'. Considering I had had many waiting room moments, I saw this as a relatively easy part to play physically, and something in which I could easily participate. This was not to be, as I was informed on enquiry that there was no part written for a person with a disability. I envisaged the theme to be based upon conversation and interaction whilst people wait. Well, I do that, and it may be surprising to some, but I even occasionally participate in conversation and general banter, at all levels.

What I am about to suggest next is politically sensitive and I understand that in many circles it will be vehemently opposed, but as I grow older and become increasingly familiar with the way most individuals with disability are treated in our society my views on abortion seem to strengthen. I think parents should carefully consider whether or not to abort the embryo of a disabled foetus.

"How can she say that?" I hear the populous baying. "That's murder … she has no right … !" Don't I? May I suggest that with what I have been asked to endure for much of my life, and witnessed in others, I have absolutely every right to advocate abortion and would even suggest the 'do-gooders' who oppose this course of action don't know the first thing about living with disability. In fact I believe strongly that the broader community has two choices.

Choice 1: Get serious about providing necessary support levels and employment opportunities for those with disability to ensure every single individual is given a chance to feel worthy in our materialistic, self-centred society.

Choice 2: Encourage parents with a disabled child in the womb to abort the embryo.

It's that simple – get serious or abort.

***

As mentioned earlier there was a school of thought that my deformities may have been caused by the German drug thalidomide. From a legal perspective this was eliminated because thalidomide had not been registered in Australia when I was born, however it is possible my mother was given the drug by a German/Jewish doctor who lived In Lakes Entrance when she was pregnant. When the thalidomide case was being fought in the courts I went through a phase where I would think about it and get angry at the fact my life possibly turned out as it has because my mother was given a drug that should never have been allowed on the market. These thoughts came at a difficult time, not long after Mum had passed away, so I wasn't in a very good space.

Then it appeared I was likely to get compensation and although the money would never make up for aspects of life that most people take for granted, at least I wouldn't have to struggle financially and would not be a burden to anyone as I get older. But this didn't happen because I was born outside the time thalidomide was registered in Australia.

Did it cause my physical deformities? Who knows. One thing I do know is that I am identical to others who look just like me and their deformities have been directly linked to thalidomide. Lynette Rowe and I are the same … Mary Henley and I are the same. It does seem highly unusual that I look just like Mary, who is thalidomide, yet according to the law I'm not.

Somewhere in life as I moved into the art world and started researching other artists with disability I discovered a woman named Alison Lapper who, like myself, was born with what the medical profession referred to as phocomelia, a congenital disorder with classic symptoms of what was later known as thalidomide deformities. What really took my interest was a sculpture of her titled 'Alison Lapper Pregnant', which showed her nude and heavily pregnant and stood in Trafalgar Square from September 2005 until late 2007. Physically the statue is a replica of me, and it makes me smile as I feel there is no need for me to do any nude shots to show how beautiful I am. A large replica of the sculpture was also featured in the 2012 Summer Paralympics opening ceremony. I think of this as a milestone in social acceptance of the beauty and abilities possessed by those of us who happen to be born physically different.

Alison, who is about eight years younger than me, was institutionalised during her childhood and when I hear about something like that happening I feel so much gratitude for my loving parents who took me home and taught me independence. Interestingly, just like me, Alison was fitted with artificial arms but abandoned them and, like myself, learned to live without external aids. She is now a renowned English artist and in 2003 was awarded an MBE for her services to art. Alison says that her deformities were not from thalidomide, so it's possible mine aren't either.

This information helped me heaps as all my life I had moved along with a smile and my little quote from Bob Dylan, but then came the lawyers who told me I had someone to blame. Then within months I was being told I had no-one to blame and I was dropped like a hot cake, returned to the country and continued with life and a head full of doubt that someone actually was to blame. At times I'm not sure if it's age or bitterness, or purely location, keeping me home. Thankfully, older age has brought with it rationalising and a sense of having someone to be angry with, as against not having someone to be angry with. I have reached a stage where it was not worth worrying about or fighting over. This is who I am and it's pointless blaming anyone.

As I said right back at the start, as a Bob Dylan fan I have lived by his famous song 'A Simple Twist of Fate'. That's what I am and this approach has helped me retain a positive attitude for most of my life. As the years have progressed so has my depression and occasionally anger; I certainly was angry during the thalidomide case when I wondered whether my life could have been different. The cause of my deformities may have been arrogant people who allowed this drug to be distributed to pregnant women like my innocent Mum, who may or may not have been given a few morning sickness pills that were not even legally permitted in Australia. I'd also get angry when I thought about medical professionals who ignored the warning signs and continued prescribing the drug despite mounting evidence of the consequences.

But for most of my life I've been able to switch my mind back to Dylan's 'Simple Twist of Fate' in the understanding that negative thoughts do not achieve anything. I lived by the mantra that it does not matter what cards in life you are dealt, the only way to play them is with a positive attitude. That's a message for everyone, regardless of whether or not you live with disability, and it's one I have tried desperately to reinvent in myself.

CHAPTER 19

Let's get positive

I want my book to finish on a positive note. I have vented my spleen and will not shirk the serious issues about disability support, and particularly in employment, that society needs to address, but I do not want the negative aspects of recent times to engulf the previous 50 years.

Throughout life I have generally adopted a positive attitude and, as I've said, been prepared to express my views and opinions. On occasions I am more forthright than some people are comfortable with, however it's an approach which has helped me survive and be living today in my own comfortable home that I built with the unwavering help and support of brother Jim. Many people thought I was financially carried by Jim, though this was not the case. He helped, for sure, but his huge generosity and personal habits meant he lived pay to pay, at the same time as ensuring we lived and socialised to a pretty high standard. We designed the home together and for the second time in my life I had easy access to water, as we allowed for a low sink. The sink and the vanity were the only modifications to the norm.

As I reflect back I can say with some pride that I have accomplished nearly everything that a person with arms could want to achieve. It's been done with lots of tenacity, an occasional sprinkling of cheekiness and a firm belief in what I am capable of doing. The fact some people talk about my achievements as being amazing has at times been a bit confronting. Sure, it can be more difficult than 'normal' if you have no arms and are only 44 inches high, but all I've really done is what I wanted to do, the same as any astute woman living on her own.

I don't take for granted the inspiration I have been able to provide, especially when I was on the speaking circuit and addressing school groups and other business staff on their personal development days. I understand that when people say "it's bloody amazing how your toes work and how you use your chin and shoulder", that they genuinely believe it to be so. Yet all I'm doing is making best use of my working parts, and yes it can be a frustration in life to watch good strong capable bodies doing nothing. When I wanted a beer I couldn't pick up a stubby with my hand and take a swig, so I would simply pick it up with my front teeth. This method did make it difficult not to scull, as the liquid amber ran straight down my throat. Hence, in my 20s and early 30s I did spend many nights intoxicated.

It's the same with any other task I had to perform … it's all about compromise and using my strengths. For most people, toes are pretty damn useless. In my case, they're just like normal fingers and they were genetically wired to do be that way. I never had any lessons to use my toes, they just developed with finger-like dexterity.

So I've done my best to foster a 'can do' attitude and adapt the strengths I was born with to the best of my ability … stay positive and think about that 'simple twist of fate'. It has helped overcome some of the bitterness when a person looks at me and I say to myself, 'stop looking at me as if I'm a Martian'. I'm unique … I know that. But I'm not a bloody Martian!

It's not easy coping with some of the visual examination which comes your way when you look different to 'normal' people, and I acknowledge now that for a long time that's exactly what I wanted to be seen as … 'normal'. I fought all my life to be seen as a normal woman with a normal day to day existence.

From a relationship perspective, until David came along I had been denied a connection which most women take for granted. I didn't have the chance to care and look out for 'my man', so to speak … to feel needed. I did for David. As he worked I found it a pleasure to be able to cook the meals, wash the clothes and generally look after the home and all his needs. I know he appreciated my efforts and loved me deeply, as I loved him, but it all came crashing down when I discovered he did not want to be a father. I was quite devastated and spent some time crying on the shoulder of my new American friend, Shaleen Feasby. I had often dreamed of the day I would be a mother, and the thought that this may never become reality was heartbreaking. I believe I have adapted to what I was born with very well and developed strong independence, yet along the way there have been parts of everyday life which I've been denied. The more I thought about it, having a child was not going to be another one.

The fact David did not want to be a father was something that life threw at me from left field, but wasn't an issue I was prepared to duck and weave from. Maybe David's strong attitude against fathering a child was the reason he fell in love with me. I have wondered whether he loved me more because he thought "she's a sure thing not to want a kid". After our relationship broke down I thought "there has to be something weird about him". So, instantly I felt I knew that's why he fell in love with me. I was convinced he never thought we would be talking about having children. Yet it was something I wanted with all my heart from a young age. When I was seven years old Mum gave me a doll; it turned out to be a favourite which I gave all the care and attention it could possibly get from any little girl, and I decided way back then, just like some of my girlfriends, I was going to be a Mum. I practised on that doll and waited for Mr Right to come along. Eventually he did, in America, but he didn't want to be part of my dream.

When I informed him of my investigations and consequent options, it became non-negotiable; I felt that fate had brought me to this point and at 35 years old I could not let this opportunity pass by. He was out of our relationship pretty quickly. There was no more affection, let alone sex. I explained my lifelong maternal desires, but from his perspective children were not on the agenda and never would be. Strangely, however, he was very supportive.

I remember that even when our relationship was at its strongest I was guarded and feared David would one day discard me, probably because that had happened in my relationships so many times before.

And here I am, more than 30 years later, still living on my own and realising David is the only man I really, truly loved and in some respects that love still exists. Over the years I have longed for another genuine loving relationship, but they're hard to find in general, and more so when you're different.

As you get older you tend to dwell on the best things in your life which, in my case, was David; apart from Jim and Emma, of course. Jim was still alive when I met David and there was a bit of rivalry there, though only on David's side. For a while it created a double-edged sword as each hankered for their part in my life. Things were never easy, but I refused to let this issue cause any huge problems.

Now, when it comes to a loving partner, all I have are memories. And yes, I know, many others are in the same boat. However, it still saddens me that I did not have someone to share all my adventures with … to laugh and love. But I still realised my maternal desire to be a Mum. And the little doll I cherished when I was just seven years old is still sitting in my bedroom.

***

From when I was young I loved art, whether it was drawing or painting. After spending many years as a hobby artist drawing with a pencil I was convinced by a friend, who was a professional artist, to take up more serious study. At the time I was a frustrated and dismayed unemployed person and thought this may provide me with opportunities to work on community art projects which, from time to time, receive government funding.

My course was through East Gippsland TAFE in Bairnsdale, from where I graduated in 2004 with a Diploma of Visual Arts. I love my painting and it has helped me overcome my fight against depression and loneliness which I have struggled with, especially after the deaths of my adorable young brother Jim In 1995, Mum in 2009, Dad in 2014 and Geoff in 2016.

Creating artworks has helped me find a renewed confidence. It is a talent which runs in the family ... my brother Geoff was a good artist, so was my father and his father, and even more so my maternal grandfather. I developed an eye for drawing when I was young and it doesn't matter if you don't have arms because art is in the eye, regardless of whether the strokes are made with feet or hands.

Some people are surprised with my artwork and I understand this view as I reflect on the way most civilised quadrupeds keep their feet smothered and untrained in shoes. I know my feet are very clever – certainly more so than most – but if they hold and manipulate a spoon or a pen, why should it be such a shock when they use a paintbrush? I have the eye and the perspective in my head which my feet are innately able to express.

When people see this as some sort of miracle, expressing "she did that with her FEEEETTT!!!" in excited amazement, I take a breath and think "can you just accept the fact I'm a good artist?" It's the reason I have never joined the mouth and foot artists, because I don't want to be put in that basket, although in some ways this has probably been to my detriment because it could have provided more avenues to promote my work.

Sue, or 'Patto' as she is affectionately known, is the artistic coordinator of The Colour Gang, a group of artists who paint with the support of Noweyung Ltd. which is a provider of disability support services. Anyway, Sue is a friend of mine going back probably 40 years who knew I was a keen artist, but was not as artistically active as I would be if I had a little physical support. She suggested I should hire an art space at the Butter Factory and make my studio day on a Monday when, whilst attending to The Colour Gang clients, she would be happy to fulfil some of my needs, such as pulling lids off paint containers or brush washing and other water supplies. To my own detriment I kept putting it off, primarily because I did not want to be seen as a Day Care client. Hiring, cheaply, a small area within the Butter Factory, I had no qualms about working in the same area as people with disabilities; it's the social expectation, assumption and comments that I am

ASSUMED to be a part of the Day Care system which was the issue. The assumption really pissed me off

Many years ago I finally accepted Sue's offer and arranged, with the art space director Peter Neill, to hire a small area within the studio to practice my art. Really, it's been a saviour. I do not feel like a client. However, there have been many comments along the lines of "are you off to school today? How nice that you're with The Colour Gang." Mind you, several community artists have used the space just as I do, and I bet their space is referred to as studio.

When I arrive on Monday mornings the Colour Gang artists are always so happy and genuinely pleased to see me. We have our occasional banter, including Al who calls me a puppy dog because I carry things in my mouth. With anyone else I would have been offended, but It's the type of environment where it's all harmless fun and no offence is taken. They are also very helpful, carrying an easel or opening paints if that's what I need. I fully believe that a part of their joy in my attending the space is that they can help me. They're not being, so called, 'told what to do' they are helping someone. I have not a patronising bone in my body; everyone's got a 'boat to row' and I use language and expression as I do with everyone. I swear a little, and articulate my expectations and needs, and communicate without a pat on the head or arm around their shoulder. I don't get in their face.

Peter Neill is a fellow artist who has always made me feel welcome, charged very little for my space and asked about any physical support I may need and has always 'gone the extra mile' to ensure I have a suitable environment. He even provided a two gallon container of water with tap and wash dish to catch drips and empty dirty water into, and set up a little table and kettle so I can make myself a cuppa. Everyone at the Butter Factory is so obliging, yet without creating any fuss.

In 2012 I had a painting included in an exhibition as part of the Toyota Community Spirit Gallery, in Port Melbourne. It was inspired by the fact I am an Aussie gal with a great love for my daughter and the Aussie bush, with the peaceful feeling and freedom it offers. It sold for $200 … I felt chuffed!!

One day I will have enough paintings for my own exhibition, but that's down the track a bit as I am rather fussy when it comes to exhibition quality. I want people to buy my paintings because they see the quality, not because they've been painted with toes instead of fingers.

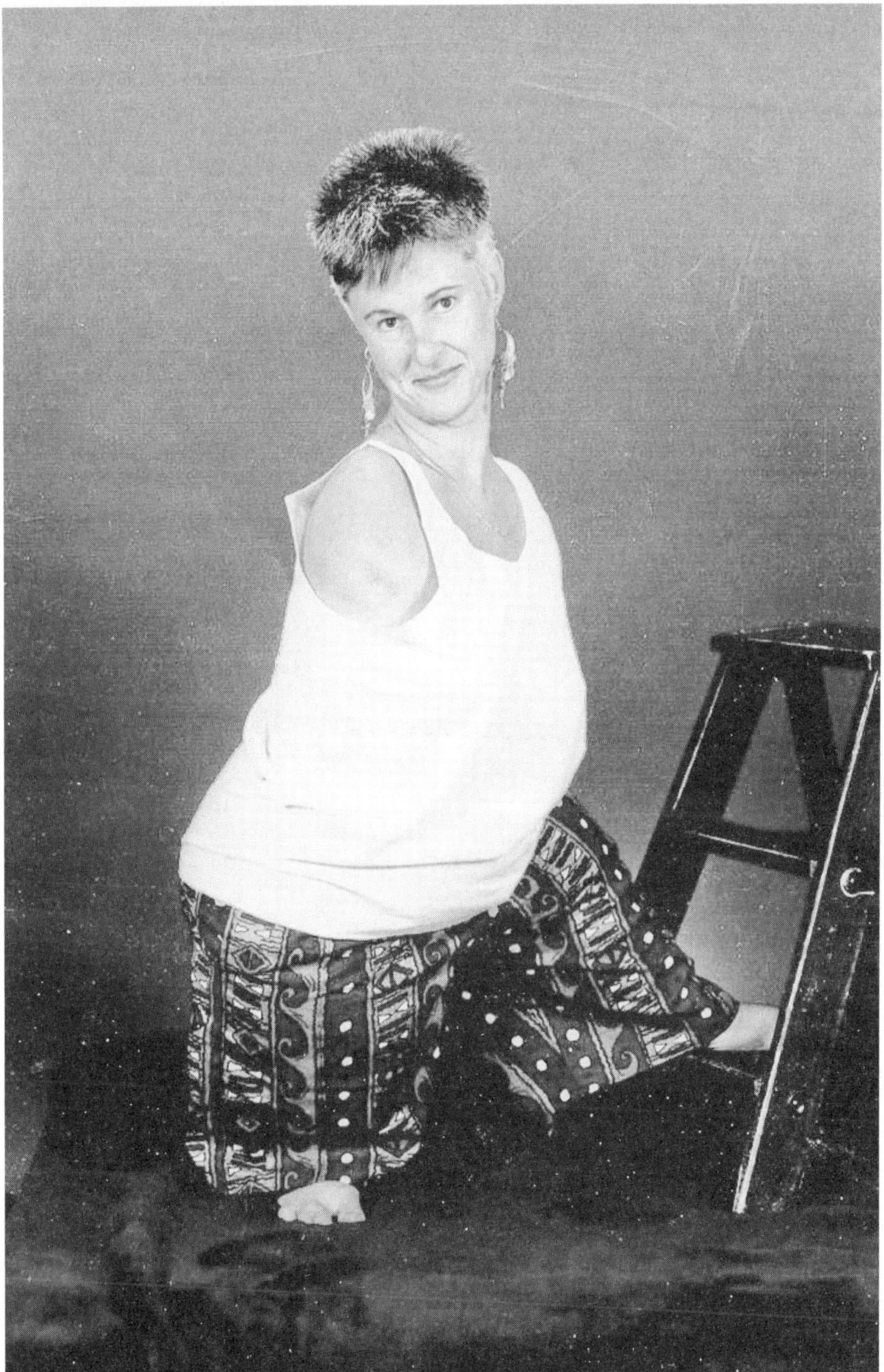

Above: 1991 Crescent City Modelling, hahaha.

Left: With my dear Mum.

1957

FISHERMENS CO OP
JOE PETHO AUTOWORKS
1957

LONE STAR
STEAKHOUSE & SALOON
VARIETY VICBASH
1998
VARIETY CLUB OF VICTORIA
the children's charity

LAKES ENTRANCE
FISHERMENS CO OP
JOE PETHO AUTOWORKS
BAIRNSDALE
TWO WAY RADIO
RENTALS
9584 9666
BELLEVUE
LAKES ENTRANCE
SKUNK WEAR
1957
apa
LAKES WELD
Mobil

Above: 1998 VicBash Hawaiian Night, Partner attached.

Top left: 1996 Variety Club Bash Car in the red!!! Dust n' Mud that is…

Middle left: 1998 Variety Club VicBash Broome, Cable Beach.

Bottom left: 1998 Variety Club VicBash to Broome.

milk

Above: Serving a cup of tea.

Photos left: Making a cuppa.

By Phut

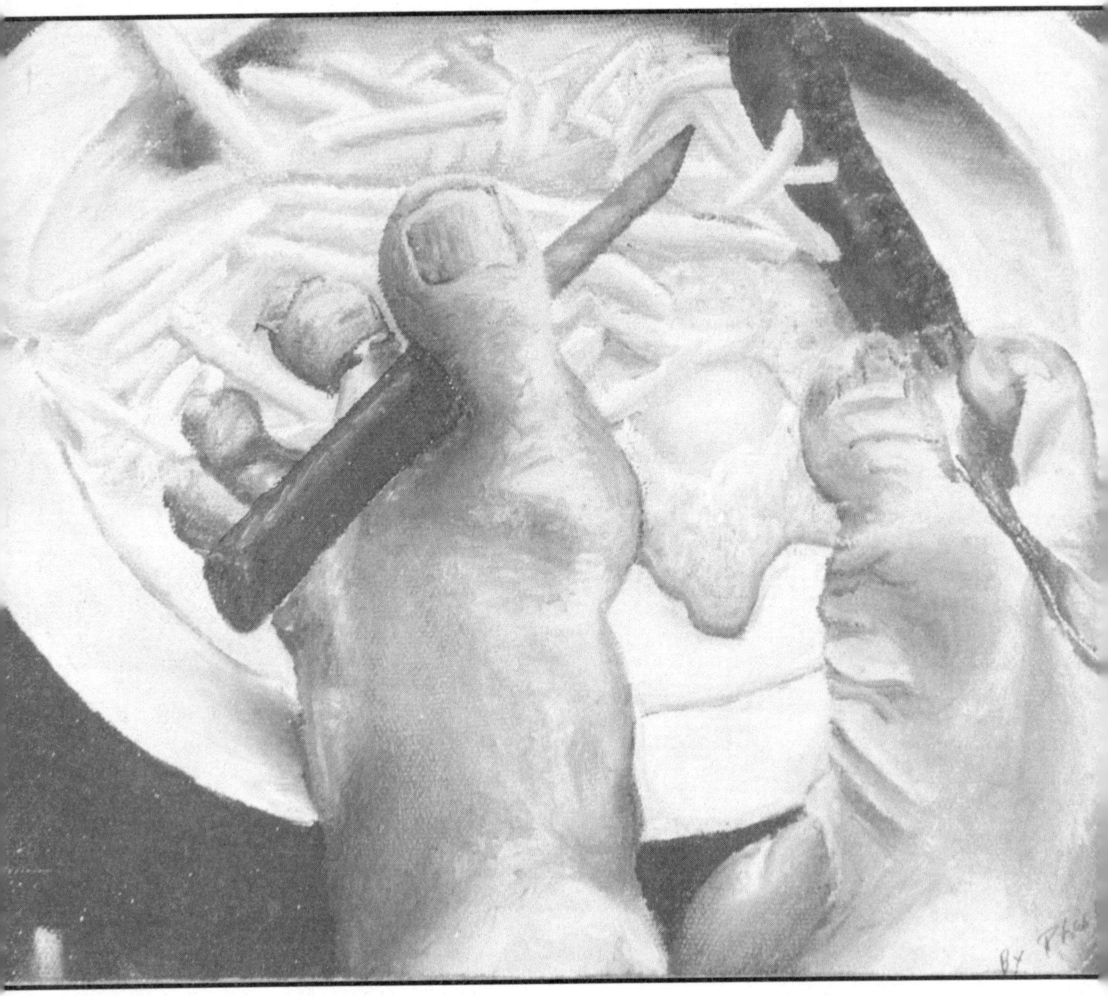

Above: One of my paintings, titled 'The Meal'.

Left: Another one of my paintings, 'Cup of Tea'.

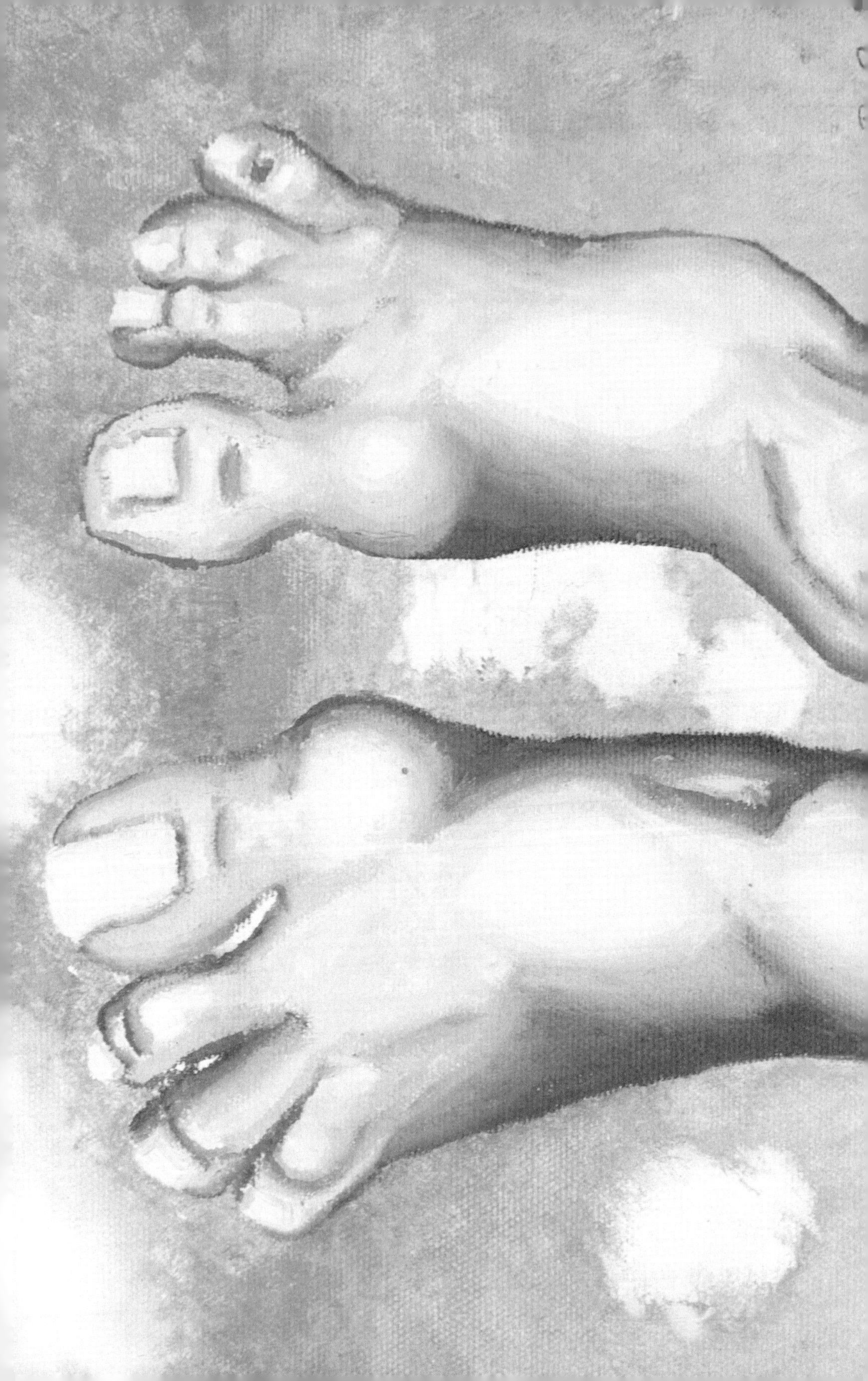

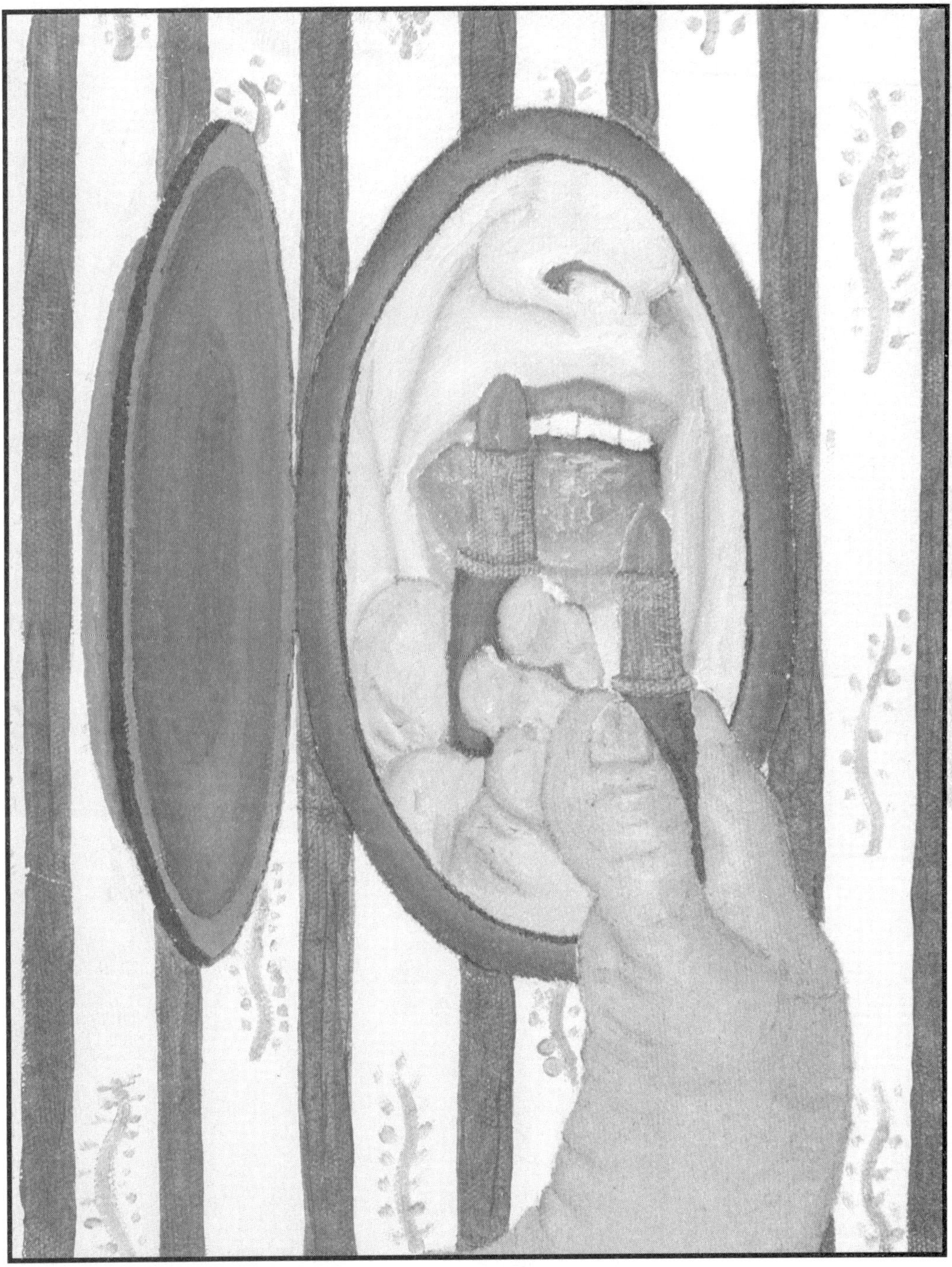

Left and above: Two more of my paintings. At left is 'Feet In The Clouds' and above is 'Lipstick It'.

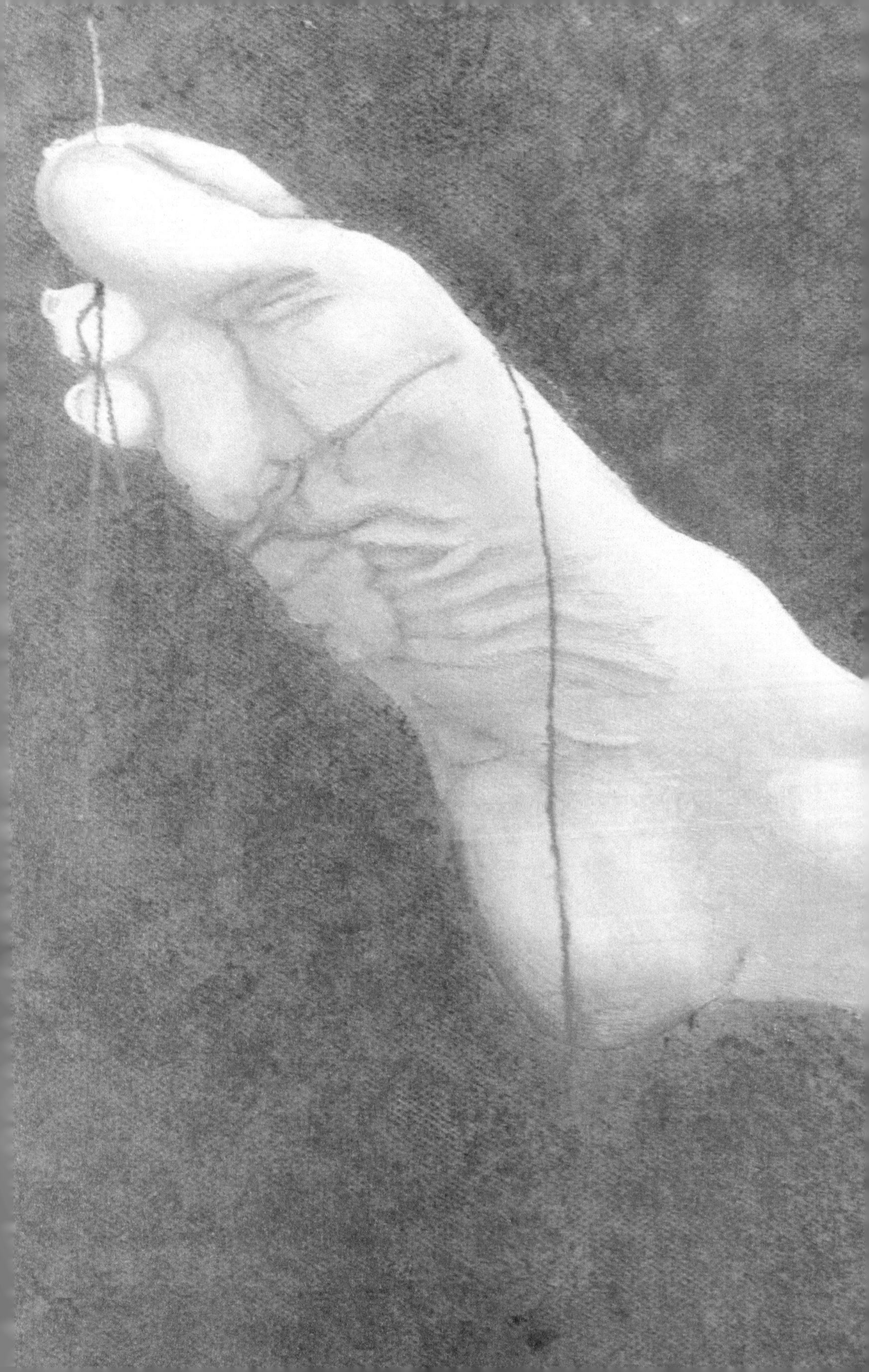

Above: Enjoying some time on my back veranda.

Left: My painting, titled 'Sew what'.

Above: Top left: Sitting out the back with our dogs.

Left: Two recent photos taken at home by my friend Lisa.

Photo above: Taking a break.

CHAPTER 20

Simple twist of fate

So where am I now? Well, I'm pleased to report that after a couple of challenging years Deb Gray is back on top of the world. Well, maybe not on top but at least closer to the peak of the mountain than I've been for a while. There was a dark tunnel, especially after my Dad died, but eventually I found light at the end of it.

I made a conscious decision to stop moping around and make things happen in my life, and that's what I am trying to do … forcing change and taking notice of the Dalai Lama's teaching. He tells us everything that happens in life comes from within, and things happen because you instigated them in one form or another. I accept that! He also teaches us the purpose of life is to be happy and you don't achieve that by sitting at home and worrying. So my thanks to the Dalai Lama for helping me understand that I had to take control of my destiny, and for enabling me to finish this book on a positive note, reflecting my present attitude to life.

It would have been disappointing if the final chapter was one filled with sadness and depression because that is not a true indication of my journey. Mind you, there have been some heartbreaking times, with another one occurring on, of all days, April 1, back in 2016. It was a lovely day on which to be ending a week away with my friend Ann in Bendigo and we were heading to a motel in North Melbourne where we intended spending the night. I was heading back to Lakes Entrance the next day and Ann was returning to Bendigo, so we were in separate cars. We left an aged care facility in Preston after I had popped in to visit an older friend when Ann pulled over in front of me, so I also stopped. She approached and jumped in the front seat of my car, sitting there rather strangely, and said she had something to tell me. I was then told about the sudden passing of my brother Geoff, who I, regardless of a recent dysfunctional relationship, loved very much. Although we were amiable and civil, regrettably we had not been on the same wave for some years and with more recent will estate problems I guess it made the love hard to see.

The sudden loss of Geoff left me wondering, "why am I the only person in my family still alive?" In 1995 I lost my brother Jim, who was almost my twin; then in 2009 my dear Mum was suddenly gone. I nursed Dad to his cancerous death and now just as suddenly as Mum and Jim was the loss of big brother Geoff. Like so many families when wills and estates have to be sorted, problems arise and there are disagreements. Unfortunately, and typical of that scenario, Geoff and I were not on good terms and we did not get the opportunity to come back together and reminisce about our good childhood, even though Geoff may have had a different tale to tell after I was born. Sadly, his story was spat at me just prior to Dad's passing when he said that he felt he "lost his parents the day I was born" and felt his children had lost their grandparents the day Emma was born. This saddened me, but unfortunately appeared to be out of my control. Now, we'll never be able to patch up our differences. So if you are having a strained relationship with a sibling, please don't put off any chance to mend it, because the opportunity may suddenly be ripped away.

I have grieved the loss of Geoff on my own and there will forever be another empty space in my heart - alongside Mum, Dad and Jim – but I am determined to fight on. I've had enough sadness and depression and will resist with all my powers whenever they try to take over my mind.

Predominantly my life has been one of vibrancy, independence and an absolute commitment to living a good life, and while I remain on this earth my resolve to be positive and enjoy any remaining years may get dented, but I will not allow it to be defeated. I've been on a roller-coaster, through good times and bad. Early in 2016 the ride was racing upwards, then Geoff's death, compounded by what I perceived as selfish extended family relationships, sent me plummeting down, but I had no intention of staying there.

I also continue to occasionally think about how much I would love a partner with whom to share life's experiences, but try to overcome this by focusing my thoughts on how lucky I am to have my daughter Emma, and cherish the relationship that we have. I understand it must be difficult for her when I am in a depressed state. After all, who wants to phone or visit a misery guts? Sadly, for some years I lost sight of what I had, as my mind concentrated on what I didn't have. Thanks for this goes largely to the thalidomide lawyers who gave me someone to blame with a rainbow of financial support for my future, then tossed me aside. But that's all in the past.

I try to get out of bed each morning in a positive frame of mind, knowing there are many people in this world far worse off, whether through a disability or their life's circumstances. I think often about places I have seen in my travels and remember some of the shocking poverty. Even in Australia we have people living on the streets and in heinous conditions. One time when I was in Sydney I tried to assist a poor homeless man. I couldn't leave him because I initially thought he was dead, so I stayed and comforted this impoverished human being until an ambulance arrived.

So I have now accepted I'm not too deprived, though it did take a reality check and telling myself, 'for fuck's sake get off your sooky bloody bum, 'cause life ain't that bad'.

My attitude has been boosted by loyal old friends, spread around the country and globe, and newfound friends at The Butter Factory Art Space, where I often spend three days a week. On Mondays I attend my studio space at the Butter Factory, this being a day The Colour Gang use their space, and I am in interesting and fun company, On Wednesdays I provide administrative support in order to assist the marketing, promotion, and cataloguing of the wonderful artworks produced .

I was also asked to join the East Gippsland Shire Disability Advisory Committee, and although it is not yet active I am hoping this will allow me to have an active and valuable involvement with advice to the shire, via this committee, ultimately paving the way for a more accessible and inclusive community.

These additional activities and my renewed positivity after a grey – or should that be 'Gray'? – period have turned around my outlook on life and I am determined this will be maintained. Unfortunately, the sad passing of those around me is something I have had to live with all too often since my teenage years. As I have read drafts of this book certain sections bring tears to my eyes, and they roll down my cheeks as I remember lost friends and relatives. And as I reflect back, particularly over the past 40 odd years, I think about the influence of drugs and alcohol in too many of these deaths, whether from drunk drivers or heroin addiction.

Personally, I cannot understand why our society condones alcohol yet bans marijuana. I've used 'pot' as my Valium and I do not believe it has caused me any harm. I believe I have been a well respected member of this community. Lots of my friends, many with responsible jobs, have a puff and there are no adverse effects on their life or work performance, although I can't say the same for others who drink too much alcohol. Generally, I've seen smoking 'pot' as having a calming influence, yet alcohol makes people obnoxious and dangerous. Anyway, for what it's worth I cannot see why alcohol is acceptable in our community despite the aggression and damage it causes, whereas marijuana, which is more a relaxant, continues to be illegal. And don't give me that rubbish about marijuana leading to use of 'harder' drugs, because that has not been my experience. If people seek harder drugs, it's because softer drugs are harder to get.

***

If you've made it this far you have read an open and honest account of my views on life, being the perspective of a little person with no arms who has tried so desperately to enjoy life. I trust you may understand many of my unique experiences which are a direct result of not being 'normal'. During my 'down' times I have turned around negative thoughts by remembering some of these experiences and I occasionally laugh at numerous offbeat encounters, like the night I jumped into the limousine and looked up to see a very startled Prince.

On another occasion, at a concert in San Francisco, famous American blues' artist Albert Collins jumped off the stage, knelt down in front of me and played the most amazing lead on the electric guitar. It was breathtaking. It's almost another book to explain how I came to be in possession of a photograph of that moment, forehead to forehead, as he pumps out a guitar solo. How many people can boast an experience like that? In fact, it is the cover of this book!

My love of music has been the catalyst for many memorable occasions. During my years following the band circuit in Melbourne I was a great fan of Cold Chisel and used to hang out with band members. A couple of times, when they were playing in Melbourne, I had a phone call from either Jimmy or Jane Barnes to say, "hey Deb, we're coming down. Do you want to come to the concert or hang out with Jane?" So I would either go and boogie to the band or spend time in the hotel with Jane and their daughter Mahalia, who was just a toddler at the time. I recall one night being in a dressing room with Jimmy, with his rather elderly, Scottish Mum and, I do believe, his stepdad sitting quietly in a corner. They were so proud of their wild boy Jim! In later years, during an encounter at an event, he reminded me and informed the patrons of my under-the-weather, behind the wheel antics around St Kilda with his wife Jane as my passenger.

I'd love to see Jimmy and Jane again because they were so kind and accepting, yet never patronising and oh so much fun. I was treated no differently to anyone else, which I appreciated, and it helped give me a sense of normality. Jimmy used to say, 'ah, you're armless' and in doing so acknowledged my disability, but in a non-offensive way. And, of course, it was because of the disability that I was able to get back stage and to band parties where many other young ladies would dearly love to have been. At one of these parties I had a 'pash' with Ian Moss … I reckon there are thousands of fans who'd tell you they would give their right and left arms for that experience. Well, perhaps I had, and it was worth it! Haha!

When I was young, experiences such as these gave me a thrill and added to the fun and excitement that I was always chasing. But more than that, they made life worth living and helped dispel negativity on the occasions when depressive thoughts started taking over my brain. These people treated me like a real person and gave me moments to treasure.

They also made some of the hardships that go hand in hand with my physicality a little easier to handle and helped keep me going when times were tough. Back then, and still today, I would see some poor guy on the street and think, 'he doesn't even have a roof over his head'. I've never been left with nowhere to live, so in that respect I've been pretty damn lucky.

Even now I can look back on many of the good times and think, 'shit, you've had some fun over the years'. At 65+ years of age I may not be the vibrant, energetic bundle from 30 or 40 years ago, something everyone has to cope with as they get older, but I still have my sometimes warped sense of humour and high spirit for life and a deep desire to help things be better for anyone who crosses my path, no matter what the cause.

So just like everyone else I have to adjust and get used to the fact that there's less bounce in my body compared to younger days when I was able to jump around the dance floor, get tossed up onto a bar stool and party all night long, or simply throw a leg up to get on a standard chair.

I'm hoping my next chapter will be touring around promoting this book and finding platforms to spout the disability with dignity and self determination issues yet to be addressed, which in many ways is going to be yet another challenge for this ageing, three feet eight and a half inches tall (don't forget the 'half'!) person with no arms. I see exciting times ahead, especially when my book is finally completed because it's a project I have been working on for well over 30 years and, to be honest, I didn't think it would be finished in my lifetime.

I am determined to maintain a positive frame of mind, despite the challenges that life keeps throwing up. I want to paint more, learn and live more and keep trying to give back to the world I love, wherever possible sharing my experiences in an educational way, in the hope that society will understand there are better ways to treat those among us who live with disability. We need to give every individual purpose and opportunity and wipe out the view in many quarters that 'normal' is a combination of two arms, two legs and a functioning brain.

Maybe along the way, as my journey in life approaches its twilight, I'll meet some handsome old man (it's probably getting a bit late for a young one … maybe not!) who will sweep me off my feet, take me for long rides through great places and love me forever.

And when he says, "so tell me about yourself, Deb" I'll look him in the eye and give him that line from Dylan. "I'm just a simple twist of fate." Or sell him a copy of this book……hahahaha Hahahaha!!